BETWEEN THESE WALLS

MICHAEL NEWMAN

 FriesenPress

Suite 300 - 990 Fort St
Victoria, BC, V8V 3K2
Canada

www.friesenpress.com

Copyright © 2020 by Michael Newman
First Edition — 2020

Between These Walls is a work of historical fiction set against a background of real historical events. Its characters are born of the author's imagination as are their individual stories in this book, and bear no resemblance to persons living or dead. For authenticity purposes historical personages have been utilised throughout. A few have been integrated into the storyline, but without contradicting historical facts.

ISBN
978-1-5255-4883-3 (Hardcover)
978-1-5255-4884-0 (Paperback)
978-1-5255-4885-7 (eBook)

1. FICTION, HISTORICAL, WORLD WAR II

Distributed to the trade by The Ingram Book Company

I want to thank my wife Dixie for her patience in endlessly reviewing and her sage advice during the writing of this book

This book is dedicated to my Father George Newman,
who spent eight terrible months during 1944/45 as a prisoner of the
Nazis at Mauthausen concentration camp in Austria.

BETWEEN THESE WALLS

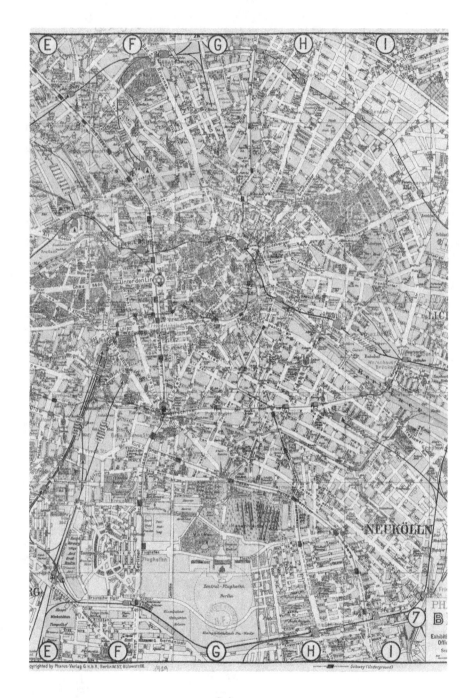

Berlin 1939

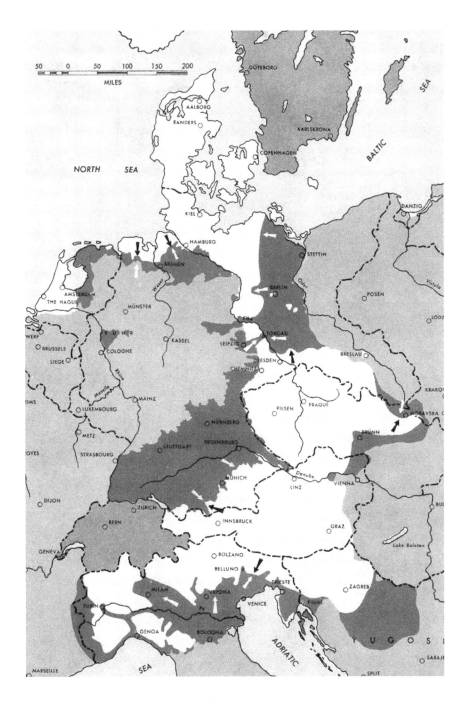

Germany 1945

ISRAEL AND
THE OCCUPIED
TERRITORIES

✪	National capital
◉	District (meḥoz) centre
○	City, town
✈	Airport
—··—	International boundary
—·—·	Boundary of former Palestine Mandate
————	Armistice Demarcation Line
—···—··—	District (meḥoz) boundary
	Main road
	Secondary road
+—+—+	Railroad
·—·—·	Oil pipeline

LEBANON

36°

UNIFIL

UNDOF

SYRIA

Tyre

Qiryat
Shemona

Al Qunayṭirah

Nahariyya

GOLAN

'Akko

NORTHERN

Lake Tiberias

Haifa

Tiberias

Nazareth

Dar'ā

Afula

Irbid

HAIFA

Hadera

Netanya

Ṭūlkarm

Jarash

CENTRAL

Nābulus

Herzliyya

Az Zarqā'

TEL AVIV

Tel Aviv-Yafo

WEST BANK

Bat Yam

Rām
Allāh

Amman

Ramla

Jericho

Ashdod

Mādabā

Ashqelon

Jerusalem

JERUSALEM

Bethlehem

MEDITERRANEAN

Dead
Sea

JORDAN

SEA

Gaza

Qiryat
Gat

Hebron

GAZA

Khān Yūnis

Al Qaṭrānah

Beersheba

Al Arīsh

SOUTHERN

Ak Karak

Zefa'

Bi'r Lahfān

Dimona

Aṣ Ṣāfī

Abū
'Ujaylah

'Ayn al
Quṣaymah

Zin

Bi'r Ḥasanah

Mizpe
Ramon

NEGEV

Al Jafr

Ma'ān

EGYPT

Ra's
an Naqb

S I N A I

Al Kuntillah

An Nakhl

Yotvata

Elat

Ṭābā

Al 'Aqabah

0	10	20	30	40	50	60 km
0		10	20	30		40 mi

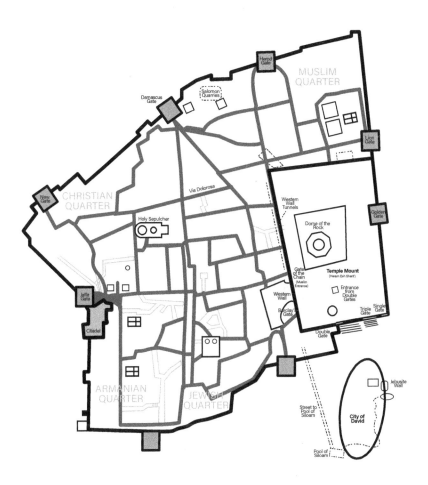

Jerusalem 1948

FOREWORD

Toronto, Canada-September 24, 2019

My inspiration to write this book had its genesis on a trip my wife and I took to Berlin, Germany in the summer of 2015. While walking along one of the residential streets in the Charlottenburg district of the city, we came upon small bronze plaques imbedded in the sidewalk in front of an apartment building. It was a silent witness commemorating a family that had lived in that apartment building and had in 1944 been forcibly removed and sent to a concentration camp by the Nazis.

I started to wonder who these people had been, under what circumstances had they been removed, what happened to them, and what happened to their apartment? Who was living there now, and how did they come into possession of the apartment?

After our visit to Berlin, we for the fourth time travelled to Salzburg, Austria. On a day excursion from Salzburg we went to visit the Eagles Nest on the Obersalzberg, Adolf Hitler's summer residence. As well, from Salzburg we took a train to Mauthausen, where my Father was incarcerated as a prisoner of the Nazis in the concentration camp on the outskirts of this small Austrian village during 1944/45. I had heard stories of the horrendous conditions that he had endured and how he survived.

This is when I first thought about writing a book of historical fiction combining the elements and aura of all three locations, and the parts they played in history. The idea then gelled in my mind to round out the novel building upon my surreptitious trip to Israel during the

Second Lebanon War in 2006 that was written about in the Toronto Star and National Post.

The book is based on a lot of "what ifs" and its main characters are figures of fiction, the background and many elements are historical facts. Daniel and the Singer family, as well as Bruno Schmidt and the Schmidt family, along with Arnold Weiss and his family are all fictional, created by my imagination. Many of the events described in the book however actually took place at the time and locations described. The horror that Adolf Hitler and his Nazi followers visited upon the Jews of Europe are well documented, as is the activity of former Nazi scientists on behalf of Egypt after the war and the battle by israel's Mossad spy agency to eliminate them.

Michael Newman

CHAPTER 1

A US Army Jeep, with the white star painted on its hood bouncing and vibrating through each pothole, rambled along the single-lane dirt track on the west side of the river Elbe. Mixed stands of beech, spruce, pine, and oak encroached on the winding, dusty clay path, sometimes wrapping the road in mid-morning shadow. The shade and openness of the Jeep were a welcome respite from the brilliant sunshine and heat of an early Saxon summer.

Germany had already lost the war. Berlin had been captured by the Soviets. Adolf Hitler and his mistress Eva Braun were dead, their bodies burned in the garden of the Führerbunker. Chief of the Nazis' vaunted U-Boat fleet, and Hitler's successor as Germany's ruler, Grand Admiral Karl Dönitz, was preparing to sign the instrument of unconditional surrender on behalf of the Third Reich in Flensburg on the Baltic Sea.

One of the most important waterways of Europe, the Elbe runs from Czechoslovakia to the North Sea. One week earlier, the American and Russian armies had met at the German town of Torgau, agreeing that the Elbe's west side would become the American Zone of Occupation. The officer in the Jeep, Lt. Colonel Dr. Samuel Singer, was returning from a meeting with the Soviets on protocols surrounding the treatment of wounded non-combatants in their respective zones of occupation.

Sam Singer had left his position as Assistant Head of Surgery at Brooklyn's Zion Hospital to enlist in the US Army Medical Corps. Tall and slightly overweight, with thinning brown hair, an infectious smile, and an unlit meerschaum pipe loosely hanging from his lower lip, he looked more like someone's friendly uncle than a senior military officer.

"Still feeling the effects of the vodka?" Singer asked his driver with an amused look. "The Russkies consume enormous quantities of that vile spirit. Can't keep up to them; we're just not used to drinking that much."

Corporal Joe Murphy, a stout, dark-haired Irishman from Philadelphia, had been in the war since 1942. He had been driving for Colonel Singer for four months and enjoyed the officer's easy-going rapport with enlisted men.

"Nah, I'm good," he answered, the tone in his voice belying the way he felt. "My dad was from the Emerald Isle, and though I grew up in Pennsylvania, my brothers and I learned how to drink like we were from the old country. So I was weaned on whisky, with a little Guinness thrown in."

Suddenly, both men were shaken out of their abstraction by the deep roar of a fighter aircraft just above their heads, flying at treetop level towards the Russian zone. The silver-grey plane, its super-charged engine screaming at full throttle, arose out of the west and almost instantly disappeared, the red star on the underside of its wing being the only recognizable identifier.

"Holy fuck!" shouted Murphy. "Sorry about the language, sir. I was just caught by surprise."

"No need to apologise, Corporal. Those were the two exact words I was thinking to myself. That Russian plane is flying from the wrong direction. He's over our lines! What the hell does that mean?"

"Big blue sky up there, sir," answered Murphy. "Easy to get lost."

"I understand that, but the Elbe is a large river, not difficult to recognize from the air. I wonder what he was doing on our side."

A mile farther, they emerged from the canopied dirt side-road onto the paved Autobahn. They could see smoke ahead of them before they could confirm its source. A black, convertible Mercedes staff car bearing SS insignia had plowed into the ditch, dark-grey smoke curling skyward from under its hood.

"Looks like the Sturmovik found its mark," said Singer as Murphy slowed the Jeep to a stop beside the burning wreck. Both men rushed to the disabled Mercedes.

The first person they noticed within the crash debris was the driver, in a black SS uniform, lying in the ditch halfway under the car's undercarriage. He was in a bad way—both legs broken and one shoulder shattered by a bullet, his arm hanging down, held only by the blood-saturated sleeve of his jacket. Another 23 mm round had gone clean through his upper thigh. Blood flowed freely down his leg, soaking his pants.

A second figure, dressed in greenish-grey Wehrmacht colours, lay a couple of yards away, crumpled against a tree. It appeared he had been ejected from the vehicle when it hit the ditch, his head smashing against one of the sturdy roadside oaks, breaking his neck, killing him instantly.

"Corporal Murphy, look after the wounded man, and pull him away from the burning car. I'll see if there's anyone else in the vehicle."

The engine fire had significantly increased and there was an imminent threat of explosion. The driver moaned loudly as Murphy pulled him clear of the wreck.

Singer looked in the back of the car. Sprawled on the grey leather seat was a young woman, seemingly in her early twenties, with a silver-dollar-sized hole through her forehead. Blood from the wound had dyed her long blonde hair red. Her lifeless blue eyes stared up at the now-empty sky.

"This one's dead," he yelled to the corporal, not even worrying about searching for a pulse. No one could survive a head injury of that magnitude and live. "How's the other one?"

"In lousy shape, sir, but he might make it if we can get him back to the aid station quickly enough. Let's go before this thing blows!"

"Okay!" As he turned to help the corporal tend to the driver's wounds, the woman's body moved. "No, she's dead, this can't be," he muttered to himself in a moment of sheer panic. Then it shifted again, ever so slightly.

Singer quickly grabbed the woman's blood-soaked coat and started to lift her off the seat. "Now, what have we here?" he exclaimed, his barely audible words getting stuck in his throat as the car's gas tank exploded, shooting a column of bright-orange flame skyward.

CHAPTER 2

Daniel looked at the envelope, which was postmarked July 9, 1988.

The sender's particulars were unfamiliar to him: Kellermann, Czinner und Hugo Rechtsanwaltkanzlei, Kurfürstendamm 193, viii/3B, 10481 Berlin, Bundesrepublik, Deutschland. The postage stamp bore a likeness of Willy Brandt, former mayor of West Berlin and former West German Chancellor.

Daniel Singer's name and address were correct, however. The envelope had been registered, and he had picked it up at the post office on his way home late that afternoon. It was a large brown package sealed with security tape. After a couple of minutes of struggling with the tape, he finally used a pair of scissors to cut open the bottom of the envelope.

Its contents spilled onto the tiled floor, creating a messy pile. He bent over to retrieve the documents, immediately noticing a faded black-and-white photograph of a building paper-clipped to the top of a page. An address was written in marker across the bottom of the sheet of paper, and an arrow, also in marker, pointed to a fourth-floor window. There was an official-looking seal covering part of the picture and address.

WOHNUNG
SCHMIDT
#4

14 MEINEKE STRASSE

Daniel lifted the remaining pages from the floor. Since they were in German—at least, it looked like they were in German, though he couldn't be sure because he had no familiarity with the language—he simply tossed the pile onto the kitchen table.

He was hungry. He had skipped lunch, and preparing dinner was a far greater priority than examining some mysterious report. During the lunch hour he had been called to look at some 17th-century Italian etchings at an antique art gallery on East 57th Avenue.

Daniel was assistant curator of "European Old Masters" at the Metropolitan Museum of Art in New York City. The Algerian/French proprietor of an antique art gallery had acquired a portfolio purchase from an Armenian intermediary with attractive prices, but a dubious reputation. The owner was concerned that he had obtained some very authentic-looking fakes.

Daniel, being an acknowledged expert in his field and the proprietor of the gallery a minor patron of the New York art scene, felt compelled to rush over and examine the items in question. After close study, and much to the relief of the gallery owner, he pronounced all but two of the seventeen works of art by Canaletto, Guido Reni, and the Tiepolo brothers authentic.

By the time he finished, it was too late to eat. Since his girlfriend, Madelaine, was soon arriving for dinner, he now needed to quickly begin preparation.

They had been dating for four years, and for that entirety she had constantly complained about his lack of housekeeping skills. He wanted her to move in with him, but she refused until he met her Good Housekeeping Seal of Approval. He was incessantly teased about the fact that she could never find a clean plate in any of his kitchen cupboards.

Daniel picked up an unmatched pair of socks and a sweat-stained t-shirt from the bedroom carpet and tried stuffing them into the over-flowing laundry hamper in the corner. No luck. He tried pushing harder, but the wicker basket's sides gave way and its contents spilt onto the floor.

"Shit!" He grabbed the smelly clothes and deposited them into the bathtub, drawing the shower curtain to hide the whole mess. He went back into the kitchen and opened a cupboard, its door barely hanging by two loose hinges, and pulled out a bottle of 1979 Silver Oak cabernet sauvignon from his "wine rack"—simply a few red-clay drainpipes laid on their sides. After opening the bottle, he took a glass from the drying rack beside the sink, blew into it vigorously to get rid of the dust that had settled, and poured himself a generous portion.

He didn't bother with a taste, but instead emptied half the glass. He put it down on the papers he had placed on top of the table, spilling a drop in the process. He wiped it off with his thumb and couldn't help but look at the picture of the building once again. He wondered what the documents were all about and whether it was just a case of someone having sent it to the wrong name and address. He looked at the envelope much more carefully. *Nope, name and address match.* He rifled through the papers to find the cover page. Without a knowledge of German, he couldn't make head or tails of the letter. The sender seemed to be a law or accounting partnership with a West Berlin address.

He took another drink of wine and turned his attention back to the papers. His own name, and those of Helmut Johann Eckler, Heinrich Karl, Karl Bruno Schmidt, and Margit Angelika Hootveg appeared a number of times throughout the document, along with the address of the building in the picture. However, he had no way of figuring out their connection to him, each other, the document, or the building. Strangely, though, the name Bruno Schmidt jogged something in his memory from fifteen years before. *Nah, it couldn't be. Schmidt, like Smith in the US, must be a very common name in Germany.*

The loud, incessant buzzing of the apartment intercom shook him out of his preoccupation. He looked at his watch then rushed to let Madelaine into the building, muttering, "Hell, it's six-thirty already, and boy, am I in trouble!"

The kitchen was even messier than usual, due to the papers spread out on the table along with a leaking cardboard box that had contained the lobsters he prepared for dinner.

"I see another five-star Michelin restaurant in the making." Madelaine snickered sarcastically, surveying the chaos in front of her.

"A glass of wine?" Daniel asked half apologetically.

"No thanks, not right now, but some water would be great," she said, her breathing heavy from climbing the three sets of stairs to the apartment building's top floor.

He handed Madelaine a glass of water, refilled his own with wine, and asked how her day was. She wrinkled her nose from the slight chlorine smell as she took a sip. "Usual BS. Everyone wants everything at the same time, then gets pissed off if they're not the first ones to get it."

Madelaine was attractive in an understated fashion, with dark hair and sparkling green eyes. She lacked a Victoria's Secret figure, shunning the gym in favour of anything with an unhealthy dose of sugar.

Her looks were in total contrast to Daniel's. He was handsome, blue-eyed, thin, and tall, with an unruly mop of blond hair that was starting to turn white. He tried unsuccessfully to comb it in a manner that would hide his thinning crown.

Madelaine draped the jacket of her light blue business suit over one of the kitchen chairs as she kept talking. "How about you? How come you're just getting started?"

"Oh, had to go look over a couple of Italian Renaissance prints for Rougier on East 57th. He was hyperventilating because he thought he'd been swindled out of eighty grand. All's good, though," he continued. "Most of the etchings are lifetime originals."

He took a frying pan from under the sink, put some butter in it, and placed it on the stove. He turned back to Madelaine and gave her a light kiss on the forehead.

"Might cook faster if you lit the element under it." She giggled, giving him a hug.

After dinner, he opened a window, letting some early evening air inside. Outside a fine summer rain started to fall, and the dying cacophony of rush-hour traffic was replaced by the Moody Blues' "Nights in White Satin" from the cassette player on top of the refrigerator. The lights of New York City began to twinkle, illuminating a darkening sky, while the clouds played hide and go seek with a full moon.

All in all, a great day. Daniel drained the last of the wine from his glass and began to gently massage Madelaine's shoulders.

"Aaah, that feels good," she sighed, leaning her head back as Daniel went on with his gentle ministrations.

However, the mystery of the brown envelope continued to haunt his subconscious. *What could all this be about? I can't help but think that there might be something important here.*

CHAPTER 3

NOVEMBER 1938,

MUNICH, GERMANY

Sturmbannführer (Major) Bruno Schmidt of the SS (Schutzstaffel) or Protection Squadron bounded up the front steps of the elegant, neo-classic, marble-colonnaded edifice that was the SS, Gestapo, and Reich Main Security Building at 8 Prinz-Albrecht-Strasse in Berlin. It was a chilly, grey fall morning at the beginning of November 1938, and he was there to report to the office of his superior officer, Reinhard Heydrich, head of the combined German Secret Police apparatus.

That morning, Berlin was abuzz with news of the assassination of the First Secretary at the German embassy in Paris, by a young Polish Jew, and Bruno Schmidt had been summoned on Hitler's direct orders. There was a palpable atmosphere of impending crisis in the air in the capital. As Reich minister of propaganda Josef Goebbels said in his radio speech that evening, "The country's Jews will pay a heavy price for this heinous, dastardly act."

The SS guards, smartly attired in black uniforms, snapped to attention, raising their arms in the Hitler salute as Schmidt swept past them through the double doors of Heydrich's high-ceilinged, ornately furnished office. Schmidt was known in Nazi circles as an ambitious "up and comer." It didn't hurt his career trajectory in the Third Reich, either, that he was married to the sister of Arthur Nebe, head of the Criminal Investigation Police of the Reich Main Security

Office. Dressed in black, with silver SS runes on his collars, he was what Heinrich Himmler, minister of state security, referred to as the ultimate Aryan.

Tall, blond, muscular, and well-tanned with piercing blue eyes, he had been admitted to Ludwig Maximilian University of Munich. After his first year of general arts, he transferred to the law faculty to pursue a master's degree in criminal law. There he was befriended by, and came under the influence of, Hans Frank, three years his senior, who was the lawyer for the then-emerging National Socialist Workers Party (NSDAP), and would later become Adolf Hitler's personal attorney.

In 1924, the year of his graduation and calling to the Bavarian State bar, and as part of the practical component of his studies, he attended the trial of the defendants in the Munich Beer Hall Putsch (or *Hitlerputsch*) of 1923. During the attempted *putsch*, Adolf Hitler and his motley band of SA Stormtroopers, including Ernst Röhm, Hermann Göring, and Rudolf Hess, tried to overthrow the legally elected government of Bavaria. The trial started in February 1924, and Adolf Hitler was the chief defendant.

Bruno had been so impressed by Hitler's performance in court that he decided to contact him after the conclusion of the trial. Hitler was sentenced to five years for treason in *Festungshaft* (literally "fortress confinement") at Landsberg Prison. One of his frequent guests during his incarceration was the young lawyer Bruno Schmidt.

The two of them sat for hours in the anteroom of Hitler's comfortable cell, surrounded by some of Hitler's acolytes like Ernst Röhm, who was head of the Brownshirts, Hermann Göring, who was a World War I highly decorated fighter pilot and war hero, and Rudolf Hess, who would later become Deputy Führer. Schmidt and Hitler would discuss the *putsch*, Nazi and Aryan ideology, the war, and most frequently the "Jewish problem." Bruno was puzzled by Hitler's rabid fascination with the Jews. One evening, in the summer of 1925, in Hitler's dimly lit cell he asked, "Herr Hitler, why do you feel the Jews, being such a small percentage of Germany's population, pose such a big problem for us?"

"My young, naïve friend, you didn't personally experience the pain of our Fatherland being stabbed in the back by these blood-sucking Jewish profiteering vermin as we soldiers did at the front," Hitler shouted, so that everyone within the prison walls could hear him.

"But Herr Hitler, I went to university with a number of Jewish students, some of whom were war veterans returning to their studies. They seemed no different than me or the other Christian students."

"See, that's where they trick you, my young and gullible Bruno." Hitler's voice increased in volume. "They make you believe that they got there on merit. But oh no! Their parents bought their way into the school, bribing school officials with the profits from their ill-gotten gains on the backs of decent Germans. The Jews' and the Communists' aim is to enslave the German people and use them to increase their dominance of the banks and industry. Look around you. They control everything!"

They would debate late into the night, with Bruno sometimes falling asleep on the floor, and Hitler, a night owl, working on his book.

"Herr Hitler, your book *Mein Kampf (My Struggle)* is a blueprint for a Nazi future, not only for Germany, but the entire world. How are you going to accomplish that with only a few hundred followers?" Bruno would ask in a concerned tone of voice.

"As my good friend Herr Goebbels will tell you, today ideas are stronger than weapons, and slogans mightier than armies. We will win over ordinary Germans who have no jobs and no hope with our plan for the future greatness of our beloved Fatherland." Despite his ambivalence towards Jews, and his lack of the rabid anti-Semitism displayed by his compatriots in Hitler's inner circle, the young Schmidt was slowly drawn into the Nazi vortex. He attended Nazi rallies and also provided pro bono legal advice to Brownshirts who may have been arrested and jailed overnight for disturbing the peace. He also acted as a go-between for Hitler with Munich's right-leaning judiciary.

In 1925, Hitler was released from Landsberg, having served a little over eight months of his sentence and paying a 500 Reichsmark fine.

Bruno was then hired by a Munich law firm, with Hitler's sponsorship and recommendation.

Schmidt's love affair with Hitler and the Nazis, however, bought him into constant conflict at home. His father was a dyed-in-the-wool trade unionist and a member of the German Communist Party (KPD). Father and son would often clash, frequently at the dinner table, over their diverging alliances.

"How can a son of mine listen to the drivel of a fanatic anti-Semite and believe the filth that comes out of this idiot's mouth?" Karl Schmidt Sr. screamed at the top of his lungs. "I, who have been a member of the German trade union movement for thirty years, who has earned an honest living and provided for you and your mother, now has to share a meal with a brown-shirted street thug?"

Invariably, Frau Schmidt intervened before the two came to blows and gently escorted her son out the door. "Bruno, you know how upset your father gets about your friendship with these terrible people. Why don't you distance yourself from them? You are smart. You can find a good job with another law firm."

"Mutti, just pay attention! Herr Hitler and his group are destined for great things. Father's been working for thirty years, and all we have to show for it is this filthy apartment. The Fuhrer and the Party will change all that. They'll take money from the wealthy Jewish bankers and industrialists and give it to the honest little people. You just watch! And you better warn Father to beware who he gets mixed up with. He and his Marxist cronies are being closely watched."

"Son, your father is a good man, and you should show him some respect."

He slammed the door without saying goodbye to his father, heading down to the local beer hall to meet his less-than-savoury Nazi associates. The distance between him and his parents grew in direct relationship to the ascendancy of the NSDAP, until they no longer saw each other at all. By 1930, he had joined the Nazi Party. As a protégé of Hans Frank, he became a junior partner in the law firm of Axman, Streicher und

Wolff, who were at the forefront of dealing with legal and constitutional matters on behalf of Hitler and the NSDAP.

In the general elections of 1930, the Nazi Party dramatically increased its number of seats from 12 to 107, while the KPD (Communists) gained 23 seats to 77. Over the next three years, there were frequent street battles between Nazi SA Brownshirts and Communist trade unionists, with injuries and sometimes fatalities on both sides. The police would, more often than not, look the other way, especially when it was the SA's thugs administering the beatings.

In 1932, Bruno began an affair with Stefania "Steffi" Hartmann, the wife of Rolf Hartmann, one of Ernst Röhm's deputy SA commanders. Rolf was in his mid-fifties, had risen through the ranks of the SA participating in, and often leading, street battles between his Brownshirts, the Bavarian State Police, and the rival Marxists during the time of the Weimar Republic. He was a decorated officer in Kaiser Wilhelm's army, fighting on the Russian front during the First World War. A short, rotund man, Rolf had a swarthy, reddish complexion, such as one would see on people who had drunk more than their fair share of beer in their lifetime. His head, topped by a greying buzz cut, seemed too small for his body. He had large hands, with short, fat fingers, one of which was missing as a result of a knife cut sustained in a street fight.

Steffi Hartmann was the sister of Arthur Nebe, head of the Criminal Investigation Police of the Reich Main Security Office, and the daughter of wealthy Bavarian landowners who traced their lineage back to the twelfth-century Wittelsbach Dynasty. Not much love was lost between Nebe and his brother-in-law, whom he considered a low-class boor.

Bruno and Steffi met at a cocktail party hosted by Bruno's law firm for members of the Bavarian police force and SA stormtrooper officers in an effort to smooth out relations between the two.

Although he was eighteen years her junior, Steffi was immediately taken by the young, tall, and handsome lawyer with the piercing blue eyes who was surrounded by a bevy of fawning young secretaries.

"You certainly seem to enjoy the attention, Herr Schmidt."

"Oh yes, it does wonders for one's ego, but I prefer women with whom one can conduct an intelligent conversation outside of the bedroom."

"Well, that's certainly different than what most of the men with raging hormones in this room would prefer." Steffi stole a sideways glance at her husband, who was in deep conversation with his boss, the corpulent and scar-faced Ernst Röhm, while openly stroking the back of a short, plump, blonde secretary.

"So, what kind of law do you practise, Herr Schmidt?"

"Please, call me Bruno. I mostly defend your husband's associates when they get into trouble with the police for one transgression or other. And you, what do you occupy your time with, Madame?"

"When not at an official charity function or fundraiser for the Party with the other poor, neglected SA officers' wives, I lie on my back and fill the space between the mattress and him," she replied sarcastically, with a contemptuous look in the direction of her spouse.

Just then Hans Frank approached and whispered in Bruno's ear.

"Frau Hartmann, duty calls." Bruno excused himself, clicking his heels together and bending down and planting a kiss on Frau Hartmann's outstretched hand. He lowered his voice, saying, "It was a pleasure. Perhaps we can continue our conversation at some other time?"

"That would be delightful, Herr Schmidt. Why don't you come by our house for dinner with my husband and I one evening? That is, if you find yourself without more exciting company." She smiled at him.

Bruno couldn't get the conversation or the visage of Steffi Hartmann out of his head as he walked home to his small apartment in Munich's Schwabing artists' quarter. She was slim and tall, with long auburn hair worn in a bun and sleepy hazel eyes. A week later he found himself at the Hartmanns' dinner table in Altstadt, or Old Town, enjoying pork roast with sour cabbage prepared by the Hartmanns' Nazi-Party-supplied maid.

After dinner, accompanied by copious amounts of Moselland Bernkasteler Kurfurstlay riesling, the three of them sat in the salon, nursing glasses of sour-cherry schnapps and listening to *Tannhäuser*, an opera by Richard Wagner, the Nazis' favourite composer, on the gramophone.

Rolf was stretched out in a large, comfortable, leather-upholstered armchair, with Steffi sitting on one arm, with her long, shapely legs hanging down, her stocking tops just showing beneath her skirt. She made no effort to adjust her position, despite the fact that Bruno was in a chair opposite her and quite obviously enjoying the view. If her husband noticed, he didn't show any sign of it. Her long hair cascaded over her shoulders, with a few strands falling across her forehead that she continually swept away as she engaged in animated conversation about the role of women in the "New" Germany.

"Tell me, Schmidt, do you have a girlfriend? Someone with your Aryan good looks and position should have his pick of eligible Fräuleins." Rolf smiled.

"Frankly, Herr Hartmann, I just haven't found the right one yet. These young ones all have stars in their eyes, and I am too preoccupied with my work to take the time to train them."

Rolf chuckled at that comment. "Old roosters, young hens. That's what I always say."

"No, what I am looking for is a woman, not a girl," Bruno responded.

He snuck a sideways glance at Steffi as he finished. Their eyes met for a moment, and the die was cast.

The next morning, Bruno's telephone rang. "Hello, Herr Schmidt."

He immediately recognised the voice.

"Thank you for coming by last evening and thank you especially for the dozen beautiful white roses. Their fragrance fills our entire apartment. I was wondering if you would like to meet for a coffee later this afternoon? Maybe we can continue our conversation from the other evening. I know of a wonderful little patisserie in Schwabing, not too far from where you live, I believe."

Quite surprisingly, he, the consummate attorney and talker, was speechless for a moment.

"Ahem, ahem," he stuttered. "Yes, I would really like that. What is the name of the place?"

"The Poor Artist's Café at half past two, then?"

"Yes, I know where it is. I am looking forward to seeing you again."

For the next year, the two of them conducted an illicit affair, meeting in hotels and restaurants or going for walks in the countryside, away from probing eyes. They would also bump into each other at various Nazi Party functions, but kept their distance, lest their secret was discovered.

On one occasion, however, they were nearly outed. They ran into each other at a masquerade ball at Nymphenburg Palace in October 1932 celebrating Joseph Goebbels' thirty-fifth birthday.

With no one else around, Bruno grabbed Steffi's arm and pulled her into the men's washroom. No words were needed as their lips met, and he lifted her skirt, pulling her silken underwear to her knees in one swift motion. She struggled with the multi-buttoned fly of his trousers and swore under her breath at the Uhlan Cavalry officer's costume that he had rented for the ball. She had just about freed his manhood from its constraints when they heard voices outside, and the outer door of the washroom opened.

They were lucky, as whoever was coming in stopped to converse with someone else, giving Steffi just enough time to sneak into a cleaner's closet, and for Bruno to pretend to have just relieved himself and do up the fly of his trouser.

Two inebriated men—one dressed as a Viking, the other in a clown costume—entered and tried to strike up a conversation. Bruno demurred and quickly exited to await Steffi outside the door. After what seemed like eternity, the two drunks also came out, followed a few minutes later by her. Steffi and Bruno looked at each other, laughing hysterically as they returned to the ballroom through separate entrances.

Most times they would end up in Bruno's modest apartment satisfying their physical yearning for each other. They made love in the afternoons, after which Steffi would hurry home to wait for Rolf's return from work, which became later and later.

It was 1933 and the fortunes of the NSDAP were on the rise, along with those of its Stormtroopers of the SA. In addition to the increased activity within his organisation, Rolf had also taken up with a nineteen-year-old secretary from his office. She, a simple country girl, had become infatuated with Hartmann's political power and sphere of control over events in Munich. For Germany, 1933 was to be a watershed year, one of enormous changes and ominous upheavals that would bring Adolf Hitler and the Nazis to power for the next twelve years.

CHAPTER 4

Arnold Weisz moved stealthily along the dark street leading to Budapester Strasse and the Tiergarten (zoo) on a blustery January 1944 evening in Berlin. He carefully picked his way through the ruins, not wanting to be noticed by any of the other dark figures creeping like ghosts in the blackout. They were likely on the same desperate mission as he. The light of the full moon—what pilots referred to as a Bomber's Moon—reflected off the thin veneer of snow covering the street and debris, sparkling like small diamonds on an ermine blanket. Arnold wondered whether the RAF, whose Lancasters and Halifaxes made their bombing runs at night while the Americans performed the daylight raids, would be back to pay them another visit that evening.

Earlier that day, a squadron of three hundred four-engined B-24 Liberator bombers of the Americans' Eighth Air Force had dropped their twelve hundred tons of high-explosive payloads over Berlin. According to Dr. Joseph Goebbels, the Third Reich's enlightenment and propaganda minister, in his radio speech following the air raid, "the damage inflicted by the bombers was superficial and would not impact Germany's war effort." Having listened to Goebbels' speech earlier on a clandestine radio, Arnold could only snicker as he picked his way in the dark over the rubble obstructing his path. Spots of blue flame from broken gas mains provided some illumination, as did smouldering fires here and there amongst the destruction. *Superficial damage?* Two whole city blocks around his apartment building were obliterated, turned into rubble and dust. He wasn't quite sure what they were after, since there were no military installations nearby, but he thanked God, as irreligious as he was, that other than a few cracked window panes, his apartment in Charlottenburg didn't suffer any damage.

Arnold had been a patent lawyer, and a very good one at that. "Had been" because, being a Jew, the Nazis' Nuremberg race laws of 1935 stripped him not only of his livelihood and dignity, but also of the Doctor of Law degree he had obtained after five long years of study at the prestigious University of Heidelberg. Now he, his wife, Ingrid, their eight-year-old son, Max, and their red-headed four-year-old twins, Elsa and Rachel, were in hiding. Fugitives in the land of their birth, they lived in daily fear of discovery, arrest, and deportation to one of the many extermination camps dotting Eastern Europe's war-torn landscape. All of their Jewish neighbours had long ago been arrested by the Gestapo and hustled off to Grunewald railway station for "resettlement" in the East, never to be heard from again.

His father-in-law, Alexander "Papa" Grossman, had used the proceeds of the sale of one of his two Grossman Menswear and Haberdashery stores in Berlin to purchase the large apartment in Berlin's Charlottenburg upper-middle-class neighbourhood. Papa Grossman had returned from the First World War, having fought for two years on the Western Front, as a subaltern with the 173rd Field Artillery Battalion and was cited for bravery during the Battle of the Somme. Apprenticed as a tailor before the war, he seized the opportunity to own a haberdashery in the chaos and turmoil of post-war Berlin.

Two menswear stores had come up for sale by the widow of the owner, who had been a casualty of one of the British gas attacks during the last year of the conflict in Belgium. One store was located just outside Berlin's city limits in the exclusive suburb of Potsdam, and the other was on Wieland Strasse near Kurfürstendamm, one of Berlin's wide and fashionable main thoroughfares. Alexander's wife, Esther, had given birth in 1914 to their daughter Ingrid, named after her paternal grandmother; she was the couple's only child after Esther had suffered a number of miscarriages.

Arnold and Ingrid met in 1930 when she was just sixteen. She was short and thin, with a light complexion and wispy black hair. Her most prominent and noticeable feature was her emerald-green eyes whose colours were even more pronounced due to her fair skin. She was intelligent, having graduated at the top of her class, was valedictorian, and along with her mother turned out to be an excellent piano player, winning several competitions. She had been lucky enough, in the midst of the Great Depression, to be offered a summer job at the prestigious Berlin law firm of Guthausen, Braunstein und Pockler through a client of her father's. It was in this office that Arnold Weisz started articling at the same time.

CHAPTER 5

Arnold was nine when the Great War broke out. He had been born into a privileged family with a long history in the legal profession. His grandfather had been a trusted adviser to Chancellor Bismarck, and his father, Maximillian, joined the staff of the Advocate General of Kaiser Wilhelm's army at the outbreak of hostilities. Seeing his contemporaries enlisting in various branches of the military, and leaving for active duty at the front, while he was in a safe and comfortable desk job, he resigned his posting in Berlin and joined the Imperial German Navy. Two months after being commissioned as a lieutenant and assigned to the modern battle cruiser *SMS Lützow* as a gunnery officer, he was killed when his ship was sunk by the Royal Navy at the Battle of Skagerrak in May 1916. He was posthumously awarded the Iron Cross 2nd Class.

As a consequence of being the son of a decorated war hero killed in action, the German State provided Arnold with the best education at the most prestigious schools in Germany. Despite the difficulties of life without a father and the challenge of being Jewish in a country with an inbred cultural undercurrent of anti-Semitism, Arnold graduated at the head of his class from the law faculty of the University of Heidelberg.

He was short and stocky, with dark curly hair and a nose broken in a fight with some Jew-baiting classmates. He exuded an air of confidence and was well liked by his colleagues for his ever-present sense of humour. At the age of twenty-four, he joined one of Germany's most respected patent and trademark legal firms as an articling student. And it was here that he first laid eyes on Ingrid, his future wife. The attraction was immediate and mutual. Arnold was called to the bar in 1932, and the two married a year later.

After their honeymoon in Tuscany, and at Esther and Papa's insistence, they moved into their in-laws' apartment. It was an idyllic existence that frequently found the four of them spending evenings together having dinner, with Esther and Ingrid playing the piano in the art-deco-furnished salon afterwards. Their maid, Heldi, would often hum along with the music, much to Esther's well-camouflaged annoyance, while she cleaned up in the dining room adjacent to the salon. The melodious music of Mozart, Schubert, or Bartok would drift into the oak-panelled, book-lined study where Papa and Arnold busied themselves with a game of chess or discussed the day's political events while inhaling the heady aroma of some Cuban cigars and sipping their vintage Berentzen Winter Apfle schnapps. Their favourite topic of political conversation those days was the recent rise to the chancellorship of Adolf Hitler, the "Austrian Corporal" as Papa liked to refer to him. The two held quite opposing views.

"Do you for a moment think the German population is so stupid as to let this moustachioed little man with the funny hair stay in power for more than a month or two? Either that or Herr Hitler will need to change his tune, especially about us Jews. He needs us to help him run the finances of this bankrupt country," Papa said, exhaling a cloud of smoke from his Cohiba.

"Don't underestimate the man, and don't overestimate the political awareness of our poor, unemployed working class, Alex. Bad days are yet to come," Arnold shot back.

"Oh, you lawyers are always so pessimistic, forever complaining that the glass is half empty. Our economy is starting to bounce back, and people are returning to work. Why, the other day a gentleman came into the shop and ordered two made- to-measure suits. That hasn't happened since the twenties. Believe me, my boy, this Nazi stuff is just a passing infatuation."

"I hope that you're right Alex, but I've heard whispers around the firm that the Justice Ministry asked us to provide them the names and addresses of all of our Jewish partners. Now, why would they do that?"

Their conversations often ended with Papa dozing off and loudly snoring, his half-smoked cigar smouldering in the ashtray on the table beside him. Arnold would then quietly head into the kitchen to get Heldi to brew him a cup of Italian espresso before returning to the salon to join his wife and mother-in-law.

Heldi came to Berlin from Salzburg at the age of twenty-one and was one of six daughters born to a deeply religious Austrian dairy farmer and his wife. She came from the grassy meadows at the foot of the Alps to the hustle and bustle of cosmopolitan Berlin to find employment. Heldi had been working for the Grossmans from the time Ingrid was three, and had been hired as a nanny, cook, and cleaning lady. Although Catholic, and not living with them in their apartment, she was treated as one of the family. On weekends they would all go for pleasure boat rides on the River Spree or walks in the Tiergarten. But it was 1933, and dark clouds were gathering on the horizon as Adolf Hitler and his NSDAP were about to usurp the mantle of power in the Reichstag.

As Arnold stumbled and felt his way around the rubble in the dark, his memory strayed back to those wonderful, carefree days, which now seemed a millennium ago. He could hardly believe that it had only been a decade since the four of them had happily strolled through this pulverized neighbourhood on their way for lunch at one of the elegant restaurants at Berlin's zoo. Oh! How Ingrid and her father loved those animals. Especially the majestic big cats from Africa and India.

And now Arnold was headed back there, not for enjoyment and wonderment, but for a very basic necessity. Food! From rumours rushing like a wildfire through the neighbourhood that afternoon, it appeared that some of the bombs dropped by the Americans that morning had missed their target by a wide margin and had hit the Tiergarten grounds, destroying many of the animals' enclosures and killing a large number of its four-legged residents, as well as a lot of exotic birds from around the globe.

In 1944 the average Berliner was subsisting on only 794 calories per day. Most of the food intake consisted of root vegetables like beets and potatoes, some fat, and bread baked from any flour-like ingredient, including sawdust. Meat was a luxury only enjoyed by those in the higher echelons of the Nazi Party.

Ordinary Berliners would stand in queues for hours in all kinds of weather in front of a butcher shop to buy a chicken thigh, a bit of pork hock, or a gristly, tiny chunk of beef to feed to their emaciated children. Skinny horses used to cart freight around the city, for lack of petrol, were a favourite target of many desperate city dwellers. Often, the horses would drop from exhaustion, or be killed or wounded in an air raid, only to be set upon by hordes of men and women spilling out like so many ants from nearby homes, most in ruins, brandishing kitchen knives and even scissors, desperate for a piece of horse flesh to sustain them and their families for another day. Many a bloody fight had broken out over a scrawny equine appendage. It was with this mindset that the carnage at Berlin's zoo, world famous before the war for the variety and number of its wild animals from all corners of the world, became a magnet for its starving populace.

Arnold shook his head, trying to chase away the images of those halcyon days from his mind in order to concentrate on his desperate, gruesome objective. The other ghostly interlopers around him all had the same goal in sight. Hopefully there would still be some scraps left of the carcasses of the wild animals killed in the raid for them to take back home. *We are back to the Stone Age*, he mused to himself. Unbeknownst to him, worse was yet to come.

CHAPTER 6

SUMMER 1988,

NEW YORK CITY—SINGER FAMILY HISTORY

"I am sure you baked something totally decadent for dessert," Madelaine teased Daniel as she took another sip of her wine.

"I was going to but didn't have time to pick up anything. Maybe we can go for a walk and stop in at Zucker's Bakery for a cappuccino and apple strudel. Another of my mother's favourites."

"You do miss your mother, don't you?" Madelaine sadly but matter-of-factly enquired, cocking her head to the side.

Agnes (Agatha) Singer had been the pillar of strength in Daniel's life. She was born in 1915 in Brooklyn into a well-to-do Jewish family. Her father, Bernard, was a surgeon at Brooklyn's Zion Hospital. Her mother, Sarah, was a budding mystery writer who spent her days following Brooklyn cops on their beat, hoping to pick up ideas and clues for mystery novels she hoped to write. She had some short stories published in the *Brooklyn Daily Eagle*, but never actually finished writing a complete book. Agnes's birth interrupted Sarah's writing career (her mother insisted that she change her name to Agatha at the age of eight, after Agatha Christie, the famous British mystery writer) and she never again sat down at her Underwood typewriter.

In 1936, Agatha married Samuel Singer, a colleague of her father's at Zion Hospital. He was thirteen years Agatha's senior, a handsome, pipe-smoking giant of a man with a greying and receding hairline, who looked older than his thirty-three years. Samuel's parents had emigrated from Meissen, Germany, on the river Elbe in the late 1800s, settling down in Corning, New York, where his father continued his profession as a glass blower at the famous Corning Glass Works.

Samuel graduated from medical School at Cornell University in 1928. After their marriage, Samuel and Agatha settled down in a small, two-bedroom house in the Queens neighbourhood of New York City. After the Japanese attack on Pearl Harbor on December 7, 1941, he resigned his position at the hospital and volunteered for the US Army Medical Corps. He was commissioned as a captain, and after training at Carlisle Barracks in Pennsylvania, was posted to the 18th Mobile Surgical Unit in the south of England in early 1944. He landed at Utah Beach in Normandy with a field hospital two weeks after D-Day, having been promoted to major the day before they sailed from Southampton. In France, his unit was attached to General Omar Bradley's 12th Army Group.

CHAPTER 7

Daniel and Madelaine huddled under the umbrella as they hurried through the evening crowds on the busy Friday night. With Daniel being a frequent customer at Zucker's, they managed to skip the lineup outside and made their way to a small table near the window. The sound of Billy Joel's 1977 hit "Scenes from an Italian Restaurant" over the antiquated audio system provided the musical background to the hubbub of the crowded eatery.

"An apple strudel with whipped cream, two forks and two cappuccinos, please." Daniel smiled as a waiter approached their table. "How have you been, Howard?"

"Staying out of trouble since that last episode with the cab driver," the waiter replied.

"Well, keep it that way, kid. I don't want to lose my favourite waiter and fellow Yankees fan." Daniel laughed, then turned back to Madelaine. "It's been really hard since Mother died. You only met her once and didn't really have a chance to get to know her."

"That's unfortunate, because she must have been an incredible lady from all you told me."

"That she was! You know, she and Grandpa Bernard used to come here for dinner in the forties. But I guess I've told you that before."

"Only every time we come here." She chuckled, a broad smile crossing her face.

Daniel moved a lock of hair from her face with his hand, giving her a kiss on the lips.

"You know I love you, and if you could ever clean up that messy place of yours, I might even consider moving in with you," she said, her voice serious.

As their strudel and cappuccinos arrived, Daniel said, "You know, Maddie, shivers run down my spine every time I come in here and imagine my mom and Grandpa Bernard sitting where we are."

"Tell me more about what happened back then." She dropped three cubes of sugar into her coffee.

Back then was 1945, the year in which Agatha and Samuel Singer adopted baby Daniel at the age of one.

"Well, as Mom told me the story just before she passed away last year, she and my father had always wanted children, but she, due to some medical issues she didn't elaborate upon, had difficulty conceiving. She wanted to become a clinical psychologist but never got past completing her application to Sarah Lawrence College.

"In 1944, Dad was still overseas. In late July, Grandpa Bernard delivered a baby boy through a Caesarian section. They had run into some difficulties during the delivery, and the mother, a widow whose husband, a US Army sergeant, had been killed in action at Anzio in Italy earlier that year, died on the operating table right after delivery. The nurses at Zion Hospital looked after the baby during the first year of his life.

"My mother, on frequent visits to my grandfather at the hospital, would look in on the little blond-haired, blue-eyed baby and spend hours playing with him, feeding him and changing his diaper. On the occasional weekend, she would take him back to Westchester with them. Spending time away from the baby became more and more difficult for her. When Dad returned from Europe in late 1945, Mom and he decided to adopt me. They named me Daniel after a wartime friend of my dad's. I didn't know that I had been adopted until after my father passed away and shortly before Mother died. My father, for some strange reason, didn't want me to know, and Mother went along with keeping it a secret until he was no longer alive."

Daniel took a sip from his cappuccino and continued.

"Anyhow, I grew up the typical Jewish kid in Larchmont, playing baseball in Little League as a catcher. My Grandpa Bernard would come to every one of my games. My father would pick us up after, and the three of us would go out for ice cream to Egger's Ice Cream Parlor on Staten Island."

"I love that story," Madelaine gushed as she put her arms around Daniel's shoulders and gave him a hug and a kiss.

"I regret to this day that I wasn't able to get to my mother's bedside in time when she called from the hospital. She apparently wanted to let me know that there was another aspect of my adoption that she still had to reveal to me."

"You know, Daniel, we all have our little secrets locked away in our hearts," she said.

"I am not sure what she meant by that. I was just getting ready to leave for LaGuardia for my flight to Rome to look at some Michelangelo drawings at the Vatican archives, and I thought I could visit her when I got back. Sadly, she took a turn for the worse while I was gone, and by the time I returned, she'd slipped into a coma. She never came out of it, so to this day I continue to wonder what that 'little secret' was. I was deeply saddened by her passing and very much regretted not seeing her before she died and finding out what aspect of my adoption she still wanted to disclose to me," Daniel explained with a sad look darkening his face.

Madelaine took Daniel's hand in hers and slowly caressed his fingers with her lips. The two sat in silence as the rain cascaded down Zucker's shop window and the Friday evening stream of revellers and theatregoers outside started to thin out.

After a few moments, Daniel went on. "I've searched the hospital and city records on births and adoptions in 1944 and 1945, and found a copy of my adoption certificate, but could find no trace of a baby boy being born at Zion around what was supposed to be my birthday. When I looked through my mother's things after she passed away, there was a letter that my dad had written to her and I when he snuck off to Israel in 1948. It mentioned something about being forever grateful to 'Mickey,' the friend of my dad's that I was named after. According to the letter, he had made my adoption possible by interceding with then-General Eisenhower. Unfortunately, 'Mickey' was killed in the 1948 Arab–Israeli War in Israel, so I couldn't follow up with him. I attended his funeral at Arlington National Cemetery with my parents. I was only four, so I don't remember much."

"Anything else for you two lovebirds before we close shop?" Howard's query came like a thunderclap out of nowhere, breaking the quiet that had settled over the little corner table by the window. Daniel and Madelaine looked around the restaurant and were surprised to find that most of the other patrons had already left, and staff were cleaning the tables.

"Wow! I didn't think we'd been here that long. What time is it?"

Madelaine looked at her watch. "It's a quarter after midnight."

Daniel quickly drained what was left of his cappuccino and, leaving a twenty-dollar bill on the table, took Madelaine's hand as they slipped out the door.

"Have a good night, and try to stay dry," Howard yelled after them.

Their umbrella provided little protection from the sheets of rain as they hugged the sides of the buildings, trying to keep from getting completely soaked. Back at Daniel's apartment, Daniel went to the bathroom and got out of his wet clothes, threw them into the bathtub on top of his dirty laundry, and changed into a New York Yankees logoed track suit.

Madelaine took off her suit jacket and pants and draped them over one of the kitchen chairs. Then, in bra and underwear, she decided to clean up the dirty dishes. While piling them into the sink, she noticed a sheaf of papers on the counter under the window. They were stuck together from the rain that had come in through the opening Daniel had forgotten to close before they left.

"Hey, Mr. Clean, what do you want me to do with these soaked papers?" she yelled into the bathroom.

Daniel entered the kitchen and handed Madelaine a towel. "Here, you better dry your hair before it goes all curly on you." He chuckled, knowing how much Madelaine hated her natural curls. "As for the papers, just spread them out on the table and they should dry out by morning."

In bed later, Daniel hugged Madelaine and slowly started to stroke her breasts, removing her bra in the process. They kissed tenderly, their tongues intertwining. Daniel moved his hand down to her belly.

"Stop, mister," Madelaine whispered. "I haven't taken a shower since this morning."

Daniel knew from past experience he shouldn't push her, as she wouldn't make love to him without first having taken a bath or shower. So, he discontinued his amorous advances and rolled onto his back.

Madelaine turned on her side and, raising her head, leaned over. "What are the papers on the counter all about? They look official," she whispered in the dark, not sure if Daniel was still awake.

"Huh?" he responded, only partly comprehending the question as he was drifting off to sleep. "Oh, I don't know. They're in German." He yawned, quickly falling back asleep, leaving Madelaine to wonder about the meaning of the documents.

CHAPTER 8

In Germany, 1936 was the third year of rule by the NSDAP or National Socialist Workers Party (Nazi). Adolph Hitler's anti-Semitic rabble had come to power in 1933 through the ballot box. Everything that Arnold Weisz had warned his father-in-law about three years before had come to pass. The last few years had indeed been dark days for the Jews of Berlin after the passage in the Reichstag of the Nurnberg Race Laws of 1935. One of these edicts forbade the practice of law in Germany by Jews.

Arnold was dismissed from his junior partnership position in the law firm, which by then was called Guthausen und Pockler, having rid itself of Mendel Braunstein, the Jewish senior partner, in order to comply with the new Nazi edicts. Had it not been for the generosity of Ziggy Guthausen, who in 1934, sensing what was yet to come, paid a handsome bribe to a Berlin city clerk to excise his own Jewish ancestor from the Guthausen family's records at City Hall Archives, Arnold would not have received any compensation at all for his percentage of the partnership.

On the day in early 1936 that Arnold left the firm for the last time, Ziggy Guthausen called him into his office. "Look, Arnold, I don't like this dirty Nazi business either, but we have no choice in the matter. We either let all the Jewish partners and law clerks go, or the Ministry shuts the firm down. I am sure that this little bit of Jew-baiting hysteria will die down once Herr Hitler gets booted from office in the next election. But until then, one needs to lay low. Here are three thousand Reichsmark for your piece of the partnership. Take my advice, my friend, buy your way out of Germany."

Guthausen didn't look Arnold in the eye but rather cast his gaze down at the floor as he spoke, visibly regretting the action he was forced to take with his junior partner, worried about the man and his family's future in a country quickly sliding toward the abyss.

"Thank you for your generous offer, Herr Guthausen, but I can't leave Germany. I have my wife here, and she's in her ninth month of pregnancy. My mother's in a clinic, hovering between life and death, and my in-laws, the Grossmans, will never leave this country. Anyway, where would we all go? No country that I know of is taking in Jews these days."

Arnold responded quietly, with a resigned look on his face, also avoiding eye contact with his senior partner. "Okay, son. Take the money I am offering you, and I will try to get you some outside contract work to give you some cash-flow, as long as we don't put your name on it. A filthy mess, this is." With a sad look, he shook his head, with its shock of grey hair, and pressed the banknotes into Arnold's palm, laying his arm on his former junior partner's shoulder as he bade him what he thought would be a final farewell.

Arnold was in a daze as he exited the building. He didn't want to go home to face the family with the devastating news that he no longer had the ability to provide for them. He wandered from one street to the next without clear direction. It was late afternoon by the time he ended up on the Unter den Linden. There was a large demonstration in progress in front of the Athlon Hotel, just up from the Brandenburg Gate.

He was caught up and swept along with the crowd who were loudly singing the "Horst-Wessel-Lied," the Nazi Party's marching anthem: "Clear the streets for the brown battalions, Clear the streets for the storm division! Millions are looking upon the swastika full of hope …"

The words were enough to propel him back to reality. A light, powdery spring snow had started to fall as the procession continued down the wide boulevard bordered by linden trees on either side. A lot of the demonstrators were carrying crude homemade signs that read *Juden Raus* (Jews Out), with caricatures of hook-nosed men, blood on their teeth, wearing Jewish skullcaps.

Passing the open entrance of a brew pub by the name of The Jolly Blond Maiden, he quickly ducked inside. He stumbled down the stairs into a small, smoke-filled room with a bar and around half a dozen tables.

"Look what the wind blew in," a booming voice hollered from somewhere behind the bar.

Arnold felt all eyes in the crowded place focussing in on him as he leaned for support against the door frame. The smell of beer, sweat, and cigarette smoke invaded his senses.

"A filthy Jew from the looks of him," yelled another voice.

Because of the haze that obscured his view, Arnold couldn't dodge the punch that flew at him out of nowhere, hitting him square in the forehead over his left eye, shattering his glasses. Blood started to trickle down his face as he turned and half- crawled, half-ran back upstairs and out through the entrance. The crowd had passed, although he could still hear their singing in the distance, the words faintly carried on the wind, *"For the struggle, we all stand prepared. Already Hitler's banners fly over all streets … "*

He was quite alone as he leaned against the building's brickwork. Blood ran down his face, staining the snow that had started to accumulate on the sidewalk. *Welcome to the new Germany,* he thought. He took out his handkerchief and tried to wipe as much of the congealing blood as he could from his face. The world around him was a blur as he put the intact pieces of his glasses into his coat pocket.

The sky darkened and the gas lights along Unter der Linden began to glow blue. He walked towards the nearest S-Bahn (commuter train) stop. As he got on the crowded carriage, it was as if the gazes of all the other passengers were in his direction. Never in his life had he felt so vulnerable.

He got off at the Kurfürstendamm station across from the Zoological Gardens and hurried on the slippery pavement as fast as his feet would carry him. Curious crowds had gathered by the shop windows along the avenue, and the loud, haranguing voice of Adolph Hitler boomed from the radios inside. Despite the cold, those listening outside seemed riveted to the pavement and mesmerised by the Führer's voice, rising to a crescendo. Arnold only heard snippets of it as he moved ever faster: *"Citizens of the Fatherland ... our troops are on the march to reoccupy the Rhineland ... perfidious Jews who stabbed our great nation ... Sieg Heil, Sieg Heil ..."*

He tried to blend into the background, afraid of being noticed, as the men, women, and children all raised their right arms, some with red, white, and black swastika arm bands above their right elbows, in the Nazi salute and yelled in unison with Hitler, and each other, *"Sieg Heil. Sieg Heil."* Unnoticed, he crossed the street, walking down Meineke Strasse. He was thankful when he got to number 14 and put his key into the shiny steel lock of the ornate plate-glass front entrance of his building.

He was too exhausted to climb the four sets of stairs as was his usual habit. Instead, he pushed the call button for the small wood-and-glass, four-passenger elevator. The whirring sound of the lift cables and the cooking odours drifting down from one flat or other provided him with the comforting sense of having finally reached home.

"Mein Gott, Herr Weisz!" screamed Heldi as Arnold walked through the door of the apartment. "What happened to you?"

"It's my welcome to the new Germany from that passing Nazi phase that Alex keeps talking about. Where are Ingrid and my in-laws?" he asked, since none of the other inhabitants of the flat came running in response to Heldi's panicked, loud voice.

"Oh, your in-laws took Frau Weisz to the hospital," Heldi said. "She began to go into labour and the midwife couldn't get through because of some street demonstrations. They were finally able to get a taxi to take them."

"Which hospital?"

"The Königin Elisabeth on Karlhorster Strasse is the closest, and Dr. Walter Wolff is the head doctor there. He's very good."

Arnold quickly turned around to head back out the door but was stopped by Heldi.

"Herr Weisz, you need to clean up before you go. You look terrible. And where are your glasses?"

"Oh yes," he replied as he fished the broken pieces from his coat pocket. "Could you please get my other pair from the bedside table in our bedroom while I wash up?"

In the bathroom, he was shocked by the face staring back at him in the mirror.

"Here, let me look at that." Heldi was standing behind him, holding his glasses. She took a hand towel and soaked it in cold water under the tap, and then gently wiped away the blood that had by then caked on to Arnold's left eyebrow.

"It's not as bad as it first looked, Herr Weisz. I'll put some iodine and gauze over it, and you'll be as good as new."

"Thank you, Heldi. I must hurry now." He turned around and started walking back down the hall. As he opened the door, Heldi grabbed his arm.

"This might come in handy," she said as she took a small badge and pinned it on Arnold's lapel. Arnold looked down to see a round, red-and-white enamel badge with a black swastika and the letters NSDAP in the foreground. Arnold stared at her quizzically, half in disgust.

"Some Hitler Jugend were handing them out by the U-Bahn (subway) exit this morning. Don't worry, even though I am also Austrian like Adolf, as a Catholic I don't share either his views or his methods. I hope this nightmare comes to an end soon. Good luck, and please wish your wife well."

Arnold gave her a hug as he turned around and ran down the stairs.

Back towards Kurfürstendamm, the crowds had dissipated, and the snow had stopped falling. He passed a policeman on the corner who, noticing his badge, gave him a perfunctory "Heil Hitler," raising his arm in half a salute. Arnold responded in kind. He was in a hurry to catch the next U-Bahn, which would drop him off within a few hundred metres of the hospital. The subway platform was crowded with people heading home from work. Everybody was talking about Hitler's speech from earlier that evening.

"Wasn't that powerful?" one said.

"Oh yes, and we are finally kicking those Frenchies in the ass in the Rhineland," responded another.

Arnold tried to blend in, his Nazi badge giving him some cover and comfort. A small band of World War I veterans in wheelchairs or on crutches were playing the "Horst-Wessel" march in a corner of the station as passersby dropped coins into the steel bucket in front of them. The crowded train finally pulled into the station and began to disgorge its weary passengers.

A commotion had erupted somewhere down the platform. "You dirty Yid," a voice shouted as a small, elderly man, obviously Jewish by his appearance, was being escorted from the train by a burly policeman holding him by the scruff of the neck. "Jews should walk, not take space from good German burghers," the policeman yelled as he shoved the old man through the crowd.

Arnold looked around as he was being jostled by those behind him into the carriage. He noted some sympathetic faces, but by and large the people seemed apathetic, tired, and disinterested in the goings-on and he was happy when the doors closed and the train started to move.

Arnold arrived at Königin Elisabeth just as the evening shift of nurses was taking over from the day shift. He went to the reception desk to enquire as to the whereabouts of his wife. The receptionist, a large woman with blonde corn braids and apple-red cheeks, looked at him curiously. She looked at the patient admission register. "I'm sorry, but I don't see anyone by that name being admitted today."

"Perhaps under the name Grossman?" he asked.

"No, not that name either," she said impatiently. "Please wait here. I'll call one of the doctors who's still here from the afternoon shift to talk to you."

About fifteen minutes passed before a bespectacled young man in a white coat, with a stethoscope wrapped around his neck, appeared at the desk. "Good evening, sir. I'm Doctor Steinmeir." He nodded to Arnold. "I understand that you were enquiring about an Ingrid Weisz, who was supposedly admitted here earlier today, in labour?"

"That's correct. Is there anything wrong?" Arnold's agitated voice rose in volume.

"Please calm down, sir." The young man took Arnold by the arm and walked him over to a quiet corner of the white, antiseptically clean reception hall, and the two of them sat down on a bench. "How are you related to this Ingrid Weisz?"

"I'm her husband, and this is our first child. What's the matter?"

"Look, sir, I was the one who saw her when she came in, accompanied by what I believe were her parents."

"Yes." Arnold began to shake, overcome with worry and trepidation as he listened to the doctor's whispered tone.

"Look, Herr....?"

"Weisz," Arnold whispered back.

"Yes, of course. Look, you have nothing to worry about, but since last week, after Dr. Wolff was dismissed and replaced by Dr. Hahn, a member of the Nazi party, the hospital has refused to take in any Jewish patients, even in emergency situations. Myself, it's not something I agree with."

As Dr. Steinmeier spoke, Arnold couldn't help but cough nervously and fidget with the buttons of his coat as he grew more and more concerned and agitated about what had transpired earlier that day.

The doctor lowered his voice even further. "But it's the new regime with new rules and regulations. I'm truly sorry. However, I'm happy to say your wife was fine. She still had some time to go before she would give birth. I sent them over to Dr. Levy, a former colleague of mine at

Adass Yisroel Hospital on Torstrasse in Charlottenburg." With that, the doctor rose, shook Arnold's hand and walked down one of the whitewashed hallways leading from the reception area.

Tears welled up in Arnold's eyes as he walked through the revolving doors onto the street. He breathed a heavy sigh, a mixture of relief and exhaustion. It was getting late, and only a few pedestrians were out and about. He hailed a passing taxi and gave the driver his destination.

The driver, an older fellow, sought to make conversation. But Arnold just wanted to be left alone with his thoughts and worries. He sank back into the plush upholstery in the rear of the cab and dozed off as the taxi wended its way through the sparse evening traffic.

After being dropped off, despite being weak and exhausted, he bounded up the front steps of Berlin's pre-eminent Jewish hospital, founded in 1901.

In contrast to Königin Elisabeth, Adass Yisroel Hospital showed the neglect of the new government towards Jewish institutions. The paint was peeling from the entrance corridor's walls, and here and there a light bulb had burned out. Patients lay on gurneys along some of the hallways due to overcrowding as a result of other hospitals in the city turning away Jewish patients. Only one of two elevators were in working order. There was a long lineup at the reception desk. By the time his turn came, he had become highly agitated again.

"Has an Ingrid Weisz been admitted this evening?" he yelled.

"Sir, please lower your voice and let me check," the young woman at the desk icily replied, while looking down at a sheet of lined paper. "Yes, she was admitted about two hours ago. I believe that she's in the delivery room now, on the second floor, being attended to by Dr. Levy."

Without saying thank you, which was quite unusual for him, Arnold turned around and, ignoring the lineup by the only functioning elevator, headed for the dimly lit staircase. He ran up the stairs, nearly bowling over an elderly couple on their way down.

The second-floor corridor was jammed with patients, some on gurneys, surrounded by their anxious relatives or friends. The air was stale, full of the odour of antiseptic and vomit. The noise from all the whispered conversations reminded Arnold of the humming of a beehive. A loud moan or scream would now and again bring the hubbub to a stop. In the half-light he spotted his in-laws standing outside one of the doors. He hugged his mother-in-law and shook Alex's hand.

"How's Ingrid? Where is she? Is there a baby yet?" The words came like a torrent from his lips.

"Calm down, son. Ingrid's fine, as is the wonderful baby boy that she gave birth to twenty minutes ago." Papa threw his arms around his son-in-law and kissed him on both cheeks. "*Mazel tov!* You are a father now!"

"Can I go see her?" Arnold didn't wait for a response as he pushed the door to the delivery room open.

"Out!" A loud female voice yelled from within, followed by a newborn's cry. He quickly closed the door and rejoined his in-laws in the corridor.

Papa gave him a stern look. "What in God's name is that on your coat? Have you gone crazy?" he enquired in a low tone, not wanting to draw attention from anyone else in the crowded space.

For the first time that day, a smile crossed Arnold's face. "Oh that, it's a long story." He pulled the pin from his coat and put it in his pocket.

The door opened and a grey-haired nurse stuck her head out. "You can come in now," she whispered. The three of them shuffled into the room, well-lit in comparison to the hallway.

"Good evening, I'm Doctor Levy. Everything is fine. Mother is a little weak, but otherwise all right, and the baby is a healthy little boy with big lungs, as you can hear."

Dr. Levy was a young, handsome obstetrician overwhelmed by the volume of patients suddenly under his care but continued to maintain a calm and cool demeanour.

Arnold moved forward to embrace Ingrid.

"What on earth happened to your eye?" she asked, a concerned look clouding her tired face. The hours of labour delivering the baby and going from one hospital to the next had exhausted her.

"A present from the Führer." He laughed as he planted a kiss on her forehead and looked down at the swaddled baby lying on her breast. He bent down and gently put his lips to the baby's cheek. Esther and Alex stood looking at the three of them, with tears running down their faces.

"Should we name him Maximillian, after your father?" Ingrid asked Arnold.

"That would be a wonderful name," her parents replied in unison.

"Little Max. Beautiful little Max," Ingrid whispered, looking down with a broad smile on her flushed face at the rosy-cheeked baby in her arms, who had by now gone to sleep.

CHAPTER 9

AUGUST 1988,

NEW YORK CITY—LOVE IN THE MORNING

Saturday dawned sunny and hot. The sun was just rising above the skyscrapers of Manhattan, the rain clouds of the previous evening having been chased from the sky by a warm summer wind. Daniel, true to habit, got out of bed as the sun rose. He tried to be quiet, but his movements stirred Madelaine awake for a moment.

"What time is it?"

"It's 6:30, and I am going for my run," Daniel whispered. "Go back to sleep."

"Ahem," she responded, turning over and pulling the covers over her head.

He entered the bathroom and rummaged around in the bathtub, finally finding a t-shirt and a pair of shorts. He laced up his running shoes and went into the kitchen for some orange juice, which he drank straight out of its wax paper container. Ten minutes later he was jogging along West 110th Street in the direction of Central Park for his usual morning run. The air was clear, the sky blue and cloudless. He avoided a couple of puddles left over from the previous evening's rainfall and stopped for a second, petting a passerby's German Shepherd.

He loved dogs. Unfortunately, he couldn't have one in his apartment. As he continued running, his mind wandered back thirty years to when he was fourteen. It was late June 1958, and he had just graduated from grade school. He had his report card in his backpack and was anxious to share his straight "A" grades with his parents. When he got to their house, he bounded up the front steps, opening the screen door that had been left open, letting the early summer breeze in.

He had noticed his Grandfather Bernard's green, 1956 Chevrolet Bel Air in the driveway and wondered what he was doing there. The answer came quickly and elicited a loud and happy yell from Daniel. For there, sitting on the couch, was his grandfather with a tiny, gold-coloured cocker spaniel puppy in his lap, licking his face. It was the realization of a promise that Bernard had made to buy him a dog when he finished grade school with excellent marks. Daniel threw his arms around his grandfather and scooped the puppy from his lap.

From that moment on, and for the next fourteen years, "Shadow" truly became Daniel's shadow, accompanying him everywhere. It was to Shadow that he confessed his first high-school crush, it was the dog that he held in his arms when Grandpa Bernard's coffin was lowered into the ground on a wet and windy fall day in 1963. Nine years later, he held Shadow's head to his face as the dog peacefully breathed his last and slipped away from the effect of the heart-stopping injection coursing through his veins administered by the veterinarian. Daniel still had trouble holding back his tears whenever he thought back to that cold winter's day.

He was jolted out of his journey down memory lane by the shrill honking of an oncoming car that just avoided hitting him as he crossed 5th Avenue into Central Park. He ran for an hour through the park, breathing in the fresh air and absorbing the sunshine, working up a sweat before returning to his apartment.

Madelaine rose shortly after Daniel left, put on a pot of coffee and took a shower. She was sitting at the table wearing one of Daniel's blue dress shirts, with a towel wrapped around her still-wet hair, drinking her coffee when Daniel came through the door. He just avoided tripping over the mound of dirty laundry she had piled in front of it. The papers that had arrived the day before lay spread out on the table.

"They're all dry," she said, pointing at the documents. "But I can't figure any of it out either. Looks like some kind of will. I made you some coffee, but the milk you had in the fridge has gone sour. I am drinking mine black. Oh, and I also took your dirty laundry out of the tub so I could take a shower. It was disgusting. I think that some of it had already started to crawl out on its own." She giggled. "About the papers, if you want me to, I can call Eric Bender over at Deutsche Bank. He speaks fluent German. He could translate it for you. He owes me a favour for some research I did for him on a merger we were working on at Goldman. Besides that, he's cute, and I think he has the hots for me," she teased Daniel as he removed his shirt and shorts and threw them on the pile before heading into the bathroom to take a shower.

"Whatever," he shot back. "Sure, give him a call." He slammed the door behind himself.

The phone rang four times before the answering machine came on. "You have reached the office of Eric Bender. I am not at my desk right now, but please leave a message and I will get back to you ASAP."

"Good morning, Eric, it's Madelaine Young from Goldman. I thought I might be able to catch you at your office. I know it's a Saturday morning, but I was hoping you might still be working on that merger transaction that's supposed to close on Monday. If you get this message, please call me back."

Daniel came out of the bathroom and into the kitchen, a towel wrapped around his waist. He poured himself a cup of coffee and was just about to sit down when the phone rang.

"Daniel, it's Eric Bender. How are you?"

"Good, and you?"

"Fine, is Maddy there? She called me a few minutes ago."

"Yeah, hold on a minute." Daniel gave Madelaine an annoyed look and handed her the phone.

"Eric, thanks for getting back to me so quickly. I thought I might catch you there. How's the deal coming along?"

"Okay, I guess. I got home at 2:00 a.m., as I hoped to sleep in my own bed instead of the couch in my office for a change. Also, I hadn't seen the kids in a few days and wanted to be here when they woke up on the weekend. What's up?"

"Well, Daniel got these official-looking documents by registered mail yesterday, and we're trying to figure them out. They're in German, and neither of us speak it, so I thought you might be able to help."

"Sure, no problem. I should be finished here by around four. Why don't we meet at the coffee shop downstairs on the main floor of our building?"

"That's at 60 Wall Street, right?"

"Yeah, I'll see you two there."

She got up and went to the bathroom to dry and straighten her hair. Daniel snuck up behind her, moving his hands to her front to unbutton her shirt. He started nuzzling and kissing her neck as he gently massaged her breasts. She looked at him in the mirror.

"You're not getting jealous, are you?" she asked, playfully aiming the blow-dryer at his face.

"No, but we've both showered, and you were wasting my playtime talking to that guy." He laughed.

She turned, embracing him, throwing her legs around his waist. His towel dropped to the floor as he carried her into the bedroom, their lips locked in a passionate kiss.

After their lovemaking, they lay exhausted on the bed, her head on his shoulders, her right hand entwined in the hair on his chest. "You know, I never asked before, but if you're Jewish, how come you're not circumcised? I thought all Jewish men were."

"Apparently, as I heard from my mother, both my father and grandfather, being surgeons, felt that it was archaic and unnecessary. Beside that, neither one was very religious. The only concession they made to religion was to have me bar mitzvahed at Ben-David Synagogue in Westchester when I turned thirteen. Since I was already one year old when I was adopted, they wanted to spare me the pain of having my penis remodelled. But most importantly, my life was probably saved by the 'skin of my dick' in Cairo in July 1973," he said to her with a laugh. As she would later find out, in reality, it was no joke.

CHAPTER 10

JUNE 1967,

NEW YORK CITY—WAR BREAKS OUT IN THE MIDDLE EAST

Daniel graduated from Columbia University in Upper Manhattan with a Bachelor of Arts degree in 1962. He had majored in Art History and Romance Languages, French and Italian, with a minor in World History. In early 1963, he enrolled in City University of New York (CUNY) on 5th Avenue to obtain his PhD in Art. Unfortunately for him, the course was already full for that semester, so he sought employment in the interim, walking the streets of Manhattan with Shadow in tow, dropping off resumes at all the well-known art galleries, institutes, and museums.

Two weeks after starting his search, he was offered a position as an appraiser of European drawings, etchings, and engravings at New York Fine Art Appraisers on Park Avenue. He moved into a rented small bachelor pad upstairs from the gallery. He stayed at that job for two years longer than he had intended to and didn't enter the PhD program at CUNY until mid-1966. That same year, as the war in Vietnam was starting to escalate, he received his draft notice to the army. He got a deferment based on his university studies and by joining the university's Reserve Officer's Training Program (ROTC).

And then at sunrise on June 5, 1967, Israeli Air Force Phantom and Mirage jet fighters and bombers, flying in from the Mediterranean with the sun at their backs, surprised the Egyptian Air Force on the ground, destroying 90 percent of its aircraft. That signalled the beginning of the third war in the Middle East between Israel and five Arab nations in less than twenty years.

Early that morning, as Daniel awoke to the alarm of his radio, he heard the news of the outbreak of hostilities. Jumping out of bed, he called his father.

"Hi Dad, how are you and Mom? Would you have time for a coffee this afternoon somewhere near the UN building?"

"Sure, but don't you have classes?"

"Yeah, but this is important. There is a little bagel shop on 2nd Avenue, around the corner from the UN. Let's say at two-thirty?"

"I've got surgery in the morning, so I may be a little late. What's so important?"

"We'll talk when I see you. Have to run to class now. Love you. Bye." He skipped classes that morning and headed straight for the offices of the Consulate General of Israel on 2nd Avenue. By the time he got there, a line was snaking around the corner and down East 42nd Street.

Samuel Singer was just shy of sixty-four when he met his son at the bagel shop that June afternoon. He had a concerned look on his face as he walked into the restaurant and spotted Daniel sitting in a corner nursing a coffee. "So, what's so important that you skip classes?"

"Well, Dad, you know what's going on in Israel. It's another David and Goliath scenario. I can't just sit by and see them get pushed into the sea and not do anything. This morning I went to the Israeli Consul General on 2nd Avenue and volunteered to go over there and do whatever I can do to help."

Samuel sat there for a minute, chewing on the stem of his well-worn meerschaum pipe, which had gone out hours ago, just shaking his head. "You know what this will do to your mother, no?"

"But Dad, you did exactly the same thing in '48."

And indeed he had! And there was no way his father could hide that fact, since a movie about Mickey Marcus, starring Kirk Douglas and Yul Brynner, titled *Cast a Giant Shadow* was released by MGM in theatres the year before. His father's close friendship with Marcus had been featured in the movie.

CHAPTER 11

APRIL 1948,

NEW YORK—A FATEFUL TELEPHONE CALL

After landing in Normandy a few weeks after D-Day, Samuel, a major at the time, commanding a US Army field hospital of the 71st. Infantry Division, campaigned with General Omar Bradley's 1st Army from the Cotentin Peninsula in northern France in 1944 to hooking up with the Soviets' 58th Guard Division on the river Elbe at the conclusion of the war in May 1945. He had been awarded two Purple Hearts, the first one for a wound inflicted by an enemy sniper with "bad aim," as he would later recall, and the second for wounds sustained during the Rhine crossing in March 1945 as part of Operation Varsity, when a German 88 shell exploded near the mobile surgical tent where he was performing an operation.

At the end of the war, he returned to Agatha and his job as assistant chief surgeon at Zion Hospital, and the boredom of civilian life in New York. After adopting Daniel, they moved from their small bungalow in Queens into a four-bedroom side-split in Larchmont, Westchester County, to be near Agatha's father, Bernard. They settled into the mundane everyday life of an ordinary American family. Then, in early 1948, life for them changed once again when the State of Israel was born through a resolution of the United Nations in New York.

On a cold and blustery April morning, Samuel was reading the *New York Times*, while Agatha chased around their house playing hide-and-go-seek with four-year-old Daniel. The phone rang and Agatha answered it, breathless from chasing the little boy.

AT&T's New York long-distance operator's voice came on the line. "Madam, we have an overseas long distance call from Palestine for Mr. Samuel Singer, is he the … ?

"Good morning, Agatha," came the deep male voice from the other end of the line who'd cut into the operator's introduction before she could finish her sentence. "How are things in New York this morning?"

Agatha immediately recognised the voice as that of Mickey Marcus. "We are all well thank you, and you? What are you doing in Palestine?"

"Eating oranges right off the tree in Jaffa." He chuckled. "Is Sam there? Can I talk to him?"

Agatha handed the receiver to Samuel. "It's Mickey Marcus calling from Palestine."

"What the hell is he doing there?" Samuel looked quizzically at Agatha. He and Mickey had been lifelong friends, having gone to grade school and high school together in Brooklyn, and both joined Michael, the oldest of the Marcus children, when he formed a self-defence group that protected elderly Jews from neighbourhood street gangs. After graduation, their paths diverged, only to come together again in the maelstrom of the Second World War.

CHAPTER 12

1944,

NORMANDY—MICKEY MARCUS

At the end of June 1944, during the US Army's VII Corps assault on the port of Cherbourg under Major General Lawton Collins, Samuel was in the midst of trying to save a GI's life at a forward aid station when the canvas flap at the entrance to the tent flew open and a sergeant walked in supporting a colonel on a crutch. Samuel didn't bother to look up. He was dressed in a white medical apron over khaki fatigues and covered in blood up to his elbows as he concentrated on extracting shards of shrapnel from the badly wounded GI's abdomen with a pair forceps.

"Doctor, I have a colonel here with a bullet through his leg that needs some attention," the sergeant yelled, his voice drowned out by the screaming of the GI on the operating table and the loud rumble of artillery in the background.

"Can't you see that I am trying to save a man's life, not some colonel's leg?" responded Samuel without turning around, and with annoyance in his voice. After successfully removing the jagged chunk of metal from the GI's stomach, sewing up the wound, and wiping the blood off his hands, Samuel turned around. As he did, a wide grin crossed his face, and then he embraced the colonel leaning on crutches in front of him. "Mickey, it's you!"

For a moment the tall, balding colonel didn't recognise the towering figure of the man whose arms were around his shoulders. Samuel was covered in blood with two weeks of stubble on his face, partially covered by a surgical mask and cap on his head. Then that deep voice from the past provided recognition.

"Sammy? Good Lord, what a small world!"

"What have you been up to?" Samuel asked Mickey.

"Oh, just looking around," Mickey replied with a laugh, adding, "I think we have the Krauts on the run. We'll be in Berlin in a month."

"Good, just in time for my anniversary. Here, sit down. Let me look at that leg. Nasty, but you're lucky. The bullet missed the bone and exited clear through. You'll get a Purple Heart but no ticket home," Samuel said.

David Daniel "Mickey" Marcus, a tough Brooklyn street kid, was born to immigrant parents in 1902. Marcus grew up in the Brownsville section of Brooklyn where, to defend himself against neighbourhood toughs, he learned to box.

While Samuel was studying medicine at the Columbia College of Physicians and Surgeons in New York, Mickey, due to his high-school athletic and academic record, won admission to West Point in 1920, from which he graduated with impressive scores. He became a favourite cadet of Brigadier General Douglas Macarthur, who was the commandant of West Point at the time. After completing his required army service, Marcus went to law school and spent most of the 1930s as a federal attorney in New York, helping to bring "Lucky" Luciano to justice. As a reward, Mayor LaGuardia named Marcus Commissioner of Corrections for New York City.

Convinced that war was imminent, Marcus voluntarily went back into army uniform in 1940, and after the Japanese attack on Pearl Harbor, served as executive officer to the military governor of Hawaii. In 1942, he was named commandant of the Army's new Ranger school. Like Samuel, he was sent to England in early 1944. On the eve of D-Day, he voluntarily parachuted into Normandy with the troops of the 101st Airborne Division.

After getting his leg stitched up, Mickey and the sergeant that bought him in bade their farewells to Samuel, who had once again become preoccupied with the flow of wounded being bought in on stretchers.

"Thanks, and see you in Berlin," he yelled, and he waved at Samuel.

"Keep out of the way of bullets in the future," Samuel shouted back with a wave of his right arm then turned his attention back to another GI being placed on the operating table.

After the campaigns through France, Belgium, and Germany, and at the closing stages of the war, Mickey Marcus helped draw up the surrender terms for Italy and Germany and became part of the occupation government in Berlin. Admiring colleagues identified him as one of the War Department's best brains.

In 1944, Marcus's awakening of himself as a Jew took a dramatic turn when he was given responsibility to clear out the Nazi death camps. Here, Marcus came face to face with the survivors of Nazi atrocities and saw with his own eyes the piles of uncounted Jewish corpses in Europe's death camps. Following that assignment, Marcus was named chief of the War Crimes Division, planning legal and security procedures for the Nuremberg trials. Through these experiences, he got to understand the depths of European anti-Semitism.

Though never previously a Zionist, Marcus became convinced that the only hope for the remnants of European Jewry lay in a Jewish homeland in Palestine.

In 1947, Marcus returned to civilian life. A few months later, the United Nations authorized the partition of Palestine and the eventual creation of a Jewish state. Within days, David Ben-Gurion, then Israel's prime minister, asked Marcus to recruit an American officer to serve as military adviser to Israel. Failing in his attempts to recruit one of his friends, Marcus decided to volunteer himself. The US War Department granted Marcus, who was a reservist, permission to accept the offer, provided Marcus not use his own name or rank and on the condition that he disguise his military record.

Thus, one "Michael Stone" arrived in Tel Aviv in January 1948 to confront a nearly impossible situation. The widely separated Jewish settlements in Palestine were surrounded by a sea of hostile Arabs. The newly created Israel would have no defensible borders, no air power, a few tanks and ancient artillery pieces, and almost no arms or ammunition. The Haganah was an effective underground organization, but it had no experience as a regular national army.

Facing it were well-supplied Arab armies determined to drive the Jews into the sea. The pro-Arab British administration in Palestine prevented the importation of military supplies to the Israelis. Undaunted, Stone designed a command structure for Israel's new army and wrote manuals to train it, adapting his experience at Ranger school to the Haganah's special needs. He identified Israel's weakest points as the scattered settlements in the Negev and the new quarter of Jerusalem. When Israel declared independence and the Arab armies attacked in May 1948, Israel was ready, thanks to Stone's planning.

CHAPTER 13

"Mickey, how are you, and what are you doing in Jaffa?" Samuel asked his long-time friend.

"I'm here to help build and defend this new country called Israel. A place that us Jews can finally call home. I'll never be able to erase from my mind's eye the piles of Jewish corpses at Dachau, Mauthausen, and Bergen-Belsen, and I can't let it happen again, Sam, without raising a finger!"

"Haven't you had enough of war yet? Didn't that bullet through your leg in France teach you anything? The next one could be through your head, and I won't be there to help you."

"Sammy, that's what I'm calling you about."

Samuel listened in silence as the voice at the other end came through, despite occasional static.

"Look, Sammy, this war's going to heat up soon. There are five Arab armies just waiting to invade. Our asses are against the Mediterranean, and we don't have any experienced battlefield surgeons to care for our wounded. I know it's much to ask, but we need you here."

"Look, Mickey, I am married. Daniel's growing up. I can't just pick up and go halfway around the world and have my head blown off. What would happen to Agatha and Daniel?"

As soon as his words left his mouth, he knew how shallow he sounded. *How could he refuse to help the one individual who had such a great impact on all their lives? Who was in large part responsible for the happiness their son bought them?*

"Let me talk to Aggie and Bernard. I can't do anything without discussing it with them first. Where can I get back to you?"

"You can't. I'll call you back tomorrow evening. My love to Agatha and Daniel. *Shalom.*" He hung up without giving Samuel the chance to say goodbye.

Samuel walked into the kitchen and put on the kettle to make himself a cup of coffee. He then sat down, burying his head in his hands. Conflicting thoughts raced through his mind.

"What did Mickey want?" Agatha asked, walking through the kitchen door with little Daniel in tow.

Samuel thought for a moment and decided not to tell Agatha the true reason for the telephone call. "Oh, he asked me to round up some medical supplies for the new army being formed over there. They need everything from Aspirin to bandages to morphine. He wants me to talk to all the Jewish congregations in New York to raise money to pay for it. I'll also talk to your father tomorrow to see how he can help."

"Good! Knowing Mickey, for a minute there I thought he was asking you to do something foolish."

Samuel couldn't get to sleep that night, tossing and turning, finally getting out of bed at 5:00 a.m. He couldn't get his earlier conversation with Mickey, nor his friend's plea, out of his mind. Sitting on the front steps of the house, trying to smoke his pipe, he looked at the brightening sky in the east, the rising sun's rays painting it a reddish hue, remembering the old proverb, "Red sky at morning, sailors take warning."

He had to constantly try to relight his pipe, as the cold, early-morning April wind kept extinguishing the flame in the bowl, finally giving up and just chewing on the stem. *How can I refuse Mickey's request?*

After all, if it wasn't for him, we would never have been able to adopt Daniel. And they obviously need surgeons like me in Israel, or Mickey wouldn't have asked. I have to go. I must go. Thoughts cascaded through his brain. *But how do I tell Aggie?*

I won't tell her! Just make travel arrangements and get on an overseas flight, leaving her a note. Then I can talk to Bernard. He'll be able to keep a secret until I'm gone. Bernard will then be there for Agatha and Daniel while I'm gone. Simple, it's done.

He was so overwhelmed by his decision, he didn't notice that he was sitting outside on the front steps in his pyjamas, in bare feet. The morning copy of the *New York Times* came flying through the air, nearly hitting him square in the head.

"Good morning, Mister Singer," the paper boy yelled as he continued to ride his bike down the street.

Samuel stood up and stretched, picked up the *New York Times* and walked back into the house. Everything was quiet. He put a pot of coffee on the stove, sat down, and opened the newspaper. The headline read "Middle East Crisis to Be Debated At UN." He read through the rest of the news until Agatha and Daniel came downstairs.

"Morning, Daddy." Daniel went to hug his father.

"You were up early this morning," added Agatha. "Can I make you some breakfast?"

"Sure, thank you. I'm going to go upstairs and wash up, and then go over to your father's to talk to him about Mickey and his wish list of medical supplies."

"Why don't you take Daniel with you? You know how much Dad loves to have him around."

"Yes, Daddy," squealed Daniel. "And Grandpa can take me to the park!"

The two of them arrived at Bernard's mid-morning. He was listening to the news on the radio.

"How's my little guy this morning?" Bernard beamed as he lifted Daniel way up in the air, much to the youngster's squealing delight.

"Bernard, can we go into the kitchen?' Sam asked. "I need to talk to you about something, but not in front of the child."

"Sure, I'll put some coffee on. Do you want some cookies or something?"

Hearing the word "cookies" perked little Daniel's ears up. "Can I have some cookies too, Grandpa? And maybe you can make me some hot chocolate, too."

Bernard stood by the stove heating up a pot of coffee for Samuel and himself, and some milk for Daniel's hot chocolate.

"So, Sam, what's this important matter you want to entrust to your father-in-law? And have you discussed it with Agatha?"

"I have not, and when I tell you, you'll realize why. Since my parents passed away, you're the only one besides Aggie that I can confide in, and this is one thing I can't tell her just yet," Samuel continued.

"Go ahead. As much as I don't like to keep secrets from my daughter, I'll respect your confidence."

Finally, being inside, Samuel didn't have to fight the elements as he lit his pipe. He said, "Do you mind?" Without waiting for a response, he took a deep draw, exhaling a cloud of bluish smoke.

"I had a phone call from Mickey Marcus in Jaffa, Palestine, last night. He has taken some command position with the Jewish army over there. They're waiting to be attacked by a million Arabs. He needs medical supplies for his soldiers, and I would like your help in securing them."

"Oh, that's something I would be glad to help him with. I'll call around to a couple of my Jewish colleagues, especially ones at the Jewish hospitals like Mount Sinai. I am sure we can get him fixed up, hopefully with more than he'll require."

"Thank you, Bernard. I knew I could count on you for that. But that's not all that he wanted. He asked, no, pleaded, that I come over because they don't have any experienced battlefield surgeons, and he thinks they'll need them."

"Go on, I think I know where this is headed." Bernard raised his eyebrows as Samuel was about to continue but was cut short by Daniel.

"Grandpa, I'm hungry. Can we go to the park now for some pretzels?"

"I am talking to your dad, Daniel. We'll go when we're finished." He turned to his son-in-law. "Go on, Samuel."

Daniel pouted, upset by his grandfather's tone, but moved closer to the older man anyway.

"Well …" Sam started to chew on the well-worn stem of his pipe, as was his habit whenever confronted with a difficult decision.

"I don't want to tell Aggie because she will beg, cry, threaten all kinds of dire consequences and would probably succeed in talking me out of it, especially on account of Daniel. I also can't turn Mickey down. He's been a lifelong friend, and as you know, without him we wouldn't have Daniel. The kid's been a ray of sunshine in all our lives.

"I must go, I really don't have a choice in the matter. Mickey needs me there, and I can't let him down, but neither can I tell Aggie of my decision."

His father-in-law listened without interrupting, slowly bouncing Daniel on his knee.

Samuel went on, "Bernard, she was there to comfort you when Esther died, and you were there to do the same for her when I went overseas during the war."

"I remember that only too well. The shoulder of my jacket was soaked by her tears every night," Bernard cut in.

"I'm going to need you to assume that role once again."

"What are your plans?" Bernard asked.

"I was hoping to catch a flight to London tomorrow evening and then on to Athens, and from there to Tel Aviv, or perhaps take the ferry from Piraeus to Haifa. The Brits are not making the trip to Palestine too easy with their blockade. I plan to go see the Pan Am offices in New York later this afternoon and then British Overseas Airways after that. If I think on this too long, I might change my mind.

"Mickey's calling tonight, and I'll need to give him an answer. In any case, I would appreciate it if you could stay with Aggie while I am gone. She'll put your shoulders to good use once again, I'm sure."

Bernard lifted his grandson off his knee, stood up, and gave his son-in-law a tight bear hug. "Keep safe, son. If I wasn't as old as I am, I would gladly join you. Rest assured that she and Daniel will be well taken care of while you're away."

"Could you please look after him while I go into the city?"

"Of course. Daniel, let's put on your coat and start for the park. Should we take a ball along?" Bernard patted his beaming grandson on the head as they started out the door.

Samuel lifted his son up and gave him a warm hug and kiss. "Now, Daniel, be good for Grandpa, and don't eat too much."

The three of them walked out the door, Bernard and Daniel heading for the park across the street, and Samuel to his car for the drive into Manhattan.

Bernard shouted after him, "Give my best to Mickey, that rascal!"

CHAPTER 14

Samuel returned home early that evening with airline tickets to Athens through London in his pocket. He couldn't obtain air passage from Athens to Tel Aviv, so decided to take his chances once he got to Greece. *If worse comes to worse,* he thought, *I can always take the boat.* Although he hated sea travel, having become violently sick during his passage on a troopship from New York to Southampton during the war, and then again on his way back after the end of the war. The Channel crossing a couple of weeks after D-Day had been less traumatic, so he was hoping for the best on the short trip across the Aegean to Israel, if it was the only way he could get there.

"Where have you been until now?" queried Agatha. "Dad bought Daniel home about an hour ago and is just upstairs reading him a book."

Samuel was saved by the ringing of the telephone.

"That's probably Mickey. He already called earlier," Agatha said suspiciously.

He picked up the receiver. "Hello?"

"Mr. Samuel Singer? This is the AT&T operator with an overseas call from Palestine."

"Yes, this is Samuel Singer."

"One moment, sir. I will connect your caller. Go ahead, sir."

"Sam, how did things go with Agatha?"

"Hmmm, oh, okay."

"I'm assuming from that, not too well."

Samuel paused for a minute and took his pipe from his pocket.

"Sam, are you there?"

"Yes, yes. Everything is fine." He started chewing the stem of his pipe without even making an attempt to light it.

"So you'll be coming over?"

"Yes."

Agatha was hovering close by, trying to somehow overhear her husband's conversation with his friend in Palestine. Luckily for Samuel, just at that moment, Bernard descended the stairs

"Aggie, Daniel asked for a glass of water and wants you to tuck him in."

With his wife out of earshot, Samuel lowered his voice and whispered to Mickey of his plan to catch a Pan Am flight to London. Then after a twenty-four hour layover he would get on the British European Airways flight from London to Athens. He would figure out how to get from the Greek capital to Palestine once he got there.

"Great, Sam! It'll be wonderful to see you again. By the way, there's a private flying boat charter service out of Piraeus that you might want to try if you can't get Hellenic Air or a ferry to get you here. It's a bumpy ride and expensive, but they fly from there to Haifa every evening other than on Fridays.

"Once you're in Greece, give me a telephone call to let me know how you're getting here, so I can meet you. The best way to get a hold of me is to leave a message with the front desk at the King David Hotel in Jerusalem. We really need you here! This is a great country, on the verge of being born. *Shalom*."

After hanging up the phone, once again without the opportunity to say goodbye, Samuel went into the kitchen where his father-in-law was drinking a coffee and eating one of Agatha's chocolate chip cookies.

"Where's Aggie?"

"Upstairs, saying good night to Daniel. Sooo, what's the latest?"

Samuel lowered his voice once again, "I have a Pan Am flight booked to London tomorrow evening, and then on to Athens the following night. I'll figure out how to get to Tel Aviv or Haifa from there. Instead of going to work tomorrow, I'm going to leave the car at your house and then take a taxi to LaGuardia."

They heard Agatha's footsteps coming down the stairs and quickly changed the subject to pre-season baseball trades.

"So, what did Mickey want this time?" Agatha, with her hands on her hips, gave her husband a stern look.

"Just to see how your father and I are coming along with gathering the medical supplies they will need over there."

Bernard stood up to get his jacket and head home, providing Samuel with a bit of breathing space before his daughter could continue her questioning.

Agatha walked her father to the door and closed it behind him. "Bye, Dad. Love you," she yelled into the cold night air as Bernard descended the front steps.

The next day also dawned cold and windy, with some light, powdery snow blowing about. Samuel couldn't sleep all night, but he stayed in bed until Daniel and Agatha awoke.

"Are you okay? You tossed and turned the whole night."

Samuel didn't get a chance to respond, as his son jumped on him with a loud yell.

After a couple of minutes of horseplay, father and son headed downstairs, with Daniel perched on his father's shoulders. Following a breakfast of scrambled eggs and coffee, Samuel went back upstairs to draw himself a hot bath. Sitting in the tub, he leaned back and closed his eyes, letting the steam from the hot water engulf him and momentarily dissipate his worries about the upcoming journey. Visions of his wartime experiences and what he had seen crowded his mind.

Can I do this again? How will I react? What if I'm killed? What'll happen to Agatha and Daniel? His thoughts were interrupted by Agatha and Daniel standing at the bathroom door.

"Hey, mister, aren't you going to be late for work?"

Agatha patted Samuel on the head as she spoke.

"No, I don't have to be there until noon. No surgeries planned for today, only some pre-op consultations. However, I may stay overnight down at the Carlyle, as I have some early surgeries scheduled for tomorrow morning," he lied.

It didn't raise any suspicions with her, as he had done that a number of times before.

"Okay, dear. I'm going to take Daniel with me to shop for groceries, and then I promised Mrs. Green to drop in for tea and to discuss the Hadassah clothing drive for Palestine that's coming up next month. Daniel can just play with their two little dogs while I talk to her. He loves those two little … whatever mix they are."

She leaned down to give her husband a goodbye kiss. Samuel half rose out of the tub and put his wet arms around her and gave her a long and passionate kiss.

"Ooh, maybe I should stay," she whispered in his ear.

Samuel took her two hands, grasped them tightly and planted a kiss on each.

She then turned and walked out of the bathroom shaking her head as Daniel came to the door.

"Come here, Daniel. Daddy wants a hug."

"You're not going to pull me into the bath, are you?" Daniel asked.

"No, son, not this time."

Daniel came over, and Samuel leaned out of the tub and gave his son a tight embrace, wetting the boy's shirt in the process. "Now you be good, and help Mom with the groceries," he yelled after them.

Agatha left with her son, but a strange, unfamiliar feeling came over her. *I wonder what that's all about?* Samuel had never in the past been overly demonstrative, or indeed, at all emotional. He was the epitome of the "cool as a cucumber" surgeon. The thoughts quickly dissipated from her mind as she and Daniel walked down the street, heading for Cohen's Fruit and Vegetable Market in the middle of town.

After packing a small suitcase, Samuel jumped into his black 1946 Hudson Commodore, which he'd bought from the money he had saved from his wartime Army pay. It was his pride and joy, and the envy of the neighbourhood and his colleagues at Zion Hospital. Arriving at his father-in-law's house after a ten-minute drive, he went over his will and his bank accounts with Bernard.

"Look, Bernard, I fully expect to return here within a month or two. I went through a year of combat in Europe, and other than the two scratches, no serious harm came to me. But one never knows. I've written a short note to Agatha and Daniel. Please, give it to them only after I send you a telegram that I've safely arrived in Palestine."

He handed Bernard the small white envelope with "To My Loving Wife and Son" printed by hand on it.

My Darling Wife,

By the time you get this letter, I will have already landed in Haifa or Tel Aviv. First of all, amongst other things that I need to apologise to you for, the first is for not telling you of my plans. I didn't want to get into arguments, justifications, and recriminations. It may be awfully selfish of me, but it is something that I must do, whatever the consequences. I didn't leave with an easy heart, especially not in the light of not even having said goodbye to anyone other than your dad. Goodbyes are always so painful, and you never want people to remember you through tears in their eyes, nor do I want to remember them in that way. I will try to call you on a regular basis to let you know that I am well and keep you updated as to what's happening over here. Now to the rest of my mea culpas.

I know that for most of our marriage I wasn't the model husband or lover you either wished me to be, or that I could have been. But that is me. So far from perfect, but so near to you. I don't need to detail all the areas of my failures; they are only too well-known to you. Unfortunately, the ancient adage that you can't train a dog to do new tricks applies in this case.

However, I do believe that we established and nurtured a true bond of love, caring, and friendship. Despite the everyday stress of my work and your caring for Daniel, we still managed to kiss each other good morning and good night every day. You don't know how important that was to me and how knowing that you loved and cared for me comforted me through our life together. I know that I don't need to explain to you why I have done what I have done, because you know me too well for that. Our people have suffered since time immemorial due to having been born into the Jewish religion.

As everyone knows, I am not a religious individual. And this journey is a personal one, without religious overtones. Other than having served my country in time of war and attending to the sick, I have not done anything that I could really be proud of in my life. Doing this gives me a sense that I am giving something back to the world. That I am doing something that is unselfish, ethical, and morally right. I need to honour my commitments to my lifelong friend Mickey, without whom our lives would be less fulfilling and happy, and finally take a step that at least will not render our people's murder and suffering at Auschwitz, Bergen-Belsen, and Mauthausen a mockery. I am sure that I will be fine, as I have been in tighter spots before.

Should anything unforeseen happen, I want you to remember that you unselfishly gave me the best years of my life, and for that I will love you and be in your debt forever. Please take care of Daniel, our gift from God, in my absence. Please don't blame your father for not having told you of my plans, but I swore him to secrecy, which I knew he wouldn't breach. And please don't be angry with Mickey, as I am sure he would have understood had I turned him down. But after what he and I have been through in our lives and with his intercession with Eisenhower on behalf of Daniel's adoption, there was no way I could refuse. We shall forever be grateful to him for that.

I love you, and will forever,
Your loving husband, Samuel

My Dearest Son Daniel,

I know that you're way too young to understand what your father has done at this time, but you may understand as you get older and have a family of your own. Please remember that Daddy is helping our people in a far- away land that you may someday visit, people who are today in peril of being annihilated. Daddy also owes to a friend of his to go over there and help to heal sick soldiers. Without this friend, who you were named after, you wouldn't be part of our family. Please take care of Mommy and listen to Grandpa. We will have lots of time to play when I get back. Be a good boy and remember that Daddy loves you.

Your loving Father

CHAPTER 15

APRIL 1948,

LONDON & ATHENS—SAMUEL'S JOURNEY

Samuel's Pan Am, Lockheed Constellation landed at London's Croydon Airport the next evening after an eighteen-hour flight from New York. He was dead tired, having hardly slept on the trip over. He dozed off every now and again but was constantly awoken by nightmares about the war and by his seatmate's loud snoring. *How the hell can this guy sleep like that, with the turbulence, the noise of the engines, and the groaning of the passenger in front of us, who's violently airsick?*

At the terminal, he asked the young Pan Am clerk at the service desk to direct him to a nearby hotel. The pretty girl, with a wide, friendly smile and a strong Cockney accent, yelled over to one of the pilots who had just disembarked from the Pan Am flight, "Hey Captain America, do you know where this Yank can find a bed for the night?"

The tall, blond Pan Am captain, smartly dressed in a dark-blue uniform with four gold stripes on his sleeves, shouted back, "Irene, we're heading over to the Waverley Inn. That fleabag always has rooms available. He can ride on the bus with us. And darlin', you can join us in the pub for drinks when you're through here."

"You wish! In your dreams," she responded, laughing off the airman's flirtatious remark and holding up her left hand with a wedding band on one finger.

"No harm trying," he muttered under his breath. The captain then nodded to Samuel and headed towards the exit, saying, "Follow us."

During the ride to the Waverly Inn near the airport, Samuel found out that the Pan Am captain, Randolph Hughes III of Lubbock, Texas, had been a fighter bomber pilot, flying Republic P-47 Thunderbolts over Belgium and Germany during the war. On Christmas Day 1944, he was credited with shooting down two Luftwaffe Me-109s during the Wehrmacht's Adrennes Offensive.

After arriving at the hotel, and before heading off to bed, the two of them shared a bottle of Cutty Sark whisky on the rocks and regaled each other with their wartime experiences.

Since he wasn't scheduled to fly out until later the next evening, Samuel slept in the following morning. Having dozed only intermittently on the flight over, and with the alcohol kicking in, he quickly drifted off into a fitful sleep. Not having been in London since early 1944, the next morning he decided to take the train from Croydon into the British capital to try to look up his old friend, Major Douglas Jamieson.

Major Jamieson had been a family practitioner in London before the outbreak of war and then joined the Royal Medical Corps. Like Samuel, he'd became a battlefield surgeon, serving with the British 1st Special Service Brigade during the Rhine crossing in March 1945. Samuel had no trouble locating him in the London telephone book. When he called, the phone was picked up on the second ring. "Hello, is this the Jamieson residence?"

"Yes, it's Dr. Jamieson speaking."

"Dougie, it's Sam Singer from New York."

"Sammy, old boy, where are you calling from?"

"Around the corner, so to speak. I am in your fair city for the day and would love to catch up over a couple of pints. It's been a long time."

"Sure has. Glad to hear your voice, old chap. How about the Dog and Duck in Mayfair, around the corner from the British Museum, in an hour?"

"Okay, we should have a few hours to reminisce. I'll grab a taxi. I don't trust my sense of direction in the Tube."

Soon, the two wartime comrades settled into comfortable leather-upholstered armchairs in the dimly lit, storied drinking establishment. Originally built in 1734 where the Duke of Monmouth's home had stood, John Constable, the painter and George Orwell, the author, had been patrons over the years. They ordered two mugs of John Smith's ales and started to catch up.

"So how's Madge and your little girl? I'm sorry, but I can't remember her name."

"Oh, two girls! Jenny's now going on nine and Abigail's nearly three. And you? It's Agatha, right? Any children?"

"A four-year-old boy, Daniel, who we adopted after the war. Where are you practicing these days?

"I'm not. Madge's father owns a medical supply company and I'm the vice-president of sales. And you?"

"Oh, they took me back in my old position as assistant head of surgery at Zion Hospital after returning from Europe. But good for you! Probably better pay, and shorter hours than cutting into people and then stitching them up again."

"And a whole lot less stressful," Douglas responded with a snicker.

Samuel took out his pipe while Douglas lit up a Camel cigarette, a habit he'd acquired during the war. The thick smoke shrouded them in a bluish haze.

Douglas began to chuckle. "Sam, I can still remember the last time I saw you. You were swearing a blue streak. The blast from the shell of that German 88 on the other side of the river blew your uniform right off, you were covered in dirt, and your hair was singed. When I got to you, I thought that you'd been hit in the backside, as blood seemed to be running down the back of your thigh and leg, but you'd actually shit yourself." Douglas couldn't stop laughing.

Then it was quiet for a few minutes as the two former comrades in arms downed the last of their stout and let their minds wander back to their wartime adventures.

It wasn't funny then, and it isn't funny now, Samuel thought to himself.

Douglas broke the silence, coughing from inhaling his cigarette too deeply. "So what are you doing in London?"

"Just passing through on my way to Athens to visit some friends."

They parted with a handshake and embrace, Samuel towering over the stocky red-headed Englishman.

BEA flight #67 landed in Athens mid-morning. Samuel immediately approached the registration desk of Hellenic Airlines to see if he could get a flight to either Tel Aviv or Haifa. Much to his disappointment, he was told that Hellenic Airlines didn't fly to either destination due to the political situation there. The clerk at the desk, lowering her voice so her supervisor wouldn't hear her, said there was a private charter flying boat service from Piraeus to Haifa, operated by a former RAF bomber pilot and his wartime navigator. But Samuel would have to go down to the port to arrange passage.

Samuel thought that since he would probably have to get down there in any case, since that was also where the ferry terminal was located, he might just as well try to find it at the same time. Before leaving the airport, he headed to the Greek Post & Telephone office, located in the terminal building. Not being sure of how good the communication facilities in Tel Aviv or Haifa were, he decided to send Bernard a telegram advising him of his safe arrival in Greece.

Taking the form at the desk, he wrote, "Safely arrived in Athens. My love to all, Samuel."

He handed the form to the telegraph operator behind the desk and waited until she keyed it into the teletype machine. After paying the per-word overseas telegram charge, he headed out of the building.

Walking out into the warm noon sunshine, Samuel was surprised by the array of military hardware guarding the airport. Tanks, armoured cars, Bren Gun Carriers, and a sea of British Tommies in light-beige tropical kit, brandishing Lee–Enfield 303s and STEN guns. When picking Athens as his final point of departure for Palestine, he had forgotten that a civil war had been in full swing in Greece since 1946.

A moustachioed captain of the British Paratroop Regiment, red beret on his head, swagger stick under one arm, and a holstered Browning 9mm at his side, approached him. The captain saluted Samuel. "Sir, may I see your passport please?"

"Certainly, but I've already passed through passport control inside."

"I understand, sir, but this is military security," he said, extending his arm to reach for the passport. After a cursory look through the document, he smartly saluted once again. "On your way then, sir."

The captain then turned and marched away towards a crowd of local taxi drivers standing by their vehicles and having a loud, heated conversation, gesticulating with their hands to emphasize their points of view.

Samuel waved his arm towards the group to hail a taxi. After what seemed an eternity, and some more loud dialogue amongst the Greeks and the British officer, one of them jumped into his ancient, rusty Citroën, and with thick black smoke billowing from the exhaust and loud grinding noises from under the hood, pulled up beside the tall American.

"Where to, mister?" the portly driver enquired with a thick accent as Samuel opened the door and got into the back.

"Heading down to the harbour in Piraeus, hoping to find the chap with the flying boats."

"Oh, you're heading to Palestine?" The driver raised his eyebrows, looking back at Samuel. "We've had quite a few of your people travelling in that direction lately. With the English blockade … " At that point, the driver spit out the window, showing his disdain for the British.

"It's the fastest and best way." He winked at Samuel. "I know where to find him."

They continued the rest of the way in silence, passing through a number of military checkpoints. The guards obviously knew the driver, as they nonchalantly waved him through. After leaving the city and driving through dusty backroads to avoid additional British Army checkpoints, they arrived on the promenade by the azure Aegean. The driver stopped at a small, white-stone building surrounded by red and pink bougainvilleas, with a blue-and-white, hand-painted sign in Greek and English hanging in the solitary window: Aegean Flying Boat Service, Single or Group Charters.

Samuel got out, paid his fare and a generous tip, then tried to open the wooden door of the building. It was locked. Then he noticed a small, handwritten sign tucked into the tight space between the door and its frame. "Out to lunch. Back soon." He took his small bag and decided to walk around the jetty while he waited for someone to get back and open up the office.

Beyond the brightly coloured fishing boats gently bobbing on the water's surface in the inner harbour, and past the outer breakwater, he noticed the gleaming aluminum fuselage of the Saunders-Roe A.19 Cloud. Since it was the only aircraft visible, he presumed it was "the" flying boat owned by the charter company.

He decided to sit down on his suitcase and light up his pipe. It was a warm, glorious afternoon with the sun shining down, and nary a cloud in the light-blue sky. The whole idyllic scene reminded him of the pre-war travel posters beguiling travellers to the Greek Islands, displayed in New York's more elegant hotel lobbies. He deeply drew on his pipe and watched the puff of smoke from it curl upwards as he exhaled. He was having trouble keeping his eyes open after three days of travel, and was beginning to doze off when he was jolted back to full consciousness by a heavy Australian accent behind him.

"A beauty, ain't she?" the voice said.

Samuel turned around and saw a tall, thin figure in khaki fatigues with a well-worn RAF officer's hat on his head and dark aviator sunglasses covering his eyes. As the sun was beaming down from behind the man, and right into his eyes, all Samuel could discern was a silhouette, and he couldn't make out the details of the face looking at him. He stood up, turning to get a better view of the individual.

As he was to find out later, in front of him stood one Squadron Leader Ian Robertson, formerly of No. 10 Squadron, Royal Australian Air Force (RAAF). Born in Perth, Australia, the thirty-three-year-old man was tall and slim, with wavy, flaming-red hair, a handlebar moustache of the same colour, and an abundance of freckles that covered his sunburned face. He had been awarded the Distinguished Flying Cross in 1943 for the destruction with depth charges of U-331, one of Grand Admiral Doenitz's submarines, off the Irish coast.

"Good afternoon. Am I to presume from your comment that the silver-skinned beauty out there belongs to you?"

The red-haired man thrust out his chest with pride. "That it does, sir! Ian Robertson, at your service. Most friends call me Robbie." He shook Samuel's hand with a firm handshake.

"Samuel, Samuel Singer. I'm looking to get to Haifa as expeditiously as possible. I understand you make the trip every evening."

"You are well informed, Sam. May I call you that?" He continued without waiting for an answer. "By your accent, I take you for a Yank."

"Yes, an American, from New York."

"The four-and-a-half-hour trip will cost you eighty quid or ... "

Robbie stopped for a second, and seemed to go into deep deliberation, quietly humming "Waltzing Matilda" at the same time.

"Two hundred American dollars," he finally blurted out. "But I don't have room on the flight tonight, and tomorrow being Friday, I don't fly."

"Well, that's a pity. I guess I'll see what's available on one of the ferries." Samuel picked up his suitcase and started to walk away.

Seeing his fare escaping, Robertson grabbed Samuel's arm. "Just one minute, Sam. For an extra fifty, I think I might be able to squeeze you into the co-pilot's seat. I can fly this baby by myself, and Pete, my partner, would probably be thankful for a night off."

Samuel had to think for a minute. He hadn't as yet seen a ferry schedule and didn't know what the cost would be. However, he also wasn't looking forward to a crossing by water. Taking the flight this evening would get him into Haifa two days earlier.

Sensing his potential passenger's hesitation, Robertson interrupted Samuel's train of thought. "Okay, you know what? I'll make it an extra forty. That's a real bargain, as you Yankees would say! The ferry's fifty quid, doesn't leave until noon tomorrow, could be intercepted and delayed by a Royal Navy destroyer, and it's fairly rough out there at this time of year."

The last comment convinced Samuel to accept Robertson's offer. "You've got a deal. What time do we leave?"

"I'll see you back at the white building in three hours. But first, could you please come with me so I can collect your fare?"

"Would you happen to have a telephone I could use?"

"Certainly, right after you pay for your flight." Robertson smiled at Samuel. When they opened the door, a small, white-and-beige fox terrier ran outside and promptly watered the bougainvillea at the side of the building. It then ran back inside and started to bark and run in circles around Samuel.

"That's Pete's dog, Gypsy. Just ignore him."

In the small, stuffy office with maps and airplane photographs on the walls, and papers covering every flat surface, Samuel picked up the phone and dialled the overseas operator in Athens, who put him through to the switchboard at the King David Hotel in Jerusalem.

"King David Hotel, how may I help you?" the hotel operator's voice enquired in flawless English.

"May I have Mr. Marcus's room, please?"

"Oh, General Marcus doesn't stay here, may I take a message for him?"

At this point, Gypsy started humping Samuel's leg, momentarily distracting him. "Oh ... oh ... yes, certainly. Please let him know that Samuel Singer will be arriving by flying boat in Haifa this evening around midnight."

"Thank you, Mister Singer."

Samuel hung up the receiver, shook a persevering Gypsy off his leg, and walked outside, the dog following closely behind.

Robertson was sitting on the wharf smoking a pipe, letting his feet dangle above the water. The wind had picked up a bit as the sun started its declining arc in the western sky. Samuel decided to light up again as well.

"Thank you for the use of the phone. How many other passengers will be on our flight tonight?"

"We have seating capacity for eight in the back, along with freight," Robertson responded curtly, making it obvious he wasn't looking for further conversation.

"One more thing. I haven't eaten all day, where can I get some decent food?"

Robertson looked at him, annoyed, as if to say, *I'm done talking, now go away*. "Walk back the way your taxi drove you down here about two hundred yards. There's a small restaurant with tables outside. The fresh fish is about the only thing edible that won't give you the runs. Order beer, the wine's undrinkable."

And with that, he turned his back on Samuel and stared out to sea, continuously puffing on his pipe. Gypsy came and lay down beside him, putting his head in Robertson's lap.

CHAPTER 16

The sky had turned a dark orange as the sun dipped below the horizon, and it seemed to sink into the azure sea, creating a purplish haze above it. It was starting to get dark, with the first few faint stars appearing above, as Samuel walked back to the white building.

The eight other passengers were already there, along with Peter "Pete" Cook, Robertson's navigator and partner in Aegean Seaplane Charter Service. Robertson and Peter were in a deep discussion inside the building, going over charts and weather reports. As Peter would not be along on this trip, Robertson was getting a refresher course on the navigation instruments of the aircraft.

The other passengers were standing at the edge of the wharf, talking quietly in French, while smoking Gitanes, a French cigarette brand that had a very distinct, sweet aroma. The musical sound of a bouzouki drifted over the water from somewhere along the wharf, and the lights of the fishing boats, bobbing up and down, reflected off the surface of the dark water.

After about fifteen minutes, Pete gathered the group around him and provided a brief outline of what they could expect on the flight over. "So, do we all understand English?"

One of the group responded in the positive, in a thick French accent. "I understand, Monsieur, and I will ... how do you say? Translate for my friends. But please speak not too fast."

Pete then went over all the fine points of the flight, the route, the potential but unlikely event of being forced down by an RAF aircraft enforcing the British blockade, and emergency evacuation procedures. He then handed all the embarking passengers a Mae West, yellow life preserver, with "Property of the US Navy" stencilled on it, and led them in single file to a rusty metal ladder loosely attached to the side of the jetty.

"*Mon Dieu*," sighed one of the French passengers, looking down into the small motor launch tied to a cleat at the top.

"Gentlemen, follow me. Watch your step and take your seats evenly on each side."

The Frenchman, known as Gabriel, translated the instructions to his companions. They were all Jews, survivors of German concentration camps, some of them having fought with the resistance, recruited by the Jewish Agency to help Israel's fight for survival.

The motor launch, driven by Pete, with Robertson in the bow holding a flashlight, swiftly reached the aircraft and tied off to one of the pontoon struts. Robertson nimbly ascended the ladder, opened the pilot's door and hoisted himself in.

The rest of the group, with Pete's flashlight lighting the way, awkwardly scrambled up the ladder, with one of them slipping halfway up and nearly falling into the water. They had to bend down to go from the cockpit into the fuselage through the narrow opening between the two compartments. A single, small red bulb illuminated the inside of the plane. Antoine, the tallest of the group, yelled out, "*Merde!*" and rubbed his head as he bumped heavily into the top of the entryway.

Robertson grabbed Samuel as he came through and roughly shoved him into the co-pilot's canvas seat. Once everyone was seated, Robertson shook his partner's hand and closed the door. Pete untied the line holding the aircraft to its anchor buoy and, waving goodbye, sped off.

Everyone watched as the boat's silhouette melted into the darkness. It represented their last connection to dry land. Robertson pumped the choke and pushed the start button on the airplane's instrument panel, and first the starboard engine, and then the port, sputtered to life, coughing thick smoke. He then gingerly depressed the throttles and with his feet on the pedals, turned the plane into the westerly wind. Waves buffeted the plane as it picked up speed and for a few minutes bounced along the crest of the waves, before slowly lifting off into the crisp night air.

A small murmur of relief arose in the passenger compartment. Robertson tried to lift the nose of the A.19 Cloud but was having trouble gaining altitude. The plane shook as he applied more power.

For the first time since they'd left dry land, Robertson spoke. "Now I wish I hadn't agreed to take that load of Mausers and ZK-383s for Gideon."

As he explained to Samuel in the co-pilot's seat beside him, he had accepted one hundred contraband Austrian-manufactured Mauser 7.62 mm rifles and fifty ZK-383 Czech-made submachine guns, to be smuggled to a Major Gideon, who was going to meet him on touchdown in the harbour in Haifa.

"It's all very complex, mate, this business with the Jews. I am doing it because my girlfriend is a Greek Jew. Her parents were from Salonika, and the Germans sent them to Auschwitz. She was eighteen and a waitress in a bar in Athens when I met her. She is an orphan and had been living on the street. It was through her that I met Avner Gideon on my first trip to Haifa. I'm telling you, mate, this thing with the Jews is very complicated."

He didn't get a chance to elaborate, as he required all his strength and attention to get the heavily laden aircraft up to altitude, leaving Samuel to wonder what "this complicated thing" with the Jews was.

They were now well above the swells below, with the lights of Piraeus and Athens slowly disappearing in the darkness off their port side. The plane's engines hummed in unison, and the sound of snoring from the passenger compartment accompanied their rhythm.

Five hours later, past midnight, the twinkling lights of Haifa came into view through scattered clouds. It had been a fairly smooth flight, with little turbulence and good visibility, and the aircraft started to descend. Samuel had also fallen asleep and was just opening his eyes when the plane's radio came crackling to life with heavily Hebrew-accented English. "Robbie, this is Gideon. I can see your lights. The sea's calm. You should have an easy landing. Do you have the goods?"

"Aye, mate, and what have you got for me?"

"Everything you need, my friend," came the response from Major Gideon. "One more thing, Robbie, do you have a passenger named Samuel Singer on board?"

Robertson looked at the man sitting beside him who was still rubbing the sleep from his eyes.

Samuel nodded. "I do."

"Good, make sure he doesn't get his feet wet." Gideon laughed.

Robertson then turned around and yelled loudly into the back to the half-asleep French passengers. "*Mes amis*, hang on tightly to whatever you can grab. We are going to land in a minute."

Robertson levelled the aircraft off just above the whitecaps, pulled back on the throttles, and as the pontoons hit the water, bounced along the Mediterranean's surface, leaving a fluorescent wake behind them. The plane continued taxiing towards the dark outline of the outer breakwater protecting Haifa's natural harbour.

Two large motor launches, their searchlights like giant fingers seeking out the airplane, were speeding in the aircraft's direction, their bows creating a white phosphorescent froth as they approached. Pulling alongside the airplane on each side, men in the bows tied the launches to the pontoon struts with heavy lines.

Robertson scrambled through the aircraft's fuselage, shaking hands and patting the backs of the Frenchmen as they began to move through the pilot's open door and down the ladder into one of the waiting launches. He then swung the rear cargo door open and from the back, began to haul the first of the fifteen crates containing the rifles and submachine guns over to it.

Someone from one of the launches, with a heavy Israeli accent, yelled up, "Where is the American?"

Samuel leaned out the co-pilot's window and yelled back, "Right here."

"Okay, go to the back and get in the launch loading the crates."

Samuel squeezed his bulky frame through the opening, making sure to lower his head so he wouldn't suffer the same fate as the tall Frenchman Antoine had. He came to the door just as Robertson was shoving the last of the crates down to the two burly dockhands standing in the boat below. Samuel went to shake Robertson's hand and started to put his feet through the door to climb down as well.

"Not so fast, mate!" Robertson yelled. "There is still cargo coming this way and maybe your VIP-ness could help."

At that moment, the other launch untied from the plane, and with its engines stirring up the water, sped off towards shore, creating a wave that nearly tipped the now much lighter airplane over. The plane, its cargo door open, leaned precariously over to port, launching Samuel, who was halfway out the door, into the dark water below.

One of the dockhands reached over and grabbed the collar of Samuel's jacket as he bobbed to the surface and hauled him, soaked, spitting water and swearing, into the boat.

Above, Robertson couldn't stop himself from laughing.

While Samuel sat shivering in the bow, the men in the boat quickly hoisted the cases of rum, whisky, gin and Marlboro and Lucky Strike cigarettes up to Robertson standing in the door of the aircraft. The goods, purloined from British Army warehouses in Palestine by the

Jewish underground, were payment for the transport of the Mausers and Czech submachine guns.

Robertson looked around the aircraft before closing the door, and, spotting Samuel's suitcase, threw it into the bottom of the boat, where it landed in the water that had accumulated there. Beaming a broad smile down at Samuel and lifting his hand to the peak of his cap in a mock salute, Robertson shouted, "Hey, Yank. Good luck in the Promised Land."

The boat pulled away from the airplane and began moving towards Haifa, picking up speed as it went. Samuel looked back at the plane rising and falling in the boat's wake, its propellers slowly starting to rotate as it started its takeoff run, the sound of its engines drowned out by those of the motor launch. He turned and waved, hoping Robertson would see it through the darkness and the sea spray. They had reached the inner harbour by the time Samuel saw the wingtip navigation lights of the airplane moving higher into the night sky to disappear amongst millions of stars.

The boat pulled alongside the seawall far from the area of the port used for the unloading of merchant ships. It was in total darkness. The other boat, which had taken the Frenchmen to shore, had also tied up along the stone jetty, but was empty of its human cargo. The men in the boat helped the still-waterlogged Samuel climb up the ladder, where an athletic-looking young man with dark curly hair and dressed in British army fatigues stood. He extended his arm to shake hands with Samuel.

"Welcome to Palestine, Dr. Singer. I am Major Avner Gideon. General Marcus asked me to meet you, as unfortunately he was not able to. Once we have finished unloading, we will be on our way to meet him in Jerusalem."

It was then that he noticed Samuel's drenched attire. "I, did you swim to shore Dr. Singer?"

Samuel didn't appreciate the humour. "Major Gideon, could you please get me some dry clothes before I die of hypothermia!"

"Oh, please call me Avner. I am sure we can find you something to wear, although you're definitely on the plus side." He laughed.

After scrounging up a pair of khaki shorts and a blue denim shirt one size too small, along with a full-length, beige trench coat, the two of them set out for Jerusalem in a green US Army surplus Dodge ¾ ton 4x4 truck. The fifteen cases of Mausers and submachine guns were in the back of the vehicle, hidden under canvas bags filled with potatoes. They laid the wet contents of Samuel's suitcase on top of the bags of potatoes to dry out. Samuel searched his wet jacket for his pipe, lighter, and tobacco. Fortunately, both pipe and lighter were there, but the tobacco was saturated with sea water and totally useless. Samuel desperately wanted to light up his pipe, but without tobacco, settled for chewing on the stem. They set out, driving along the Mediterranean coast, their headlights dimmed.

Avner spoke first. "General Marcus has told me a lot about you. We in Palestine truly appreciate your bravery in coming here to help us. Do you know a lot about our country?"

"Very little, in fact. Only what I heard from Mickey, and what I've read in the New York newspapers. By the way, Avner, where did you learn your excellent English?"

"I was a lieutenant in the Jewish Brigade of the British 8th Army under Field Marshal Montgomery in Italy during the war."

"How long have you lived in Palestine?"

"I was born here, in Kibbutz Degania Alef, by the Kinneret, to you, the Sea of Galilee. My parents emigrated here from Ukraine in the twenties."

They drove along in silence, watching the sky starting to lighten in the east. Samuel would nod off every now and again but would periodically be awoken by the truck hitting a bump or hole in the uneven coastal road. They turned off the main road at Netanya, and Avner pulled the truck over to the side of the road.

He got out, heading into some bushes and shouting back to Samuel, "If you need to pee, now is a good time to do it!"

When Avner came back, he reached behind the driver's seat and pulled out a Thompson submachine gun and a Webley .455 calibre British Army service revolver. He handed the revolver to Samuel. "You probably know how to use this. We will be driving through some Arab villages on our way into Jerusalem, and it is good to be prepared." He grabbed the top of the truck's doorway and swung into his seat, placing the Thompson between himself and Samuel.

Samuel examined the Webley as they got back on the dirt road that would take them to one of the holiest cities in Judaism, Islam, and Christianity, fought over for many centuries by a multiplicity of religions. As dawn broke over the Judaean Hills, the sky a bright pink, Samuel was thinking that night would still be enveloping those back home.

Avner slowed down to let a sleepy Arab shepherd with his flock of baa-ing sheep cross the road in front of him. He then realized his mistake and gunned the truck, swerving around the panicked animals, kicking up a cloud of yellowish-brown dust.

A shot rang out from somewhere in the treeline beside the road, and then two more.

Both of them ducked instinctively as the bullets from an Arab sniper whizzed by them harmlessly. Avner contemplated stopping the truck for a moment and jumping out and spraying the treeline behind him with his Thompson, but then thought better of it, and kept his foot on the gas. Once past the village, Avner spoke up. "That's pretty regular. The good thing is that they have old rifles and really bad aim. They couldn't hit anything smaller than a cow. We've lost some people to them, mostly because they stop when they hear a gunshot and try to figure out where it came from. The Arabs get the shepherds to cross the road in front of you to get you to slow down. Best thing to do is to keep driving, even if you have to run over a few sheep or an Arab shepherd doing so."

They continued down the road without further incident, and soon the golden Dome of the Rock came into view, with the rising sun blindingly reflecting off it. The magnificent view took Samuel's breath away, and he could only stare.

"You know, Samuel, that was built one thousand two hundred and fifty years ago by Caliph Abd al-Malik. It is said that Muhammad ascended to heaven from there. The earliest Jewish tradition regarding Jerusalem states that Adam, the first man, was created from the same place where in future the altar would stand in the Holy Temple in Jerusalem. After he was ejected from the Garden of Eden, he returned to this spot to offer a sacrifice to God. Cain and Abel also brought their offerings on this altar. It is believed that Adam lived in Jerusalem for all his life. The altar in Jerusalem remained as a permanent shrine where all people could worship God, until it was destroyed by the Flood."

"Avner, you sure seem to know your history."

"I should. I have a master's degree in Middle Eastern History and taught it in high school in Tel Aviv in peace time. But enough of ancient history. Let's concentrate on where we are going, or we will end up in the wrong neighbourhood. And in this part of the world, that can be deadly!"

"You know," Avner continued, "the Jewish half of Jerusalem had been under blockade by Arab irregulars from the surrounding villages since 1947. Entering the city has become a precarious enterprise for Jews."

Fortunately for them, their destination, the King David Hotel, was located outside the city's ancient stone walls on King David Street, overlooking the Old City and Mount Zion. From its construction, the King David Hotel had hosted royalty: the dowager empress of Persia, Queen Mother Nazli of Egypt and King Abdullah I of Jordan stayed at the hotel, and three heads of state exiled from their countries had taken up residence there: King Alfonso XIII of Spain, forced to abdicate in 1931; Emperor Haile Selassie of Ethiopia, driven out by Italian armed forces in 1936; and King George II of Greece, who had been forced to flee after the Nazi occupation of his country in 1942. During the British Mandate, the southern wing of the hotel was turned into a

British administrative and military headquarters. It was also where Mickey would greet visitors who came at his behest from overseas, and whom he would lobby for assistance in obtaining clandestine weapons, medical supplies, volunteers, and financial donations for the fledgling Jewish army.

As Avner drove the truck through heavy traffic, Samuel looked, amazed, at the variety of conveyances, from horse carts and riders astride donkeys, to British tracked military vehicles and dilapidated old Austin taxis. His ears were assaulted by the loud cacophony generated by all of them.

They parked the truck at the back of the hotel away from prying eyes, and Avner went in through a service entrance, leaving Samuel to guard the vehicle. He emerged a few minutes later followed by two tanned, muscular young men in coveralls, who jumped into the truck and drove off.

Avner then took Samuel by the arm and they walked through the lush landscaping surrounding the hotel to the front entrance. Scaffolding partially hid the collapsed southwestern corner of the building, which had been partly destroyed on July 22, 1946, by a bomb planted by Irgun, the outlawed Jewish underground. Coming through the front doors into the expansive lobby, Samuel immediately spotted a well-tanned Mickey in army khakis without rank insignia, who was in deep conversation with several well-dressed elderly gentlemen. As soon as he noticed Samuel, he broke away from the group and with long strides came to embrace him.

"Sammy, finally!" He then took a step back, looked at his friend, and burst out laughing. "My God, what happened to you? Who dressed you this morning?"

It was then that Samuel realized he was still wearing the ill-fitting clothes he had borrowed the night before. His own wet clothes were still draped over the potato sacks in the back of the truck where they had been left to dry out.

A few minutes later, Mickey and the elderly gentlemen were sitting around a small, green-felt-covered table, drinking gin and tonics and enjoying some locally grown fresh fruits. Mickey pulled out an empty chair for Samuel and introduced him.

"Gentlemen, may I introduce you to a dear, dear childhood friend of mine, Dr. Samuel Singer, from New York. Dr. Singer and I served together in Europe during the war, and he has unselfishly left family in the USA to come and help in our cause. He's an experienced battlefield surgeon, and I am sure will save many Jewish lives in the upcoming struggle."

Murmurs of admiration and appreciation passed through the group.

"Sammy, these gentlemen are from the Jewish Agency offices in Geneva, and I am trying to impress upon them the gravity of our situation, with Jerusalem surrounded and five Arab armies ready to pounce."

"Nice meeting you, gentlemen, but I must excuse myself."

With that, Samuel drew Mickey aside and whispered, "I must get in touch with Agatha and let her know I got here safely. God only knows what's going through her mind right now."

"Sure, there's a little private room just behind the switchboard. Just give them the number and they will put you through. Thanks for coming, Sam." He then embraced his friend and turned back to his guests once again.

After his telegram from Athens, Samuel assumed that by then Bernard would have handed his letter to his wife revealing his plans, and he wanted to let her know that he had made it safely to Palestine. It was around eight in the morning in Larchmont when he called home.

Agatha answered on the first ring, saying, "Hello." Her voice was tired and teary.

"Aggie, it's Samuel ... "

A long silence ensued. "You selfish bastard."

It was the first time in their twelve-year marriage that Samuel had heard his wife swear. It took him aback, and he didn't know how to continue. Then the dam broke, and a torrent of recriminations poured forth from the other end of the line.

"I haven't slept in three nights. I cry all day and night. Poor Daniel keeps asking 'Where did Daddy go? When is he coming back? Doesn't he love us anymore?' My father's been here since he came over the day after you'd left and handed me your mea culpa nonsense.

"Samuel, how could you do this to us? I am going to be a wreck until, or rather *if*, you get back. Don't you think I did enough worrying for a lifetime while you were in Europe for two years?"

At that point she broke down and couldn't talk anymore.

Her father came on the line. "Samuel, she can't talk to you right now. We are happy to know that you are safe. Please stay that way and call us later."

He then whispered, "Now that she knows where you are, and that you're safe, she'll settle down in time. Here, Daniel wants to say hello."

"Daddy, when are you coming home? What did you buy me?"

A broad smile crossed Samuel's face. "Hi Daniel, I am in Jerusalem, very far away, perhaps Grandpa can show you on a map. I will be coming home in a couple of weeks. Be a good boy and listen to Mommy and Grandpa. I love you."

He hung up the phone, and a wave of doubt about his actions washed over him. *Did I do right? Did I do it in the right way? Should I have told her?*

His silent self-recriminations were interrupted by Avner. "Mickey wants us to join him out back. Operations against the Arab Legion are about to begin, and he wants to familiarize you with the plans."

They entered the walled city through Jaffa Gate in a camouflaged surplus US Army Jeep, passing by Herod's Citadel and the Tower of David. The words of Benjamin Disraeli, Queen Victoria's foreign secretary in the late 1800s, rang in Samuel's ears: "The view of Jerusalem is the history of the world; it is more, it is the history of heaven and earth."

Mickey drove, with Samuel in the passenger seat and Avner in the back, the Thompson submachine gun cradled in his lap. Following a slow drive through the Christian, Armenian, and Jewish quarters of the city, impeded by slow-moving pedestrians and merchants hauling their wares on two-wheeled carts or overloaded donkeys, they sped through Damascus Gate, with the Muslim quarter on their right.

"We're lucky. We didn't get shot at today. Usually we get a couple of pot shots taken at us from the Arab Legion guards posted on the walls. Fortunately, they're terrible marksmen," remarked Mickey.

They then drove into the Judaean Hills overlooking the ancient city, arriving at an encampment in a clearing amongst a grove of olive trees. The encampment was a hive of feverish activity, with men and women, young and old, outfitted in various paramilitary dress, pitching tents, digging trenches, and unloading equipment from trucks and horse-drawn wagons. It didn't take Samuel long to spot the truck he had left his clothes in to dry, and he went to retrieve them. Mickey gathered his staff around a folding table beside his Jeep.

From their high vantage point above Jerusalem, overlooking the Kidron Valley, they could see the Old City and the Arab villages scattered around the lush green countryside. The late-spring afternoon sunshine enveloped the entire scenery in a golden glow. Mickey, with the rank of general in the Israeli Army, was only an adviser to it, with the active role assumed by regular Palmach or Haganah officers, many with British Army backgrounds.

Mickey had spread a map of the Central Front, the area surrounding Jerusalem, with arrows indicating both Jewish and Arab planned and anticipated troop movements, on the table. All the officers were gathered around, most smoking cigarettes and paying rapt attention to Marcus as he went over details of the battle strategy in English, his fingers forcefully jabbing at various points on the map. General Yigal Allon, the officer commanding Central Front, translated his words into Hebrew.

Mickey drew everyone's attention to the fortified Arab town of Latrun. "This is the cork in the bottle. It's the gateway between our forces in Tel Aviv and our besieged brothers and sisters in Jerusalem. We have to remove the cork so that we can have safe passage between the two. Yigal here will provide all the section leaders with their orders for the coming fight."

He then turned to Samuel. "Sammy, so great to see you again. Let's go and talk somewhere private."

Throwing his arm around Samuel's shoulder, they walked up a small, grass-covered hill, with Avner following a short distance behind, and sat down under a large cypress tree.

"Avi, could you please go down and grab a bottle of red wine and a couple of glasses out of my tent and bring them up here? There should be a corkscrew by the bottles."

"Oh, and Avner, could you please scare up some pipe tobacco from somewhere? Maybe some of your men are pipe smokers? I'm going out of my mind. I haven't had a smoke in three days," added Samuel.

Mickey then turned to Samuel. "Sam, I am truly concerned about the coming days. The situation does not look good. And these gentlemen from Geneva are scared of their own shadows. You'd swear they think we're trying to steal their last dime when we ask them for help." He shook his head. "Unfortunately, I am afraid we're going to need your services more than I'd like. But tell me, what's going on at home?"

His talking was interrupted by Avner's return; he was carrying a bottle and two small drinking glasses. "Here you go, sir. I hope you don't mind but I opened the bottle down at the tent, and these are the only glasses I could find."

Avner then bent down and gave Samuel, who was sitting on the ground leaning against the tree trunk, a small paper bag. "I was in luck, Dr. Singer. One of our sergeants is also a pipe smoker, and he sent you this with his regards."

"Thank you, Avner. Please pass on my thanks."

Avner jogged back down the hill, leaving the two friends to themselves.

Mickey took the bottle and poured each of them a full glass. They touched glasses and whispered, "*L'chaim*. To life."

The rays of the slowly setting sun filtered through the tree's branches, turning the dark red wine in their glasses a translucent, velvety crimson as they raised them to their lips. For a moment, the two of them sat in silence, slowly sipping their drinks, their eyes taking in the vista below them. The sky turned from a bright orange to a glowing red, as if a bloody curtain had been draped over all of Jerusalem, foretelling the terrible days of conflict to come. The call of the muezzin summoning the faithful to evening prayer drifted over the hills from a hundred minarets around the countryside as the lights in the city were turned on.

Mickey spoke first, forgetting his last question about events at home, and continuing about the dire situation of the Israelis in the Holy Land to provide Samuel with an understanding of the combat that lay ahead. "The operation itself will begin tomorrow morning in the Latrun area"

He handed Samuel his binoculars, stretched out his arm and pointed at a grouping of dim lights just beyond the dark silhouette of the ancient walls of Jerusalem. "With Haganah forces taking over the Wadi al-Sarrar camp, Arab Hulda, and Deir Muheisen. Parallel to this, the village of Bayt Mahsir in the region of Bab el-Wad over to your left will be attacked by the Palmach, thus clearing the mountain road to Jerusalem."

He looked at his friend and smiled.

"Unfortunately, as that famous German General Helmuth von Moltke said, 'No plan of battle ever survives contact with the enemy.' I am praying for the best. We had to delay the start of the operation because we were waiting for the arrival of the hundred Mausers and 50 ZK-383s, courtesy of that Aussie pilot, Ian Robertson. He's a real gem. He's doing this for his Jewish girlfriend, you know."

"Yeah, and for crates of gin and smokes." Samuel laughed.

They both lay back, Samuel in a half-sitting position against the tree trunk so he could once again enjoy his meerschaum, the glowing embers of which cast a dim light on his face as he drew in the sweet-scented tobacco. Mickey lay with his arms supporting his head, looking up as a multitude of stars twinkled in the rapidly darkening sky above them. Their quiet conversation turned to days past.

Finally, with a yawn, Mickey stood up, stretched out his arms, and said, "Well, it's the eve of battle. Time to go to sleep. They've set up a cot for you in my tent. Hope you don't mind."

"I've slept in worse places, and at least the tent doesn't move," Samuel replied.

The two of them walked down the hill in the direction of the small campfires scattered throughout the troops' bivouac area.

Young and old, men and women from cities and villages around Palestine, others recently arrived on refugee ships like the *SS Exodus*, the survivors of Auschwitz, Treblinka, Sobibor, and another dozen hells on earth, were sitting by the flames, their faces illuminated, smoking, talking, and some singing patriotic songs about the new State of Israel in Yiddish and Hebrew.

Mickey went through the encampment saying goodnight to his charges, while Samuel retired to their tent. The wine had its effect, and he just wanted to go to sleep and not dwell on what was to come when the sun rose once again. He dropped on to his cot without bothering to undress, drawing his trench coat over himself, and dreamt of home.

CHAPTER 17

MAY 1948,

LATRUN AND THE BATTLE FOR JERUSALEM

It was 4:00 a.m. and the eastern sky was still dark, with only a thin, pink border hinting at sunrise. A bright crescent moon and an even brighter Venus were high in the sky as they traversed the heavens above the Holy Land. General Yigal Allon had gathered his troops around him in a clearing in the midst of the olive trees. Rabbi Yitzhak HaLevi Herzog, Ashkenazi Chief Rabbi of Israel, was standing behind him, ready to recite the *Schacharit*, or morning prayers. Some of the troops wore full vestments, others just prayer shawls, while others only wore *kippas*. The majority didn't wear any signs of religiosity whatsoever. Many were fidgeting with their weapons, others rubbing the sleep from their eyes.

Allon spoke first in Hebrew, "Men and women of my command, you are all children of Israel, ready to lay down your lives for a homeland for our people, who have been persecuted since time immemorial in the four corners of the world. After Hitler's hellfire, those of us left are ready to forge a new nation, as was promised in the scriptures. As we go into battle today to relieve the siege of our historic capital, Jerusalem, remember that our cause is right. It's just and holy. Tomorrow in Jerusalem!"

Those gathered around murmured as one along with Allon, the ancient Jewish greeting that had been passed down over the millennia, "Tomorrow in Jerusalem."

Then Rabbi Herzog stepped forward, and in his booming voice, read from handwritten notes. "Psalm 137:5–6. 'If I forget you, O Jerusalem, let my right hand forget its skill! If I do not remember you, let my tongue cling to the roof of my mouth if I do not exalt Jerusalem above my chief joy.'"

Mickey and Samuel had been standing quietly off to the side, listening to Allon and the rabbi. Although neither spoke nor understood Hebrew, they both understood the importance of what had been said.

"Let's go get some coffee and something to eat," Mickey said, as the troops began to disperse and head off to the mobile kitchens parked nearby.

"You know, Mickey, this reminds me of Utah Beach a few years ago. The same dynamics at work. You can smell the fear, the food, the gasoline exhaust, the privies, and the sweat, all of it overtaking the refreshing, clear air of these hills and the scent of the olive trees. Patton was right. 'War is Hell.'"

They joined the lineup of men and women receiving what for many of them might be their last meal. Conversations had died down, with each lost in their own thoughts, contemplating what was yet to come, their roles and how they would face the challenges. They returned to Mickey's tent to finish their coffees, both sitting on the side of Samuel's cot. It was 5:00 a.m. and the slowly rising sun showed itself just above the horizon and shone through the entrance into the tent. The start of the operation was scheduled for 6:00 a.m.

The various military conveyances revved their engines, the smoke from their exhausts creating a blue haze above the trees. There were trucks, Jeeps, jerry-rigged armoured cars with metal plates welded on to their chassis, a few Bren Gun Carriers, and some US Army surplus armoured personnel carriers mounting heavy .50 calibre machine guns. The troops had started to climb into their assigned vehicles when Avner drove up to their tent with Yigal Allon in the passenger seat. An ambulance with a red Star of David in a white circle painted on it followed.

"Good morning, gentlemen." Allon smiled at the two. "Are we ready to go to war? Mickey, you ride with me in the back. Dr. Singer, you will ride with Gabriel in the ambulance."

Mickey put the GI helmet that had stood him in good stead throughout France and Germany on his head and jumped into the back of the Jeep beside Yitzhak, the HQ radio operator.

Samuel hoisted himself into the passenger seat of the ambulance and immediately recognised the driver, Gabriel, one of his French fellow passengers from the flight over from Piraeus.

"*Bonjour, docteur*," Gabriel said with a smile. "I guess all roads lead to Jerusalem."

"Indeed, they seem to." Samuel smiled back.

It was getting close to six o'clock, and Allon stood up in his Jeep as they drove down the slight incline and took position at the head of the column of vehicles that had assembled in the clearing.

"Thank God the Arabs don't have an air force in the area, or this operation would be over before it started." Allon turned to Mickey.

At exactly the appointed hour, as the high-pitched voice of the muezzin called the Muslim faithful to morning prayers from a hundred loudspeakers in Jerusalem and the surrounding villages of the valley, and the sun started its ascent into a clear blue sky, General Allon stood up, raising his right arm and pumping it up and down. It was the signal to start moving. The deep rumble of myriad engines drowned out the warble of the songbirds happily winging their way through the trees, looking for maturing buds on the branches, as the vehicles snaked down the dirt track leading from the Judaean Hills in the direction of Latrun.

The battle at Latrun, commanding the strategic highway from Tel Aviv to Jerusalem, raged for several weeks afterwards, with both the Israeli and Arab high commands pouring increasing numbers of men and materials into the struggle. Despite assaulting Latrun on five separate occasions, Israel was ultimately unable to capture Latrun, and it remained under Jordanian control. The Battle of Latrun left its imprint on the Israeli collective imagination. The attacks cost the lives of 168 Israeli soldiers, and more than 1,000 were wounded.

Throughout the battles, Samuel operated from his mobile aid station on the Israeli wounded, with the able assistance of Gabriel and four Viennese nurses, all survivors of Bergen-Belsen concentration camp, until the end of May.

He also made the perilous journey by armoured car to Jerusalem to help the overworked doctors at Bikur Cholim Hospital deal with the daily casualties from the fighting around Jerusalem.

Since a convoy bringing supplies and medical staff to Hadassah Medical Center on Mount Scopus had been ambushed by Arab forces on April 13, 1948, killing many of them, there had been a shortage of medical personnel in the Jewish half of the city to deal with the wounded and sick, so Samuel jumped in to fill the breach as best he could.

Mickey Marcus continued to provide advice and direction on all the battle fronts from Jordan to Egypt, to Lebanon and Syria, during the closing stages of Israel's War of Independence, as the conflict came to be called. He would drive in his Jeep or fly in a surplus US Army Stinson L-5 liaison airplane, piloted by a former US Air Force fighter pilot.

On June 10, 1948, he returned to the Latrun area, setting up camp at Abu Ghosh, on the outskirts of Jerusalem. A ceasefire had been negotiated between Jews and Arabs through Count Folke Bernadotte, the Swedish diplomat representing the United Nations, to commence the next day.

Samuel was just leaving the operating room of the hospital when he bumped into Avner.

"Dr. Singer, you're just the man I am looking for." Avner warmly shook Samuel's hand, not noticing that it was still encased in a rubber surgical glove.

"General Marcus asked me to come and take you to Abu Ghosh for a celebratory dinner with him this evening. You know, a ceasefire is supposed to start tomorrow morning at 9:00 a.m. Maybe this craziness will be over."

"Well, give me half an hour to clean up."

He and Avner drove along the "Burma Road" established by Shlomo Shamir as an alternative route from Jerusalem to Tel Aviv, which avoided villages controlled by the Arab Legion.

They arrived at Mickey's encampment near the Church of Notre Dame, where Mickey strode out to greet them. He hugged Samuel. "We have quite a spread laid out for this evening, with lots of wine from Galilee. Maybe this mess is over after all and us Jews will be able to enjoy peace in our own land for a while."

They walked around an apple orchard and got caught up on each of their most recent activities.

"You know, Sammy, we're winning this war. I feel terrible for some of our boys. Just out of a concentration camp, into a refugee camp, and then on to some rickety old freighter and into the front lines in Palestine. These kids deserve a better life. You and I get a chance to go home at some point, but they'll be fighting for theirs forever unless we are strong enough to discourage the Arabs from continuing with this shit."

He reached up to pluck a ripe apple from a low-hanging branch and handed it to Samuel, then took another for himself.

Before Samuel had a chance to take his first bite, a sergeant, out of breath, ran up to Mickey.

"General, we are all set up. When should I call the troops for dinner?"

"What time is it?"

Samuel looked at his watch. "It's coming up to 6:30."

"Sergeant, let's start at seven."

It was an evening for celebration. A few shots were heard in the distance, but by and large, the conflict had died down in anticipation of the next day's ceasefire. The men and women sitting around the hastily set up tables were in a good mood. The wine flowed freely.

Mickey got up to make a speech, and Avner translated.

"Friends, men and women of the Palmach and the Haganah. We are for the first time celebrating the coming of peace to our own land. You, your families, and your friends shed their blood to achieve it. Your children shall, God willing, harvest its fruits. It has been my privilege to serve with every one of you."

He then raised his glass. "*L'chaim.*"

There was applause all around as everyone raised their glasses in response. Someone bought out a violin and started playing the mournful notes of the new Israeli national anthem "Hatikvah" ("The Hope"). All those gathered by the campfire joined in, their voices rising with their emotions:

> *As long as the Jewish spirit is yearning deep in the heart,*
> *With eyes turned toward the East, looking toward Zion,*
> *Then our hope — the two-thousand-year-old hope — will not be lost:*
> *To be a free people in our land,*
> *The land of Zion and Jerusalem.*

Without exception, all eyes welled up with tears. Once again, men, women, boys and girls, young and old—the persecuted survivors of all of Europe's Jewry—joined in celebrating having a land to call their own.

With the strains of "Hatikvah" still ringing in his ears, Mickey turned to Samuel. "I'm cold and tired. I'm going to go get some sleep. I'll see you in the morning. Avner, make sure we have sentries posted. This is not over yet."

He then turned and started walking to his tent through the mist that had arrived with the cold night air.

Samuel and Avner returned to sit by one of the fires the troops had gathered around. There was an exciting buzz in the air. Everyone recounted their own stories of struggle and survival and hopes in a brighter future. Finally, around midnight, Samuel decided to turn in as well, and went to join Mickey in their tent. Once again, a cot had been provided for him. *Boy, I'll be happy when I can have a real bed to sleep in where I don't have anyone else to share space with,* he thought to himself.

Mickey was fast asleep and snoring loudly when Samuel entered, blew out the candle on the ammunition crate beside his cot, and lay down.

Around 2:00 a.m. he awoke to Mickey sitting up then wrapping his blanket around himself, standing up and walking out of the tent, murmuring something about not being able to sleep.

Samuel turned over to go back to sleep when he heard a single gunshot. He didn't know what to make of it but figured it was probably someone discharging their firearm by mistake. A minute later Avner flew through the opening to the tent

"Samuel, come quick. Mickey's been shot!"

Although still in the twilight between sleep and consciousness, he jumped to his feet and followed Avner. The rest of the encampment had also come to life, the beams of flashlights criss-crossing the darkness and the low-lying mist. Avner and Samuel arrived at a clearing on the edge of the apple orchard to find Mickey wrapped in his blanket, lying on his back, surrounded by a couple of sleepy-eyed troops yelling excitedly at each other.

Avner shoved them aside to make a path for Samuel, who knelt beside Mickey and felt for a pulse. There was none. He then noticed a small hole in the blanket, through which blood had started to flow. He looked up at Avner and shook his head. With the help of a couple of men, they lifted Mickey's body and walked it back to the tent, laying him on his cot.

Avner knelt down by Mickey's head and started to cry uncontrollably. Samuel joined him, wrapping his arm around Avner's shoulder.

Avner's report the following morning, ten minutes after the commencement of the ceasefire, to Prime Minister Ben-Gurion and General Allon read: "I regret to inform you that, tragically, General Marcus did not live to see the peace. Last night, six hours before the ceasefire began, in the village of Abu Ghosh near Jerusalem, he was unable to sleep, and he walked beyond the guarded perimeter wrapped in his bedsheet. One of our sentries saw a white-robed figure approaching in the mist and, not understanding the general's response to his challenge, fired a single shot, which hit him in the heart, causing instant death."

Two days later, at the airport in Jaffa, by the shores of the Mediterranean Sea, where only a month earlier he had been picking oranges off a tree, Mickey Marcus's coffin was slowly marched to a waiting C-47 US Air Force transport plane. Lining the tarmac were the new nation of Israel's political and military elite. Future prime ministers and generals were all in attendance to say goodbye to a true Jewish hero who had given his life so a new nation to provide a homeland for Europe's persecuted could be born.

The hastily assembled band played "Hatikvah" as the casket was carried to the plane. Avner and Samuel were amongst the eight pallbearers, who included Yigal Allon, Moishe Dayan (future minister of defense), Yigael Yadin (commander of the Israeli Armed Forces), and Ezer Weizmann (grandson of the founding father of the State of Israel, former RAF fighter pilot, future commander of the Israeli Air Force, and future president of the State of Israel). General Moishe Dayan, along with Samuel, accompanied the coffin to London and then on to New York.

Samuel had one arm around Agatha's waist, with the other hand holding Daniel's as Mickey's coffin was lowered into the ground at Arlington National Cemetery in Virginia. The guard of honour from West Point fired their rifles into the air as "Taps" was played by a solitary bugler. A Jewish US Army chaplain recited Kaddish, the Jewish prayer for the dead, which ended with the words "May His great name be blessed for ever, and to all eternity."

Mickey's comrades from the invasion of Normandy, including General Maxwell Taylor of the 101st "Screaming Eagles" Airborne Division and General James Gavin of the 82nd Airborne, all came to pay their respects. His gravestone read "A Soldier for All Humanity."

CHAPTER 18

JUNE 1967,
NEW YORK CITY

"Dad, have you heard anything I've said?" Daniel's question was answered by silence from his father, who was sitting across the donut shop table from him.

Samuel's face was vacant, his eyes seemingly thousands of miles away. He had heard Daniel's every word but couldn't extricate his mind from the past and pay attention to the present. All those memories from 1948 came flooding back. And now his only son, not flesh and blood, mind you, but loved and cherished just the same, wanted to risk his life in the same cause that had seen his best friend sacrifice his barely twenty years before. How could he allow that?

"Dad, are you okay?" Daniel's shrill voice cut through the fog of the past.

"Yes, Daniel, I heard what you said. I am not sure I can dissuade you from what you seem intent on doing. Your cause is right, the same as mine was twenty years ago, but I still remember the harm it caused in my and your mother's relationship for many years to come."

"Yeah, but you never told her you were going. You just left her and I alone, and for days we didn't know that you were flying off to a war zone. I'm letting both of you know up front. In any case, my mind's made up, and I am over twenty-one, so I can do as I damned well please. I have to go back to the Israeli Consul tomorrow morning, and

I thought I could get your blessing and maybe some contacts I could visit in Israel."

With that, he got up and walked through the door.

Samuel sat for a while, replaying once again in his head the journey that had brought Daniel and him to this point. He understood but couldn't rid himself of the fear and doubt that Daniel's proposed journey engendered in him.

The next morning, Daniel once again joined a long line of mainly young men outside the Israeli Consulate. All those, including Daniel, that couldn't make it in the previous afternoon had been given numbers and told to show up again the next morning. Daniel struck up a conversation with two young men standing in line in front him. They were both Israeli citizens studying in the US. They had received their military call-up notices and were reporting to the consulate to obtain travel passes. After about two and a half hours of standing on the street, Daniel finally made it to the reception desk inside.

"Name?"

"Daniel Singer."

"Citizenship?"

"American."

"Religion?"

"Jewish."

"Age?"

"Twenty-three."

The young clerk, with a blank look on her face, typed Daniel's answers on a standard query form without once looking up at him. She handed the form to him. "Please go to the second floor, room 208, and hand this form to the consular officer up there. Next?"

Daniel headed up the white marble staircase and once again found himself in a lineup by room 208. After another hour of waiting, he handed the form to a tall, dark-complexioned and muscular young man wearing a grey business suit that was a size too small, prominently showing the bulge of a shoulder holster beneath his jacket. The man exchanged Daniel's form for another one and directed him to an empty chair and desk.

"Please fill out the form, and someone will be with you shortly," the man said in heavily accented English. Shortly turned out to be another hour, when an older, bald, bespectacled man wearing an open-necked sports shirt sat down at the desk across from him.

"*Shalom*," the man said as he shook Daniel's hand and carried on speaking in fast-paced Hebrew.

Daniel stopped him mid-sentence. "I am sorry, but I don't speak Hebrew."

The man looked down at the form in front of him and put an x beside one of the questions on the form. "Well, that's a negative." He smiled up at Daniel. "Military experience?"

"Two years of ROTC at CUNY."

"Well, that's a plus."

The rest of the fifteen-minute interview followed in the same vein, with the man not saying anything beyond "Well, that's a negative" or "Well, that's a positive." At the end of the process, the man said, "So, Mr. Singer, you are seeking to join the Israel Defense Forces, correct?"

"Yes, sir."

"What special talents, knowledge or expertise do you possess that you feel the IDF would be able to take advantage of during the current hostilities?"

Daniel was stumped as he searched his brain to provide a cogent response.

Breaking the silence, the man said, "I see here that you have a master's degree in fine arts and Romance languages. Won't be able to apply much of that on the battlefield. Would you be prepared to be a cleaner, a cook, or a warehouse worker to free up other, more qualified individuals to man the front lines?"

Daniel's disappointment showed clearly on his face. He was hoping he could do more than clean latrines and peel potatoes so many thousands of miles from home.

The man, sensing Daniel's hesitation, said, "Look, Mr. Singer, why don't you leave this form with me and think it over. We'll keep it on file. You can come back, or not, after you've had some time, but your lack of Hebrew and active military experience would disqualify you from front-line service. Unfortunately, you also don't possess any unique skills that would help in our current fight. Thank you, and good afternoon."

With that, the man stood up and walked over to talk to the young, grey-suited man securing the room's entrance, ignoring Daniel, who followed him out, and then walking down the stairs and into the street bathed in late afternoon sunshine.

Well that's that, Daniel thought. He had been hoping to join the IDF and participate in some of the action taking place in that faraway country, like his father had done at Israel's birth twenty years earlier.

He headed home and took Shadow for a walk in the park across from his apartment. Upset and angry at what he perceived as cavalier treatment from a country's representative to whom he volunteered his services, he felt the disappointing turn of events would probably remove a heavy burden from his father's shoulders.

A week later, the Arab–Israeli conflict, the third in twenty years, was over, with Israel having achieved an overwhelming victory over five Arab armies and increasing the size of territory under its control six-fold. Daniel went over to his parents' house in Larchmont for dinner the evening following the cessation of hostilities.

Agatha was in the kitchen cooking one of his favourite dishes, beef stroganoff. He gave her a hug and kiss and handed her a bouquet of the pink carnations she was so fond of, which he'd bought from a street vendor on his way over.

"Where's Dad?"

"He's on the porch smoking his pipe, drinking a martini, and reading the newspaper." He found his father sitting out back, immersed in that day's edition of the *New York Times*.

The headline screamed "Cease-Fire in Syria Accepted, Israel Victorious in Six-Day War."

Further down the page, it read, "A few days ago, Israeli paratroopers, under the command of General Mordechai Gur, seized the parts of Jerusalem under Jordanian control, uniting the Holy City, and for the first time in 2,000 years Israelis could once again pray at the Western Wall. Other IDF units, after vicious fire fights with Jordanian armoured units, retook the police fortress of Latrun on the outskirts of Jerusalem that had been under Arab control since the war of 1948."

Samuel gave Daniel a sad look. "History has come full circle, son. I am sure that Mickey's smiling right now. May he rest in peace." A tear came to his eyes as he hugged his son and whispered in his ear, "Let's not discuss the other day with your mom. We'll keep it between us."

CHAPTER 19

SPRING 1933,

BERLIN AND MUNICH—HITLER COMES TO POWER

On January 30, 1933, Adolf Hitler, leader of NSDAP (National Socialist German Workers Party), was appointed Reich Chancellor by the Reich President, Paul von Hindenburg.

On February 27, 1933, the German Reichstag (parliament building) burned down. A young Communist, Marinus van der Lubbe, was accused of arson. Van der Lubbe was arrested, and the Nazis convinced President von Hindenburg to sign the so-called "Reichstag Fire Decree," which was in fact "Decree by the Reich President for the Defence of People and State" on February 28, 1933. In reality, this decree gave Hitler almost unrestricted powers to imprison any political opponent. Hitler used these powers to have Communists arrested and thus forced out of the upcoming elections.

On March 23, 1933, the Nazis succeeded in passing a law that made the Reichstag lose its powers. The "Enabling Act" invested Hitler, as Reich Chancellor, with powers to issue legislation on equal terms with the Reichstag. In other words, he was personally in control of both the executive and the legislative power. Bruno Schmidt's law firm played a key role in the drafting of both the Reichstag Fire Decree and the Enabling Act.

On an unusually warm spring morning in 1933, Frau Schmidt showed up at the offices of Axman, Streicher und Wolff with tears running down her face. The receptionist, not used to having crying ladies enter the offices of the firm, quietly asked who she was there to see.

"May I see my son, Herr Bruno Schmidt?" the shabbily attired elderly woman sobbed.

"Why, of course. Please sit down. Can I get you a glass of water, perhaps?" asked the solicitous, well-dressed receptionist.

"No, thank you. I just want to see my son."

Frau Schmidt looked around the dark, wood-panelled reception area. A large photograph adorned one wall, showing the partners of the firm assembled on either side of a broadly smiling Adolf Hitler. On another wall hung an oil portrait of Field Marshal Paul von Hindenburg, German president, by the famous portrait painter Max Beckmann. The receptionist quietly tapped on Bruno Schmidt's private office door.

"Come in," came a voice from the other side.

"Herr Schmidt, I am truly sorry to bother you, but an elderly lady claiming to be your mother is in reception, and she's in a very bad state."

Bruno stood up, quickly starting for the door.

As she saw him come through the door, Frau Schmidt rose from the leather-upholstered chair she had been sitting in, wrapped her arms around her son, and continued to cry uncontrollably.

Bruno took the handkerchief from his breast pocket and handed it to her. The receptionist, not wanting to intrude on such a private family moment, quietly walked to the large picture window at the opposite end of the office and, drawing the lace curtain aside, looked at the street below.

"Come, Mutti. Come into my office." Bruno closed the door behind them.

"Your father's dead. He's been murdered by your brown-shirted friends," Frau Schmidt sobbed, collapsing on the couch by Bruno's desk. "When he didn't come home last night, I went looking for him. I found him on Handler Gasse, around the corner, collapsed on the sidewalk. His face was a bloody mess, and he wasn't breathing. Two of his comrades from the trade union were with him, and they were also in terrible shape. They told me that the three of them had been putting up election posters when they were ambushed by a gang of Brownshirts. It's your so-called friends that did this to him!"

At that, she got off the couch and, clenching her fists, set upon her only son, screaming at the top of her voice. "You Nazi murderer. You murdering scum! I should never have brought you into this world!"

Bruno tried to calm her down, to no avail. Finally, after fifteen minutes of crying and screaming, he managed to put his arm around her and slowly walk her through reception to the elevator.

"Fräulein Oltman," he instructed the receptionist, "please have Eckler bring the car to the front."

Helmut Eckler had been a classmate of Bruno's at university but was forced to drop out due to his parents' poor financial state. His father was unemployed, and his mother earned a meagre living as a cleaning lady. The Depression took a heavy toll on the Eckler family, as it did on millions of other Germans. He took on a job as a lorry driver for a furniture-moving company so he could help support his parents and two younger sisters.

He and Bruno remained friends and would occasionally get together for a beer and discuss politics. Eckler blamed his family's misfortunes on the bourgeois, or moneyed class. He and Bruno could have been mistaken for twins, as not only did they share many physical attributes that Heinrich Himmler idolised as the perfect Aryan model, with both of them being tall and blonde with piercing blue eyes, but they also shared similar political prejudices. One evening, in the fall of 1930, the two of them met at a beer pub after Bruno had attended a Nazi rally.

"You know, Helmut, I just came from a meeting with Herr Hitler and his associates. The man is a genius! He understands and captures our discontent and grievances and is able to inspire the masses into action by his words alone. And the vision he has for our country is fantastic. A job for everyone, and redistribution of the wealth of the Jews and their fellow bloodsuckers to the poor, ordinary, and suffering workers. I want you to come to the next gathering with me so that I can introduce you to him."

Several weeks later, Helmut attended a rally of the local wing of the NSDAP and was enraptured by Hitler's oratory. He joined the Nazi Party on the spot, plunking down a week's salary for his membership. In 1931, when the firm of Axman, Streicher und Wolff fired their chauffeur for being a card-carrying member of the Communist Party, Bruno recommended Helmut for the job.

Bruno escorted his weeping, distraught mother to the curb, where Helmut had pulled up in the firm's shiny black 1931 Mercedes-Benz Cabriolet.

"Mutti, this is Herr Eckler. He will drive you home now, and I will come by later."

"Don't bother, I would rather be alone than with the likes of you."

Bruno gave Helmut his mother's address, turned heel, and walked back into the building without a backward glance.

Helmut and Frau Schmidt drove in silence through the sunny streets filled with afternoon traffic. Helmut helped the elderly woman out of the car and up the stairs to the third-floor apartment she had shared with her tool-and-die-maker husband. He solicitously asked whether there was anything he could get her, but she just shrugged, and said, "Yes, bring my husband back."

That evening Bruno stopped by his mother's flat, bringing her some pastries, which she promptly dumped into the garbage, although she'd not had anything to eat all day.

"You know, Mutti, I told both of you that he was hanging around with the wrong crowd, and that it would not end well. Now, here we are. When and where is the funeral?"

He reached into his pocket, taking out his wallet. "Here is three hundred Reichsmark. This should cover the funeral expenses."

He extended his hand with the money in it, but she pushed it away. "I don't need the Nazis' dirty money! The trade union is taking care of it all. He's being buried the day after tomorrow in Alter Südfriedhof (Old South Cemetery). Out of respect for your father, I don't expect you to show your face. You know, Bruno, this will be the first time in forty years that I won't be sleeping next to your father."

She broke down and started crying again. "Now go. I want to rest!"

Before he turned to leave, he said, "You know, you should go and stay with your sister, Aunt Hanna, in Dresden for a while. I will send Helmut around next week to pick you up and drive you. Please, at least let me do that."

"I'll think about it." And with that, she slammed the door behind her son.

The funeral two days later was solemn and low key. Bruno's mother was there, as were four trade union comrades of the elder Schmidt. It was raining hard as two burly cemetery workers lowered the simple wooden coffin into the ground. As Karl Schmidt, a Communist at heart, avoided anything that smacked of religion, there was no priest or minister officiating. It seemed that because of the downpour everyone wanted to get the burial over with quickly. Each of the trade unionists threw a shovelful of wet earth on the coffin after it had been placed in the ground, with the last one handing the shovel to Frau Schmidt.

On a small rise behind some trees and the mausoleum of Alois Senefelder, the inventor of lithography, a black Mercedes was parked, hidden from sight of the mourners. Helmut Eckler was in the driver's seat, with Bruno Schmidt in the back, tears in his eyes, holding a dozen white roses. He had remembered his mother's words: "Your father is a good man." Once the mourners were gone, he slowly walked down to the fresh mound of dirt, knelt, and placed the flowers on top. He whispered, "Father, why did you not listen to me?"

With that, he stood up, wiped the mud from the knees of his trousers, and returned to the car.

"Helmut, let's go to the Augustiner-Bräustuben. I need a drink."

A week later, Helmut stopped off at Bruno's mother's flat to pick her up and drive her to her sister's home in Dresden. Bruno would never see her alive again. On February 14, 1945, 722 heavy bombers of the British Royal Air Force, and 527 of the United States Army Air Force, dropped more than 3,900 tons of high-explosive bombs and incendiary devices on the city. The bombing and the resulting firestorm destroyed over 1,600 acres of the city centre. An estimated 22,700 to 25,000 people were killed, including Bruno's mother, her sister Hannah, and her two nieces, who had been nineteen and twenty-two.

The rest of 1933 would turn out to be busy for Bruno Schmidt. Adolf Hitler's ascension to power in early March and his proclamation of the Third Reich on the fifteenth of the month brought new opportunities for Bruno to continue climbing the ladder of success, both in the law practice and within the Nazi Party. The law firm, where at the beginning of the year he had achieved senior partner status, played a key role in drafting the myriad new laws being promulgated by the Nazis in the Reichstag.

Despite his busy schedule, filled with lengthy meetings with his partners, judges, court and NSDAP officials, and assorted Party hacks, he didn't allow his ardour for Steffi to languish. They met in cafés, at hotels and his apartment. He moved out of the Artists Quarter and into a large, two-bedroom suite in the more upscale, fashionable Lehel district of Munich. Bruno on occasion gave Helmut the afternoon or evening off from his chauffeuring duties and took the car to meet Steffi somewhere out of the way. They would often end up outside the city limits, making love in the back of the Mercedes or, in the summer months, on a blanket amongst the thick patches of forests in one of the city's many parks.

Frequently, Bruno would get invited to the Hartmanns' expansive home. It seemed that Rolf was either oblivious to his wife's dalliance with the much- younger Bruno or he didn't care, as long as it didn't come into the open and expose him as a cuckold. At the same time, Hartmann was carrying on a torrid affair with Ditta, one of the young secretaries from his office, that he didn't do a very good job of hiding.

As the Nazis did well, Rolf Hartmann would do that much better. He was starting to amass a collection of antique paintings, furniture, and sculptures, as well as foreign currency seized from the estates of Jews, Communists, and the Nazis' other political opponents whom his SA roughnecks had beaten and thrown into the newly created Dachau concentration camp on the outskirts of Munich.

The SA had become a law unto itself, much to the consternation of Hitler's conservative, bourgeois, banker and industrialist backers. Their aggressive head-bashing tactics, homosexual orgies, and bacchanalian parties were embarrassing to the Party, and threatened to rend asunder the coalition of right-wing political and social entities that Hitler and Franz von Papen, Hitler's vice-chancellor, had struggled so hard to build.

On New Year's Eve in 1933, Hitler's inner circle met at Reichsmarschall Hermann Göring's palatial summer home at Bad Reichenhall in the Alps near the Austrian border to celebrate the coming of a new year. Martin Bormann, Hitler's secretary, was present, along with Hans Frank, Bruno's mentor and Hitler's personal attorney, as were Josef Goebbels (his minister of propaganda), Heinrich Himmler (head of the newly created SS), Rudolf Hess (Deputy Fuehrer), and Albert Speer (Hitler's architect). A host of politicians, industrialists, and bankers were there, all looking to curry favour with Germany's new supreme ruler. Bruno Schmidt was also in attendance, having been invited by Franz Gurtner, Germany's minister of justice.

Prior to the start of the New Year's festivities, they were all gathered in the great Hunters' Hall of the expansive residence, standing in a semicircle around Hitler, who was holding court, seated in a large armchair. They were hanging on to his every word as he outlined his fantastic plans for the "Thousand-Year Reich." It seemed that even the heads of wild animals—sharp-tusked boars, stags with magnificent antlers, ferocious-looking bears and wolves, all trophies of Reichsmarschall Göring's famous hunting expeditions mounted on the walls— were paying rapt attention to the Fuehrer.

Afterward, they all broke into small groups, nursing their drinks, waiting to be called to the sumptuous midnight feast prepared by some of the best chefs to be found in the country. Hitler, Himmler, Borman, Gurtner, Hermann Schmitz (president of the chemical giant IG Farben), Gustav Krupp of the German steel and arms manufacturing behemoth bearing his name, and Bruno were all standing by the roaring marble fireplace when the justice minister broached the topic of the SA's recent excesses.

"Mein Führer, my colleagues and I are very concerned with the recent activities of Röhm's Brownshirts. These ruffians, and I am not sure what else I can call them, are causing great alarm within our nation's civilized circles with their pillaging and roughneck tactics. If they can't somehow be reined in, I am not sure that we can continue to count on the support of a very important segment of the population."

Nods of approval and murmurs of consent were seen and heard from those standing around Hitler.

"My dear friends, Major Röhm has done the Party and the Reich a great service during our struggle to achieve power over the past ten years. It is only natural that the SA troopers want to seize their share of the ill-gotten profits from those they feel betrayed their country during the Great War. They believe what wealth the Jews accumulated by dishonesty rightly belongs to them. And who are we to argue with such Aryan logic?"

Hitler laughed cynically in response.

"But tonight is not the time to discuss these matters. We are here to celebrate the dawning of a new golden age that belongs to Germany!"

Hitler then turned to Himmler. "Heinrich, why don't you set up a meeting with your people and some others from the judiciary in the new year and see what can be done to curb Ernst and his so-called ruffians?" He shot an angry glance at Gurtner as he spoke.

CHAPTER 20

Since it was a beautiful sunny day, Daniel and Madelaine wanted to walk to meet Eric Baur of Deutsche Bank at the coffee shop at the bottom of the bank's building at 60 Wall Street. They walked holding hands and doing some window shopping along Broadway. The lovers decided to stop for a quick lunch on the patio of a little Italian bistro on the corner of Broadway and Wall Street.

As they sat in the bright sunshine drinking their chardonnay, Madelaine turned to Daniel. "I hope you don't think I'm intruding into your private family affairs by getting Eric involved? It's just so exciting! These mysterious documents just showing up from Europe, it's like a detective novel! I thought you would be much more excited than you seem to be, with your grandmother having been a detective story writer and all."

"Frankly, I just think it's a case of mistaken identity, with some papers sent to the wrong address. I've never been to Germany and don't know anyone who lives there. Your friend Eric will clear it all up for us, I'm sure."

They continued chatting as they ate their pizza, and then after drinking their cappuccinos, they headed to their meeting.

Eric Bender was a vice-president at Deutsche Bank, in the Mergers and Acquisitions department. He had climbed the corporate ladder rapidly through hard work, long hours and a canny talent for remembering numbers. At the age of thirty-four, he was the second-youngest VP at the bank's American operations. He had been born in East Germany at the height of the Cold War, and his parents escaped with him to the West when he was only three years old.

He had been transferred from the bank's head office in Frankfurt in 1983, and met Madelaine, who at the time was working as an investment banker at Goldman Sachs, a year later. He was a handsome, energetic, and athletic father of two young kids, married to an attractive Chinese woman whom he had met while studying for his MBA at the London School of Economics.

The three of them arrived at the coffee shop at the same time. Eric gave Madelaine a warm hug and shook hands with Daniel.

"Good to see you guys." Eric smiled as he led them to a table in the corner of the coffee shop. "You want a coffee, donut, or muffin?"

"No thanks, we just had lunch and a couple of cappuccinos."

"Well, don't mind if I grab a coffee? I need it to stay awake."

Daniel shot his girlfriend an angry look as Eric went to get his coffee. "That was quite the hug!"

"Oh, lay off, already. We're just friends."

"Well, let's see these German documents," Eric said as he pulled up a chair and took a sip of his coffee.

Daniel took the envelope and, turning it upside down, spilled the papers onto the table. As he started to leaf through them, a much smaller, thicker card fell to the floor. It seemed that due to the papers having gotten wet from the rain coming in through Daniel's kitchen window, it had gotten stuck to the back of one of the pages, which is why Daniel and Madelaine hadn't noticed it before.

Eric bent down to retrieve the yellowed, faded, dog-eared document. It had the Nazi eagle with the swastika clenched in its talons at the top, with Gothic writing in German below. "Well, let's see what this is all about!"

Daniel and Madelaine leaned over the table to better see the card Eric was holding. He translated as he read, saying, "It's a birth certificate issued by the German State, certifying the birth of one Heinrich Gunther Schmidt, on July 28, 1944. The father is Karl Bruno Schmidt, a German citizen, the mother Margit Angelika Hootveg, a Dutch citizen. The father's occupation is listed as an 'Obersturmbannführer' or senior colonel in the SS. Must have been a real stand-up guy!" he snickered. "The mother's as a housewife. The birth took place at 14 Meineke Strasse in Berlin, and the godfather and witness was a Helmut Johann Eckler. And according to a handwritten note on the back, there was also a midwife present, but she's not named."

Geburtsurkunde
Deutsches_Reich

Neugeborenen Name: Heinrich, Karl
Geburtsdatum: 28 Juli, 1944
Familienname: Schmidt
Name des Vaters: Schmidt, Karl Bruno
Vaters Staatsbürgerschaft: Deutsche
Name der Mutter (Mädchenname): Hootveg, Margit Angelika
Mutters Staatsbürgerschaft: Niederländer
Beruf des Vaters: Standartenfiuehrer, des Schutzstaffel (SS)
Mutter Besetzung: Hausfrau
Geburtsort: Meineke Strasse 14, Charlottenburg, Berlin, Deutsches_Reich
Name des Paten / Zeugen: Eckler, Helmut Johannv

Eric looked up when he had finished translating the card to see Daniel sitting there as if in a trance. Although Daniel had seen the name Karl Bruno Schmidt in the document previously, and it rang familiar, it didn't hit him with full force until Schmidt's occupation as senior colonel of the SS was read out by Eric. The blood drained from Daniel's face and his mind raced back fifteen years, to May 1973.

CHAPTER 21

May 14, 1973 was the twenty-fifth anniversary of Israel's independence. For such an auspicious occasion, the Israeli government and military had sent invitations to all those now living in foreign lands who had contributed to the founding of the State of Israel to attend the planned celebrations. One of those invited was Dr. Samuel Singer. He was invited not only as someone who had played a key part in Israel's victory in the 1948 War of Independence, but also as a representative of the State of New York. After all, it was in the City of New York at the General Assembly of the United Nations on the Hudson River in May 1948 that the State of Israel was born by a vote of thirty-three to thirteen, with ten abstentions.

The invitation was delivered by registered mail to Samuel at his office and was postmarked from the Israeli Embassy in Washington, DC. He lit his pipe before opening it and let the bluish smoke from it envelop him as he did so. Along with the smoke, his memories drifted back to those desperate days in the spring of 1948 when life was in the balance on a daily basis.

He then thought of Daniel's failed attempt to join Israel's fight in the Six-Day War in 1967. He picked up the phone and called Information.

"Could you please get me the telephone number of the Israeli Embassy in Washington?"

"Certainly, sir. Please stand by. Here it is: 1 202-364-5500. Anything else we can help you with today?"

"No, thank you." He then dialled the number.

"Embassy of the State of Israel, how may I direct your call?"

"Could you please connect me with your military attaché?"

"Certainly, I'll put you through to his office."

"Colonel Gonen's office, may I help you?"

"Yes, my name is Dr. Samuel Singer, and I received an invitation to attend the twenty-fifth anniversary of the founding of the State of Israel."

"Yes, one moment, please," said the secretary to Colonel Gonen, Israel's military attaché in the US. "Yes, Dr. Singer, I see your name here. Will you be attending?"

"Well, yes, and that's what I wanted to talk to Colonel Gonen about."

"Perhaps I can help you," came the cheery response.

"I would like to see if it would be all right for me to bring my son Daniel with me. He's twenty-nine. You see, he volunteered to go over there during the 1967 War, but never made it, and I would like him to see Israel, and show him places that are special to me."

"That's very thoughtful of you, Dr. Singer, and I am sure that it won't be a problem. Let me just check with the colonel, and I'll get back to you. Could I have your phone number, please?"

The next morning, Samuel got a call back from the secretary confirming that not only would it not be difficult for Daniel to accompany him, but they would assign an English-speaking army officer to be their guide during the planned ceremonies in Jerusalem and the battlefield tours afterward. They were also to attend the nighttime swearing-in ceremonies of new officers to the Israeli Army at the ancient hilltop fortress of Masada. Daniel was thrilled when his father broke the news to him. Finally, he would get to see the places in the Holy Land that he had only heard about, where his father and Uncle Mickey had helped shape the new country's history.

The El-Al charter flight from New York to Tel Aviv was full of men and a few women in their fifties, sixties, and seventies, with some even in their eighties. Daniel was the "kid" on the Boeing 747. They had all participated in some way in the turbulent and bloody creation of Israel in 1948, and they all had stories to tell. The country was rolling out the red carpet for all those who had helped in its creation and fought in its battles for survival through its twenty-five years of independence.

As the plane winged its way across the Atlantic, Daniel sat back sipping a glass of Cabernet Franc from Carmel in the Judaean Hills. *Not a Silver Oak,* he thought, *but not bad.* He watched his father rekindling twenty-five-year-old friendships. With an unlit pipe dangling from the corner of his mouth, Samuel was engaged in animated conversation with other veterans of the various battles around Israel in 1948. The name of Mickey Marcus came up in most of the discussions.

As darkness fell and the old-timers started to doze off, filling the aircraft with the rhythmic drone of snoring, Samuel reclined and thought back to the last time he had made this trip. The snoring of others seemed to be his ever-present companion when he was airborne.

Daniel got up to use the bathroom and gently covered his father's sleeping figure with the blanket that had slipped to the floor. There was so much of his father's past that he had been unaware of.

The Boeing 747 landed at Tel Aviv's Ben Gurion Airport at noon. The sun was shining and there was not a cloud to be seen in the deep-blue sky. A Combined Forces military band was playing as the passengers disembarked, some walking with the help of canes, some others in wheelchairs. At the bottom of the stairs, they were greeted by Yigal Allon on behalf of the government, and by General Mordechai Hod, Commander of the Israeli Air Force, on behalf of the military. As they walked the length of the red carpet laid on the tarmac in their honour, they were welcomed individually with bouquets of twenty-five red roses by young officers of the three armed services. They were to be their guides during their week-long stay in Israel.

"*Shalom*, and welcome to Israel. My name is Naomi." A very pretty young army lieutenant greeted the father and son. She was dressed in a khaki skirt and white blouse topped off with a peaked cap bearing the gold sword and olive branch within a Star of David, badge of the IDF.

"*Shalom*, I am Dr. Samuel Singer, and this is my son, Daniel. We're from New York."

"Yes, I know, Dr. Singer. I have heard a lot about your work in Israel during our War of Independence in 1948." Her English was impeccable, without trace of an accent. "How was your flight?"

"Oh, much, much more comfortable than on my first visit." Samuel chuckled.

They stopped for a moment before entering the terminal building so Samuel could light his pipe.

"Usually they frown upon smoking in the terminal, but in your case, I think they will make an exception." Naomi smiled at him.

Up to this time, Daniel hadn't uttered a word, just walking along behind his father and Naomi, admiring her shapely figure from the back. After picking up their luggage, they headed outside where an Israeli Army Jeep awaited them for the drive to Jerusalem.

They would be staying at the newly renovated King David Hotel in the Holy City, one that Samuel was quite familiar with from his previous trip to Israel. They drove along Highway #1 with Naomi and their driver, Benjamin, in the front, and the Singers in the back, enjoying the sun and wind in the open vehicle. Naomi pointed out various historical sites as they drove through the lush countryside, stopping every so often to take a closer look at a monument, particular flower, or a fruit tree by the side of the road.

Finally, Daniel spoke up. "How is it, Naomi, that you speak such perfect English?"

"Oh, I spent my summer vacations at my uncle's house in Los Angeles during my high-school years."

"And your family, do they live in Israel?"

"No, I have no family outside of my American uncle. My family was from Szeged in Hungary. My father, a rabbi, and my brother died in Bergen-Belsen. My mother and I survived until the English liberated the camp, but she died of typhus shortly after. My uncle bought me to Israel, but wanted to immigrate to the US, and as a single male, was not allowed to take me with him. I grew up in an orphanage on a kibbutz near Beersheba in the Negev."

"I am so sorry," Daniel stammered, looking for something emphatic to say, but unable to find the words.

They drove on in silence until they came to the road junction at the abandoned police fort in Latrun. The damage from the fighting in the Six-Day War of 1967 was still evident, with the rusting hulk of a Jordanian M48 Patton tank partly concealed by the growing vegetation around the fort. They all got out of the Jeep to walk the perimeter of the now-silent, crumbling, shell-scarred concrete building.

Samuel asked if he could be left alone for a few minutes so he could walk over the sand dunes to where his mobile surgical tent had been set up twenty-five years before. Naomi and Daniel went to sit on a large rock, while Benjamin went back to the Jeep and listened to some music on his transistor radio. Wanting to make conversation, and to try to get beyond what had been said earlier, Daniel asked, "So, how's life for a young woman in the Israeli Army?"

"You have got to be kidding me! Is that as lame a question as you can come up with?" Naomi laughed.

Daniel looked at her sheepishly. She had taken off her cap and shaken out her long, jet-black hair, letting it fall loosely on her shoulders. *She's beautiful, sparkling green eyes, short and slim, wonder how old?*

She guessed what he was thinking. "I am thirty-one, an old woman compared to you."

"I am 29 ... and—"

"Yes, I know, I read your CV, Mister Art historian and Student of Romance languages." She cast her eyes to the ground and then raised her eyebrows with an impish smile on her face, afraid she had bruised his ego. The tension was broken by Benjamin's yell in Hebrew from his Jeep.

"He wants to know if we would like a bottle of water."

"Yeah, that would be great. Let me go get them." Daniel trotted off to get the water, kicking up the sand as he ran.

There is something very sweet, innocent … even vulnerable about him. Doesn't look very Jewish, though, with that blond mop and blue eyes, she thought.

Samuel arrived back from his walk behind the dunes at the same time Daniel did with the water.

"Boy, not much has changed in the last twenty-odd years." Samuel was holding something in his hand.

"What did you find, Dad?"

Samuel opened his palm to show them two rusty bullet casings from the Mausers he helped deliver so many years ago.

"Well, we'd better get moving, gentlemen. We have a welcome dinner buffet waiting for us at the King David."

They approached the outskirts of Jerusalem just as the sun started to set in the west, its rays bouncing off the golden Dome of the Rock. *A mirror image of the first time I set eyes on it,* Samuel thought.

Naomi recounted for them the same story about its history as Avner had on that warm May morning in 1948. They arrived at the front entrance of the King David this time, instead of in the back. There was no sign of the damage from the 1946 Irgun bomb explosion—two floors had been added and the façade totally restored since Israel occupied the whole of Jerusalem in 1967.

"Dr. Singer, there is a surprise waiting for you inside." Naomi took his arm and set out at a brisk pace for the revolving front doors of the hotel, with Benjamin and Daniel following with their suitcases.

As they entered the high-ceilinged, ornate lobby, a shout rang out. "Sammy, welcome back!" There, sitting in a wheelchair, with Gabriel standing behind him, was Avner.

Samuel bent down and enveloped his old friend in a bear hug and gave him a kiss on each cheek. He then embraced Gabriel and shook his hand.

"How are you, my friend? It's been a long time!"

"I see you've lost my trench coat, and without those khaki shorts and undersized shirt, you even look somewhat respectable," Avner kidded Samuel.

"Come here, Daniel. Let me look at you. You were twenty-two when I last saw you in New York. Boy, you haven't changed a bit."

Avner gave Daniel a hug as Samuel also introduced him to Gabriel.

"Is our lieutenant taking good care of you, boys?"

He smiled at Naomi, who blushed at the question.

"Well, why don't you go to your room, freshen up and then join us in the dining room along with the others for dinner?"

Naomi walked them to the check-in counter and gave them their keys. "I hope you do not mind but you will be sharing a room as there were none left because of the anniversary celebrations."

Samuel laughed in response. "No, I am quite used to sharing a tent when in the Promised Land." Samuel turned to his son in the elevator. "Quite the beauty, no?"

Daniel just nodded as they reached their floor.

✠

Dinner turned out to be a raucous affair, with veteran after veteran getting up and recounting stories from their time in Israel during the War of Independence. With each story came a toast: *"L'chaim."* ("To Life.") These men and women who had shared their struggles, laughter and tears, life and death those many years ago were tied to each other by an unbreakable bond.

When it was getting close to midnight, Samuel stood up and raised his glass of Glenfiddich. "To Mickey Marcus, may he live in our hearts and memory forever."

He was followed in the toast by the rest of the hardy and mostly inebriated souls still left at the tables. He then turned to Naomi and Daniel, sitting on either side of him.

"I think I've had too much to drink. I'm going to bed." He rose and, on unsteady legs, headed for the lobby elevator.

Those remaining continued their reminiscing about days past, in small groups. Avner, sitting at the head of the table and trying to match everyone drink for drink, kept falling asleep in his wheelchair, but refused to go to bed. Gabriel dutifully kept him company.

Naomi turned to Daniel and asked, "Are you heading to bed as well, or would you like to take your drink and we can walk through the gardens? They are beautiful at this time of year with all the flowers in bloom."

"No, I'm not tired. Let's go."

The two of them walked out into the cool night air filled with the sweet scent of the flowers, and with a full moon shining down. They walked along the gravel paths between the flower beds and chatted. Daniel talked of his love of art and his childhood years in New York, his parents, Samuel and Agatha, and Grandfather Bernard. He told her of his heartbreak at the death of his beloved Shadow.

They were on their second circuit of the gardens before she had a chance to speak.

"I am so sorry, I haven't let you get a word in edgewise."

"Oh, that is okay. I love hearing about life in the States."

"But what about you?"

"It was not so bad growing up in an orphanage, other than I missed my parents and brother Janos terribly. There were about sixty of us orphans on the kibbutz, all survivors of the camps. Having shared a common past, we all grew very close and looked out for each other. The adults, whether they had children or not, would take care of us as if we were their own. It was a bond born out of sadness for the loss of our relatives and from what we all went through in the camps. I am still good friends with most of them. If you have never experienced it, you would not be able to feel it, to comprehend it."

They were on their third round of walking through the gardens when she wiped away a tear that appeared at the corner of her eyes as she finished speaking. "You know, I am tired, and we have an early morning, so I think I will go to bed. You should as well. Goodnight."

And she just turned around and walked back in through the lobby doors. He stood there for a minute, alone in the moonlight, not knowing what to think or say.

"A pretty girl, but a hard one." The voice came from behind him. It was Gabriel.

"I'm sorry, but I overheard some of what she said. It's true, Daniel, the camps never let you go, no matter how hard you try to not remember, to not think about it. We are all prisoners to our past, and hostages to our memories. As if spending time in the camps weren't enough, they consume the rest of your life as well. It's a sadness that never leaves you. You lose a lot of your feelings of love and compassion, you lose a part of yourself that you never get back. All you're left with is an everlasting sadness and the smell of smoke from the crematoria in your nostrils. If it weren't for my Claudette and my beautiful children, I would have ended it a long time ago."

He put his arm around Daniel's shoulder.

"Your father tells me that you speak fluent French. Let's go and have a nightcap in the bar and continue our conversation *en français*. Other than with my wife, I don't get an opportunity to speak it."

It was well past one o'clock by the time Daniel stealthily stole into their room, thankful that Samuel was snoring so loud he didn't hear Daniel knock over the bedside lamp as he climbed into bed.

The next day dawned quite like the previous one. Sunny, without a cloud in a brilliant blue sky. Samuel was still fast asleep as Daniel quietly put on his shorts, T-shirt, and running shoes to go for his usual early-morning jog. He wasn't going to miss the opportunity of circling the thousands-years-old walls of Jerusalem.

In the lobby, he ran into Alexei Dubayevsky, a short and stocky, tough-as-nails Russian with pale blue eyes and snow-white hair. They had chatted briefly the evening before. Although more than twenty years Daniel's senior, he had the strength and stamina of a much younger man.

As a twenty-year-old conscript, he had fought the Germans in the gutted, bombed-out ruins of Stalingrad and pursued them all the way to Berlin, rising to the rank of captain in the 37th Guards Rifle Division. His entire family from Minsk had perished during the war at the hands of the German *Einsatzgruppen*. Not having anything, or anyone, to return to, Alexei deserted the army after the fall of Berlin, stowing away on a freighter heading to Palestine, after having made his way to Marseilles.

Upon arriving in Haifa, he joined the Irgun, the outlawed Israeli underground, under future prime minister Menachem Begin, and participated in many sabotage actions against the British. He was captured and spent time in jail until the creation of the State of Israel. He enlisted in the nascent Israeli Army after independence and fought in both the 1956 Sinai campaign and the Six-Day War in 1967. He held the rank of colonel when he retired and joined the Mossad (the Institute), Israel's famous foreign intelligence agency. He was deputy director of Section VI, responsible for Egyptian Affairs, when he ran into Daniel in the King David's lobby.

"Good morning, Daniel. Do you mind if I join you?" he asked in heavily Russian-accented English. Without waiting for an answer, he continued. "A good run around the ancient walls of Jerusalem will do you a world of good, will keep you young. It's also an opportunity to take a step back a couple of hundred years into the Eternal City's past."

It was an early weekday morning, but the streets were already crowded with traffic, both pedestrian and motorized, by the time they exited the hotel grounds. They continued talking as they ran.

"I met your father briefly in 1948 at Abu Ghosh, when General Marcus was shot. Mickey was quite the man, as is your father. You should be proud." Alexei kept running and talking without breathing hard.

"Did you fight with them at Latrun?"

"No, I regret to say not. I spent most of my time during the War of Independence in a British jail, being interrogated by MI6. I got out a couple of weeks before the state was born. I had hoped that '48 would be the last war we would have to fight. Boy, was I wrong."

"Do you think there'll be another war?"

"Most definitely. I think that Sadat is itching to get the Sinai back. He's not like Nasser was, wanting to throw the Jews into the sea, but he needs to show his people that he can recapture territory they lost in the war. And the Syrians want the Golan back. I think that they are both preparing to resume hostilities at any time they think our resolve has weakened."

"And how will it end?"

"The same as the last three, with many young people dead on both sides. Young men and women who should have been studying in universities, starting families, going on picnics. I was studying electrical engineering in Moscow when the Germans invaded. I never got the chance to graduate. Maybe my grandson will go to the Technion in Haifa and get a degree, if he doesn't also get ground up in the mills of war. I am sorry to be so pessimistic, but in my fifty years I have seen it all, and I have nothing to be optimistic about."

By now they had covered most of the ancient walls of the city that had been rebuilt by Suleiman the Magnificent between 1537 and 1541 from the original, constructed by King David's son, Solomon, around 500 BC.

"You know, Daniel, I can imagine myself back here two thousand years ago. It seems that very little has changed."

They arrived back at the King David just as people were starting to filter into the dining room, Daniel breathing heavily and soaked in sweat, Alexei as if he had only been out for a leisurely stroll. They ran into Samuel and Naomi just as the two were getting off the elevator.

The four greeted each other.

"I'll be down in twenty minutes," Daniel yelled as the elevator doors closed.

"See you downstairs, Alexei. Thanks for the company this morning."

"My pleasure, young man. You need to train a little harder, though, if you want to keep up with me." The Russian smiled.

Daniel went to take a shower. Downstairs, Alexei was already seated at a table with Samuel and Naomi, digging into a large bowl of cereal and fruit. Samuel was sipping his coffee. When he got there, Daniel gave his father a hug and sat down in the empty chair to Naomi's left.

"Well, that was quite a run this morning. Alexei is quite the marathoner."

"Where did you two run?" she asked.

"Did the walls," Alexei cut in.

"I hope you did not exhaust young Mister Singer too much. We have a full day ahead of us." Naomi laughed, glancing at Daniel with a broad smile on her face. "Here's our itinerary for the next couple of days." She handed a photocopied page out to them, just as Avner, pushed along in his wheelchair by Gabriel, approached their table.

"Lady and gentlemen, good morning. What are you two innocents doing in the company of these cloak-and-dagger types?" Avner asked, looking at Naomi and Alexei and laughing out loudly.

Daniel shot a quizzical look in Naomi's direction.

She ignored Avner's comment. "Today we are going to drive around the Sea of Galilee, stopping at a couple of spots of historical and religious significance and then up to the Golan Heights to view the Syrian fortifications and the scenes of the battles from 1967. General Gideon here," she glanced at Avner, "who was an armoured corps commander at the time, will be conducting the tour. Then it will be down to Haifa for dinner aboard one of the Navy's SAAR-class missile boats. Afterwards, we will drive back to Jerusalem for a good night's sleep.

"After breakfast we will be joining government officials, including the prime minister and her cabinet and defense staff, on the reviewing stand for the Armed Forces parade. In the early evening, we will head to Masada to witness the swearing-in of new officer recruits to the Israeli Defense Forces. Then, the following day, we will visit the Sinai battlefront with a stop for lunch at one of the Bar Lev Line fortifications. You will be taking your luggage with you, as that evening you will be departing for your flights back to your homes from Ben Gurion Airport in Tel Aviv. Any questions?"

CHAPTER 22

MAY 1973,

GALILEE, GOLAN HEIGHTS, AND HAIFA

There were thirty people on the bus, including six Israeli Army escorts. They drove north, skirting the West Bank of the River Jordan, captured by Israel in 1967. First stop was Tiberias on the western shore of the Sea of Galilee.

On board, Daniel had tried to jump into the seat beside Naomi but was beaten to it by another one of the army escorts. She had curly, flaming red hair, hazel eyes, and a face full of freckles. She looked a couple of years older than Naomi.

"Daniel, this is my friend Rivka," Naomi said. "We grew up together in the orphanage on the kibbutz. She was like a big sister to me."

"Nice to meet you, Mr. Singer."

Rivka stood up and gave Daniel a very firm, manly handshake. Daniel noticed the five-digit tattoo on Rivka's forearm, a sure sign she had spent time in a concentration camp.

After a brief refreshment stop and a visit to the grave of famed medieval Jewish philosopher and astronomer Maimonides, they got back on the bus.

"Our next stop will be Capernaum and the Church of the Apostles," announced Yonathan, the leader of the escorts, from the front of the bus. He then added, "We will have typical Israeli field rations for lunch once we hit the Golan."

Daniel ended up sitting beside a seventy-five-year-old veteran of the '48 war from Poughkeepsie. The old man was hard of hearing and too vain to wear a hearing aid, so he was constantly asking Daniel, "What did he say? What did he say?"

As Captain Yonathan continued with his travelogue, the bus rumbled along the coastal road.

"You know, young man, when I was your age I was fighting in the Pacific, on Palau and Guadalcanal. I was a Marine, you know. No fancy, air-conditioned buses for us." Since he couldn't hear Yonathan in any case, he just rambled on to Daniel about his Second World War exploits.

"You should have seen them Japs. Now, they were tough sons of bitches, but we showed them. I was a Marine, you know."

According to Rivka, who was escorting the septuagenarian and three of his like-aged companions, the old man had fought on the Egyptian front during the War of Independence and been wounded.

Samuel was seated on a bench seat at the front of the bus between a strapped-in Avner and Gabriel. They were involved in an animated conversation about the current state of the IDF.

When they arrived at Capernaum, all the passengers other than Daniel and Naomi dismounted the coach and walked around the ancient ruins. They followed Yonathan as he recounted the history of the town.

Naomi and Daniel stayed back at a refreshment stand drinking fresh-squeezed orange juice.

"As an art historian, are you not interested in seeing these ancient works of art? They are quite remarkable, you know."

"I'm much more interested in finding out some more about a much more modern work of art."

Naomi blushed but couldn't think of anything witty enough to respond with, so she left it alone.

"So, what was Avner implying when he referred to you and Alexei as 'cloak and dagger' guys?"

"Did Alexei not tell you that he is a deputy director of Mossad?"

"No, but what does that have to do with you?"

"I work for Alexei, as do the rest of the escorts."

"They are all Mossad?"

"Yes. They were picked because they speak English, and at least one other language besides Hebrew. In our work, we are used to dealing with civilians and people from foreign countries and can pick up on anything that may not arouse suspicion in others."

"So, you're spying on us?"

"No, not really. Just keeping our eyes and ears open in several different languages. We do have some veterans along that still live in the Soviet Union, and today, one never knows where loyalties lie."

Daniel, emboldened by Naomi's openness, then decided to probe a little further into Naomi's personal life. "I saw you and Captain Yonathan exchanging looks on the bus, are you two an item?"

She laughed. "No, definitely not!"

Their conversation was interrupted by the group's return from their excursion.

"Daniel, you missed a wonderful walk!" Samuel shouted to his son as he returned. "What were you doing that you didn't come along?"

"Oh, Lieutenant Naomi and I were chatting about the rest of our itinerary and time just flew by," Daniel said. When they got back on the bus, Daniel took a seat beside Alexei.

"I understand you're pretty high up in the Mossad, Alexei?" It was part question, part statement of fact.

"So rumour has it," he replied with a grin. "But being the age I am, I'm only in an administrative position. No real secret agent stuff, just routine 'check this, check that' shit."

Avner's voice came over the bus's loudspeaker system. "I've been asked to conduct the next part of our tour up to the Golan Heights. I will be pointing out places of interest as we go, but for now, sit back and relax."

He then handed out photocopied maps of the Golan Heights showing the movement of Israeli and Syrian forces during the battles of June 1967.

The bus drove north, through kilometre upon kilometre of apple, peach, and mango orchards, and vineyard after vineyard, interrupted here and there by Jewish and Arab villages. Once they began their drive through the Hula Valley and the Heights came into view, Avner once again took over the microphone.

"As I met most of you during those fateful months of 1948, I don't think I need to introduce myself. I've been asked to speak to you about the battle for the Golan Heights during the Six-Day War, prior to us actually arriving there. I was a tank battalion commander in the Northern Command of the IDF, facing Syrian forces with thirty-six modified Sherman and Centurion tanks under my command, when war broke out on June 5. My Centurion was destroyed by a Syrian T-62, and I lost both my legs."

He then went on to describe the vicious battles that took place between the Israeli and Syrian armour on the Heights.

As he came to the end of his presentation, the bus passed the rusted hulks of two Syrian T-54/55 tanks, their barrels peeled back like bananas, pointing skyward.

After negotiating a curve in the road with still-active minefields surrounded by barbed wire and yellow-and-red caution signs on either side, they pulled up beside a partially destroyed Syrian pillbox, which had been mostly hidden by the thick vegetation that had enveloped it in the six years since hostilities ended. After a short visit to the portable washrooms, they walked through the devastated Syrian fortification, with a rusted anti-tank gun still protruding from a slit in the stonework.

After a lunch composed of Israeli Army field rations and some fine wines from the region, they once again climbed aboard their coach for the drive down to Haifa for dinner as guests of the Israeli Navy. This time, Daniel got a seat beside Naomi's friend Rivka, while Naomi sat down beside Samuel. It didn't take long for most of the aged passengers to fall asleep from the gentle rocking of the bus as it descended from the Heights and headed south.

"You grew up with Naomi at the orphanage, right?" Daniel queried her.

"Yes. Since I am a couple of years older than her, and I lost my twin sister in the war, I sort of took care of her as if she were my little sister. I missed her during the summers when she went to Los Angeles to spend time with her uncle."

"Did you join the army together? Is she in a ..."

The bus lurched to avoid a tractor pulling a load of hay, throwing a couple of the elderly veterans into the aisle. After a chain of profanities in English, Hebrew, Yiddish, and Russian, it was determined that no major injuries had been caused, and they resumed their journey. However, Rivka left her seat to attend to some minor scratches and bruises on her elderly, shaken-up veteran from Poughkeepsie.

Daniel filed away his question regarding Naomi's relationship status, thinking he would ask her at a later time.

As the late afternoon gave way to early evening, the Port City of Haifa and the Mediterranean came into view. The sky had clouded over, and the setting sun painted the city and the sea with a pinkish hue. Haifa is built in tiers extending from the Mediterranean up the north slope of Mount Carmel. As they drove through the city to its naval base in the port area, they passed its most iconic sites: the immaculately landscaped terraces of the Bahá'í Gardens and, at their heart, the gold-domed Shrine of the Báb.

As Samuel looked out the window, he remembered the first time he had set eyes on the city, on a dark night in May 1948, exactly twenty-five years ago. He had been soaked to the skin after several days of harrowing travel.

He again took out his pipe and without lighting it, in deference to his fellow passengers, chewed on the stem, as he had done those two-and-a-half decades ago. He and Avner exchanged knowing glances as the bus came to a stop at the entrance to the base.

The gate was opened by a smartly dressed naval sentry, and they pulled up beside the battleship-grey hull of the Israeli Navy's SAAR-class fast missile boat.

It was one of the boats that on Christmas Eve, 1969, Israeli naval commandos clandestinely boarded and sailed out of the French port of Cherbourg on a very stormy night, after French president General Charles de Gaulle imposed an arms embargo on Israel. France called it an "act of piracy," while Israel decorated its homecoming heroes.

A naval guard of honour in parade whites was assembled on the gangway to welcome the veterans.

"Quite a different greeting party than the last time," Samuel remarked to Avner with a smile.

Once aboard, they toured the ship's engine room, modern Combat Information Center, and weapons displays, after which they were escorted to the officers' wardroom by their host, Admiral Ze'ev Almog. During a delicious dinner of local fish, once again accompanied by wines from several Israeli vineyards from the nearby Carmel Hills, the ship's executive officer, Commander Benjamin Nesher, gave a talk on the navy's role in the 1956 and 1967 wars and their state of preparation for any future conflicts.

After a round of *Slivovitz* (kosher plum brandy), the veterans, on unsteady legs, disembarked and climbed aboard the bus, headed once again for Jerusalem. Samuel and Avner sat beside each other on the front bench seat again and recounted their previous journey as they retraced their route from 1948. They both laughed when they passed the tree line from where they had been fired upon back then.

"We were lucky that the sniper was probably half asleep at that time of the morning," Avner whispered, not wanting to wake the other passengers. "Or we wouldn't be sitting here tonight."

It was dark when they reached the outer suburbs of Jerusalem. Daniel had finally managed to get a seat beside Naomi and was quite intent on probing a little further into her personal life, but the effect of too much wine and *Slivovitz* resulted in him falling asleep even before the vehicle started to move. Occasionally, his head would slump over onto her shoulder, and drool from his mouth would stain her shirt. She kept smiling at Rivka and Yonathan, seated across the aisle, giving them the look of someone involuntarily carrying a heavy burden.

They pulled up in front of the King David, and with Samuel and Gabriel supporting him on either side, helped a less-than-sober Daniel to his room. Everyone else headed upstairs to get a good night's sleep, as the following day would also be a long one, commencing with the Independence Day parade at noon.

Alexei smoked a cigarette, and Yonathan, Naomi, and Rivka decided to take a walk through the landscaped grounds to discuss plans for the next day's activities before heading off to bed.

CHAPTER 23

APRIL 1934,

GERMANY—CONSPIRACIES IN HIGH PLACES

It wasn't until early March 1934 that the group that had assembled in front of the outsized fireplace at Hermann Göring's palatial country home in Reichenhall on New Year's Eve 1933 was able to get together again. They were there to continue their discussion about what steps were going to be taken to rein in the out-of- control, brown-shirted goons under the command of Ernst Röhm, Rolf Hartmann, and their underlings. Present at the meeting at the headquarters of the Secret State Police (forerunner of the Gestapo), formerly the School of Industrial Arts & Crafts, at 8 Prinz-Albrecht-Strasse in Berlin, were high-ranking officers of the SS, Gestapo, Secret Police and Reichswehr (Army), as well as senior officials from the Justice Ministry and representatives of Germany's wealthy bankers and industrialists.

Bruno Schmidt was there representing the Nazi Party and to provide input from the legal profession. Field Marshall Werner Thomas Ludwig Freiherr von Fritsch, the commander in chief of the Reichswehr, kicked off the discussion by enumerating recent acts of violence by the SA, which reflected negatively on the members of the regular army and in the eyes of ordinary Germans. He went down the list one by one.

"Murder; inflicting serious, sometime fatal injury on political opponents; disorderly conduct; public drunkenness; vandalism; fist fights in public places; desecration of places of worship; urinating and defecating in public parks. Gentlemen, the transgressions go on and on. The Brownshirts are holding our citizens hostage to terror. People are afraid to go out after dark for fear of being attacked or worse. Terror rules our streets."

Gustav Krupp, head of the giant Krupp steel and arms conglomerate, chimed in. "Our workers are afraid to work the late shifts for fear of being accosted on their way home. We are losing money at some of our factories. Our overall profitability is being affected."

Nodding his head in agreement was Hermann Schmitz, president of the chemical giant IG Farben. "It's shameful, and we must put an end to it, or we will lose the support of the working class. This is not how civilized people conduct their affairs."

At this point, Heinrich Himmler, head of the newly established SS, cut in. "Gentlemen, we have here Herr Bruno Schmidt." He then pointed to Bruno, who glanced around the room, acknowledging the introduction. "He is one of our country's foremost constitutional lawyers and is very familiar with all the issues surrounding Herr Röhm and his unsavoury associates, having defended many of them in court prior to us being elected to government.

"Why don't we let him, and my deputy, Obergruppenführer (Colonel) Reinhard Heydrich devise a plan to deal with this unfortunate distraction and present it to us and the Führer in a month's time? I am sure they will be able to find a way to resolve these issues peacefully. And if not peacefully, then ... " Himmler gave a conspiratorial smile to those around the room.

"I don't think that we need to spend any more of our time on these matters, so now let us go and eat lunch in our newly renovated cafeteria, as our cooks have prepared an excellent meal."

Bruno and Heydrich sat together at a corner table, along with Arthur Nebe, head of the Criminal Investigation Police and Steffi Hartmann's brother, and Josef Wegman, Heydrich's adjutant.

Heydrich turned to Bruno and said, "Well, counsellor, what are your thoughts on how to deal with these unsavoury characters?"

He gave a sideways glance at Nebe, knowing that his brother-in-law Rolf was a high-up member of the SA, and would likely be feeling a considerable amount of heat as a consequence of any decisions made at the table.

"Herr Obergruppenführer, we obviously need to thoroughly investigate constitutional and legal options open to us in order to put a limit on their activities, perhaps even outlaw their organization."

"What if I told you that Röhm and his Stormtroopers are in fact planning a *putsch* to overthrow the legally elected government?" Wegman asked Bruno.

"Do you have any proof of this?"

"No, but there are a lot of rumours floating around, much to the Führer's consternation. And where there's smoke, you will usually find some burning embers!"

"If these rumours were to be confirmed, then it's obviously another much more serious matter."

"And even if they are not substantiated, it could be an acceptable *casus belli*," Heydrich added, "if we can't end their rampage peacefully."

At that moment, Heinrich Himmler came over to their table. "Gentlemen, how are we doing? Everyone enjoy the food? Excellent, isn't it? Did we come to any conclusions regarding the SA? You all know that Röhm is one of the Führer's favourites, no? He has been one of his most loyal and ardent followers. When it comes to Ernst, the Führer has blinders on. Röhm is the only senior Nazi who is allowed to address him as 'Adolf' as opposed to 'Mein Führer.'

"In his eyes, the SA is doing everything correctly to bring about the conditions that would result in the ideal state, as he outlined in *Mein Kampf*. No Jews, no Communists, no half-wits! He doesn't realize the damage that's being done to the Party, to the State, to those that control finance and industry in this country. I hope that the four of you can come up with a solution."

To some, such as Himmler, Röhm was drifting offline and away from what he believed to be pure national socialism.

It was early evening by the time the meetings broke up and everyone started heading home. Under the gas lights, Bruno and Nebe walked side by side down Prinz-Albrecht Strasse, chatting, Nebe smoking a cigar, their greatcoats pulled up around their ears to shield them from the cold March wind.

Helmut Eckler was waiting around the corner in the driver's seat of the Mercedes. "Arthur, let me give you a lift home."

"Thank you, Bruno, that's appreciated. I gave my driver the night off."

They continued talking as they got into the back of the sedan. "Heydrich talked to me the other day, wanting to know if I thought you might be interested in joining the SS once this nasty business with the SA was over. You should consider it, Bruno. The SS is the elite, the cream of the crop, the future, and Heydrich has taken a liking to you. And Hans Frank would certainly vouch for you with the Führer. Think about it. You never know, you might take over my dimwit brother-in-law's well-paying position." Eckler gave Bruno a knowing wink.

Early the next morning, Bruno called his secretary, Fräulein Oltman, and gave her instructions to gather the constitutional law experts at the firm to research what options they had to legally curb the SA's excesses.

After finishing with her, he lifted the phone and dialled Steffi's number. She picked it up on the first ring.

"Steffi, I miss you."

"I miss you, too, darling."

"So why don't you get on the afternoon train and come down to Berlin? We could spend a wonderful evening and night together, go to the zoo tomorrow, and then Helmut can drive us back to Munich in the late afternoon."

"Sounds wonderful, darling, but what do I tell my husband? Do I just say, 'Excuse me, dear, but my lover wants to spend the next two days and nights in bed with me. Is that fine with you?'"

"Well, I guess you have a point there. But when can I see you? It's been a long time since I held that stunning body of yours next to mine!"

She giggled at his brazen openness about his physical attraction to her. "Rolf will be attending some torchlight parade or book burning in Leipzig this coming Saturday. He should be gone the whole weekend. I am sure that little blonde tramp from his office will be keeping him company."

"All right, I'll plan something totally decadent for us!"

"Will it involve wine, chocolate and the Kama Sutra?"

He laughed as he said goodbye and hung up the phone. After shaving, showering, and dressing in the expensive pin-striped dark grey suit he'd had tailor-made for his trip to Berlin, he headed back to the Reich Security Main Office to meet once again with Heydrich's inner circle, to plan their response to the SA conundrum.

As they broke for a late lunch of beer and sausages, an SS secretary delivered a sheaf of teletype pages to Bruno. It was the report from his associates at the firm in Munich. Excusing himself, he sat alone at a corner table, leafing through the pages, quickly glancing over the materials as he ate his lunch. After about twenty minutes of reading, he rejoined the others.

"Fellows." He took a deep swallow from his beer, which went down his throat the wrong way, causing him to start choking and coughing.

Nebe slapped him on the back a couple of times.

Once he had recovered his composure, he continued. "Reading through the report from our constitutional legal experts back in Munich, I don't have good news. There is nothing in the current constitution that would provide us with any legal avenues to put a stop to what's going on. We'll need to explore other means."

"Well, that does it, then," Heydrich said. "I'll have to report back to Reichsführer Himmler as to our conclusion and let him and the Führer come up with a resolution. Thank you all. Heil Hitler!" He raised his arm, turned, and left the room.

Bruno, Nebe, and Wegman remained at the table, continuing to drink their beer and discussing what might transpire in the future based on what Himmler and Hitler would decide.

It was early morning when Heydrich, Himmler, and Göring met at Göring's office in the Air Ministry and decided to seek an audience with Adolf Hitler after their meeting with Schmidt, Nebe, and Wegman the previous evening. They drove to the small hamlet of Berchtesgaden in the Bavarian Alps, Hitler's favourite retreat when weighty decisions needed to be made. In the 1920s, just out of prison, he had checked into an alpine hut up there to finish his manifesto, *Mein Kampf*. Because it was there that he claimed to be inspired and laid out his vision, some called Berchtesgaden the "cradle of the Third Reich."

Light snow was falling when they arrived at *Alpener Adler Hof* (Alpine Eagle House) Hotel that evening. Their progress had been slow due to the heavy accumulation of snow along the highways and through the mountain passes. They all gathered around the roaring fire in the fireplace in the hotel's empty main room, the manager having cleared out everyone else in deference to his illustrious visitor. Hans Frank, Hitler's personal attorney, was also staying at the hotel, but quietly hung back, standing with his arms crossed behind a seated Hitler and listening to the arguments.

Göring had spread out his bulky frame, puffing a cigar and sipping a glass of schnapps, while Heydrich and Himmler vehemently made their point to Hitler about the dangers of not putting a stop to Röhm's activities by any means, possibly including violence. They emphasized the need for the Führer to first get the army on side, and then convinced him that Röhm, encouraged by France, was plotting a *coup d'état* against Hitler. Heydrich had gotten his *casus belli*.

Hitler, being a teetotaller, stayed with them, listening to their forceful arguments for only a short time, then excusing himself around midnight and retiring to his room to work on an upcoming speech to the Reichstag. Hans Frank joined Hitler and bade the others good night. For once, the Führer seemed indecisive; however, he did commit to meet with senior military brass as soon as possible to discuss the role of the SA in the future of the Fatherland.

The three conspirators drank and talked well into the morning hours, with Göring falling asleep on a comfortable leather couch beside the fireplace with its dying embers. His two companions left him there until sunrise, when the first maid reported in for work and got the shock of her life in finding the portly Reichsmarschall still sleeping in full Luftwaffe Air Marshall's regalia, medals and all, and snoring loudly.

The next day, the three stopped in Munich on their way back to Berlin to bring Bruno Schmidt up to date on their meeting with the Führer, as they wanted to make sure the country's judiciary would at least give a veneer of legality to the actions they were contemplating.

Bruno, who had also arrived back in town that morning, after a long drive from Berlin, greeted them with cups of hot chocolate at his office, served by Fräulein Oltman. A pretty redhead, she seemed to have quite a mesmerizing effect on Göring, whose large, bulging brown eyes followed her every move around Bruno's office.

"So, my friends, what was accomplished at Berchtesgaden?"

"The Führer didn't say no! He has promised to meet with the General Staff shortly, and to decide on what action to authorize based on input from the Armed Forces Chiefs," Himmler responded.

"What role would the legal community, including the judiciary, be asked to play?" Bruno enquired.

"My dear Bruno, we want to ensure that you and your esteemed, black-robed colleagues fully appreciate the gravity of the situation, and while interpreting the laws, act in the State's—no, I correct myself—in the Führer's best interests." Heydrich said with a conspiratorial smile, distorting the left side of his face where a sabre slash he received years ago, in a university duel, ran the length of his cheek.

What a macabre sight, Bruno thought. "Rest assured, Herr Gruppenführer, that our Fatherland's legal experts will always be on the right side when interpreting our constitutional statutes."

They were ready to leave when Göring drew Bruno to the side. He reeked of cigar smoke, schnapps and cheap cologne, not having bathed prior to setting out from Berchtesgaden and still wearing his uniform from the day before.

"Tell me, Schmidt, your secretary, what's her name?"

"Fräulein Oltman."

"Oh, yes. She's quite attractive. Nice hips. Do you think you could arrange for me to have dinner with her the next time I visit Munich?"

Bruno had trouble holding back his laughter, but answered, saying, "I will do my best, Herr Reichsmarschall."

He was anxious to usher his visitors out the door as quickly as he could, so as to be able to finish his work at the office and meet Steffi at a small, intimate, out-of-the-way restaurant on Munich's outskirts. A glorious weekend of lovemaking lay ahead.

He ran himself a hot bath and luxuriated in its warmth, while whistling along with a tune from Hungarian composer Franz Lehár's operetta, *Land of Smiles*, playing on the radio.

At her home, Frau Hartmann, ever the dutiful wife, folded her husband's shirts and placed them along with his underwear, socks, and suspenders in the suitcase that he was taking to Leipzig for a torchlight parade, book burning, picnic and general rabble-rousing with his brown-shirted SA comrades in that beautiful medieval city, capital of Saxony and birthplace of Adolf Hitler's favourite composer, Richard Wagner.

She hugged and kissed her husband on the cheek as he got into the black SA staff car, driven by his sergeant at arms Siegfried Hoff, and then ran upstairs to pack her most alluring and flimsiest silk undergarments for her rendezvous and illicit weekend getaway with her young lover Bruno.

On an overcast April 11, 1934, just before his forty-fifth birthday, Hitler met with senior armed forces staff on board the pocket battleship *Deutschland* in Kiel Harbour. He was courting them to get their support for when President Hindenburg died. He wanted to become not just chancellor but president—and he needed the army's backing for this.

However, the political instability felt by many in Germany was not in Hitler's favour. He knew he had to act swiftly when he learned that the ageing field marshal, President Hindenburg, due to the countrywide chaos created by the SA, was threatening to declare martial law in Germany, with the army being given the power to run the country. Himmler in black SS uniform, Göring in Luftwaffe white, and Rudolf Hess, Deputy Führer, were all gathered around the Führer on the quarterdeck of the *Deutschland* mingling with the generals and admirals of the General Staff.

A sumptuous feast had been laid on for the occasion, prepared by the best chefs of the Navy, along with wines from Germany's various wine-growing regions. Partway through their meal, a fine rain began to fall, and they all retired to the officers' wardroom to continue their delicate negotiations. Seated at a long rectangular table, they were lined up as if on a chessboard. The military players were on one side, the Nazi Party, with the Führer in the middle, on the other.

The military chiefs didn't mince their words. According to them, Roehm probably made his worst mistake in February 1934 when he insisted that the German Army should be incorporated into the SA. Senior army leaders had been horrified at the suggestion. Although Hitler had no love for senior army commanders, he knew he needed to keep the army on his side and that meant rejecting what Röhm proposed. They now made it clear to Hitler that the price for their continued support, and that of the industrialists, would be the disbanding of the SA and the arrest and imprisonment of its leaders for treason.

Before responding, Hitler asked Captain Hans Langsdorff, commanding officer of the pocket battleship, if he and those with him could use the captain's cabin for a private conference. Lamsdorf posted two armed guards outside the cabin to make sure they wouldn't be disturbed.

"These pompous desk jockeys! They were probably hiding behind their mothers' skirts in Berlin while Ernst was in hand-to-hand combat against the French at Verdun! The man was severely wounded twice and is the recipient of the Iron Cross! And now they want me to arrest him for treason?" Hitler's voice continued to rise as he pounded the small round table in the cabin with his fist, his straight black hair falling across his forehead.

"Mein Führer, please lower your voice, or all of Kiel will hear you," pleaded Himmler.

Hess, who always had a calming influence on his leader, placed his hand on Hitler's shoulder, which had the desired effect.

"So, Heinrich and Hermann, what do you think of the army's preposterous proposal?" Hitler, cocking his head to the side, asked.

Both of them had ulterior motives for supporting the military. Röhm was a threat to the dominance that Himmler wanted, as his SS was much smaller in numeric terms than the SA, and Göring was worried that he wanted to absorb the Luftwaffe, as well as the Reichswehr, into the SA.

"*Mein Führer*, we know that you still very much support Ernst and the SA despite the negative press they received for their behaviour in and out of uniform. However, they see themselves as being above the law when it comes to their outrageous indiscretions. Our party leaders believe that they are bringing discredit to our party, especially the dalliances of Röhm and his deputy, Edmund Heines, both acknowledged homosexuals."

The reference by Himmler to Röhm's sexual orientation had an immediate and totally negative effect on Hitler's attitude towards his close and loyal acolyte. He was known to be vehemently opposed to any non-heterosexual deviations. Due to their long, symbiotic relationship, he had closed his eyes and mind to Röhm's homosexuality. Now, with it being brought into the open by his two top lieutenants, he could no longer ignore it. It also gave him a convenient excuse to abandon Röhm and gain the continued support of the armed forces, bankers, and industrialists.

"You are sure that Ernst is a 'fancy bird'?" he asked, using the pejorative slang expression for a homosexual to communicate his disgust.

"The Gestapo has photographic proof from one of their weekend outings. He and a very 'pretty' young Stormtrooper," Himmler responded.

"In that case, go and tell those dilettantes in the wardroom that we agree to their demands, subject to the army taking a personal oath to the Führer, once the SA is no longer in the picture."

"Are you not going to tell them yourself?"

"No, I have no desire right now to meet with them in their fancy uniforms again. You go inform them. Now, let's get this mess behind us."

With a bit of subterfuge, Göring and Himmler had convinced Hitler that he had no other choice but to close down Röhm and the SA's violent activities if he wanted the Nazi Party to stay in power. When they got back to the Prinz-Albrecht-Strasse Headquarters of the SS and Gestapo in Berlin, Göring and Himmler immediately caucused with Heydrich and Nebe and instructed them to set the Security Services machinery in motion to carry out the Führer's orders to deal with the brown-shirted SA.

Heydrich laughingly seized on Hitler's "fancy bird" comment and suggested that they name the action against the SA Operation Hummingbird. The others smilingly agreed. Nebe contacted Bruno and asked him to join them, even though it was already past midnight.

Bruno threw a trench coat over his pyjamas, called Helmut Eckler, and had him drive him to the meeting. The earlier misty rain had turned to a heavy downpour by the time he got there and found the other three drinking hot cocoa and poring over mimeographed lists.

"Don't drip on the papers," Nebe cautioned Bruno as he leaned over Heydrich's shoulder to better see the lists.

"These are complete lists of every SA officer above the rank of Sturmbannführer. We have the home addresses of all the people in the lists. The Führer has authorized the arrest of all of them. Bruno, we need you to make sure that all of this is well-documented and that all of the legal steps in order to accomplish it are in place and adhered to."

Nebe asked Bruno, "And what happens if any of them resist arrest?"

Heydrich chimed in, looking over at Himmler. "Arthur, you're a policeman, what would you advise? Use armed force?"

"That would be the police force's standard procedure," Nebe responded. "I have a major concern. With over 30,000 names in these lists, the police force, not even with co-operation from the Gestapo and the SS, will have sufficient number of agents to simultaneously carry out the arrests. We need to think of some other way."

"All we need is to cut off the snake's head and the rest of the body will wither," Himmler added as he cleaned his pince-nez glasses with his handkerchief. "We arrest the top one hundred and the rest will lose their enthusiasm."

"I've got an idea. We get the top command together in one place, have them surrounded and arrested," Bruno explained. "There must be some torchlight parade or book burning coming up that they will all be attending."

"I will try to get one of our agents on the inside to find out when that possibility might arise," Nebe answered.

"We can't wait for that. Things are getting out of hand quickly, and I think that old man Hindenburg will not allow that to go on forever," Himmler added.

"I'll get an audience with the Führer next week, and perhaps he can arrange to set up a meeting with Röhm and his higher-ups somewhere secure and isolated. Röhm would never turn down that kind of request from the Führer."

"Gentlemen, let's follow that plan. It's getting very late, and we should all be going home," Heydrich concluded. The stage had now been set for what was to be called Operation Hummingbird and would end in the "Night of the Long Knives," a seminal event in the twelve-year history of the Thousand Year Third Reich, and indeed the history of the world.

✠

Life at the Grossman and Weiss household was also in turmoil during the upheavals within the Nazi Party in the spring of 1934. Papa Grossman's volume of business at his remaining haberdashery dropped precipitously after the ascension of the Nazis to power. His Gentile customers, many of whom he considered long-time friends, crossed the street in front of his shop to avoid bumping into him. His only remaining ones were all Jewish, with ever-shrinking incomes. He was now selling more suits on credit, with the forlorn hope that times might change, than for cash.

Arnold's list of law clients at the firm were also more and more likely to shift their case to the non-Jewish partners, consequently cutting Arnold's retainers in half. In order to supplement it, he took work outside of the firm from Jewish clients at less than a quarter of his hourly rates. He toured the lower courts of Berlin, pleading the case of his newly impoverished clients with unsympathetic, even hostile magistrates recently appointed to the bench by the Nazis. After all, one of Bruno Schmidt's tasks was to make sure the new judges being appointed met current "Nazification" standards and approval from him and his partners.

By this time, the women of the household would not go out during the day, and more and more of the food shopping and other chores of the day fell on Heldi's shoulders. Despite the fact that they had to reduce her wages, Heldi stuck to the simple morals of her Catholic upbringing in the foothills of the Austrian Alps and refused to abandon her Jewish employers.

The evening conversations between Papa Grossman and Arnold in the salon at Meineke Strasse 14 became more and more rancorous as time went on, and the excesses of Röhm's Brownshirts grew in frequency. Alex's unbridled optimism clashed head-on with Arnold's pessimistic measure of reality. The discussions over their favourite schnapps, which they could ill afford, always followed the same, familiar pattern.

"Arnold, I tell you, this Nazi nonsense will soon come to an end. The politicians will come to the realization that they can't run this country without us Jews. And President Hindenburg is no anti-Semite. He served with Jewish officers during the war. Why, I think he even had a Jewish adjutant—Pearlstein, I believe?"

"Alex, old man Hindenburg doesn't run the country anymore. He's sick and senile and is only a comfortable figurehead that Adolf and his cronies can hide behind. They're slowly choking the air out of our lungs with their various restrictive decrees. You can't even buy alcohol or your cigars anymore, and must have Heldi do it for you, because they won't serve Jews in those stores. We are not welcome in this country any longer, Alex, and we need to make some big decisions as to our future."

"I refuse to even contemplate leaving this country. Our family has lived in Germany for hundreds of years, from before Martin Luther and the Reformation, and has given its loyal service to its rulers during that time. I am not about to let that little Austrian corporal with the funny moustache chase us out of here. And, by the way, I can still go into Mandelbaum's Tobacco Shop and buy my Monte Cristos. He keeps a stash of them under the counter just for me. You want another shot?"

"No, thanks." Arnold stood up and left the room, shaking his head.

Later that night, Ingrid and Arnold were lying in bed discussing their family's situation. Her head lay across his shoulder, with his arm embracing her, and her long hair across his bare chest. The light of the half moon beaming through the lace curtain bathed the dark room in a soft glow.

"My mother asked again when we are going to give them some grandchildren."

"What sane person would want to bring a child into the world around us today? Your father and I have difficulty even providing for the four of us, never mind the expenses of a baby."

"But father says that the current troubles are only temporary, and that everything will return to normal again soon. And I don't want to have children when I am much older."

"I don't know, darling. I just don't know. I want to have kids as much as you do, but bringing them into this chaos just makes no sense. I am afraid to say, but your father, God love him, is an old, naïve, and optimistic fool. He hasn't sold a yard of fabric or even a tie in a month. The money he keeps giving your mother comes from selling parts of his stamp collection and not from sales at the store, as he keeps fooling her. Let's see where matters go in the next couple of months."

He started to kiss her neck and slipping his hand under the top of her nightgown, and began gently massaging her breast, eliciting a low moan from her lips.

"Mr. Weiss, you better stop that or there will be consequences!"

"Oh yes, and what kind of consequences would that be?" he asked with a quiet laugh.

"A beautiful addition to our little family." She giggled as she sought to push her small hand past the waistband of her husband's pyjamas.

CHAPTER 24

Daniel made it down to the lobby of the King David earlier than every-one else. He was still too hung over from the previous day's alcoholic beverages to attempt his usual morning run. He was desperately looking for a cup of coffee. He had left his father up in the room, taking a shower and loudly singing, off-key, Frank Sinatra's version of "The Impossible Dream" from *Man of La Mancha*.

He finally tracked down a half pot of tepid coffee in the hotel's kitchen and, much to the protestations of one of the kitchen help, poured its contents into a large cup, downing it in one swallow. It was just past seven when the rest of the group started to filter into the sunlit dining room. Some were wearing an ill-fitting assortment of military uniforms from their soldiering days twenty-five years ago, while others wore a variety of open-necked sports shirts and sport jackets, or suits and ties. The few women amongst them wore skirts and blouses, with a heavy veneer of makeup, trying to recapture their younger days. Their Israeli military escorts wore crisp, well-ironed uniforms of the various branches—the navy in white, the air force in blue, and the army in khaki, with unit badges and decorations on their chests.

Samuel and Gabriel both wore light-beige summer suits without ties, while Avner was dressed in army colours, wearing his combat medals. Samuel proudly displayed his two US Army Purple Hearts. After everyone was assembled downstairs and picking away at their breakfast of fruits and bagels with lox and cream cheese, Alexei, wearing a dark-blue suit and tie, the Soviet army decorations for the battles of Stalingrad and Berlin on his chest, addressed them in his Russian-accented English.

"Dear friends, comrades, honoured guests. Today the State of Israel celebrates the twenty-fifth anniversary of its founding. Many of you gathered here today bravely participated in the battles to make this a reality. Too many of our brothers, sisters, friends, and comrades from those desperate times are now lying in the military cemetery on Mount Herzl. Today, we honour their sacrifice and celebrate the reality of an everlasting homeland for the Jewish people."

There wasn't a dry eye in the audience as they all rose, applauding his words.

Yonathan then took over, outlining the day's agenda. "It's now half-past eight. There will be Jeeps waiting for you outside in half an hour to take you to the parade reviewing stand. The parade starts at ten. There will be two visitors and one guide to each of the Jeeps. After the parade, we will have lunch at the Knesset (Israeli Parliament) as guests of all the members of the Knesset. After lunch, we will visit and lay wreaths at the memorial to the fallen heroes of Israel's wars on Mount Herzl. You will then be taken back to your hotel for a brief rest, after which your Jeeps will pick you up once again for the drive to Masada to observe the officers' swearing-in ceremony. Are there any questions?"

The veteran from Poughkeepsie spoke up again. "Tell me, young man, with all this riding in Jeeps, will we have time to go to the bathroom?"

The room broke out in loud laughter, drowning out Yonathan's response, prompting the old man to ask, "What did he say? What did he say?"

Someone from the group answered him, to another round of laughter. "He said that there'll be a large bucket in the back of every Jeep."

More than 300,000 people lined the four-and-a-half-mile route of march in 90-degree weather that morning to watch a display of Israel's military might in the longest, largest, and most spectacular Independence Day parade in the nation's twenty-five-year history. President Zalman Shazar, Prime Minister Golda Meir, and former Prime Minister David Ben-Gurion watched the parade from the official reviewing stand, facing police headquarters in the Sheikh Jarrah quarter of East Jerusalem.

Mrs. Meir wore a white handkerchief around her head to shield her eyes from the blazing sun. They sat in the stand for ninety minutes while the three main elements of the parade passed in review–the Air Force fly-past with their American-built F-4 Phantoms and A-4 Skyhawks, and French Mirage IIIs, the armoured corps rumbling along the pavement with the British-built Centurions and American-produced M60 Pattons spewing heavy black exhaust fumes, and finally the infantry. Israeli Air Force F-4 Phantom Jets flew overhead in a formation depicting the six-pointed Star of David to close the show.

After the end of the parade, once all the military units had dispersed, the group got back in their Jeeps and headed for lunch as guests of the various Israeli political parties at the Knesset. During the extravagant luncheon banquet, they met the Israeli cabinet, including Prime Minister Golda Meir and Defense Minister Moshe Dayan.

Samuel and General Dayan, with the famous black eyepatch covering the loss of an eye in Syria during the Second World War, hugged each other warmly.

"Dr. Singer, it's nice of you to visit us once again. We are honoured," General Dayan said.

After lunch, they were driven to the military cemetery on Mount Herzl, where they laid a wreath at the memorial for all those killed while fighting for the State of Israel in three previous wars, in 1948, 1956, and 1967.

By mid-afternoon, they were all back at their hotel, with the more elderly of the group heading to their rooms for a quick nap, while others either took a leisurely walk through the gardens or sat in the bar having drinks. Daniel and Naomi took their glasses of chardonnay and sat on a low stone wall around the corner from the front entrance, under a cherry tree just coming into bloom.

"So, what did you think of the parade today? Were you impressed?"

"Oh yes, it was quite the show."

He was once again readying himself to ask her about her personal life, when Rivka and Yonathan showed up.

"Hello, you two, do you mind if we join you?" Yonathan asked, and immediately sat down on the wall beside Naomi.

Rivka continued to stand in front of the three, sipping on her lemonade.

Am I ever going to get the opportunity to get her alone? Daniel thought. He had become infatuated with the dark-haired, mysterious beauty.

As the sun began its descent in the western sky, bathing Jerusalem in a golden glow, thirty Jeeps set out from Jerusalem heading north towards the eastern edge of the Judean desert to the ancient hilltop fortress of Masada, overlooking the Dead Sea. This time, Samuel rode in a Jeep with Avner, Gabriel, and Alexei, while Yonathan drove another Jeep with Naomi in front, and much to Daniel's disappointment, Rivka in the back with him. She recited the history of Masada and the suicide of the Jewish zealots for Daniel's benefit.

By the time Rivka finished telling the story of the death of the defenders of Masada, they had arrived at the base of the Rock, with the ruins of the fortress at the top, fifty metres above sea level. They waited there for the rest of the Jeeps to arrive, after which they ascended the hill in small groups by cable car. When they were finally all assembled on the middle terrace of the fort, the sun had dipped below the horizon, but the sky's pinkish hue was still reflecting off the glistening, mirrored surface of the Dead Sea below. A small military band positioned on the upper terrace was playing Schubert's "Marche Militaire" as the group of dignitaries and relatives of the IDF officers to be sworn in gathered on the reddish earthen surface of the lower terrace.

At exactly eight o'clock, the band launched into "The March of the Israeli Defense Force," the IDF's anthem, and the officer cadets about to graduate smartly marched forward in a line and took up position in front of the dais. A full moon had by then risen in the sky and illuminated the entire scene.

The band had stopped playing and the brigadier general atop the reviewing stand read out the names of the graduating officers one by one. They each stepped forward, came to attention and saluted the general. A sergeant major would then affix the single small metal bar, signifying the rank of lieutenant, to each of the cadet's shoulder flashes.

When the last cadet had been inducted, all present turned, lifted their heads and faced the top of the fortress where Israel's white and blue flag with the Star of David in the middle fluttered in a gentle breeze, lit up by a battery of searchlights.

The general, in a booming voice, then called out, "Graduates, welcome as officers to the greatest army in the world. Remember to honour all those that have passed here before you, and never forget the lesson of Masada."

Then as the band played "Hatikvah," Israel's national anthem, two soldiers slowly lowered the flag. Wine and snacks were served, and the new officers and their parents, wives, or husbands mingled with the dignitaries and those foreign veterans that had fought their country's wars before them and hoped that this new crop of officers wouldn't have to follow in their footsteps.

Samuel was in deep conversation with one of the newly graduated officers whose parents he had started talking to prior to the ceremony. "So, Roni, your parents tell me that you want to be assigned to the medical corps."

"That's right, sir," the beaming twenty-year-old responded.

"You know, son, I served in the US Army as a battlefield surgeon in the Second World War and in our War of Independence, and I saw things that no one should ever witness. You better think it over and make sure it's what you want, because once the firing starts, you can't change your mind."

"Yes, I'll remember that."

"But there's no better feeling on this earth than saving a man's life, so remember that as well." He gave the young man a hug and walked to the edge of the terrace and lit up his pipe. The past—in France, in Germany, and in Palestine—once again rushed over him. The young men whose lives he saved, and the ones he couldn't.

Daniel came up to him. "Are you all right?"

"Yes, just a lot of ghosts coming back to visit up here," he said with a sad smile. They stood in silence, looking out at the moon's rays dancing on the surface of the dark water down below, the blue smoke from Samuel's pipe slowly curling upward.

The silence was broken by Naomi coming over from a group of escorts that had been standing off to the side. "Dr. Singer, do you mind if I kidnap your son? I would like to show him something special before we head back to Jerusalem. I'm taking the Jeep, so is it okay if Rivka, Yonathan, and our driver go back with you?"

With that, she looked at Daniel. "Are you coming?"

He followed her to the Jeep like a happy puppy, looking back and flashing his father a smile. Samuel smiled back and gave his son a knowing wink.

"So, where are you taking me?"

"Oh, it's a surprise." She laughed mischievously as she got behind the wheel of the Jeep. They drove through the darkness, their way down the dirt road lit by the moon and the Jeep's headlights. Daniel put his arm on the back of Naomi's seat as the Jeep bounced along the uneven surface.

After about fifteen minutes, Naomi pulled the Jeep to a stop in the sand at the edge of the Dead Sea. It was a beautiful, warm, moonlit night with the moon's rays bouncing off the still surface of the water.

"Come on, let us go for a swim," Naomi yelled to Daniel as she jumped out of the Jeep, shedding her clothes on the sand as she ran into the water.

Daniel was dumbstruck.

"Hey, I don't have a bathing suit," he yelled out to Naomi, who was standing up to her waist, completely nude, in the very salty water of the sea.

"You do not need one! Are you shy?"

Daniel didn't need further invitation, tearing off his sport jacket, shirt, pants, and underwear as he ran and dove headlong into the dark water. He quickly popped back up, struggling to stay balanced in the water, and spitting out the salty liquid he had inadvertently swallowed.

Naomi looked at him and couldn't keep from laughing.

"How do you swim in this stuff?" he yelled to her.

"You do not. Because of the high salt content, it has way too much buoyancy. Just float on your back."

She did the same. They floated side by side, looking up at the moon and the millions of stars decorating the heavens above them.

"Quite a surprise," Daniel said as he tried to look over at her but lost his balance once more and got turned onto his stomach. He was spitting salty water once again when he got himself righted.

They drifted in the darkness and silence, only interrupted by the occasional headlight along the coastal road or the sound of a gently breaking wave on shore. Finally, Naomi stood up and walked out of the water, standing on the sand and waiting for Daniel to do the same, as he struggled to stand up. He looked at her, drinking in her full naked beauty bathed in the moonlight. Her long, wet hair hung down over her shoulders, partially covering her small, pert breasts. She made no attempt to hide her nakedness as she waited for Daniel to exit the sea. When he was finally upright, and only up to his knees in the water, she turned and started running.

"Where are you going?"

"Come on to the showers."

There were a number of upright metal pipes with shower heads at the top located on shore to allow bathers to wash off the salt that had accumulated on their bodies. She was already under one, with the water cascading down her well-tanned body by the time Daniel got there.

"Come, get under the water," she invited him.

He approached her slowly, his excitement clearly showing. He put his arms around her and pulled her close as his lips searched for hers, their naked bodies tight to each other.

She shook her head and pushed him away, whispering, "No, No." She looked down at him and said, "Mister, you better put that away."

Daniel didn't understand and tried to embrace her again, but she turned and walked away.

"I have some towels in the Jeep," she said.

"What's the matter, Naomi? Is there someone else? Are you in a relationship? What did I say or do wrong?" he quizzed her as he followed.

"Nothing, but yes, there is someone else."

She seemed reluctant to continue, but he pushed her. "Is it Yonathan?"

"Oh no." She laughed.

He kept at her. "Well, who is it, and how serious is it?"

"It is Rivka," she whispered.

At that moment, more than just Daniel's ego deflated. *Holy shit! I come all the way to Israel only to fall for a lesbian.*

"I know what you are thinking. Like all the men in this country, you think that I am sick, that there is something wrong with me, but believe me, it is not like that at all!" She started to cry. Now he was feeling sorry, and he took one of the towels and moved to wrap it around her. The tears continued to flow as she put her head on his shoulder.

"I will tell you the whole story on the way back," she sobbed as they dried themselves off. It was close to midnight when they drove off the beach and onto the coastal road heading back in the direction of Jerusalem.

"It was in the orphanage at the kibbutz that I first met Rivka. She was a precocious and lively girl, with curly red hair and lots of freckles. She was three years older than me and was from Berlin. Her parents died in Auschwitz, as did her twin sister, Elsa, from having medical experiments performed on her by that monster, Dr. Mengele. She also had an older brother named Maximillian, but does not remember much about him, nor what happened to him after she and the rest of her family were taken away by the Gestapo and shipped off to Poland in 1944.

"Rivka was already at the orphanage when I got there, and she immediately took me under her wing and adopted me as her 'little sister.' We would play together, bathe together, and sleep together. We were inseparable."

Naomi then went on to describe their teenage years going to the school established on the kibbutz.

"Neither of us could ever develop an emotional bond with the opposite sex after what we endured at the camps, so we relied on each other for closeness and comfort. She was twenty and I was seventeen when we discovered that we had a physical attraction and deep feelings for each other that far exceeded the boundaries of pure friendship. We were taking a shower together one evening and playfully lathering each other up when matters suddenly went beyond play. And how do they say it? The rest is history."

From then on, they drove in silence through the dark desert, without encountering any other vehicles until they got to Jerusalem's outskirts.

"Do your comrades know?"

"They suspect, but everyone is afraid to go there. Because of our violent history, Israel is the world headquarters of male chauvinism. And that is okay with Rivka and I, as long as we are left alone."

He hugged her and put his arms around her waist as they walked back into the hotel around two thirty in the morning, with each heading to their own room.

Now I feel like a big brother, he regretfully thought as he climbed into bed. Samuel, as usual, was snoring loudly in the next bed, but that wasn't what kept Daniel awake that night. It had been quite an evening, going from an emotional and physical high to a gut-wrenching low, finally settling somewhere around a plateau of ambivalence.

Naomi took the elevator to her floor but didn't enter the room she shared with Rivka, instead going back down to the hotel's lobby to use the pay phone located there.

At 3:00 a.m., the telephone rang in Alexei's apartment in Tel Aviv. He woke with a start, knocking the glass of water on his night table to the floor. He searched for the phone in the darkness for a moment before turning on the bedside lamp and picking up the receiver.

"Alexei, it is Naomi." Her voice was low and excited.

"And what can I do for you at this ungodly hour?" he asked hoarsely, clearing his throat. By now he was fully awake.

"I think we found our man for Operation Berlin on the Nile."

Hearing that, he sat upright. "How so?"

"Our boy, Singer Jr., fits what we've been looking for to a T. Do not ask me how I know, but he is not circumcised, does not look Jewish with that blond mop and blue eyes, and he is fluent in French."

"Must have been quite a graduation ceremony." He chuckled. "Can you bring him into the office tomorrow morning? I'll see if I can get Lotz in to meet him as well. Good work. Now get some sleep."

She hung up the phone, went back to her room, and climbed into bed beside Rivka.

As if in a dream, Rivka felt Naomi's lips and tongue lightly nibbling her neck then moving down to her breasts, encircling one nipple then the other. She hovered in that nether world between dream and reality, letting out a soft moan, finally surrendering to her eager partner's ardour. They fell asleep in each other's arms, as they had done since their childhood days at the orphanage.

Alexei couldn't get back to sleep after hearing from Naomi, so he poured himself a glass of Glenlivet and took out a thick dossier marked "High Priority/Top Secret" from the safe on the wall behind a Chagall print and started leafing through the photographs and documents in it. The first photograph was of Adolf Eichmann sitting in the prisoners' dock in the courtroom in Jerusalem. There was an "X" in black marker across his face.

CHAPTER 25

MAY 9, 1973,
TEL AVIV—THE SPYING GAME

Early the next morning, Samuel came out of the bathroom to answer the quiet tapping on the door of his suite, a towel around his waist and shaving foam on half his face.

"Good morning, Naomi. You're up bright and early," he whispered, not wanting to wake the deeply sleeping Daniel.

"Good morning, Dr. Singer. I am sorry for bothering you, but I need to speak with Daniel. It is urgent and important. Could you please wake him and tell him to meet me in the coffee shop downstairs in twenty minutes?"

"Okay, but the bus isn't leaving for Sinai for another two hours."

"I know, but he may not be going to the Sinai today."

"All right, I'll go wake him," he answered, shaking his head, not knowing what to make of the young woman's comment.

"Son, wake up." He shook Daniel.

"What, what? It's still early. I need to get some more sleep."

"You must have had a hell of a good time last night with this lovely creature if she's already looking for you this early in the morning."

Daniel laughed. "You don't know the half of it, Dad. You just don't know." He sighed as he turned over and tried to go back to sleep, pulling the cover over his head. "What did she want?" he murmured from underneath, his head buried in his pillow.

"She didn't say. She just wants you to meet her downstairs in the coffee shop in twenty minutes."

"Shit!" Daniel sat up and rubbed the sleep from his eyes.

"Oh, she did say something about you possibly not coming to the Sinai with the rest of us today."

"Hmmm." Daniel wondered what that was all about as he got out of bed and shuffled into the bathroom.

After a fast shave and shower, he hurried downstairs to meet Naomi.

"So, what's so important that you wake me up in the middle of the night?"

"I am sorry for last evening. I should have let you know earlier."

"Shhh, Naomi, you've got nothing to be sorry about. Now, Dad told me that I'm not going to the Sinai with him today, why not?"

"Because you're coming to Tel Aviv with me to meet Alexei."

"Another surprise like yesterday?"

"A surprise, but not quite like last night." She smiled. "Are you ready to go?"

"What about my luggage?"

"It will be taken to the airport."

They got into the Jeep and drove at speed through a Jerusalem just waking up, with Naomi dodging vehicle traffic and pedestrians. Once they hit Highway #1, the route to Tel Aviv, she really stepped on the gas. During the drive, they made small talk about Israeli and American politics and their favourite movies and books, both avoiding the topic of what transpired the previous evening.

"Why are we meeting Alexei?"

"He will explain it all to you when we get there."

"And where is 'there'?"

"His office at Mossad HQ."

"Wow, this sounds very mysterious, very 'cloak and daggery.' Will we be meeting James Bond there?" He laughed.

"Close," she answered. "The Israeli version."

They stopped for fresh orange juice at a service station at the junction of the highway and Route 443, just outside of Lod, before driving past Ben Gurion Airport and into the modern suburbs of Tel Aviv. They then drove north, arriving at the "Institute," as the Mossad is popularly referred to, near Glilot Junction.

✠

They drove through two sentry posts, where both their documents were checked and the Jeep searched, before driving down into an underground parking garage. From there, they took the elevator to the second floor, where they were searched by an armed guard then subjected to an x-ray scan and finally issued security badges.

"Hey, how come they put you through this? I thought you worked for them."

"I do, but not in this section."

They were ushered into a windowless room with a whiteboard on one wall and a projection screen on another. A young female corporal came into the room to ask them if they wanted water, coffee, or juice. They then sat down at the rectangular wooden table and waited in silence.

A few minutes later, after lightly knocking on the door, Alexei entered the room. "Good morning, Daniel. How are you? How have you enjoyed your time in Israel?"

"Good morning Alexei. I am well, and you? My time in the Holy Land has been excellent! Full of the unexpected!"

"Well, thanks for skipping the Sinai part of the trip. It's pretty boring anyway—just a lot of sand, camels and Bedouin."

Alexei replied with a smirk.

Naomi looked at Alexei and motioned with her head towards the door.

"Daniel, would you please excuse Naomi and I for a minute?"

Outside in the corridor, Naomi asked Alexei, "Is Lotz coming?"

"Yes, he should be here shortly. Yves as well. And I have a surprise guest coming. He should be landing in about an hour at Ben Gurion from Vienna, courtesy of the IAF."

"Boy, you are really putting on a show!"

"We have to, my dear. From what I hear from the 'Angel' in Cairo, it may be our last chance before Sadat pulls the trigger. We've reports of heavy traffic on the other side of the Suez Canal, across from the Bar Lev fortifications. And the artillery barrages have picked up in the last week as well."

Daniel paced the room back and forth, wondering what the Mossad—one of the most deadly and secretive intelligence agencies around the globe—would want to glean from a New York art historian and appraiser. *Maybe they want my help in liberating the* Mona Lisa *from the Louvre,* he chuckled.

There came another knock on the door and the corporal entered with a pot of espresso coffee, some biscuits and a bowl of fresh fruit, followed by Naomi and Alexei. "I know you're wondering why you're here," Alexei began.

"That you can be sure of," Daniel responded.

"Let me start by saying that as far as anyone outside of this room is concerned, you are not in this building and never have been. Any conversations in this room are never to be repeated to anyone, and no notes or recordings are being taken. We know that you attempted to travel to Israel to join our armed forces in 1967, so we believe that you have a certain loyalty and affinity for the State of Israel. Your father's service to the State in 1948 also gives us confidence as to your belief in Israel as a Jewish homeland. Am I correct so far?"

"Yes."

"Good. I want you to answer me honestly the question that I am about to ask you. If your answer is no, our meeting today is finished, we shall drive you to the airport to meet up with your father to fly back home, and that will be the end of it. There is no shame and no repercussions should your answer be a no.

"Others have been in the same position as you currently are and have given a negative response to my question, and are today walking the streets of Tel Aviv, Paris, London, and New York without fear or embarrassment."

Alexei looked Daniel straight in the eye, trying to guess what Daniel's answer would be. He was not sure what his own answer would be were the roles reversed.

He had asked the same question from many potential candidates over the years of his service in the Institute, and in most cases his experience had taught him to divine the answer he could expect from each. Not this time. There was no outward sign on Daniel's face or in his body language as he took a sip of his coffee. Other than the sound of their breathing and the quiet whirr of an overhead fan, the room was silent.

"Would you be prepared to risk your life to perform a highly dangerous mission to assist the State of Israel? There will be no public recognition of your service, and if your mission fails, you will be on your own."

Daniel gave no indication that he heard or comprehended anything Alexei had said. They could have heard the proverbial pin drop. Myriad thoughts raced through his brain. He wished he could be given time to contemplate the potential consequences of a "yes" beyond the possible dire outcome painted by the stocky, white-haired Russian Jew in front of him. He looked at Naomi, who was leaning against the wall, a glass of orange juice in her hand. Her face was blank, her eyes averting his, showing no emotion. He realized he was on his own and would have to live with whatever decision he made.

Not only was his decision being influenced by his loyalty to Israel as a Jew and his affinity for the underdog, but also by his knowledge and understanding of what his father had risked in 1948 by coming to serve in the fledgling Jewish army. He didn't want to let his father down by refusal.

Finally, looking straight back into Alexei's pale blue eyes, he responded, "Count me in."

"Well, then, let's get down to business." Alexei went and opened the door and yelled out, "Is Yoel here yet?"

"Coming," came the answer with a French accent from the hallway outside. In walked a youngish-looking, slender, dark-haired man of medium build, dressed in light-coloured slacks and a brightly patterned sport shirt. He approached Daniel with an outstretched hand

"*Bonjour, monsieur. Je m'appelle Yoel, et vous?*"

"*Je m'appelle Daniel Singer.*"

"*Énchanté de faire ta connaissance, Daniel.*"

"*Pareil pour moi,*" he responded in the perfect Parisian French he had learned at CUNY.

The man turned to Alexei. "This won't work. He talks like a Frenchman, not a Québécois. The Mukhabarat (Egyptian secret police) would pick up on it in a minute."

"Daniel, this is Yoel Cohen," Alexei said, "formerly known as Yves Cormier, from Trois-Rivières in Quebec, Canada. He married a lovely young Israeli girl five years ago, converted to Judaism, and settled down in Herzliya. He has been with the Institute's French section for three years."

Daniel nodded, wondering what all this would have to do with the mission he was being asked to undertake.

"Yoel, how long will it take you to break him of his pretty Parisian accent and adopt a Québécois one?"

"Give me two weeks and he'll be calling a Habs (Montreal Canadiens) hockey game from the Forum."

"You've got a week."

"Daniel, you'll be living at Yoel's home for the next week. You'll converse in nothing but Quebec-accented French. You'll dream it, eat it, shit it, and at the end of the week nobody will be able to tell that you weren't born and raised somewhere in Quebec. Your life may depend on it!"

Daniel wondered why he would have to adopt a French-Canadian accent for his mission and was just about to ask when there was a knock on the door.

In walked a distinguished-looking, tall, broad-chested, well-tanned, balding man, in a light-blue business suit, dark blue and burgundy-striped tie, wearing sunglasses. He and Alexei hugged each other and planted a kiss on both cheeks after the European fashion.

"Naomi, gentlemen, let me introduce you to my good friend and former associate, Mr. Wolfgang Lotz. Israel owes him a great debt of gratitude for his brave service to our country as a Mossad undercover operative in Cairo before the '67 war."

He then launched into a short history outlining Wolfgang Lotz's incredible background as a *bon vivant* and Mossad agent who in later life came to be known as the "champagne spy."

"My friend Wolfgang here was born in Germany and fled with his mother to British-ruled Palestine after Adolf Hitler's rise to power in 1933. He served with the British army during World War II and later with the Israeli Army. We recruited him to infiltrate groups of former Nazi scientists working in Egypt, where he posed as an ex-Nazi horse trainer and playboy. Wolfgang operated in Egypt from 1961 until 1965, when he was arrested and uncovered secrets that later aided our victory in the 1967 Six-Day War.

"The Egyptians imprisoned him until 1968, when we exchanged him for one thousand Egyptian POWs. I know that he's way too modest to blow his own horn, but let me say that without the critical information he gleaned at great personal risk about their air defences, our casualties in the war would have been significantly higher, especially amongst our pilots in the first wave of the attack."

Everyone around the room nodded their acknowledgement and appreciation of Lotz's actions.

"Now, Daniel, even though we're expecting one more guest, let's get started with explaining why we're gathered here today and why you are a key participant. Does anyone need to use the washroom before we start?"

Naomi excused herself and slipped out the door.

"Naomi, by the way, could you get them to order in a lunch for us?" Alexei asked Naomi.

While she was out of the room, Alexei turned on a slide projector and loaded a cartridge of slides. Yoel turned off the light in the room as the first picture appeared on the screen. It was of a dark-haired, middle-aged man with closely spaced, piercing dark eyes, wearing a black Gestapo uniform.

"Gentlemen, the picture in front of you is of Gestapo General Heinrich Müller, who was head of the Gestapo during World War Two and Adolf Eichmann's immediate superior, responsible for implementing the 'Final Solution' of the 'Jewish Question.' He was born in Munich on April 28, 1900, of Catholic parents. As head of the Gestapo, in the RSHA from 1939 to 1945, Müller was more directly involved in the Final Solution of the Jewish Question than even his superiors, Heydrich, Himmler, and Kaltenbrunner.

"Müller signed the circulating order requiring the immediate delivery to Auschwitz by 31 January 1943 of 45,000 Jews for extermination, and countless other documents of a similar nature, which reveal his zeal in carrying out orders. In the summer of 1943, he was sent to Rome to pressure the Italians, who were proving somewhat apathetic in arresting Jews. Until the end of the war, Heinrich Müller continued his remorseless prodding of subordinates to greater efforts in sending Jews to Auschwitz.

"In his hands, mass murder became an automatic administrative procedure. Müller exhibited a similar streak in his treatment of Russian prisoners of war and gave the order to shoot British officers who had escaped from detention at Sagan, near Breslau, at the end of March 1944."

The door opened, letting in a ray of light as Naomi re-entered the room, who went over to Alexei and whispered in his ear.

"Our last guest has arrived," he announced, "and will be joining us momentarily. Let us take a few minutes' break until he makes his way up here."

It was just past noon when a short, slim, balding man with grey around the temples and a salt-and-pepper pencil moustache entered, impeccably dressed in a grey suit and black tie. He and Alexei shook hands as he was introduced.

"Everyone, this is Mr. Simon Wiesenthal, head of the Jewish Documentation Centre in Vienna, which he founded, and which was in great measure responsible for the apprehension and bringing to justice of Adolf Eichmann. I am sure that his story and reputation are familiar to all of you. He has kindly agreed to fly here on short notice to attend this meeting, as it involves two individuals that his office has a great interest in tracking down."

Wiesenthal took a chair beside Daniel, and the two shook hands.

"Alexei, please carry on," Wiesenthal said.

The Russian continued. "Müller's whereabouts in May of 1945 are shrouded in mystery—he was last seen in the Führerbunker on April 28, 1945, after which he disappeared. Though his burial was recorded on May 17, 1945, when the body was later exhumed, it could not be identified. There were persistent rumours that he had defected to the East—for he had established contact with Soviet agents before the end of the war, either to Moscow, Albania, or East Germany. Müller was last seen in the bunker on April 29, 1945, the day before Hitler's suicide.

"From that day onwards, no trace of him has ever been found. He is the most senior member of the Nazi regime about whose fate nothing is known. This has naturally given rise to decades of speculation. There are three possible explanations for his disappearance.

"One is that Müller was killed, or killed himself, during the chaos of the fall of Berlin, and that his body was never found. This is what happened to Bormann, who was unaccounted for until his remains were found last year, and who is now known to have killed himself or been killed soon after leaving the bunker.

"Second is that Müller escaped from Berlin and made his way to a safe location, possibly in South America, as did Eichmann and many others, where he lived the rest of his life undetected."

Then Wiesenthal stood up and spoke in heavily German-accented English. "We at the Documentation Centre have a different theory. Based on reports gathered from German tourists and business travellers, and Egyptian POWs taken prisoner by the Israeli Army in 1967, we have reason to believe that Müller is in Cairo, in a high position with the Mukhabarat, in charge of training their agents and keeping a close eye on former Nazi scientists working for Egypt's guided missile program. And ... "

Another knock came on the door, interrupting Wiesenthal, as two secretaries entered with trays of bagels, cheeses, soft drinks, and fresh fruits.

"Why don't we continue while we eat our lunch, as Daniel will have to leave here by six to say goodbye to his father at Ben Gurion tonight," Alexei said as he struggled to insert another cartridge into the projector.

Wiesenthal shook his head and sat back down beside Daniel, whispering, "A man can't even finish a sentence without being cut off."

Daniel smiled. The man reminded him of Grandfather Bernard. How he wished the old man could have joined him and his father on this memorable journey. He wondered what sage advice his grandfather would give him at this time.

Once Alexei finished fiddling with the contraption, he continued. "Here is another member of the Nazi hierarchy that didn't show up in Nuremberg in '46, who we believe is hiding out in Cairo and working closely with Egyptian intelligence services alongside Müller."

A faded picture of a handsome, Nordic-looking, young, blue-eyed, blonde-haired officer in an SS uniform appeared on the screen along with a set of SS dog tags. Daniel looked at the picture, which was damaged by what appeared to be fire on one side and got an uneasy feeling of recognition. Although he knew he'd never set eyes on the man before, something about the face staring out from the screen looked familiar.

"His name is Colonel Bruno Schmidt. This picture is the only one we have of him. It's from his identity card from 1935, when he joined the SS. It was found in a burnt-out Mercedes staff car along with his dog tags at the end of the war. The existence of both sides of the ID discs tells us that he wasn't killed in combat. Also, in the wreck of the car was the body of a young Dutch woman. The car had been driven by Senior Sergeant Helmut Eckler, Schmidt's friend and driver. There was no trace of Schmidt.

"Klaus Bruno Schmidt Jr. was born in Hamburg in 1901. His father was a tool-and- die maker and an ardent Communist who was beaten to death by a gang of Brownshirts in 1933, I believe.

"The younger Schmidt graduated from law school in Munich in 1924, two years after Rudolf Hess, Hitler's deputy, and immediately gravitated into Hitler's inner circle after attending the 'Munich Conspirators' Trial.' He was a frequent visitor to Hitler during the latter's incarceration at Landsberg prison. From reports from that time, he seemed to have been an ambitious opportunist and not necessarily a 'true believer' in Nazi ideology, although he parroted the Party line.

"He became a very successful lawyer in Munich in the late twenties and early thirties, defending many of the SA hooligans in court, after joining an influential Nazi-affiliated law firm sponsored by Hans Frank, Hitler's personal lawyer.

"Schmidt was in large measure responsible for the drafting of the majority of the Nazi-inspired German racial laws of those years. He was also quite a bit of a womanizer, having taken up with a certain Stefania Hartmann, eighteen years his senior, the wife of Rolf Hartmann, an SA higher-up, and the sister of Arthur Nebe, chief of the Reich Main Security Office. Rumour has it that he personally shot Rolf Hartmann and his secretary cum mistress, Ditta Burg, in their bed during the "Night of the Long Knives" in 1934 and then married Frau Hartmann later that same year. It was his new brother-in-law, Arthur Nebe, who convinced him, at the urging of Reinhard Heydrich, to join the SS in 1935."

Daniel spoke up at that point. "Alexei, what was the 'Night of the Long Knives'? It's not an expression that I've heard before."

Wiesenthal stood to answer Daniel's question, as he was the one in the room most familiar with that seminal event in Nazi politics that took place in the summer of 1934.

CHAPTER 26

JUNE 30 — JULY 2, 1934,

BAD WIESSEE, GERMANY—NIGHT OF THE LONG KNIVES

The evening of June 29, 1934, Heinrich Himmler, Reinhard Heydrich, Arthur Nebe, Ernst Kaltenbrunner, Heinrich Müller, and Bruno Schmidt sat around a table inside a tent, in a farmer's field just south of Munich. A map was spread out on the table, with a battery-powered lantern weighing it down. There were a large number of military vehicles assembled outside, their engines running, their lights shielded by black tape except for a narrow slit. The crews, all seasoned SS recruits, lounged beside their transports, smoking and chatting quietly. Some had fallen asleep, either lying on the ground or propped up against their vehicles.

Himmler spoke first. "We have the Führer's agreement to move ahead with Operation Hummingbird as planned. He had telegraphed Röhm this afternoon that he would be coming down to Bad Wiessee to meet with him on a very urgent matter of great national interest. Since the Führer likes to sleep in, the meeting is set for noon tomorrow. Now, let's go over the operational plan."

He stood up and pointed to a red X on the map. "This is Bad Wiessee on the southern shore of the Tegernsee (Lake Tegern). It's about sixty kilometres south of Munich, so about forty-five minutes by car from here. We plan to arrive there at around four thirty this morning.

"I am certain that Ernst and his homosexual 'brothers' will have been preoccupied with their orgiastic bacchanalia late into the night with the wine and beer flowing freely and should be sound asleep in their beds by the time we get there. My information is that there are about sixty of them in twenty little cottages spread around the lake.

"The yellow dots show the location of the cottages. Röhm and his lover, Edmund Heines, are in the larger cottage marked with a black dot. My inside man tells me that Hartmann is also there with his chubby little whore, Ditta Burg, in the building closest to the water. There are around another twenty Brownshirts that count for something in the organization scattered around the country who couldn't attend this little party. So, Arthur's agents will be going door to door and dealing with them at the same time as we conduct our operation.

"We have a hundred and eighty of the most-trusted, long-serving members of the SS with us. They have been split into nine-man units with orders not to hesitate to shoot to kill at any sign of resistance to arrest. The operation should be wound up by noon, when the Führer is expected to arrive to meet face to face with Röhm to read him the charges against him. Of the six of us, Reinhard, Ernst, and I, along with one nine-man unit, will go deal with Röhm and Heines, while the three of you, along with your unit, will go and arrest Hartmann. It's now one thirty in the morning. We'll leave in two-and-a-half hours."

He then opened a bottle of Louis XIII Remy Martin cognac and remarked, "Only the best for my friends. Personally liberated from a bar on the Champs-Élysées in 1940 when we entered Paris."

He then poured each of them a small glass and raised his. "Gentlemen, to the Führer and success." Himmler downed the strong alcohol in one swallow. The rest of the group followed suit, then returned to their vehicles to catch a few hours of sleep before setting out on their clandestine mission.

At four a.m., the column of twenty-five vehicles, led by two BMW military motorbikes painted in green and khaki camouflage, with men in their sidecars clutching MP-40 submachine guns, roared out of the farmer's field and headed for the Autobahn. In the black of night, with clouds hiding a crescent moon, the convoy rumbled south in the direction of the Tegern See, without encountering any other traffic at that early morning hour.

In the middle of the column, Müller and Nebe sat in the rear of the black Mercedes, with Schmidt sitting in the passenger seat beside his usual driver and close friend, Helmut. They drove in silence, with the men in the back puffing on their cigarettes, blowing the smoke out the open windows. Bruno took the Walther P38 9 mm semi-automatic pistol from his trench coat's pocket and looked at it, turning it one way and then the other.

"I hope you have the safety on." Helmut smiled at him.

Bruno was not used to having a deadly weapon in his hands. He fought his battles with words and statutes in courts of law. Nebe had handed it to him along with an extra magazine before they left the tent earlier. He was hoping he wouldn't have to use it that day.

He closed his eyes and thought of Steffi, fast asleep in Bruno's bed, having spent the previous evening at dinner with him. With Rolf in Bad Wiesee, they felt comfortable being together that night, until the telephone call from Heydrich, informing him that Operation Hummingbird was on and asking to meet him at Gestapo HQ right away. He apologized to Steffi, telling her he needed to go on urgent business without providing her with any details. They kissed passionately as he bade his farewell, his hands roaming over her negligee-clad body as they stood in the doorway.

"Hurry back, darling, or I'll have to call in a substitute," she teased him, rubbing the front of his trousers.

He was shaken out of his daydream by the hard braking of the car and Helmut's loud swearing. "Fucking deer. Sorry, Bruno, but this deer came out of nowhere, and I nearly hit it."

Müller and Nebe also bolted upright in the back seat, wondering what had happened. The rest of the drive was uneventful. As they stopped outside the resort town of Bad Wiesee, a low mist covered the surface of the lake and the cottages nearest the water. It was going to be a cloudy day. A thin sliver of light showed in the east. The troops dismounted and quietly crept up to their individual targets with weapons at the ready.

Then the eerie quiet was torn asunder by the barking of a dog, quickly joined by others. Suddenly, all hell had broken loose. The sounds of rifle butts smashing down doors echoed off the mountain on the opposite side of the Tegern See. A shot rang out, followed by the staccato of a submachine gun. The gunfight reverberated from the hills surrounding the lake. It seemed that although the SA troopers were surprised by their attackers, some had time to draw their own weapons and were firing back. They had no intention of surrendering or being taken prisoner by the troops wearing camouflage outfits without any identifying insignia. For all they knew, those who had set upon them might be Communist cadres taking revenge for years of terror at the hands of the Brownshirts.

In the darkness, some tried to flee, running half-dressed in the direction of the lake, only to be mowed down by SS sharpshooters. Muzzle flashes lit the night sky. There was total pandemonium, with yelling, screaming, and swearing waking the ordinary burghers of the town.

Outside the door of the large, two-storey cottage occupied by Röhm and his lover Heines, Heydrich, Kaltenbrunner, and Himmler looked at each other in panic. Operation Hummingbird had quickly gone off the rails!

Himmler knocked on the door, but as it wasn't closed properly the night before, it swung open, and they rushed up the stairs with guns at the ready, followed by the nine SS troops assigned to accompany them.

Röhm came out of the bedroom with a bedsheet wrapped around him and a Walther automatic in his hand, with Heines cowering behind him, naked as the day he was born.

"Heinrich, what the fuck is the meaning of this?" Röhm bellowed, levelling his gun at Himmler's chest.

Himmler froze halfway up the stairs, not quite knowing what would happen next, until one of the SS men below him took aim and fired a shot, hitting Röhm in the shoulder and dropping him to the floor. He screamed in pain as Heines fainted and fell naked on top of him.

At the building closest to the water, when Bruno's group heard the firing, they didn't hesitate with any niceties but broke down the door and rushed inside, heading straight for the bedroom. They pushed the door open to find Rolf Hartmann sitting up in the bed, trying to find the light switch for the bedside lamp in the dark, and Ditta Burg attempting to pull up the blanket to cover her generous bosom.

"What's going on?" Hartmann stammered at the silhouettes of figures he couldn't recognize due to the bright lights being shined in his eyes and the absence of his spectacles on his head. He was attempting to retrieve his eyeglasses from his jacket pocket hanging on the bedpost at the corner of the headboard when Müller yelled, "He's going for his gun!"

Hearing the yell, Bruno pulled the P-38 from his coat pocket and fired a shot from about ten feet away, hitting Ditta in the throat and killing her instantly.

"You idiots, I am looking for my glasses," Hartmann screamed as Ditta's body slumped over, soaking the covers with blood.

Nebe put his arm around a shaking Bruno's shoulder and escorted him outside. "Look, it was an accident. We all thought he was pulling a gun on us."

Bruno was speechless and had trouble breathing. He handed the gun to Nebe. Sick to his stomach, Bruno stumbled to the side of the building and vomited.

Inside, Müller was instructing the SS troopers to wrap Ditta's body in a blanket and take it outside while he watched Hartmann put on his uniform.

"So this is a coup against the Führer, you little shit?" Hartmann asked Müller contemptuously as he pulled on his shirt and pants. "Where is Ernst? He'll set you straight!"

"Sorry, my fat friend, but Ernst is now a nobody, an *Unmensch*. You'll see soon enough. Now shut up and get dressed before I shoot you too, like your little whore."

It was 6:30 a.m., and a grey dawn was breaking. Some twenty bodies in various states of undress were scattered on the dew-covered grass around the cottages. The sound of moaning from the wounded outside and inside some of the buildings, the incessant barking of dogs, and the occasional gunshot broke the early morning silence.

Three women, dressed only in their undergarments, were sobbing quietly as they huddled together on the porch of one of the cottages, guarded by two SS men. The soldiers had set up their vehicles in such a way as to prevent anyone from the village approaching the scene of the massacre. Slowly, groups of dishevelled men, some wearing the brown SA uniform, others pyjamas or dressing gowns, started to emerge from the cottages, prodded along at gunpoint by SS troopers.

Some of them had been wounded in the nighttime melee and had to be supported by their comrades. They were ordered by Heydrich to sit down on the wet grass in a semicircle and to be quiet. Other Brownshirts were bringing out the bodies of those killed in the fight and laying them down beside one of the trucks.

Müller and Eckler dragged a loudly protesting Hartmann, followed by Nebe and Bruno, and dumped him in the circle with his comrades. At the same time, Kaltenbrunner and an SS NCO escorted Heines and Röhm, with a bandaged shoulder, and forced them to sit down. A couple of the SS troopers were talking in whispers as they checked to see how many of their own number had become casualties.

Everyone seemed to be milling around aimlessly, not quite sure what would happen next. A motorcycle dispatch rider, wearing a heavy black-leather trench coat, arrived and startled everyone when he shut the engine of his BMW off and it backfired with a loud noise and puff of blue-grey smoke. After dismounting, he went to find Himmler. Upon approaching him, the rider came to stiff attention and gave the

Reichsführer the Nazi salute. "Herr Reichsführer, I have an urgent message from the Führer himself"

He handed over a brown envelope, which Himmler tore open, quickly reading its contents. He then dismissed the man, telling him to return to Berlin forthwith, and inform the Führer that he understood and would follow Hitler's orders. Himmler then slowly walked over to where the rest of the group were standing and quietly chatting, with Müller, Kaltenbrunner, and Heydrich chain smoking.

He gathered them around himself and said, "A message just arrived from the Führer. He will not be coming down to Bad Wiesee. He asks us to pack the prisoners up and take them to Gestapo HQ, where he, Göring, Goebbels, and Sepp Dietrich would meet us."

He then ordered the SS guards to get all the prisoners into the trucks, except for Röhm, Heines, and Hartmann. The dead, now wrapped in bed sheets or blankets, were piled into one of the trucks, with the bulk of the ragged and tired prisoners herded into others, and the convoy started down the Autobahn in the direction of Berlin.

The early morning sun began to rise above the hills and dissipated the low-lying mist over the Tegern See as two black Mercedes limousines roared at high speed ahead of the rest of the vehicles. In one were Himmler and Heydrich with Röhm and Heines, and in the other Bruno Schmidt and Nebe, along with Hartmann and his deputy, Adolf Pruhm. Pruhm's face was covered in blood, and he had trouble breathing, having had his nose broken when he had been bludgeoned in the face with a rifle butt by one of the SS during the raid.

Hartmann wouldn't stop loudly berating Nebe and Bruno. "Arthur, you! My fucking brother-in-law, you traitor to the Führer and our cause. Wait until I get in front of him! And you, you little upstart, you ass-kissing Lothario—you don't think I know that you've been carrying on with my wife, that old wench! You enjoy used goods, eh? Well, we will see what the Führer does with you!"

Nebe and Schmidt sat impassively across from them, Nebe cradling his pistol in his lap, its barrel aimed directly at Hartmann's crotch.

"I hope we don't hit a bump and this thing goes off and amputates poor Rolf's manhood. Ditta's dead, so he won't have any more use for it, in any case." Nebe laughed.

The limousines continued at high speed through the beautiful countryside, the motion of the car and the lack of sleep causing Bruno to drift in an out of an uneasy slumber. Just after noon, they arrived at the imposing nineteenth-century building designed by famed architect Martin Gropius at 8 Prinz-Albrecht-Strasse, formerly the School and Museum of Decorative Arts and, since early 1933, the headquarters of the Gestapo and the Reich Main Security Office.

The entrance was surrounded by black-uniformed and heavily armed SS and Gestapo troops. The two limousines screeched to a halt, and the four prisoners were hustled inside. Once in the building, they were handed over to a squad of burly men in civilian clothes and hustled downstairs into the basement that housed the prisoners' cells.

A few minutes later, Adolf Hitler's limousine pulled up. Sepp Dietrich, commander of the *Leibstandarte SS Adolf Hitler,* the Führer's personal bodyguard, opened the door for Hitler, who got out, followed by Goebbels and Göring, brandishing his field marshal's baton. The SS and Gestapo troopers assembled on the front steps cleared to either side at the barked orders of the major in charge, gave the Nazi salute, and shouted "Sieg Heil" as the Führer, dressed in a black-leather trench coat, and his entourage quickly ascended the stairs up the middle. Inside, they were greeted by Himmler and Heydrich. Not aware of what had transpired at Bad Wiesee, Hitler asked Himmler, "So, how did things go?"

"Not as expected; they put up a fight. There are casualties on both sides."

Hitler raised his eyebrow. "And Röhm?"

"He's wounded, but all right. He was shot in the shoulder."

"Let's go see him!"

In the basement, a guard opened the heavy metal door to Röhm's cell, as Hitler and Himmler walked in.

"Adolf, finally!" Röhm rose from the wooden stool, the only furnishing in the windowless, grey-painted cell with damp walls and a single lightbulb in the ceiling. The tight space reeked of urine and sweat. He approached Hitler, looking to embrace his Führer with his uninjured arm, but Hitler recoiled and took a step back, bumping Himmler against the wall.

Himmler took a folded piece of paper and handed it to Hitler.

"Sit down, Ernst," Hitler ordered Röhm.

"I prefer to stand, my friend. What in God's name is going on? Some of my men have been killed. What's the meaning of this?" The words continued to pour forth from Röhm's lips without any response from either Hitler or Himmler. Finally, when Röhm stopped to take a breath, Hitler quickly began to read aloud from the piece of paper.

"Ernst Röhm, you have been found guilty of conspiring with others of the SA to overthrow the legitimately elected government of the German Reich by planning an armed *putsch*, conspiring with a foreign power, and the cold-blooded murder of the elected head of state and his cabinet."

"*Mein Führer*—" It was the first time in years that Röhm had used that term in private with Hitler, instead of the familiar Adolf. "You must not listen to the lies spread by those around you." He gave a fierce and threatening look in the direction of Himmler, who was wiping his brow with a handkerchief and looking in the opposite direction.

"I have been your loyal servant, comrade in arms, friend, and confidant since our movement was born fifteen years ago. Many of my friends gave their lives in the street battles against the Reds so that you could assume the mantle of power. I cannot believe that you would choose to believe the scum that surrounds you over my honour, loyalty, and dedication to you and the cause!"

Hitler looked up from the paper and quietly whispered, "Ernst, you will know what you have to do for your Führer and country." And with that, he turned around and walked out the cell door, into the long, dimly lit corridor, while Himmler stayed behind. Ernst tried to follow Hitler out, screaming at him, but his path was blocked by a guard.

"Look, Ernst, there is no use," Himmler said to Röhm, pulling a pistol from its holster on his belt. He walked over to the chair and put the gun on the seat, and then calmly walked out the door as well, followed by Röhm's bellowing.

"You chicken farmer piece of shit. You're not getting rid of me this easy, you coward!" Röhm's shouts echoed down the corridor where other prisoners in neighbouring cells were being harshly dealt with.

In the adjoining cell, Bruno and Nebe were listening to Hartmann's tirade, much like that of Röhm. Bruno pulled the legal declaration signed by two friendly judges listing the accusations against Hartmann from his jacket pocket, and as the legal representative of the government, read Hartmann the charges against him.

On hearing them, Hartmann started yelling at the top of his lungs, loudly proclaiming his innocence and lack of knowledge about anything connected to a *putsch* against his beloved Führer.

Nebe ordered his brother-in-law to shut up and sit down.

After Bruno finished reading, Hartmann's attitude suddenly changed. He dropped to his knees and, clutching at Nebe's pants legs, started crying and pleading, "Arthur, please, you must believe me. I have never gone against the Führer. I've been loyal all these years. You must believe me and intercede with him. You can have everything I own, the apartment, the art, the money. Everything, but please don't do this!"

Bruno hung back, leaning against the damp wall in a dark corner of the cell, watching the scene unfold between his mistress's husband and her brother.

Nebe stepped on Hartmann's fingers eliciting a loud scream, then turned around and gave his Walther P-38 to Bruno. "You want his wife and his money? You deal with him." He walked out and up the steps.

Upstairs in the high-ceilinged, ornate lobby, Hitler was standing in a corner, trying to have a quiet conversation with his lieutenants. The rest of the vehicles had arrived, and the SA men were being marched inside by their guards, led by Kaltenbrunner. It was a chaotic scene, with yelling and screaming all around.

"How's Schmidt handling all this? After all, he's a lawyer and a civilian, he isn't used to getting his hands dirty," Heydrich loudly asked Nebe.

"We will see in a few minutes," he said with a conspiratorial smile and a knowing wink.

"Sepp, you better go down and see whether Röhm has seen the light yet, or if we have to trip the switch for him," Himmler, his close-set dark eyes squinting through thick glasses, instructed General Dietrich.

Sepp Dietrich was a bull of a man, broad-shouldered with a boxer's broken nose and rugged facial features. Before meeting up with Hitler's circle, he had migrated from one job to another, including waiter, policeman, foreman, farm labourer, petrol station attendant, and customs officer, until he became Hitler's chauffeur and bodyguard. In 1928, he joined the nascent SS and quickly rose in the ranks. On January 5, 1930, he was elected to the Reichstag as a delegate for Lower Bavaria.

Röhm jumped to his feet when Dietrich entered his cell. The two of them had been comrades in arms, fighting street battles with the Communists in the 1920s and early 30s as members of the pre-Nazi Freikorps.

"Sepp, has the world gone crazy? As a military man, you understand that I would never break my vow of loyalty to our Führer. We've known each other for a long time. Please speak to him."

"Ernst, you and your men went too far. You overstepped your boundaries with your wild shenanigans, head-bashing, and homosexual orgies. That threatened the Führer's position with the people that count in this country today. Now you have to bear the consequences."

He hugged Röhm as tears started to run down the man's scarred, rugged face, marked by the wounds he'd suffered in the Great War. Dietrich picked up the pistol from the chair, cocked it, and handed it to Röhm, then turned to walk out. "You know what you must do for your Führer and Germany."

"Fuck you. I am not going to make it easy for you. You want me dead, you kill me!" And with that, he threw the gun at Dietrich's back. Dietrich spun around, pulling his service automatic from its holster as he did, squeezed the trigger, and emptied the nine-round magazine into a slumping Röhm. The sounds of the shots reverberated like thunder throughout the basement and stopped all conversation upstairs.

The loud gunfire next door gave Bruno the courage he needed to finish off Hartmann, who was still kneeling and shaking like a leaf in front of him. He pointed the gun down at the top of Hartmann's balding skull and pulled the trigger. *Click.* He pulled it again. *Click.*

The two men looked incredulously at each other, speechless. As Hartmann started to rise to his feet, Bruno hit him square in the mouth with the butt of the P38, causing Hartmann to fall backward, spitting out blood and teeth. Bruno rushed headlong out of the cell, Hartmann's groans and screams following him. He swore as he slipped in the pool of blood that had started to seep under the door of Röhm's cell.

He brushed past two sturdy guards and bounded up the stairs into the lobby, not concealing his anger at having been made a fool of. He charged at Nebe, grabbing him by his lapels, breaking off one of the silver death's head insignia on his uniform.

"You bastard! You gave me a gun with an empty magazine!" he yelled at his mentor. The room had become totally silent, with all eyes turned to the two men.

Bruno towered over the much shorter man as Nebe broke out laughing. "I wanted to see if you could actually kill a man with intention," Nebe said, "rather than accidentally, but I didn't want your pure barrister's conscience to keep you awake at night, so I emptied the magazine."

Heydrich separated the two men and calmly said, "Bruno, you passed the test, so I want you to join the SS as a full Standartenführer (major). Will you accept?"

Without waiting for an answer, Heydrich instructed Dietrich, "Sepp, please go back down and finish this ugly business with Herr Hartmann and then join us at the Golden Stag for some much-needed libations."

He put his arm around Bruno's shoulders as the group walked out of SS and Gestapo HQ and stopped at the curb to get into the waiting limousines. The cars were just pulling up when two shots were heard from the basement of the building.

Hitler, being a teetotaller, returned to his office at the Reich Chancellery with Goebbels, while the rest went to celebrate the day's events at the Golden Stag *bierstube*. So ended Operation Hummingbird, which became known in popular German culture as "The Night of the Long Knives." Heines, Pruhm, and some of the other survivors of the massacre at Bad Wiesee and the ad hoc executions in the basement of 8 Prinz-Albrecht-Strasse that July in 1934, were sent to Dachau concentration camp outside Munich, where all of them perished before the end of the war at the hands of the infamous torturer Theodor Eicke.

In September 1934, Bruno Schmidt retired from the legal profession and the law firm he had practiced at for ten years, and with the personal sponsorship of Reinhard Heydrich, joined the SS. On Christmas Eve, he and the widow Steffi Hartmann were married at Göring's country house in Bad Reichenhall, with Joseph and Magda Goebbels as best man and maid of honour. They continued to live in the Hartmanns' opulent Munich apartment, decorated with paintings and statues looted by Rolf Hartmann's SA goons from the homes of wealthy Jews. Through 1935 and 36, he attended the SS Officer School at Bad Tölz, just south of Munich.

CHAPTER 27

"And that, my friends, is what 'The Night of the Long Knives' and Bruno Schmidt's so-called 'graduation' into the SS, the most evil military unit in world history, is all about," Wiesenthal said, concluding his response to Daniel's question.

Alexei then took over once again, and went on, "But that is not the end of Colonel Bruno Schmidt's career. He's got quite a rap sheet that stretches from 1924 to the end of the war in May 1945. We are led to believe that he continues in the service of the Egyptian Mukhabarat El-Amm.

"There is not much information available on his activities in the mid-1930s, after the elimination of the SA. The next time we hear of him is in March 1938, when he accompanies Ernst Kaltenbrunner, head of the Gestapo, to Vienna during the *Ancshluss*, or German annexation of Austria. We don't have any information about what duties he performed in Vienna but believe that he participated in the violent overthrow of the legally elected government of Chancellor von Schussnigg.

"When we next pick up the thread regarding something of significance about him, is from a report by Admiral Wilhelm Canaris, head of the Abwehr, the German Army's intelligence service, prepared for the Führer. Dated the twenty-ninth of June 1938, it talks about Schmidt and another SS colonel, named Adolf Eichmann, boarding a Romanian steamship in the Port of Constanta at the end of September 1937. Here's a translated excerpt from that confidential report detailing their trip."

Alexei handed out a photocopy of the report to everyone.

Abwehr

Obersturmbannführer (Lieutenant Colonel) Adolf Eichmann and Sturmbannführer (Major) Bruno Schmidt arrived in the port of Haifa on October 2, 1937. The British restricted their stay to 48 hours, despite their tourist visas. Two days later, their Romanian steamship docked in Alexandria, Egypt. They took the train to Cairo where they failed to obtain a visa for Palestine. The British obviously did not trust the two men from Berlin. Eichmann and Schmidt initially intended to meet Grand Mufti Al-Husseini, but met one of the Mufti's representatives instead. He was a journalist from Jerusalem who travelled to Cairo. Fearing arrest by the British, the Mufti would soon flee to Lebanon. Eichmann and Schmidt, however, reported in early November 1937 that the Mufti had fled to Syria.

"It would not be the last time that Schmidt and Eichmann would meet during the war. They were together again in 1944 in Budapest, Hungary, as we will learn. The apparent purpose of this assignment in Palestine was either to research the reaction of Arab leaders to the Nazis' concept of exiling the Jews of Germany to Palestine, or the opposite; in fact, to assure them that this would not happen.

"In any case, it was during this trip that Schmidt established some contacts within the Egyptian intelligence services that would later stand him in good stead. Continuing in that vein, here's a similar excerpt from another report in the Abwehr's files on Schmidt, dated November 30, 1941, reflecting on his service to the Third Reich on behalf of the Arabs."

This time, Alexei read from a thick dossier he was holding.

Abwehr

The Mufti of Jerusalem, Mohammed Amin al-Husseini, escaped to Persia (together with Rashid Ali), where he was granted legation asylum, first by our ally Japan, and then by our Italian friends. On 8 October, after the occupation of Persia by the British, and after the new Persian government of Shah Mohammad Reza Pahlavi severed diplomatic relations with us and Italy, al-Husseini was taken under Italian protection. On the direct orders of the Fuhrer, SS Colonel Bruno Schmidt, based on his previous contact with the Mufti, was assigned to immediately travel to Persia and assist Servizio Informazioni Militare (Italian military intelligence) to spirit al-Husseini through Turkey, to Rome. Colonel Schmidt and al-Husseini arrived in Rome on 10 October 1941. There, he outlined his proposals before Alberto Ponce de Leon. On condition that we the Italians and Japanese "recognise in principle the unity, independence, and sovereignty, of an Arab state, including Iraq, Syria, Palestine, and Transjordan," he offered support in the war against Britain and stated his willingness to discuss the issues of "the Holy Places, Lebanon, the Suez Canal, and Aqaba."

The Italian foreign ministry approved al-Husseini's proposal, recommended giving him a grant of one million lire, and referred him to Il Duce Benito Mussolini, who met al-Husseini in the company of Schmidt on 27 October. According to al-Husseini's account, as conveyed by Schmidt, it was an amicable meeting in which Mussolini expressed his hostility to the Jews and Zionism. Encouraged by his meeting with the Italian leader, al-Husseini prepared a draft declaration, affirming our and our Italian ally's support for the Arabs on 3 November. In three days, the declaration, slightly amended by the Italian foreign ministry, received the formal approval of Mussolini and was forwarded to our embassy in Rome.

On 6 November, al-Husseini, once again accompanied by Schmidt, arrived in Berlin, where he discussed the text of his declaration with Ernst von Weizsäcker and other officials. In the final draft (copy attached), which differed only marginally from al-Husseini's original proposal, we along with Italy and Japan declared our readiness to approve the elimination (Beseitigung) of the Jewish National Home in Palestine. On 20 November, al-Husseini met Foreign Minister Joachim von Ribbentrop and was officially received by our Führer on November 28, 1941. It should also be noted that Major Schmidt, during his time in the Middle East travelling with the Mufti, became quite proficient in Arabic, to the extent that he could carry on conversation in that language.

Alexi went on, saying, "It was because of his impromptu participation in the Night of the Long Knives and the *Anschluss* in Austria, his rescue of the Mufti from Persia, and his quick reaction to control events on *Kristallnacht* in November 1938, that Schmidt earned the nickname 'The Führer's Fireman.' Word quickly spread throughout Berlin that 'If there was a fire, Adolf Hitler could count on Bruno Schmidt to run and put it out.' Soviet intelligence files report him near Kursk on the Eastern Front in the fall of 1943, taking a secret, personal message from Hitler to the generals commanding the German armies around Kursk.

"He played quite a strange, but key, role on *Kristallnacht* (the 'Night of Broken Glass') that seemed to demonstrate somewhat of a split personality, an enigma, if you will. He saved the lives of an elderly Jewish couple and their granddaughter, and prevented the total destruction by fire of the New Synagogue, yet had no qualms in participating in the wanton execution of a thousand men, women, and children four years later at Lidice in Czechoslovakia after the assassination of his friend and boss Reinhard Heydrich. This anomaly in his behaviour was also apparent at Mauthausen concentration camp in late 1944. We've never been too certain as to his true motivation or the depth of his anti-Jewish commitment."

CHAPTER 28

November 9, 1938, dawned grey and chilly, like most other November mornings in the German capital had that year, as Bruno Schmidt entered Reinhard Heydrich's office at 8 Prinz-Albrecht-Strasse. Berlin was abuzz that morning with the news of the assassination in Paris of a young German diplomat. In the fall of 1938, Herschel Grynszpan, a seventeen-year-old ethnically Polish Jew who had been living in France for several years, learned that the Nazis had exiled his parents to Poland from Hanover, Germany, where Herschel had been born and his family had lived for years. As retaliation, on November 7, 1938, the agitated teenager shot Ernst vom Rath, a German diplomat, in Paris. Rath died two days later from his wounds, and Hitler attended his funeral. Joseph Goebbels, the Nazi minister for public enlightenment and propaganda, immediately seized on the assassination to rile Hitler's supporters into an anti-Semitic frenzy.

Heydrich rose from behind his desk as Bruno Schmidt entered the large, high-ceilinged office, decorated with paintings of patriotic scenes from Germany's past. A large portrait of the Führer hung behind Heydrich's oversized, ornate desk, which had been carved from trees in the "Black Forest."

"Bruno, so happy to see you," he said as he warmly clasped Schmidt's outstretched hand in his own. They had long ago dispensed with the usual "Heil Hitler" commonly used by most Germans when greeting each other in this fifth year of Nazi rule.

"And how is the lovely Steffi these days?" Heydrich asked solicitously.

"She's well, thank you, working hard on raising funds for the Party. Steffi sent you this batch of homemade gingerbread cookies, remembering how much you like them."

"Ah, Steffi, always so thoughtful. But now to the important matter at hand."

The two of them sat down beside each other on the French Provincial settee by the window.

"You know that a young Polish Jew shot the first secretary at our embassy in Paris."

"Yes, it's been on the radio and in all the newspapers, and it's all you hear people on the street talking about."

"Well, he died last night, and Goebbels has been on the airwaves fanning the flames against the Jews. It could very easily get out of hand and threaten public order, and one never knows where that could lead. Rudolf Hess, Deputy Führer, called me early this morning, and on the direct orders of the Führer, requested that I get you in here immediately in order to keep events under control without letting the Jews off the hook. A sort of 'controlled boil,' he called it.

"Let the 'man in the street' vent his anger at the Jews, let them loot and destroy their property, bash in a few heads and have the police arrest a couple of thousand. But make sure it's a well-orchestrated pogrom that doesn't spill over into an uncontrollable lynch mob and spur the friends of the Jews in Paris, London, and New York to take some type of action against the Reich. The Führer has the highest confidence in you and specifically asked that you be assigned the task."

"All right. What assets do I have?" Bruno looked Heydrich straight in the eye as he asked the question.

Heydrich, averting his gaze, responded in a low voice, "Well, that's an issue now, isn't it?"

"You're damn right it is, Reinhard," said Bruno, raising his voice an octave. "Are we going to have another fuck up like we did in '34 with Röhm and his boys?"

"Look, Bruno, the regular police have been told to step back and not interfere with the rightly indignant citizenry when they mete out punishment to the Jews. We in the SS can't be seen as protecting the Jews, and yet we have to keep a lid on it. You've got twenty of my best, most experienced agents to help you."

"Twenty men in a city of four million prodded into a frenzy by Goebbels! Are you crazy?" Bruno screamed loud enough to be heard in Heydrich's office's anteroom by the secretaries working there.

"That's all I can spare, Bruno. I know you'll get the job done," Heydrich said calmly as he put his arm around Bruno's shoulder.

"So, Reinhard, what miracle do you expect me and my hastily assembled security detail to perform tonight to keep events under control?" Bruno asked Heydrich sarcastically.

"Place your men at as many strategic locations as you can and have them show the colours. That should keep the rabble rousers in check."

Heydrich then led Bruno out of his office and up the stairs to meet his twenty-man security detail.

Bruno stood before the hastily assembled group of veteran plain-clothes security men, hands on his waist, legs spread. "Well, gentlemen, we've been assigned a most important task directly by Deputy Führer Hess. All hell will be breaking loose this evening, and I expect all of you to be up to the challenge. My deputy, Scharführer Eckler here, will go through the plan and your assignments. Heil Hitler!"

With that, he turned around and left the room, slamming the door and shaking his head.

CHAPTER 29

NOVEMBER 1938,
BERLIN—SHATTERED LIVES

The struggle to maintain somewhat of a normal life at 14 Meineke Strasse had continued in the two-and-a-half years after the birth of Maximillian Weisz in 1936. Arnold was earning a living wage doing contract work for his former legal firm.

Business, too, was picking up for his father-in-law at Grossman's Menswear and Haberdashery as wages began to rise across Germany. Despite the Nazis' edict against doing business with Jews, some of Alex's previous clients started to return, recognizing the quality of fabrics and low prices being offered.

Max was the usual precocious two-and-a-half-year-old boy, keeping his parents and grandparents hopping to and fro on a daily basis. Papa Grossman would return home in the evenings, his pockets bulging with a variety of sweet treats for his only grandchild. He would sit on Max's bed and read stories to him at bedtime. Max especially enjoyed the stories of mischief of Max und Moritz and the outrageous adventures of Baron Munchausen.

Arnold, unfortunately, could only meet with his former partners and their clients in out-of-the-way locations and only after dark to avoid notice by the authorities, so he hardly ever made it home by Max's bedtime. He would come in, dead tired, and quietly go into Max's room and plant a kiss on the young boy's forehead or cheek, eliciting a low murmur and smile from the sleeping child.

Life had been harsh, but not unbearable, under the myriad anti-Jewish edicts introduced by the Nazis over the past five years. It was the beginning of November and Papa Grossman was hoping business would improve further, especially in heavier, more expensive coats, with the onset of winter. However, the news on the radio that morning had not been good. The first secretary at the German embassy in Paris had been shot by a young Polish Jew and had died the previous night. Now Goebbels was hogging the airwaves, exhorting the population of Germany to exact revenge upon their Jewish neighbours.

Hearing the news, Arnold telephoned his old partner, Ziggy Guthausen, and cancelled a meeting that was scheduled at a café in Potsdam for that evening. "My senses are telling me that it won't be safe for a Jew to be out and about for the next few days."

Alex came out of the washroom, a copy of the *Berliner Tageblatt*, the last remaining liberal German newspaper, in his hand.

Esther looked at him. "So, Mister Haberdasher, are you any smarter after spending an hour in the toilet with that rag?"

"It's crazy! This young Polish Jew shoots the first secretary, an innocent man, at our embassy in Paris, and now we Jews back home will suffer the consequences. I hope that the 'Austrian Corporal' has enough sense not to try and take advantage of this tragedy."

"Come on, Alex. Be sensible. It's the perfect excuse for Herr Goebbels to tighten the screws once again!"

"Arnold, I think that ordinary Germans are smarter than that. They'll see through his ranting and raving. Maybe we'll have some broken shop windows, but in a couple of days it'll all blow over. Now, where is my coffee and my grandson?"

Upon hearing his grandfather's voice, Max came running out from one of the back rooms and jumped into his grandfather's arm. "Can I have a sugar cube, Papa?"

"Of course you can, maybe even two." He smiled at the child with the dark curly hair.

Ingrid gave him a reprimanding look. "Dad, you spoil him. You should stop. Sugar isn't good for him."

"And why should I stop spoiling him? He's the only grandchild I've got." With that, Alex sat down and took a sugar cube from the sugar bowl, dipped it in his coffee, and quickly put it in Max's open mouth. "And now I am off to the store. I have a delivery of some very good-quality Italian suit fabrics this afternoon, and I should be there to receive it. Also, one of my wealthier clients said that he would drop by to pick up some Chinese silk ties I had ordered just for him."

He reached for his brown bowler hat and camel-hair coat but was stopped by Esther.

"Alex, you're not going anywhere," she said.

"Look, darling, I'll go, finish what I need to do and then turn around and come right home."

Arnold interjected, "Alex, don't be an old stubborn fool. It's not safe for any of us to be out on the street with Herr Goebbels screaming for Jewish blood!"

"You young, inexperienced legal beagle, this is how you talk to your father-in-law? No respect at all, under my own roof?"

With that, Alex stormed out, slamming the door behind him, and swiftly walked along Meineke Strasse towards Kurfürstendamm. He tipped his hat to the ladies he passed as he hurried down the street, ignoring the crowds gathered around shop windows reading the grim news from Paris prominently posted by Hitler Jugend.

Alex decided to drop into his favourite tobacconist, one of the last Jewish merchants left in the neighbourhood.

"Guten tag, Herr Mendelbaum," he greeted the grey-haired, bespectacled owner.

"What's so good about it, Herr Grossman? We're becoming a dying breed. If it wasn't for my Catholic wife and her Nazi-sympathizing brother, I would've been closed down long ago. I hardly have any customers left. The Hitler Jugend chase them away from my store, threatening them if they buy anything from a Jew. I think after what happened in Paris yesterday, we won't be hanging around much longer."

"You talk like my son-in-law the attorney. The sky's always grey. This will blow over as well. In any case, can I have a couple of your Monte Cristos, please? I have to hurry to my store."

Herr Mendelbaum, his back hunched over from a wound suffered in the Great War, went into a small, musty room at the rear of the shop and came out with a small package wrapped in newspaper.

"These four are my last ones, and I don't think it will be possible to get any more."

Papa Grossman placed several crumpled-up marks in the tobacconist's hands and turned to leave, tipping his hat to the merchant as he did so.

"No, this is a gift, from one old Jew to another. Who knows when, if ever, you'll be able to enjoy these again," Mendelbaum said sadly to his long-time customer, with tears in his eyes.

Papa hugged him and walked through the door onto the street that had come alive with a mob loudly chanting "Death to the Jews. Jews out of the Fatherland." He turned up the collar of his coat and quickened his pace as the unruly crowd smashed the windows of the tobacconist's store behind him.

That afternoon, in another part of Berlin, Bruno Schmidt was struggling to keep the lid on events that were quickly spiralling out of control. Crowds of ordinary Berliners, led by hooligans and egged on by uniformed members of various Nazi paramilitary organisations, had started to destroy the shop windows of Jewish-owned stores and were looting the goods within. Most had anti-Semitic graffiti scrawled on them and their signs torn down, while a few others were set on fire.

Synagogues and Jewish-owned shops were vandalized and burned throughout Berlin. Proprietors and customers were set upon, beaten with fists and sticks, kicked, their faces bloodied, their clothes torn. Watching the mayhem, Berlin police stood back and allowed the mobs to continue their destruction. With his twenty-man security detail stretched to the limit, Schmidt decided to concentrate on a few key locations in Berlin's Jewish neighbourhoods where he felt the danger to be most immediate.

One was at the junction of Berliner Allee and Lothringerstrasse in the Weissensee district—the intersection at the approach to the Jewish cemetery. Another was at the Fasanenstrasse Synagogue in the western part of Berlin, and finally by the great New Synagogue on Oranienburger Strasse. By nightfall, both synagogues were on fire, his men having been powerless to stop the rampaging mobs.

The New Synagogue building was only saved from total destruction when Bruno and Wilhelm Krützfeld, the head of the local police precinct, intervened and convinced the fire department to put out the fire because the building was an officially protected monument. The orange flames from these places of worship lit up Berlin's night sky, sending a dire warning to all Jews within the German Reich that perhaps the time had come to leave their Fatherland.

Bruno and his driver, Helmut Eckler, were parked in their black Mercedes in front of Alexanderplatz in Mitte, helplessly watching legions of Hitler Youth accompanied by older Nazi Stormtroopers pillaging the shops in this predominantly Jewish district. Suddenly, as bricks and rocks flew through the glass storefront of a Jewish-owned hardware store, showering shards of glass onto the pavement, an elderly couple, followed by a young girl emerged from the shop.

They were being chased by a gang of howling, swearing young men wearing swastika armbands and brandishing wooden sticks. As if on command, both Bruno and Helmut jumped out of their car and ran towards the fleeing family. They got to the group seconds before their pursuers. Both men, dressed in black SS uniforms, drew their automatic pistols from their holsters and aimed them at the leader of the Nazi Youth.

"One more step, and I pull the trigger," shouted Bruno at the top of his voice.

The thin, blond-haired, pimple-faced youth, wearing a brown shirt with a swastika armband, looked at Bruno quizzically. "Sir, these are filthy Jews. They need to be taught a lesson!"

The two elderly Jews were hugging each other, cowering behind Bruno and Helmut. They had fear in their eyes and were seeking reassurance from their seeming rescuers. The young girl was sobbing quietly and hanging onto the back of Helmut's uniform jacket. The crowd swelled in back of the young Nazi.

"You snot-nosed little twerp! I'll teach you a lesson!" Bruno replied, as he removed the safety on his gun.

"What are you, a Jew lover?" a shout came from somewhere in the crowd. At that point Bruno fired his gun, the bullet just passing above the heads of those in front of him.

"Now, everybody go home, or the next one's going to be aimed a lot lower," he yelled. At first, an angry murmur rose from the group, with a plethora of vicious, anti-Semitic insults being hurled at the Jews and the two SS men. However, when Helmut also removed the safety from his gun, they started to move back, and slowly but reluctantly began to disperse into the side streets and alleyways from whence they came.

The old woman, tears running down her wrinkled cheeks, moved to embrace Bruno to thank him for saving their lives from the angry mob. "*Dankeschön, dankeschön,*" she cried.

He brusquely disengaged himself from her arms and turned to her husband. "Hey, old Jew, take your wife and child home now, and run as fast as your feet will carry you. And I don't want to see you out on the street again, because next time you won't be as lucky."

Bruno nodded to Helmut, and they slowly walked back to their car. The elderly couple, with their granddaughter in tow, took off at a trot and melted into the descending twilight.

Helmut lit a cigarette as they sat in the car, and quietly asked, "Now, why did we do that?"

Bruno smiled. "I guess she reminded me of my mother when I last saw her."

"If this gets back to Heydrich or Himmler, we'll be up to our necks in shit."

"They ordered us to keep the situation under control. We did that, didn't we?" he chuckled.

✠

On Kurfürstendamm, matters didn't go so well for Papa Grossman. He had arrived at his haberdashery after picking up his cigars and quickly ducked inside through a side entrance, unseen by the many pedestrians milling about outside intent on mischief. He decided not to raise the shutters and retreated into the back dressing room.

His hands were shaking as he struck a match and lit one of his remaining, prized Monte Cristos. On the wide boulevard of Kurfürstendamm, the gas lights had started to flicker as darkness descended on the German capital. Mobs, many carrying torches, bent on mayhem and destruction had been roaming the city's predominantly Jewish neighbourhoods since early afternoon, setting fires, looting and pillaging, and in some cases injuring or even killing hapless Jews who happened to be in their vicinity.

Papa Grossman jumped up as he heard the first brick smash through the front plate-glass window of his shop. He couldn't decide whether to try and flee through the side entrance or to grab a large pair of scissors used to trim fabric and confront these hooligans. He thought, *they would never harm a veteran of the Great War who fought on the Western Front*, and unwisely chose the latter course of action.

He threw open the door from the dressing room into the front of his shop to be met by smoke and a scene of utter devastation. Mannequins had been tossed about, his finest fabrics set on fire, and a group of rowdy men, smelling of beer, were fighting over Chinese silk ties,

Egyptian-cotton shirts and Italian suits. Alex lunged at a bald, red-faced, middle-aged man with a Hitler moustache, trying to wrestle a box of shirts away from him.

The man knocked the scissors out of his hand and pinned him to the floor. "And what have we here?" he bellowed sarcastically, pulling Grossman to his feet by the collar of his well-tailored suit. Someone lifted a torch, lighting the surreal scene and shining it on Papa's face.

"Why, it's a filthy old Jew!" The shout came from someone in the crowd

"It's Grossman, the haberdasher. He's the owner."

"Well, the bastard tried to kill me with these pinking shears." The man laughed loudly, holding up the scissors.

"Let's give him a haircut!"

The mob screamed in unison. With that, they pushed him down onto the jagged, broken glass in the front of his shop window, and while two Hitler Youth held him down, the man roughly cut his white hair. The pain in his thighs and buttocks was unbearable as the glass shards cut into his flesh. Blood flowed down his legs, soaking his pants, and pooled on the pavement under his shoes. While most of the crowd had continued down Kurfürstendamm to go on with their senseless rampage, a sizeable group of gawkers remained behind to watch the spectacle of an old Jew being humiliated.

The man was pulling his hair upward and roughly cutting it with the implement designed to cut fabric, not hair. He then carelessly sliced off the top of Papa's left ear, eliciting a loud scream from the quivering lips of the old man, and a stream of crimson spurted down his neck. The spectators, with unbridled hate in their eyes, smelled blood and went berserk, yelling at the top of their voices

"That's it, kill the old Jew!"

The mass of humanity surged forward, delivering kicks and blows and trampling Papa's supine body, as two Berlin policemen stood by with arms crossed and smiles on their faces, watching the grisly scene unfold.

The end came quickly, his body in a crumpled heap, with blood streaming onto the sidewalk under him and down the street into the gutter. A half-smoked Monte Cristo lay close to his outstretched right arm.

A few of the onlookers stepped over his body and grabbed whatever remained in the looted store, with some of the expensive Italian fabrics still smouldering where they had been set on fire. The "Grossman's Menswear and Haberdashery" sign had been torn down, smashed into pieces, and haphazardly piled on top of the body of its owner.

That night, across Germany, ninety-one Jews were killed, amongst them one Alexander Emmanuel Grossman. Another thirty thousand Jews were incarcerated in SS-run concentration camps, including Leopold Mandelbaum, the tobacconist. All over Germany, there was shattered glass and broken souls.

CHAPTER 30

Alexei's audience listened attentively as he recounted the events of *Kristallnacht* thirty-five years before, and Bruno Schmidt's strange role in it.

"We don't hear much about Schmidt for the next four years. His name is mentioned in dispatches in May and July 1942, surrounding the assassination of Reinhard Heydrich, and the massacre of the thousand citizens of Lidice in Czechoslovakia, as revenge, in which he apparently took an active part.

"He surfaces again in August 1942 as we learn from a courier dispatch from Field Marshall Erwin Rommel's Afrika Korps HQ at Beda Littoria in Libya, back to OKW HQ (German Army) in Berlin, dated August 27, 1942. It's from Field Marshall Erwin Rommel to Field Marshall Wilhelm Keitel. It reads as follows, as translated by US Army intelligence from captured Afrika Korps documents, after the Afrika Korps' surrender to Allied forces in the spring of 1943."

 **Deutsches Afrika Korps**

TOP SECRET

My dear colleague, today I had the pleasure of sending back to Berlin by Luftwaffe transport aircraft one SS Obersturmbanfuhrer Bruno Schmidt. He had been assigned to an intelligence unit of my Afrika Korps in March of this year to establish a program encouraging local Arab tribesmen to join with my troops, and those of the Italian Army of Africa to expel British and American forces from North Africa. Due to his proficiency in Arabic and familiarity with local customs (which I understand he gleaned from his time escorting the Mufti of Jerusalem back to Germany), and the personal letter of introduction and endorsement from the Mufti, he was quite successful in recruiting a large number of the local Arab population to our cause. Unfortunately, these recruits proved to be less than effective in combat, as they would scatter and abandon their posts at the first shot being fired.

Another serious and highly regrettable incident occurred, which makes it impossible for me to have him continue as a member of the Korps. Nine British soldiers of General Montgomery's 8th Army were captured by one of our desert raiding parties. Colonel Schmidt, as part of the intelligence unit, took it upon himself to interrogate these POWs, some of whom were wounded during the raid. His use of methods that I personally deplore and can only guess are employed by the SS, resulted in the death of four of these unfortunate Tommies. Needless to say, my HQ staff were outraged and demanded that I order Schmidt's court-martial forthwith. My men are proud soldiers who obey the Rules of War and the Geneva Convention on Prisoners of War. Should this incident become known by our adversaries, I can foresee the atrocious treatment that our own prisoners of war would suffer at their hands. I have no jurisdiction in this theatre of war over the SS, and therefore I have ordered his immediate evacuation to the Fatherland.

I ask for your support with the Führer should there be any repercussions from Reichsführer Himmler in Berlin (who is not very fond of me, in any case) from my action on this issue.

Heil Hitler,

Signed: Field Marshall Erwin Rommel

Erwin Rommel

There was silence in the room as Alexei finished reading the translated document. He continued.

"So, in 1938, we observe Schmidt saving the lives of a Jewish family and preventing the total destruction of a Jewish place of worship, then four years later we see him responsible for the cold-blooded murder of four British POWs. By the way, this is one of the indictments, along with his participation in the Lidice massacre, that earned him a life sentence in absentia at the Nuremberg War Crimes trials in 1946. I personally have never been able to make heads nor tails of this type of enigmatic behaviour."

At this point, Simon Wiesenthal spoke up, saying, "I had the dubious and unfortunate displeasure of making the personal acquaintance of Colonel Schmidt while a prisoner in Mauthausen concentration camp near Linz in Austria, towards the end of 1944.

"On March nineteenth, 1944, German troops invaded Hungary in what was called Operation Margarethe. Hungary's regent, Admiral Miklós Horthy, was getting cold feet after the rout of the Second Hungarian Army in Russia, and had started peace talks with the Western powers and Russia to extricate Hungary from the war.

"When Hitler got wind of this, he ordered German troops to occupy Hungary, which heretofore had been a willing participant with the Axis. The occupation didn't stop Horthy's numerous approaches to the Allies, so the Germans decided to launch Operation Panzerfaust (Armoured Fist) in October 1944, in an effort to neutralise Horthy. The SS officer chosen to lead this operation was Sturmbannführer (Colonel) Otto Skorzeny, labelled the 'Most Dangerous Man in Europe' for his daring rescue of Italian dictator Benito Mussolini from a mountaintop fortress in the Apennine Mountains in 1943. Skorzeny chose as his deputy for this mission Bruno Schmidt, 'The Führer's Fireman.'" Wiesenthal stopped talking to take a drink of water.

"Okay, this is all very interesting ancient history, but what does it have to do with me, and why I was asked to miss the Sinai portion of our trip?" Daniel asked anxiously, looking around the room for an answer.

"Don't worry, Daniel. We'll come to that shortly, but you have to become familiar with all what you call 'ancient history' for you to understand why you are here," Alexei responded calmly. "Please carry on, Simon."

Wiesenthal continued in his German-accented English. "Operation Panzerfaust was mounted to kidnap Horthy's younger son, also named Miklós, and hold him hostage in order to force the Hungarians to abandon any peace talks with the Allies or Russia. Horthy's older son, Stephen, a Hungarian fighter pilot, had died under mysterious circumstances in 1943, when his airplane crashed on the Russian front. Rumour then had it that his aircraft had been sabotaged by the Germans.

"Skorzeny, Schmidt and their SS paratroop commandos accomplished their task quickly in Budapest, deposing Horthy with the help of Hungarian Nazi Arrow Cross militiamen and installing a new puppet government under the rabid anti-Semite Ferenc Szálasi. Arriving in the Hungarian capital several weeks earlier was Bruno's old friend, Colonel Adolf Eichmann, who was to act as an adviser to the new Hungarian government on carrying out the 'Final Solution' to the 'Jewish Question' in their country. A new reign of terror was about to descend on the hapless Jews of Hungary."

CHAPTER 31

NOVEMBER 1944,

BUDAPEST, HUNGARY

The air was thick with cigar and cigarette smoke in the office of Adolf
Eichmann at the Hotel Majestic on the Buda side of the river Danube,
where he had ensconced himself. He was having his first meeting with
Bruno Schmidt since their Palestinian adventure in 1938. Before the
arrival of Schmidt and Skorzeny, Eichmann, along with Gruppenführer
Otto Winkelman, and Hitler's plenipotentiary for Hungary, Edmund
Veesenmayer had met with the leaders of Budapest's Jewish Council.
When they had shuffled into his office, hats in hand, Eichmann, dressed
in the black uniform of the SS, hands on his hips, asked them, "Do
you know what I am?"

Without waiting for a response from the council members, he
answered his own question. "I am a bloodhound!"

He then made them stand for two-and-a-half hours while he and
Veesenmayer harangued them about the approaching wave of terror
for the Jewish population of Budapest.

In the middle of the one-sided lecture, a secretary knocked on
the door. "Colonel Eichmann, there are five people in the anteroom
waiting to see you, what should I do?"

"I'll just be a moment, Fräulein Hilge." He then turned back to one
of the heads of the Jewish delegation, Ottó Komoly. "Mark my words,
the Jews of Budapest will soon be keeping company to the Jews of the

Warsaw Ghetto, most of whom had gone up in smoke through the chimneys at Auschwitz II-Birkenau. Now get out of my sight!"

The eleven mostly elderly Jews, their heads hanging low, slowly walked out of the room. On their way out, they passed Schmidt, Skorzeny, and the regent's son, Miklós Horthy, guarded by two of Skorzeny's camouflage-clad paratroopers, brandishing MP40 submachine guns. The young man, jet-black hair slicked straight back, unshaven, dressed in a creased Hungarian Air Force officer's uniform, was shaking like a leaf.

"Bruno, Otto, Heil Hitler. Welcome to Paris on the Danube," Eichmann beamed solicitously, while throwing his right arm up in the Nazi salute and shouting, "Heil Hitler." Skorzeny and Bruno smiled wryly at each other, perfunctorily raising their right arms.

"It has been a long time, Adolf," Bruno responded.

"Can you believe these Jews, trying to bribe me to save some of their wealthy relatives from being shipped East and instead send them on a train to Switzerland in exchange for some jewellery and gold? Otto, make sure you tell the Führer when you get back to Berlin that I can't be bought. In a few weeks, Budapest will be *judenfrei*."

"I will certainly remember to do that."

"Now, would you like some schnapps or some sweet Tokaji wine, perhaps?" Eichmann enquired.

"I've asked Fräulein Hilge to order some pastries from Gerbeaud's but didn't want them here until that sorry band of Jews had left. But how can I help you gentlemen?"

Horthy piped up, his voice high and squeaky, saying, "I demand to immediately be put in touch with the Führer! There has been a grave misunderstanding between our governments that I need to clear up! And where is my father? I must speak to him urgently!"

The words continued to pour forth like a forest stream until Skorzeny jabbed him in the side with his elbow. "Shut up, Mouse"—the nickname given the regent's younger son—"He wasn't talking to you."

Bruno spoke up. "Adolf, we need transport to get young Miklós here to one of your camps for protective custody until his father and his cronies in the Hungarian government see the light and rejoin the fold."

"Hmmm, the closest one would be Mauthausen, just east of Linz in Upper Austria." He motioned Skorzeny and Bruno closer, out of earshot of Horthy. "Fellows, that place is a shithole. Jews and Russian POWs are dying there by the thousands every day. We do have some VIPs interned there, including some American and British OSS and SOE agents, but do you really want to throw the son of the head of the Hungarian government, an ally of Germany, in there?"

Skorzeny raised his eyebrows, giving Bruno a questioning look.

"You mean former head, Adolf. And, Otto, that's exactly where we want him! Let him see what's going to happen if his father and the rest of that chicken-shit cabinet doesn't stop talking to the Russkies!"

"Bruno will be accompanying him with four of my men. They will also need a squad of SS and two armoured cars for escort until they cross the Hungarian-Austrian border, in case they run into trouble with the Hungarian Army along the route. I will be flying back to Berlin," Skorzeny half asked, half commanded Eichmann.

Horthy started yelling once again, protesting his detention, and asking to immediately be driven back to Buda Castle, the seat of the Hungarian government, to rejoin his father.

Skorzeny turned and gave a hand signal to one of his commandos. The large man grabbed Horthy by the back of his jacket and forcefully shoved him into a red-leather armchair, and then tied his paratrooper's kerchief around Horthy's face, muffling any sound.

"Young man, you're trying our patience. Any more of this nonsense and I'll have you hogtied! Now, where were we?"

The door to Eichmann's office opened and Fraulein Hilge walked in carrying a tray of pastries from Budapest's most famous patisserie, surrounding a bottle of sweet Tokaji Aszú.

"Gentlemen, let's enjoy the best this miserable backwater has to offer." Eichmann laughed as he guided his guests to a table in the corner, leaving the young Hungarian prone in the armchair.

That evening, Bruno, accompanied by Eichmann, Skorzeny, and Veesenmayer, along with a trio of beautiful Hungarian actresses, took in Puccini's three-act opera *Turandot* at the opulent Budapest Opera House. Bruno leaned back in his seat, listening to the tenor's rendition of "Nessun Dorma," when the air raid sirens sounded.

The announcer's voice came on the public address system. "Attention, attention. Please do not panic. Leave the theatre in an orderly fashion and proceed to the nearest air-raid shelter. Thank you for your co-operation."

They hurried outside, their SS uniforms giving them a decided advantage as they shoved their way through the unruly crowd.

"Here, follow me," said Veesenmayer. "I know a little jazz club in a basement around the corner. Used to be owned by a Jew. It's not the opera, but it has a good band, alcohol, and we'll be safe there."

"And how would a good Party member know about a decadent establishment like this?" sneered Eichmann. Seeing the scared look on Veesenmayer's face, he broke out in laughter. "Just a joke, Edmund, just a joke."

His laughter was interrupted by the sound of bursting bombs several kilometres away. Orange flashes lit up the night sky. "The Yankees are after the arms and airplane factories on Csepel Island tonight. They won't be coming any closer to the city. I think we can relax."

He playfully smacked one of the blonde Hungarian actresses on her behind and followed the others down the stairs into the dimly lit, smoke-filled basement jazz club. The quartet was playing Sidney Bechet's "Wildcat Blues," music banned as decadent Negro music in Germany by Joseph Goebbels' Reich ministry of public enlightenment and propaganda.

✠

Two days later, on a chilly and foggy early winter morning, a convoy of two grey trucks without markings, with an armoured car ahead and one behind, rumbled along the Danube quay on the Pest side of the Danube, past the Baroque-style parliament buildings that had been modelled after London's House of Commons.

In the lead truck, Bruno Schmidt sat in the cab beside the driver. His orders were to deliver young Miklós Horthy to the Mauthausen concentration camp near Linz. On the express orders of Reichsführer Himmler, before returning to Berlin, he was to render any assistance requested by Standartenführer Franz Ziereis, the camp's commandant, who seemed to be in over his head.

Behind them in the truck's hold, blindfolded and tightly wrapped up in a Persian carpet, young Horthy lay on the floorboards, guarded by four of Otto Skorzeny's paratroopers.

A light snow was falling from a darkening sky as Bruno looked out the window and impassively watched columns of Jews being marched to line up in rows by the river's embankment, shepherded by armed men wearing the red, white, and green armbands of the Hungarian Nazi Arrow Cross Party.

Shots rang out and the first row of bodies tumbled into the frigid water, making a splash and turning the brownish-green water red. The bodies bobbed on the surface as the fast current carried them downstream. *Hell on earth has arrived,* Bruno thought as he settled back in his seat and shifted around, trying to make himself comfortable.

After leaving the capital, the convoy sped along the snow-slick Budapest-Vienna motorway. The vehicles passed a column of miserable-looking Hungarian Jewish women with an assortment of shovels over their shoulders, most dressed in rags, many in bare feet, being herded by Hungarian *gendarmes* in the direction of Vienna. Behind them in the ditch lay the bodies of those who couldn't keep up, who had died either of hunger, exhaustion, or from a bullet in the back of the head. Any that would survive the 160-kilometre forced march would be used as slave labour to reinforce the German defences around Vienna, awaiting the Red Army's onslaught.

The steady hum of the truck's engine lulled Bruno into a shallow, fitful sleep. He started to dream of home, of his love's blond tresses cascading over her shoulders, her sky-blue eyes full of life, and four-month-old baby Heinrich, soundly sleeping in his mother's arms.

CHAPTER 32

FALL 1942,
PARIS, FRANCE

Since the beginning of 1942, the war had been going well for the German military machine. The Afrika Korps occupied most of North Africa, advance troops of Field Marshall Paulus' 6th Army were approaching the outskirts of Stalingrad, and weapons production from Germany's arms factories was reaching its nadir.

Bruno Schmidt had returned from his stint with Rommel's Afrika Korps, his reputation unsullied by his brutal interrogation methods in Libya.

Life for Steffi back in Munich had been good in his absence, with an interminable round of parties attended by the bigwigs of the Nazi Party organizations. Frau Schmidt, the former Frau Hartmann, was in great demand in Munich and Berlin as the hostess who threw the most lavish and entertaining soirees. She had also become good friends with Magda Goebbels, wife of Joseph, the Third Reich's propaganda minster. It was a catchphrase in Berlin's Nazi social circles that "Magda Goebbels and Steffi Schmidt maintained the morale of the home front all on their own."

Upon his return in the fall, Bruno and Steffi took a week's holiday in Paris to enjoy what the City of Light had to offer after two years of German occupation. Sitting under grey, threatening skies on the outdoor patio of Le Chat Noir, a café on the Left Bank of the River Seine, Bruno took Steffi's hands in his own.

"Darling, I have a surprise for you. I know how hard you work for the Party, organizing and attending all these social events, visiting the wounded in the hospitals with the other wives, hosting all these parties, and maintaining a household for us. And with me away constantly, doing it all on your own ... "

"Sweetheart, I love doing all of this, especially because I know how important it is for your career. Now, what's my surprise? A Dachshund puppy to keep me company? You know how much I love those little wiener dogs." She giggled.

"Well, not quite. Before I went away, I asked Helmut to keep his eyes out and find us a suitable and reliable maid who could cook and clean and do the laundry. Well, he has fou—"

His words were drowned out by thunder as the skies opened up with a torrent of rain, quickly forcing the two of them inside. Shaking the rain off their coats, they looked around to see if there might be a table by the window, where they could continue their conversation and finish their cafés au lait. A young French couple were sitting at one of the tables in a tight embrace, lips locked in a passionate kiss, ignoring the world around them.

The proprietor noticed Bruno and Steffi standing by the door and came over to them. He looked over at the romantic couple, and then at Bruno in his black SS officer's uniform. "One minute, monsieur."

He walked over and grabbed the young man by the collar of his jacket from behind with one hand, and the shoulder of the girl with the other, and pulled them to their feet. He roughly shoved them through the crowded café in the direction of the exit.

When they passed Bruno and Steffi, the proprietor, in a loud voice so that everyone could hear, declared in broken German, "My apologies, but I have to throw out the stinking garbage."

And with that, he gave a hard kick to the backside of the young Frenchman, who tumbled out the door, down the steps onto the rain soaked sidewalk.

The fellow stood up, wiping the water and dirt from his torn jacket, spat on the ground, and yelled back, "*Putain d'amant de Bosch!*"

Understanding a smattering of French, and knowing that what the youth had shouted meant "fucking Kraut lover," Bruno pulled his gun from its holster and headed out the door.

Steffi grabbed his arm and pulled him back. "Let it go, Bruno. He's young."

The proprietor then led them to their recently vacated table. "I am sorry for all this disturbance; young people today have no manners. Please let me send over a bottle of champagne, on the house, of course."

Oblivious to the commotion going on around her, the middle-aged, heavily made-up dark-haired chanteuse at the beaten-up old piano in a far corner of the café continued to belt out "Mon Coeur," the latest Parisian hit, in a throaty voice reminiscent of Édith Piaf.

"Now, where were we?" Steffi smiled at Bruno while sipping her glass of champagne.

"Well, as I was saying, before I left for Africa, I had asked Helmut to look around for a maid, someone to help you around the house. And he has found someone!"

"A pretty, *young* French one, I assume," she replied with a tinge of jealousy in her tone.

"No, a Dutch woman. She was working for a Luftwaffe officer on a farm in Saxony who was killed on the Russian Front near Voronezh, and now she's unemployed."

He looked at her sheepishly, awaiting a response. "Helmut drove her down while we are in Paris, and she'll be waiting for us at home," he continued.

"I hope we'll get along. You know what it's like when a new kitten comes into the household with an old cat," she replied sarcastically.

Bruno just smiled and ignored her comment.

They continued their conversation later that evening in bed, back in their room at Le Meurice hotel, the lower floors of which also functioned as German Army headquarters for the Paris garrison.

"Bruno, we've hardly made love since you returned from Africa. I see how you look at those Parisienne mademoiselles on the street. Tell me the truth, darling, are you getting tired of me, tired of having an older wife?"

Steffi had cuddled up to him, her ample breasts spilling out from the top of her silk negligee, her nipples erect as they brushed against his chest hair.

Rather than answering her, Bruno cupped one breast and slowly started sucking on her nipple, eliciting a low moan from her closed lips as she reached over and turned off the bedside lamp, slowly surrendering to her husband's frantic effort at lovemaking. But doubt and mistrust had begun to creep into their relationship. She realized that the eighteen-year age differential had started to build a wall between them.

Two days later, they were on a train heading back to Munich from Paris after their week-long, relaxing interlude, and time away from the worries of the Home Front.

Unbeknown to Steffi, the monotonous clicking of the train's wheels along the shiny steel rails of the Deutsche Bundesbahn were counting down the kilometres that would bring her ever closer to meeting Margit Angelika Hootveg, a pretty, twenty-year-old, blonde and blue-eyed Dutch girl who would soon become her maid ... and Bruno Schmidt's mistress.

CHAPTER 33

1938 — 1939,

BERLIN—TO STAY OR TO GO?

After the gruesome lynching of Alexander Papa Grossman on Kristallnacht in November 1938, normal life seemed to have stopped for the Weiszes, with mere struggle for survival replacing it. It was their Austrian maid, Heldi, who had ventured out in the early morning after that terrible November night of "broken glass" to discover why the elderly haberdasher hadn't returned home by the time the sun started to rise over Berlin, exposing the senseless destruction of the night before. It was she who had gathered a few trusted friends to carry home Papa Grossman's badly battered body so he could have a proper religious burial in the Weissensee Jewish Cemetery.

Esther had retreated into a shell after her husband's death, refusing to see or talk to anyone.

Ingrid spent most days crying, aimlessly wandering around the large apartment clutching her father's cigar-smoke-and-apple-schnapps-saturated, dark-grey housecoat.

The only laughter to be heard in the fourth-floor apartment at 14 Meineke Strasse was little Max's. He missed Papa, but like all youngsters, soon occupied himself with childish pursuits. He and his father, Arnold, would go to one of the many lakes in and around Berlin and play with the small model boats they built out of balsa wood. On these outings, Arnold would recount the mythical exploits of the child's paternal grandfather, the gunnery officer on the battlecruiser *SMS Lützow*, killed at the Battle of Jutland in 1916.

Maximillian first came face to face with the Nazis' racial laws as a three-year-old child in the fall of 1939. War with France and Britain had just been declared after Germany invaded Poland. War fever was running high in the Third Reich, and Adolf Hitler was whipping up the flames of anti-Semitism, blaming World Jewry for the outbreak of war.

"Look, Daddy, the wind is carrying our boat to the other side," Max yelled excitedly as he watched his little wooden boat floating away.

"Don't worry, Max. We'll just walk around and get it."

"No, you won't!" came a booming voice from behind them.

As Arnold spun around to see the source of the warning, he was confronted by three youths wearing lederhosen, brown shirts and swastika arm bands. Arnold quickly grabbed Max's hand and the paper bag containing their lunch of bread, cheese, and apples prepared by Heldi. Their way was blocked by the three young Nazis.

"What's in the bag, Jew?" the tallest and seemingly oldest enquired in a threatening tone as he approached them.

"Just some lunch," replied Arnold, attempting to avoid the boy in front of him. The blond-haired Hitler Youth stuck out his leg, tripping Arnold, sending him tumbling to the grass, and pulling Max down with him. The paper bag ripped on hitting the ground and spilled its contents. The three Nazis laughed loudly, grabbing the apples and biting into them. One of them stepped on Arnold's hand as he tried to retrieve a sandwich.

"Hey, Jew, you better get used to being stepped on," he guffawed. "This is the new Germany, not a place for Yids!"

"Yes, and we don't want to see the likes of you and your little bastard around here again, or the consequences will be much worse for you," chimed in one of the others. Then they skipped up the hill chanting a Hitler Youth song, leaving Arnold and a quietly crying Max to dust themselves off and start their long walk home—walk, as Jews were no longer permitted to ride public transportation except for a few hours early in the morning and late at night.

That evening, after Ingrid had tucked Max into bed and read him his favourite bedtime story, she and Arnold sat down in the salon that held so many happier memories.

"What happened out there today, Arnold? Why were Max's eyes red and full of tears?"

"I tell you, Ingrid, we have become strangers in our own country. It is no place to bring up children," he replied, trying somewhat meekly to steer the conversation away from that afternoon's actual events. "We must leave Germany and find another home. I will go and see Ziggy Guthausen tomorrow and see if he can help us obtain exit permits."

"And where will we go? We have no relatives or friends outside of Germany. No, it's impossible. This country's the only one we've known!"

And then the tears started running down her face and dropping onto her father's old grey housecoat in her arms.

Arnold went over to put his arm around her shoulder and console her, but she stood up and walked out of the room, past the dust-covered grand piano that neither she nor her mother had sat down to play at since her father's murder. She stopped in the doorway to the hall leading to their bedroom and whispered under her breath, "Never, never."

Early the next morning, Arnold again pinned the Nazi Party badge he had received from Heldi some years earlier on the lapel of his fall coat and boarded the U-Bahn to his old office in the centre of Berlin. Though Jews were not allowed to ride public transit at this hour, he felt the small enamel pin gave him a modicum of cover. He decided to wait around the corner from the building until Ziggy Guthausen arrived, as was his habit, promptly at 8:00 a.m. Turning up the collar of his coat, he quickly approached his old law partner as the man exited the rear door of his chauffeur-driven limousine.

"Herr Guthausen," he whispered as he came up beside the taller, grey-haired, well-dressed gentleman. "Could I have a word with you, please?"

Business had been relatively good for the firm of Guthausen Pockler, providing a comfortable, prosperous lifestyle for the partnership's remaining "Aryan" partners since the Nazis' ascension to power. Guthausen glanced around to see if anyone in the vicinity was looking before responding to Arnold in a quiet but firm voice, "Good Lord, what are you doing here?"

"I must speak with you, Herr Guthausen. It's a matter of great urgency."

"Meet me in the lane out back, by the coal piles."

Arnold walked down the tight space between the buildings, followed a few minutes later by Guthausen, anxious not be seen with Arnold. The two of them stopped behind a mountain of black coal briquettes, placed there as heating fuel for the coming winter to feed the enormous coal-fired boilers of the two office buildings.

"Arnold, I told you to never come down here to see me. You're putting the welfare of the whole firm in jeopardy!"

"I am sorry, Herr Guthausen, but matters have reached a critical stage. My family must leave Germany. Now!!"

"What does that have to do with me? I advised you to do so three years ago. I am not sure what I can do for you now."

"We have run out of money to pay for exit visas, sir. My father-in-law has been murdered, my wife and her mother are daily on the verge of suicide, and my three-year-old son is afraid to go outside. I am at wit's end."

As Guthausen began to reply, a worker dressed in coveralls, with hands and face covered in black soot, pulling a small wooden wheelbarrow, with a shovel over his shoulder, came whistling down the lane. Guthausen turned towards the wall, pulling up the collar of his coat to avoid his face being seen. His whispered response was inaudible.

The worker started to shovel coal into his wheelbarrow, and Guthausen walked back up the lane without a backward glance.

Arnold felt totally abandoned and seemed rooted to the pavement, unable to move.

"Are you alright, mister?" The question came solicitously from the man with the wheelbarrow.

Arnold just nodded and slowly walked into the busy street. He wasn't quite sure how long he had been standing by the coal pile as he wandered aimlessly through central Berlin's morning traffic, finally sitting down on a park bench in Potsdamer Platz to try to figure out where or whom he could turn to next. He had not had any breakfast and felt like going to sleep, when a young man, smartly dressed in a dark-green suit, came and sat down beside him.

"Good morning, Herr Weissz. Herr Guthausen asked me to find you. You are a hard man to follow; I nearly lost you twice."

Arnold was surprised, but smiled at the man, recognizing him as Kurt, a very industrious lad who had worked in the firm's mailroom while Arnold was a partner. Judging by his attire, he had moved up the ladder since. Kurt pulled an envelope from inside his suit and handed it to Arnold.

"It's from Herr Guthausen. He asked that you please not contact him again. *Auf wiedersehen.*" With that, Kurt tipped his peaked cloth cap and walked away, joining the rest of the noon-time crowd on busy Potsdamer Platz.

Arnold looked around carefully before opening the envelope. There was a handwritten note wrapped around a stack of well-used Reichsmark. He quickly put the cash in his wallet before reading the note;

> *My dear Arnold. It pains me to see you in the state and situation that you find yourself in. It is unfortunate that you did not take my advice of three years ago and leave this country, where your kind are obviously not welcome. I was hoping that circumstances would change,*

but they seem to have gotten worse. Please accept this money as my modest contribution to help you and your family obtain exit papers. Go see Major Alois Huber at the Department of Jewish Emigration by the U-Bahn station on Behrenstrasse. Hopefully he will be able to assist you. He was a fellow student at university. I will continue to try and send some work your way, as I have done over the past several years, but please do not try to contact me in person again.

My kindest regards to your family,
Ƶ. Guthausen

Arnold stuffed the piece of paper in his coat pocket and looked around to see where he could get something to eat. He stopped by a street vendor selling hot sausages and ordered one. The man with a ruddy complexion and handle bar moustache smiled at him as he proffered the steaming sausage accompanied by a thick slice of rye bread and a dab of hot mustard on a sheet of wax paper.

Arnold sat down on the stonework surrounding a bronze statue and bit into his lunch. After finishing his meal, he headed back towards the S-Bahn and home. He felt good now that he had something to eat and some money to hopefully buy their way out of a Germany that had grown increasingly inhospitable to its Jewish citizens. After getting off the train, he bought a bouquet of fall flowers from an old lady sitting outside the station. *It will finally be a happy day at 14 Meineke Strasse,* he thought as he walked along Kurfürstendamm, his collar turned up against the cold autumn wind. Unknown to him, even happier news awaited him at home.

CHAPTER 34

MAY 9, 1973,

MOSSAD HEADQUARTERS, TEL AVIV

After explaining Schmidt's role in the kidnapping of Miklós Horthy Jr., the son of Hungary's regent, in November 1944, and Horthy's delivery into the custody of Standartenführer Franz Xavier Ziereis, commandant of Mauthausen-Gusen concentration camp, Simon Wiesenthal continued standing and recalled a story about Schmidt at the camp in Austria.

"Miklós Horthy Jr. arrived at Mauthausen concentration camp guarded by Bruno Schmidt and a fourteen-man SS detachment. At this time, there were a number of Allied VIPs, including Poles, Czechs, Britons, and Dutch being held on 'ice' as potential bargaining chips in any peace negotiations with the Allies. Horthy joined this group.

"Due to the heavy influx of Hungarian Jews and Russian POWs towards the end of 1944, Commandant Ziereis was starting to lose control of the camp. Schmidt's orders, received directly from Reichsführer Himmler, were to assist Ziereis in re-establishing order over the operations of the camp using any methods he found appropriate. Schmidt, with his legal, administrative and organizational background and attention to detail, spent two months making Mauthausen a more efficient economic production and killing machine.

"Mauthausen had originally been established as the Wiener Graben quarry, supplying building materials for road construction. Inmates of the camp were expected to haul the heavy rocks up 186 steps on their backs. They were worked, beaten, and starved to death. And those who didn't die from starvation or exhaustion were shot or gassed, their bodies burned in the crematoria.

"Schmidt, being a realist, knew by this time that Germany had most likely lost the war, so either out of compassion or in order to curry clemency at the inevitable war crimes trials that would follow an Allied victory, he once again confounds us with his actions. I didn't arrive at Mauthausen until April of '45, so I only heard this story about Schmidt second-hand from another prisoner."

Wiesenthal took another drink of water before continuing.

"A skinny little Hungarian Jew from Budapest by the name of Neumann tried to escape from the camp on Christmas Eve, 1944. Apparently, he had been close to Stalingrad as part of a forced labour battalion and retreated with the Hungarian Second Army when it was routed by the Soviets during the freezing winter of 1943. The bulk of the army was wiped out, but he survived and got back to Budapest. He laid low until the Arrow Cross seized power in October of '44, when he was arrested and put on a train with thousands of other Jews headed to the concentration camp at Mauthausen. When he got there in a cattle car in November 1944, he was skin and bones.

"By the end of December, desperation had set in amongst the prisoners, as it seemed that the Germans might be able to prolong the war with their offensive in the Ardennes, driving the Allies back and delaying the liberation of the camp.

"With the guards celebrating Christmas Eve with wine and liquor in the barracks, Neumann felt that he had nothing to lose and decided to risk his life and try the impossible—break out of Mauthausen! Others, mostly starving Russian POWs, had tried and failed, getting shot before they reached freedom or getting electrocuted on the high-voltage barbed wire fence surrounding the camp. While making his break in the dark, he got entangled in the first row of barbed wire. He was trapped, unable to move either forward or back, not reaching the electrified fence. Exhausted from the struggle to free himself, he lay trapped by the wire, listening to the loud sound of music and laughter coming from the SS barracks, waiting for the inevitable shot in the head from the first guard that discovered him."

At this point, Wiesenthal paused.

Seeing him take a breath after his lengthy dissertation, Daniel, clearly exasperated by how long it was taking the Israelis to get to the point of his involvement in all of this, seized the opportunity and quickly jumped in. "Could we please get on to what is expected of me here? None of what I've heard so far seems relevant, in my view. The war's been over for nearly thirty years."

"Patience, my friend. You need the background to be able to understand the need for your participation in this mission, the reason you were chosen, and what is expected of you," Alexei replied, giving a friendly nod in Wiesenthal's direction.

The Austrian picked up where he'd left off. "Now, where were we? Oh yes, so Neumann was unable to move, and he heard footsteps approaching. He figured that was the end as a flashlight was shined in his face."

"'What the hell are you doing?' the voice holding the flashlight asked. Quickly realizing the stupidity of his question, the man went on. 'The Americans are getting close. You will be out of here soon, so not a good time to get yourself shot. Now get your ass back into your barracks!'

"Neumann couldn't see the face of the man because of the light shining in his eyes, but he recognized an SS colonel's uniform. The colonel helped Neumann struggle free of the barbed wire and gave him a kick in the behind, sending him on his way back to his quarters. With most of the SS guards drunk from celebrating Christmas Eve in their barracks, the event was unseen by anyone else.

"The next day, at the morning roll call, with Commandant Ziereis hung over and still in his bunk, Colonel Schmidt addressed the assembled prisoners and SS guards. Neumann recognized the voice of

Schmidt as that of the SS man who had rescued him the night before, thereby saving his life.

"Was this a compassionate act by Schmidt towards another human being, as on *Kristallnacht*, or simply a calculated attempt hoping for more lenient treatment by the Allies after the end of the war? He must have known he would be charged with war crimes for the killing of the British POWs in North Africa, the massacre of civilians at Lidice, and the horrors committed under his watch at Mauthausen. Was he an evil man without a conscience, morals, or ethics, bent on the murder of anyone deemed to be an enemy of the Nazi State, or was he just a career opportunist with a redeeming spark of humanity that willed him to use his position of authority to save a number of innocent lives? We will probably never find out."

As Wiesenthal finished, Alexei stood back up. "And now, Daniel, we have finally come to the point where we can explain to you why and how you will be involved in Operation Berlin on the Nile."

CHAPTER 35

When Arnold walked through the door with his bouquet of flowers on that late fall day in 1939, he was greeted by a smiling Esther and Heldi. He was pleasantly taken aback as he hadn't seen the two of them smile since *Kristallnacht*.

"What's going on?" he queried the two giggling women.

"Herr Weisz, Frau Weisz is in the toilet throwing up!" responded Heldi.

"And that's good news? Something to laugh about?" he asked sternly.

Not able to contain her excitement, Esther blurted out, "Ingrid's pregnant, Arnold! She's going to have a baby! Isn't that exciting?"

A concerned frown crossed Arnold's face. It was not something he was expecting. Masking his concern with a broad smile, he embraced Esther and handed her the bouquet. "*Mazel tov*, Grandma."

At the sound of his father's voice, Maximillian came out of the kitchen riding a tricycle, with chocolate icing covering his lips.

"Daddy, Daddy, you're home!" shrieked the little boy, jumping off his tricycle and into his father's arms.

Later that evening, Arnold sat on the bed beside a reclining Esther, holding her hand. She had a cold compress on her head and was trying to catch a few moments of sleep before she had to get up again.

"Arnold, we will have to make an appointment to see Dr. Levy. I think that I may already be in my third month."

"Darling, I also have good news."

"What is it?"

"I went to see Ziggy Guthausen today. He gave us two thousand Reichsmarks and an introduction to an old schoolmate of his at the Jewish Emigration Office. We may be able to get our exit papers soon."

For the first time in a long while, Ingrid and Arnold were able to spend a restful night, secure in the thought that life would become more bearable in the days to come.

Early next morning, Arnold joined a long lineup of Jews of all ages anxious to obtain exit permits for them and their families to leave the Reich. The skies were grey, and the temperature had dropped several degrees overnight. Arnold engaged in conversation with an elderly couple standing and shivering in line in front of him.

"Where are you looking to immigrate to?" he asked.

"Oh, my wife has a cousin in New York who has agreed to sponsor us," the man responded.

"Yes, and I sold all my jewellery, except for this old watch, so we could pay the exit fee." The woman raised her arm, rolling up her sleeve to show Arnold.

"We are also trying to sell our flat, but with the restrictions imposed by the government, we are not having much luck getting anything reasonable for it. I am not sure how we will survive the winter if we can't leave Berlin soon." At that point, the woman put her head on her husband's shoulder and started to sob uncontrollably.

The man looked skyward and whispered to Arnold, "God help us."

The line had not moved at all in the half hour since Arnold's arrival. Two policemen walked up and down, barking commands at the crowd of miserable Jews. "Stay in line! Against the wall, so decent German citizens can pass! We will all be happy to see your filthy backsides," they said as they pushed and shoved the ever-growing crowd of people along the sidewalk.

It was well after lunch by the time Arnold finally made it through the door. The air inside was suffocating due to the crush of sweaty humanity and lack of any ventilation. There were a great variety of applicants, from families with numerous children from the countryside to elderly, ultra-orthodox couples dressed in black from head to toe, from Berlin's orthodox neighbourhoods.

There was a constant buzz from a mixture of German and Yiddish, as if from a beehive. Their line snaked around the whitewashed walls of the high-ceilinged reception hall with a single large portrait of Adolf Hitler dominating it, as if disdainfully observing the assembled crowd. When Arnold's turn came at the wooden table piled high with papers, the young woman behind it, dressed in a black Auxiliary SS uniform, sternly asked, "Name?"

"Weisz, Arnold."

"Age?"

"Thirty-two."

"I guess I don't need to ask your religion." She looked up at him through her thick-lensed eyeglasses, automatically writing "Jude" at the top of the application form with a thick black marker. "Dependents, their ages and names?"

"Wife, Ingrid, twenty-five; mother-in-law, Esther Grossman, sixty-one; and son, Maximillian, who will be four." He didn't mention the fact that Ingrid was three months pregnant, thinking it might complicate the process of obtaining exit permits.

"I am assuming that you are all citizens of the Reich," she said matter-of-factly, without looking up at him this time. Now, the name, nationality, and country of residence of your foreign sponsor,"

"We ... we ... we don't have one," he stuttered, looking at her sheepishly.

"Then why are you wasting my time, Herr Weisz?" Her voice rose in anger. "Do you not know that without a foreign sponsor you will not be able to obtain exit papers to leave the country? Are you not aware that Jews are not wanted anywhere around the globe? No government wants to take financial responsibility for you lazy people!"

She continued lecturing him as if he were a child who forgot to bring a note from his mother to school.

He tried to interrupt her, but she would have none of it, finally getting up from behind the table and grabbing the back of his coat, attempting to push Arnold roughly through the jostling crowd and out of the hall.

Seeing the commotion, a guard posted inside the building came rushing over to see what was causing the disturbance. As Arnold was being hustled along by both of them, he reached into the pocket of his jacket and pulled out the note from Ziggy Guthausen and waved it at the man.

"I am here to see Major Huber. I have a letter of introduction!" he yelled at the top of his voice.

"Why didn't you start with that, you stupid man?" came the reproach from the woman.

The guard took him by the arm and led him through the lines of desperate people and up the stairs. They came to a closed door with a sign on it: "Major Alois Huber, Director, Jewish Emigration, District 2, Berlin."

The man knocked on the door, and upon hearing a voice inviting him in, swung it open. "Heil Hitler. Major Huber, this Jew is here to see you. He says he has a letter of introduction."

"Come on in." Gestapo Major Huber, tall, thin, and aristocratic-looking with a monocle in his right eye, motioned for Arnold to sit in the chair in front of his desk.

"Thank you, sir. My name is Arnold Weisz, and I am a former law partner of Herr Guthausen. He told me that you may be of some assistance."

"Oh yes! How's old Ziggy? I heard he is doing very well in his practice. Good for him. A genuinely nice gentleman. But how can I help you?"

"Well, you see, sir, I am Jewish ... "

"That's quite obvious," Huber, wearing a dark-blue, pin-striped suit with a golden eagle clutching a swastika in its lapel, yelled with a loud, guttural laugh.

"I am looking to obtain exit papers for myself, my wife, my son, and my mother-in-law."

"Mothers-in-law. If she were mine, I'd rather leave her behind, the old witch." Huber broke into laughter again. "And do you have the exit fees and the signed legal papers to turn your assets over to the State?"

"I have two thousand marks."

Arnold reached into his pocket to retrieve the envelope Ziggy Guthausen had sent him.

"That will pay for exit visas for two people. You will need to come up with two thousand more," said Huber as he stretched his arm across his desk, taking the envelope. "I am sure that you have that much salted away in a mattress somewhere." He smiled enquiringly. "All you rich Jews do. By the way, do you also have a letter from your sponsor?" he continued, seemingly without taking a breath. "Where will you be travelling to, America?"

"We don't know yet. We don't know anyone living outside of Germany. No family and no friends. We don't yet have a sponsor," Arnold stammered.

Huber got up from behind his desk and walked to the window, his back to Arnold. Something in the street below must have caught his interest, as he didn't respond. After a minute or two of silence and not turning around, he shook his head and in a very quiet voice said, "You don't, you don't, and you don't. However, you must know that today you cannot go anywhere in this world and not be sponsored. There is not a country on the map that will admit a Jew without someone in that country taking responsibility for them. It's impossible, impossible!"

He turned around and approached a visibly shaken Arnold. "I think this interview is over," he said, raising his voice an octave.

Arnold was rooted to the chair. He started to sweat and took out his monogrammed handkerchief to wipe his brow. Arnold didn't know what to say or do, feeling as if he'd really reached the end, with no way out of a Germany that didn't want him or his family. *What will become of us? How will we survive?* All these thoughts cascaded over him.

The silence was finally interrupted by a screaming Huber. "Didn't you hear me, man? Do you want me to call for the guard to escort you out? The interview is over!"

As he slowly, on unsteady legs, rose from the chair, he turned beseechingly to Huber, and with a quivering voice pleaded, "Please, Herr Huber, I beg you as one good German to another, please help us find a way out."

Huber, like most Germans at that time, had been deeply immersed in the culture of anti-Semitism. As a member of the feared Gestapo, he was even more inclined to ignore the entreaties of a "filthy Jew." However, his past ties to Guthausen, combined with the two thousand Reichsmark in his pocket that he was intent on keeping there, softened his attitude towards Arnold. "You said you have a son?"

"Yes, sir."

"How old is he?"

"Four, Herr Huber. Here, let me show you." Arnold pulled out his wallet and extracted a small black-and-white photograph of a dark-haired young boy. "This is Maximillian."

"Well, Herr Weisz you may be in luck."

A smile came over Arnold's face as he eagerly awaited the Gestapo major's explanation of his sudden good fortune.

"I can tell you that there is currently a program in place called *Kindertransport*. Two organizations, the British Committee for the Jews of Germany and the Movement for the Care of Children from Germany, are financing the emigration of ten thousand *unaccompanied* German children of your faith to be resettled in England.

"If you wish, I can put your son's name on the waiting list. The money you gave me should be sufficient to pay for the costs related to documentation, exit charges, and travel expenses to Hamburg, the port of embarkation. The Brits are paying for transport across the Channel."

"What do you mean 'unaccompanied,' Herr Huber?" Arnold looked enquiringly at the Gestapo officer.

"It means that the parents are not allowed to go with them. They will be housed with English families until we figure out what to do with the rest of your kind in Germany. God's chosen people, *nein*? If it were up to me, I would be happy to be rid of the lot of you, but I don't call the shots in Berlin. Now, do you want me to submit his name or not?" Huber said, his voice rising, showing his impatience.

A sad look enveloped Arnold's face as he thought about Huber's proposal. *How can I send my only child, four years old, off to a foreign land to live with strange people speaking a different language? How can I know when, if ever, I will see him again?*

"Well, man? I need an answer. I have other people waiting to see me." Huber's tone had quickly changed from quiet and friendly to loud and impatient.

"I am sorry, sir, but this is not a decision I can make here and now, nor on my own. I need to discuss it with my wife."

"You have twenty-four hours. *Auf wiedersehen*." And with that, Huber strode to the door, swung it open and yelled out. "Corporal Huth, please escort Herr Weisz out of the building."

Arnold found himself out on the street again, walking past the other miserable Jewish souls lined up there to try to obtain their own exit papers. It was late afternoon and Jews were not allowed to travel by public transit until much later. He reached into his coat pocket and took out his small NSDAP badge and pinned it to his lapel.

He breathed a sigh of relief as he boarded City Bus #36 without being challenged. The bus was packed with workers on their way home. Someone on board had obviously consumed a large portion of garlic sausage and the odour permeated the entire carriage. Arnold was lost in thought, holding on to the overhead strap as the bus rumbled along busy streets, lurching from one side to the other.

He had no idea how he could even broach the subject with Ingrid of sending four-year-old Maximillian on his own to England.

What horrors is this world coming to? I could have been happy not to be one of God's chosen people, he thought. *Chosen for what?* Black clouds rapidly approaching Europe's Jews would provide the answer.

CHAPTER 36

CHRISTMAS AND NEW YEAR'S EVE, 1942,
MUNICH & BERLIN,

The languid strains of "Stille Nacht, Heilige Nacht" wafted through the Schmidts' Munich apartment on Christmas Eve 1942. The black-out curtains had been drawn and a small crowd had gathered around the piano in the salon. Helmut Eckler was at the keyboard, and the Schmidts' twenty-year-old, blonde Dutch maid, Margit, was singing the internationally loved Christmas favourite in her native tongue.

Another small group, mulled wine in hand, congregated by the radio in the dining room to listen to Propaganda Minister Joseph Goebbels' popular annual Ring Broadcast to the troops at the front. Steffi was standing by the brightly decorated Christmas tree in animated conversation with the wife of a Luftwaffe officer. The flickering light from the candles on the tree cast shadows on her face, making her look older than her fifty-nine years. Her aging had not been lost on Bruno, as he gazed in a trance at their pretty Dutch maid singing along with Helmut.

The shrill whine of the air-raid warning siren interrupted the idyllic scene as everyone started heading for the front door and down into the air-raid shelter.

"Fucking Limeys, don't they know it's Christmas?" someone yelled.

The Luftwaffe officer grabbed his wife and Steffi by the arm and quickly hustled them down the stairs as the building began to shake from the nearby bomb explosions. Steffi assumed that Bruno would be going down to the shelter by the back door of their spacious apartment. But that was not the case.

As Margit rushed around turning off all the lights in the apartment, as was her habit, Bruno stepped out from the semi-darkness, illuminated only by the candles on the Christmas tree, and grabbed her by the arm. She gasped as he roughly drew her lithe figure into his, embracing her and gazing down into her sky-blue eyes. He towered over her and she was not sure of his intentions. He placed his right index finger onto her upper lip as if to caution her to silence. Her heart was racing as he tightened his embrace and spoke in a whisper.

"Margit, you've been on my mind and in my dreams ever since I met you last month. You could not have failed to notice my eyes following your every move."

A blush unseen in the darkness enveloped her ivory features as she answered her employer haltingly. "No, no, I am sorry, but I was not aware of your interest, Herr Schmidt," she lied, as she had been instantly drawn to the handsome, older man with a surplus of charm, Nordic good looks and strength of character. Since her arrival at the Schmidts' residence after their return from Paris, she would often lie in her bed at night, her long fingers seeking out the centre of her femininity, giving herself pleasure as she fantasized about being made love to by her employer. She had also recognized the undercurrent of doubt within their marriage and thus harboured no self-guilt as to her erotic daydreams.

Towering over her, he bent his head down, and his eager lips sought out hers in a passionate kiss. He pushed her against the wall as she feebly struggled to resist.

She was no virgin, but also had not had a large number of previous encounters with the opposite sex in the small village near Eindhoven in Holland that she hailed from. She was uncertain of how to react as Bruno's hands started to fumble with the buttons of her white silk blouse.

The loud all clear signalled the end of the Allied air raid, interrupting Bruno's and Margit's frantic romantic entanglement.

"Darling, I didn't see you in the shelter. Where were you?" Steffi said.

"You know how I hate those crowded, dark and smelly basements, Steffi," Bruno replied, while Margit made herself busy in the kitchen.

New Year's Eve 1942 was not a happy one in Germany. Field Marshal Paulus' Sixth Army was surrounded by the Soviets in Stalingrad, with only days left until their surrender, signalling Hitler's first serious reverse of the war in the East. Although Goebbel's propaganda ministry tried to paint a much prettier picture, a sense of foreboding had settled upon much of the German populace.

"Bruno, I am not feeling well. I am not sure if it's something I ate on Christmas Eve or at the Speer's the next day, but my stomach's been doing cartwheels all day," Steffi said. "I don't think that I want to go to this evening's New Year's gala at the Air Ministry. Why don't you just go without me?"

"Darling, we'll just stay home and have a quiet celebration. Besides, Göring's such a bore anyway, with his fantastic stories."

"No, I insist you go! I'll be fine at home. Why don't you take Margit with you? Poor girl never gets out, and she might enjoy meeting some of those handsome and brave Luftwaffe officers."

"All right, if you're sure that you'll be fine. I've given Helmut the night off, so I'll have to drive."

Bruno whistled a couple of tunes from *Die Fledermaus* as he readied himself, getting dressed in his tuxedo. There may have been a war on but looking at the Nazi Party's bigwigs' lavish preparations to ring in 1943, the outside observer wouldn't have guessed as much.

Margit and Steffi were in the latter's dressing room, with Steffi bringing out an armful of her elegant evening gowns for the young girl to try on.

"I think you'll look just gorgeous in this one," Steffi enthused, holding up the silver and black lamé gown against Margit's slim figure. "I wore this to the wedding of Captain Junge, the Führer's adjutant. What a party that was!"

"Must have been magical, Frau Schmidt."

"Oh, it was! It'll only take me a minute to hem the bottom. Now some shoes."

Bruno and Margit drove in silence along the Munich-Berlin Autobahn as the winter sun started to slowly settle in the west. The landscape was covered in a thin blanket of white. They had several hours of driving ahead of them until they arrived at the Air Ministry complex on Wilhelm Strasse.

The modern, expansive grey block buildings covering over five acres were a monument to Hermann Göring's soaring ego. Construction started in 1936, finishing only after the beginning of the war. As they entered the eastern suburbs of Berlin, they passed some of the recent destruction wrought by the Allied air forces. Margit had fallen asleep, her head resting on Bruno's shoulder. Her left hand, nails carefully manicured by Steffi, lay across his lap.

After leaving their car to be parked by an attendant, they entered the great hall with its soaring and ornate ceiling, dominated at one end by an enormous eagle carved from alabaster, clutching a swastika in its talons. They were immediately approached by a smiling Air Marshall Milch, one of Göring's deputies.

"My dear Bruno, so happy that you could make it to our little party. Hermann will be pleased. But where is Steffi, and who is this lovely blonde apparition on your arm?"

Without waiting for an answer, the general, resplendent in his ceremonial white Luftwaffe uniform, with medals covering his entire chest, clicked his heels and bent down to plant a light kiss on Margit's outstretched hand. She blushed as she withdrew her hand. "Oh, I am

Margit Hootveg, Herr and Frau Schmidt's housekeeper. Frau Schmidt has fallen ill, and Colonel Schmidt was kind enough to invite me along to this wonderful ball."

"Splendid. Well, pass along my best for a quick recovery to the lovely Steffi, and enjoy this evening," Milch said, nodding and giving a knowing wink and a slap on the back to Bruno.

The rest of the evening was spent in small talk with other guests, listening to a wide variety of toasts from the eminent Nazi leadership, including Goebbels. Hitler was a "no show," absorbed in dreaming up fantastic strategies to try to save the situation in eastern Russia.

Rudolf Hess was absent as well, having flown to Scotland in a crazy individual attempt to try to negotiate peace with Britain the previous year. The champagne shipped in from Paris by Göring, along with foie gras, for the occasion flowed freely, helping everyone forget about the reverses in the Soviet Union, if only for one night.

Margit and Bruno cut a handsome pair as they danced to Tchaikovsky's *Sleeping Beauty* waltz as a young Luftwaffe corporal announced the ringing in of the new year with a loud blast from his trumpet.

Göring took the microphone. "Dear friends and comrades. I appreciate all of you coming to celebrate what I know will be a turning point in the history of our One Thousand Year Reich."

Everyone raised their glasses and shouted in unison, "Long live the Führer and the Thousand Year Reich!"

He raised his glass once again, "To our Führer, Adolf Hitler, and total victory."

All those in attendance were spellbound that night, screaming along with the portly Reichsmarschall at the top of their lungs, "To the Führer, and total victory. Heil Hitler!"

The band struck up once again, playing a string of Viennese waltzes by Johann Strauss the elder. Bruno held Margit close as they whirled around the dance floor. They knew this would set many jealous tongues wagging but allowed themselves to be captured by the moment.

At one point, Bruno whispered in her ear, "You know that you're like a breath of fresh mountain air that's blown into my life. I am sorry about being carried away on Christmas Eve, but I couldn't help myself. You've cast a spell over me."

She didn't get a chance to respond, as a young *Kriegsmarine* lieutenant who had obviously indulged in too much of the available libation cut in, asking her for a dance. Although he outranked him, Bruno didn't want to create a scene and graciously stepped back, allowing them to dance. It also provided a thin veneer of respectability for a high-ranking SS officer at the ball, not with his wife, but a much younger, pretty housemaid. As he stood watching the pair on the dance floor, Adolf Galland, top Luftwaffe fighter ace, approached him.

"A nice little slice of strudel you have there, Schmidt," Galland said, shaking Bruno's hand vigorously.

"I see you're chasing skirts instead of Lancasters this evening." Bruno laughed. They stood there chatting about the latest news from the front.

"So is *der dicke Hermann* (Fat Hermann) going to be able to keep his promise of parachuting 800 tons of supplies a day to our Wehrmacht comrades in besieged Stalingrad?" Bruno asked Galland.

He shrugged his shoulder, raising his eyebrows at the same time. "I am fighter pilot. I shoot them down, not drop stuff down. And I have plenty of problems getting my fighter wing supplied with sufficient petrol to keep them in the air long enough to shoot down the Yanks."

Their conversation was interrupted by Margit and the young lieutenant's return. The lieutenant saluted Bruno and Galland, clicked his heels as he kissed Margit's hand, and turned to leave.

After wishing Galland "Happy New Year and good hunting," Bruno took Margit by the hand and suggested that they wander around the magnificent complex that was the nerve centre of the Luftwaffe's worldwide air operations.

As they passed an empty office on the second floor, Bruno pulled Margit into the darkness. He threw his arms around her and held her close. He started kissing her neck, eliciting a low murmur from her closed lips. Then his tongue sought hers as a physical urgency overtook them. Bruno grabbed her waist with both hands and lifted her up on the desk in the middle of the office, then turned and kicked the door closed. He pushed her gown, the one worn by Steffi those many years ago, up above her waist, and with one deft motion pulled down her silk undergarment then dropped to his knees and thrust his head between her hose-covered, spread-eagled legs.

Margit closed her eyes, threw her legs over Bruno's shoulders and began to moan loudly as waves of pleasure washed over her. After their passionate and hurried coupling, the two of them sat on the desk in the darkness talking. A new reality had dawned for both of them, and neither knew how to deal with it. The handsome, charming, older German, capable of both tenderness and of terrible brutality in the service of the Nazi State, and the young, beautiful, and naïve Dutch peasant girl.

As they left the building holding hands, they passed other offices that, judging by the moans and grunts escaping from inside, seemed to have been employed for the same illicit purpose. The stress, the fear of what the morrow would bring, the sheer terror, the killing, and the dying of the war had taken their toll on the morale and strict Christian morality of the German people. It was, as Winston Churchill had famously said, "Not yet the beginning of the end, but indeed the end of the beginning."

CHAPTER 37

1943,

BERLIN—A NEW YEAR DAWNS AT 14 MEINEKE STRASSE

The beginning of 1943 was not quite as joyous at the Weisz residence as it had been at the Air Ministry. After having been offered the opportunity in the fall of 1939 by Major Alois Huber of the Gestapo to send four-year-old Max to England under the *Kindertransport* program, Arnold had returned home with a heavy heart, wracked by feelings of terrible guilt. Should he try to save at least one small part of his family, while surrendering the rest to whatever uncertain fate the Third Reich had in store for its Jewish citizens, or keep the family together in the hope that the future might not turn out as bleak as it seemed at the moment?

Ingrid had greeted him at the door with an expectant smile on her face and little Max in her arms. *She has never looked so good,* Arnold thought. *Pregnancy seems to agree with her.*

"Well, how did it go? When do we leave, and where are we going to?"

"Could you please have Mother or Heldi take Max? We need to talk alone," he answered in a grave tone.

The two of them then went to sit in the salon where so many happy years ago they would gather in the evenings with Arnold and his father-in-law, dissecting the day's political events over schnapps and cigars while Ingrid and Esther played the piano.

Arnold started to explain the offer made by the Gestapo major.

Ingrid didn't wait for him to finish as she stood up and broke out in tears. "Have you gone mad? How can you even think of doing such a thing? Our only child, not even four, living with strangers in a foreign land? And we may never see him again! You are crazy! It's not something we can do!"

She nearly collapsed, and Arnold had to hold her up, sobs wracking her entire body.

"No, I will not have it. You go back and tell that despicable Nazi that we are not breaking up our family. They have already murdered my father. I won't allow them to do any more harm to us!"

She let go of Arnold and on unsteady feet staggered into their bedroom, throwing herself on the bed and burying her head in her pillow.

Esther came in to comfort her crying daughter, while Heldi played a game with Max to distract him, and Arnold walked into the stairwell to have his first cigarette in over five years. He was faced with an unwinnable dilemma that his lawyer's mind just couldn't wrestle with.

In the three years since that horrible evening, matters in Germany had descended even further into the abyss for its remaining Jewish citizens. In March 1940, Ingrid had given birth to twin red-headed girls, Elsa and Rachel. Dr. Levy from Adass Yisroel Hospital, who had delivered Max four years prior, came to the apartment to deliver the twins. A week after the delivery, the hospital, the last Jewish medical institution in the Reich, was shut down by the Gestapo and its entire medical staff, including Dr. Levy, was transported to Dachau for extermination.

By the end of 1942, the majority of Berlin's Jews had been shipped off to the gas chambers and crematoria of concentration camps all over Eastern Europe. New laws had been introduced to strip those remaining within the borders of the Reich of even the smallest vestiges of wealth accumulated over centuries of hard work by them and their forebears.

And so it came to a conversation over cups of ersatz coffee in the Weisz's kitchen one evening in late 1942.

"I am at wit's end," Arnold said. "We're the only Jewish family left in our neighbourhood and I am still not sure of the reason why. Perhaps we're just lucky, or we have sympathetic and kind neighbours who haven't yet reported us to the Gestapo. Nevertheless, the situation won't last long before the knock comes on the door. We must do something to try and save ourselves. But what?"

"Herr Weisz, I have an idea," Heldi quietly answered. All eyes turned to the diminutive Austrian housemaid cum nanny. "Well, as you know, Jews in the Reich are no longer allowed to own any kind of assets, including real estate. Prior to being shipped East, they were all forced to sell everything they owned to 'good Christian Germans.'"

"That's not new, Heldi. True, but already well-known," Arnold interjected in a disappointed tone.

"Well, I have a friend who bought her employer's apartment for a very small amount of money, mere pfennigs, and then signed a document stating that when the rightful owners returned, they could get their property back for the same price. We could do that with this apartment."

"Yes, but where would we go? We know of no one within or outside Germany that we could move in with."

"And it's too late for that anyway," came the reply from Ingrid, as she and Esther hugged each other, tears flowing down their faces, their hands trembling as they tried to lift their coffee cups to their lips, hanging hopefully on every word as Heldi spoke.

"Herr and Frau Weisz and Frau Grossman, you won't have to leave."

A quizzical look, but no words, from the three others met Heldi's intriguing suggestion.

"One day, when I was at home alone, before these terrible times descended upon us, a chimney sweep came knocking on the door. He said he needed access to the chimney to clean it, as it hadn't been done in decades. To my surprise, he said there was a way to get to the roof through a trap door in the dining room. He asked me to help him move that heavy, tall dark oak cabinet that was in front of it.

"And, indeed, when we moved the piece of furniture aside, there was a nearly imperceptible line in the wallpaper that turned out to be a door. It led into quite a spacious area under the roof that it was possible to stand up in. There was also a hatch-like contraption that one would need a ladder for to get up on the roof."

A wide conspiratorial smile enveloped her face as she finished explaining the potential sanctuary to her three employers, who had listened to her with rapt attention.

"And how does this help us?" asked Esther as she cleared her throat.

"Well, Frau Grossman sells the apartment to me..."

"No, no, Papa would never forgive me, it's impossible!" Esther wailed.

"Mama, please give Heldi a chance to explain. You know that she'd never suggest anything that would bring harm to us. She's family."

Seeing Esther calm down somewhat and the trusting look in Ingrid's eyes, Heldi continued. "You would sell it to me in name only, Frau Grossman. At the same time as we sign the sale to me, I will sign it back to you. We will let a lawyer, perhaps Herr Guthausen, hold on to the copy I sign, so that when all this ugly mess is over, you can claim your apartment back."

Arnold was deep in thought as he listened. "I understand this part of it, but that still doesn't change our situation. We are still a family of Jews that Hitler is looking to get rid of one way or another. Instead of living in our own apartment, we're living in one owned by you, until the Nazis come calling for us."

"Herr Weissz, every day the Gestapo is searching all over Berlin for Jews in hiding. They order any Jews left in the city to voluntarily assemble at the railroad stations for 'resettlement' in the East, or they will face arrest and forcible deportation. So, here's my plan..."

Their discussion was cut short by Rachel, tears flowing down her flushed cheeks, a stuffed bear in her arm, appearing at the kitchen door. "Mutti, I had a bad dream," she sobbed as she went to hug Ingrid.

"Here, I'll put her back to bed, you three keep talking," Esther volunteered.

"I have several acquaintances in the Wehrmacht stationed locally. They were the ones who helped me bring Papa's body home on Kristallnacht. They are not friends of Adolf and his gang. They will come in the morning and pretend to arrest and take you away. These dark days that's quite routine, with raids to arrest Jews happening all over the city. All us good Germans pretend not to notice. We just turn our heads and carry on with our lives, seemingly oblivious to the misery that surrounds us."

Tears came to her eyes as she spoke. She paused for a moment to gather her composure, then continued, "You will stay at one of their homes until nightfall, at which time they'll bring you back here. Then you will hide in the attic space until the Nazis lose this senseless war. While you are in hiding, I will own this apartment and will seem to be the only one living in it. Life will be quite normal, with my friends coming and going. Everyone will think I made a great bargain. The neighbours will be none the wiser."

Arnold contemplated her words in silence for a few minutes, rolling the idea over and over in his head. Then, with an exasperated look on his face, he responded to the seemingly outlandish idea proposed by Heldi. "How would you expect six of us to live in such a small place for an extended period of time? How do we cook, eat and sleep? How do we go to the bathroom? This all sounds rather crazy!"

"Does a death camp sound more attractive, Herr Weisz?"

Arnold took a deep breath as Ingrid gently put her hand on his arm. "Please, let's hear her out," Ingrid said.

"You will be able to come out into the apartment at night and relax. We will obviously have to keep our voices low and to a minimum, and the lights off. The kids will have to be kept quiet and occupied. I will continue to do the cooking. I have asked two friends to split up the grocery shopping so we don't raise suspicion with the amounts of food we will be buying."

"How long will this take to set up?" Ingrid inquired.

"It won't take more than a couple of days to arrange everything in the attic space. You know—mattresses, buckets for going to the bathroom, books and toys for the children."

"All right, let's go take a look at our new home, or perhaps I should say, cave," quipped Arnold

The four of them looked around the empty space that was to be their home and refuge for the uncertain duration of the war.

"I will tap on the wall and shift the cabinet aside each night when it's safe to come out," Heldi said. "If there is an emergency and you need to come out, tap twice."

Afterwards, late in the evening and with blackouts concealing their movement, Arnold and Heldi went to see Ziggy Guthausen at his home. He came to the door rubbing sleep from his eyes, wearing a dressing gown over his pyjamas.

"Weisz, what are you doing here at this hour? And who's this with you?"

"It's our maid, Fräulein Hinklemeyer," Arnold whispered. "May we come in?"

Guthausen quietly ushered them into his library, admonishing them to be quiet as he made sure the blackout curtains were fully drawn, and he turned on his desk lamp. "Weisz, what are you still doing in Berlin? Didn't I give you money to leave Germany and a contact to arrange it?"

"It's a long story, Herr Guthausen, and now it doesn't matter," Arnold whispered sadly. "Where is Frau Guthausen?"

"She left Berlin to stay with a sister in a small village near Dusseldorf. Much safer there. What can I do for you now?" Guthausen sounded annoyed.

"We need money to stay alive. I have agreed to sell our apartment at 14 Meineker Strasse to Frau Hinklemeyer here. I don't want to impose on you, but we need to legally document it, and you're the only one I could come to get it done."

"All right, I know how this works, Weisz." Ziggy looked at Heldi and gave her a faint smile. He was going to do whatever he could to try to save his former partner's and his family's lives. Going to his antique Olympia typewriter and covering it in a blanket to muffle the sound, he prepared all the documentation required by the authorities for the transfer of real property from Jewish ownership to Aryan. After signing and sealing the paperwork, he offered his old friend and his maid some schnapps.

"I hope that this works for you and your family, Weisz. Fräulein Hinklemeyer, you are a brave woman. What's happening in this country is tragic. I just hope we all survive it. May God be with you." With that, he bade them goodbye, quietly shutting the door as the two of them disappeared into the unlit street.

A week later, at five in the morning, they were roused by loud banging on their apartment's front door.

CHAPTER 38

All eyes in the room turned to Alexei as he outlined Operation Berlin on the Nile to Daniel. "Daniel, it is our belief that Müller and Schmidt both survived the war and are today supervising and training the Egyptian secret police, the Mukhabarat. We also understand, through sources we have in Cairo, that their special assignment is to keep an eye on former Nazi rocket scientists who had been spirited out of Germany at the end of the war, who had been employed on the V-1 and V-2 rocket programs, and who are now working on guided missile technology for the Egyptian Army and Air Force.

"They are also miniaturizing timing devices to blow up airliners and supplying them to Libya's Ghaddafi and Arafat's PLO. The higher-ups in our defense establishment believe that this work is key to President Sadat feeling confident enough to launch an attack against Israel across the Suez Canal within a year. Were these scientists to be successful in completing their assignment, the existence of the State of Israel would be in mortal peril, as it would allow Egypt's Air Force to operate in Israeli air space, protected by this 'missile umbrella.'

"We know from our source, whom we will call 'Angel,' and who's a close confidante of Sadat, that many of the scientists are not working in Egypt voluntarily. They are being kept in line by Müller and Schmidt, using methods employed during the war by the SS and Gestapo when they were overseeing slave labour at various forced labour camps where the VI and V2 rockets were being assembled.

"They have both become quite proficient in Arabic, have assumed Egyptian names, and have been given the rank of brigadier general in the Mukhabarat by President Nasser, Sadat's predecessor. Their names are Abdel Gamasy and Ghazi Haloub. We are not certain which is which. Both of them have married Egyptian wives."

He paused for a moment to allow the gravity of what he had just disclosed sink in to those in attendance.

Daniel spoke up once again. "How can we be certain it's Müller and Schmidt if we have no proof they survived the war? Just rumours and the hearsay of some tourists and Egyptian POW's?

"It will be your part of the mission to visually confirm their identities," Alexei said, then he continued his outlining. "I have here a copy of a lengthy typewritten field report, filed by a medical corps colonel with the 71st Infantry Division of Patton's Third Army, dated May 5, 1945. Daniel, I think you may be familiar with the author of the report."

With that, he passed around a copy of the document.

"That report was filed by your father, Daniel. So, as you see, Colonel Schmidt's ID card was found on a dead individual who was not Colonel Schmidt. Whether that was by design or accident, we don't know, but no bodies have ever been found, since the end of the war, corresponding to either Müller's or Schmidt's known physiology. They were both sentenced in absentia during the second round of the Nuremberg War Crimes Trials in 1946. Mueller to death, Schmidt to life in prison. They continue to be on Interpol's list of 'Most Wanted.'"

Daniel sat in silence as he read the document written by his father twenty-eight years before relating to the man he presumed he has been asked to stalk and identify, perhaps assassinate.

Alexei took a drink of water, cleared his throat, and continued. "What we do know is that the wounded SS captain, Helmut Eckler, was Schmidt's driver and long-time friend from the 1930s. We also know that after his recovery from surgery at the US Army field hospital,

UNITED STATES 3RD ARMY
71ST INFANTRY DIVISION
LETTERHEAD
CONFIDENTIAL FIELD ACTION REPORT

Date: May 5, 1945
Location: 18th Field Surgical Unit, Magdeburg, Germany
Author: Lt. Col. Samuel Singer, US Army, MC
Distribution: Priority/Confidential SHAEF

On May 4, 1945, at approximately thirteen hundred hours (13:00) ETO, my
driver, Corporal Joseph Murphy, and I were returning from scheduled
meetings with officers of the Soviet 58th Rifle Division on the east side
of the river Elbe. Shortly after crossing to the west side of the river,
we came upon a badly damaged black Mercedes cabriolet. The vehicle, with
smoke pouring from under its hood, bore the insignia of the SS on its
door, and had crashed into the ditch beside the main paved Berlin-Ha-
nover motorway, just west of kilometre marker 287. We assumed that it had
been strafed and set afire by a Soviet fighter aircraft, which we had
observed flying at a low altitude in an easterly direction at least ten
miles west of the river, over the American Zone. This was a few minutes
prior to us coming upon the wreckage.

There were three individuals in and by the car. The identification
documents found on the driver, who was badly injured, identified him as
Hauptsturmführer Helmut Johann Eckler of the SS Leibstandarte Division,
and that on the deceased woman in the back of the car as Margit Angelika
Hootveg, a Dutch national. A partially burnt SS photo identification
card, found close to the dead Wehrmacht officer, bore the name of
Standartenführer Karl Bruno Schmidt. However, the picture on the ID
card did not match that of the face of the dead Wehrmacht officer.

I make this report as upon my return to the field hospital I learned that
Standartenführer Karl Bruno Schmidt's name is on a list of wanted Nazi
war criminals whose presence or capture is of a high priority to be
reported to local Military Police authorities.

Signed
Lt. Colonel Samuel Singer, US Army MC
18th Field Surgical Unit, 71st Infantry Division, US 3rd Army Corps

Samuel Singer

where his right arm was amputated, he was sent to a POW camp for
interrogation. Since he was not listed as a high-priority prisoner by
any of the Allies, he was released in 1947, shortly after which he left
Germany for South America, like many other former Nazis.

"According to Abwehr intelligence reports, Margit Hootveg was
Schmidt's mistress. Her, and the unidentified Wehrmacht officer in
Schmidt's Mercedes, both of whom died in the wreck, were buried in
Magdeburg, which reverted to the Soviet Zone of Occupation shortly
after the incident."

CHAPTER 39

MAY & JUNE 1973,

MOSSAD HQ, TEL AVIV & VALCARTIER,

QUEBEC—THE FRENCH CONNECTION

When Alexei finished reading Dr. Singer's field report, Simon Wiesenthal stood up. "I think my participation from hereon will no longer be required until we know the outcome of this mission, and I would like to fly back to Vienna this afternoon. Daniel, thank you for accepting this hazardous task. Good luck and good hunting!"

"I probably won't be needed any longer either, so I add my best wishes for success and a safe return to those of Dr. Wiesenthal." Wolfgang Lotz placed one hand on Daniel's shoulder as he spoke, and whispered in his ear, "The Mukhabarat are a vicious lot. They don't observe any niceties when it comes to their methods of interrogation."

He showed Daniel his fingers, which had been disfigured from vice grips and hammer blows administered during his captivity in Egypt.

"And I don't have to warn you about Müller and Schmidt. Not only are they brutal individuals, but they are also paranoid, being Nazis on the lam."

With that, Israel's "Champagne Spy" shook Daniel's hand, hugged Alexei, and along with Wiesenthal left the room.

"Okay, so this might also be a good time for a bathroom break," Alexei said.

Daniel and Yoel stood beside each other at the urinal. "You know, Daniel," Yoel said, "it's not going to be easy. Schmidt speaks fairly fluent French from his wartime days and would immediately recognize your Parisian accent."

"Why will I need to speak French at all?"

"Alexei will explain it," Yoel answered as he washed his hands. "In any case, you'll be spending the next week with me, twenty-four seven, learning to speak French the way the Québécois do. The only two rules I have is that no other language is spoken while you're with me, and that you stay away from my sister-in-law, Ofra. She's a beautiful brunette and always horny." He laughed.

When they re-entered the room, Naomi and Alexei were in animated conversation.

"So, Yoel, did you enlighten young Mr. Singer as to the finer points of the mission?" asked Alexei with a smile crossing his face.

"Nope, I thought I'd leave that to you," responded Yoel with a glint in his eye. "Time is tight, both for getting you to the airport to say goodbye to your father and for getting your mission underway. Our country is in impending danger and we don't know what Saddam's timeline for action is."

"I am all ears, Alexei." Daniel grinned.

"The United Nations has had a monitoring mission in Cairo since the ceasefire of the Six-Day War. Currently, a state of war exists between Israel and Egypt, with daily exchanges of artillery and air attacks. The UN is not there to interfere, but to simply monitor and report back to HQ in New York. The small monitoring team is made up of one Pole, one Canadian, and one Indonesian officer.

"The Canadian is a captain of the Royal 22nd Regiment, 'The Van Doos,' headquartered in Valcartier, Quebec, in Canada. Our military attaché in Ottawa, Canada, has an excellent relationship with the commanding officer of The Van Doos, Brigadier-General René Beaulieu. Apparently, the Canadian officer currently with the monitoring mission, a Captain Isidore Ranpuil, will be returning to

Canada for two weeks on compassionate leave, as his sister passed away unexpectedly." Alexei gave a conspiratorial wink to Daniel and Yoel as he finished the sentence. "A certain Captain Daniel Delorme from Trois-Rivières in Quebec, also known, only to us, as Daniel Singer, has been selected to take his place for the two-week period."

He looked up to see Daniel's reaction to what he'd said, but seeing no change in his blank expression, continued. "When your week with Yoel's finished, you will board a flight to Paris aboard Air France and connect to Air Canada for your flight to Montreal. You'll be met at the airport by Captain Serge Brossard, the base commandant's adjutant. He and General Beaulieu are the only ones that are aware of who you are. Brossard is married to a Jewish woman, and the general's an old friend of Israel from his time with General Burns during the UN's Sinai deployment after the 1956 Sinai War.

"You'll spend a week at Valcartier becoming familiar with The Van Doos' operating procedures and what a UN deployment entails. The Canadians are risking a lot to help us. If they're found out, their careers will be finished, and they could be court-martialled. Their global reputation as neutral peacekeepers will be ruined and Canadian diplomatic officers around the world could be in danger."

"What about documentation?" Daniel asked.

"Our documentation specialists have already prepared all the paperwork you will require, including your Canadian passport and military ID, with the exception of your photographs. Those will be taken tomorrow. We employ some of the world's best forgers, so nobody will be able to differentiate them from the genuine article.

"Now for the hard part. After your week of indoctrination at Valcartier, you will fly to Cairo aboard a Royal Canadian Air Force transport aircraft taking supplies to the UN contingent. There, you will report to Major Jan Sadowski of the Polish Army, the senior officer with the monitoring mission."

"But how do I get to Müller and Schmidt? If indeed it's them. And why do I need to? Is there no other way for you to confirm their identities?" Daniel inquired.

"No, there isn't. There is no one in our employ whom we can rely on to get close to them. We have learned from recent UN intelligence reports we acquired surreptitiously that two high-ranking Egyptian officers, who appear not to be native Egyptians, but more likely Europeans, have taken a keen interest in the activities of the monitoring mission. We assume them to be Müller and Schmidt and think this is as a result of trying to keep their preparations for an attack across the Suez Canal secret. They want to find out how much we know, so they keep close tabs on UN personnel. So, they'll probably come to you."

"Supposing that everything goes well and I get to Cairo, and somehow get to meet these two Europeans, confirm that they're indeed Müller and Schmidt, what then? Do I pull out a magic ray gun and vaporize them?" Daniel laughed at the seeming absurdity of it all. *These guys are nuts,* he thought.

Once again, Alexei read Daniel's mind. "No, we're not totally crazy. Your mission is simply to get in, make a positive identification, or not, and then get out. If your ID is positive, we will have others within the shop do what's required. You're not being trained as an assassin. Any questions before Yoel drives you out to Lod to say goodbye to your father?"

"Alexei, before I go can we have a quick word?"

"Sure."

Daniel and Alexei walked over to a corner of the room.

"You know, my father never mentioned what happened with this SS staff car at the end of the war. It's really strange, because he told me a lot of stories about his time in Europe and Palestine, but nothing about this. I think that it would have been important to him, since it involved his discovery of a Nazi war criminal. I wonder why."

CHAPTER 40

The late-winter, pink-hued sun had just begun rising over the horizon as bleary-eyed Berliners started their day after another restless night, which most of them had spent in underground bomb shelters.

The banging on the Grossmans' apartment door started with a loud knock, followed by an increasing crescendo delivered by rifle butts breaking the window pane in the heavy wooden door.

Heldi, in a bright-red housecoat, was the first to greet the squad of Wehrmacht soldiers dressed in field grey. She yelled, "It's the middle of the night. Stop the banging. You'll scare the children."

Indeed, they could already hear the cries of the three children from the back of the apartment.

Brusquely shoving aside the diminutive maid, the corporal in charge, clutching a Schmeisser machine pistol, entered the hallway and barked back at her, "We are looking for the Grossman family! They have ten minutes to pack and assemble outside!"

Having been woken by all the commotion, neighbours started peeking through curtained windows at the unfolding tragedy. A couple cracked their doors open slightly to better see and hear the goings-on.

The corporal yelled at them, "Have you never seen some filthy Jews being evicted? Keep staring and maybe you'll be able to join them!"

Most quickly withdrew back into the semi-darkness of their apartments without a word. One brave soul shouted out, before quickly closing their door, "For God's sake, have a heart! There are children in there!"

The three Weisz children—Maximillian, Elsa, and Rachel—clung to their mother's housecoat with one hand, and to small dolls with the other, and sobbed loudly.

The corporal, not bothering with niceties, began walking through the apartment, urging them to move quicker. "You won't need anything but the basic necessities. A change of underwear, toothbrushes, and combs. Everything else will be provided to you when you get to your destination. Now, let's get moving!"

Heldi helped the children get dressed and tried to calm them down with soothing words. Both Ingrid and Esther held back their tears lest it got to the children. Ingrid wrapped her belongings and a picture of her father in his grey housecoat, while Esther packed a small suitcase.

Then the six members of the Grossman and Weisz families started to bid farewell to the place they had called home for so many years and began trooping through the smashed front entrance. Heldi, tears welling up in her eyes, hugged and kissed each of them in turn, and whispered a heartfelt farewell.

By the time they got to the ground floor and went through the heavy glass front doors, a small crowd had gathered by the dark-grey Wehrmacht lorry that was to take them away. Most, with faces sullen and ashen from sleepless nights, watched without a trace of emotion as their Jewish neighbours and their children were roughly shoved and manhandled into the back of the truck along with their meagre belongings.

Someone shouted out, "Good riddance, filthy Jews."

A woman's voice was heard, as the truck, its exhaust spewing black smoke into the cold spring air started to roll away, saying, "Shut up, Hans."

In the back of the truck the corporal reached into his coat pocket and pulled out a chocolate bar and, breaking it into three pieces, gave each of the children one.

He turned to Arnold with a smile and said, "That went quite smoothly, Herr Weisz. Very convincing, *nein*?"

"That it was. That it was," Arnold answered with a deep and sad sigh of relief.

The other three soldiers broke out laughing and slapped each other on the back.

Two days later, in the black of night and in the midst of an Allied air raid, when everyone else in their neighbourhood was in the bomb shelters, the family, silent as ghosts, stole back into their apartment. Heldi was there to greet them with a warm smile and cups of well-nigh impossible to obtain hot cocoa. After hugs, and pushing aside the heavy oak cabinet, she conducted them into the secret attic hideaway that was to be their home and shelter for the duration of the war.

CHAPTER 41

MAY/JUNE 1973,

TEL AVIV, ISRAEL & VALCARTIER,

QUEBEC—THE MISSION UNFOLDS

After a short drive from Mossad Headquarters to Lod Airport to meet Samuel, Daniel, Yoel, and Naomi arrived at El-Al's overseas departure lounge. Father and son hugged each other.

"Just in time for our departure, Daniel. Where is your luggage?"

"Oh, sorry, Dad. This is Yoel Cohen. He's with the Israel Department of Antiquities and he asked if I could stay for a month to consult on an excavation project. I was happy to say yes."

"And I assume that the lovely Naomi may have played a part in your decision?" Samuel whispered in his son's ear with a knowing smile, stealing a sideways glance at the pretty young Israeli standing off to the side. "Well, good luck, and enjoy. I guess I'll have to explain it to Mom. But I'm getting used to having to make explanations to her when it comes to the Holy Land." He chuckled as he tussled Daniel's blond hair with one hand, in a way that fathers do with their adolescent sons about to go on their first overnight camp.

"Have a safe flight, Dad, and hugs and kisses to Mom."

Daniel watched as Samuel's group slowly made their way on to the Boeing 747.

Daniel turned to Yoel. "Shit, I forgot to ask him about that episode with the wrecked SS car and Schmidt."

"I really don't think you should, anyway," Yoel said. "No one's supposed to know about this mission outside of our little group."

The following week went by quickly. Daniel stayed in a spare bedroom in Yoel and his wife Erika's townhouse in Tel Aviv's suburb of Ramat-Gan. As the sun rose every morning, it found the two of them running along the city's Mediterranean seashore. After their run, they would go for a quick dip in the sea's blue waters, then grab breakfast at one of the small seaside eateries. They only conversed in French, with the Israeli Quebecer continually correcting Daniel's frequent lapses into what they laughingly called *Français Parisienne*.

Yoel would repeatedly swamp Daniel with arcane facts about life in Quebec, thereby helping Daniel establish a believable profile and background as Daniel Delorme, a Catholic Quebecer with deep roots in the province. Around ten, they would show up at Mossad HQ for familiarization with and indoctrination into the Mossad's MO. Mossad's computer nerds had developed computer-generated images of what Müller and Schmidt might look like after nearly thirty years on the run.

After one especially arduous day of training, over an afternoon beer in one of Tel Aviv's pubs, Daniel asked Alexei, "What about some weapon's training, Alexei? You know, like Bond, with some really sexy guns?"

Yoel, his eyes rolling skyward, looked sideways questioningly at the Russian, hardly able to supress a smile. "You will get that in Canada. Their standard sidearm is the 9mm Browning, which is different than our Beretta 951s. You will be issued with one of those, as it's standard equipment for Canadians serving with the UN. Hope to God you never get to use it."

Two days later, after having bid farewell to Alexei, Yoel and Naomi drove Daniel to the airport to catch an Air France flight to Paris. Upon shaking his hand at their final meeting at Mossad HQ, Alexei said, "Remember, Daniel, think twice before you do something, and then don't do it. There are already too many heroes buried on Mount Herzl."

After an uneventful flight from Tel Aviv to Paris, Daniel caught a connecting Air Canada flight to Montreal. He was greeted at Dorval International Airport in Montreal by Captain Brossard, a thirtyish, tall, red-headed man with a like-coloured handlebar moustache, carrying a duffel bag.

"*Bienvenue au Québec, Capitaine Delorme. Comment était votre voyage?*"

"*Sans incidents, merci.*"

They walked to the men's washroom, where Brossard barred the door while Daniel changed into the uniform of a captain in Canada's Royal 22nd Regiment, the famed Van Doos, that Brossard had in the duffel bag.

"*Vous êtes sensationnel. Comme un vrai soldat.*"

"*Merci, mon ami. On y va?*"

Daniel kept drifting off as they drove, mostly in silence, the 157 miles from Montreal to Quebec City, then another 16 miles north to Canadian Forces Base Valcartier. It was late evening by the time they arrived and Captain Brossard, sensing Daniel's fatigue, elected to just accompany him to his room at the base's officers quarters without stopping by at the commandant's office.

"Have a good night, Captain. I'll be by at eight in the morning, and we'll have breakfast with the general."

Daniel locked the door behind Brossard and then collapsed on the bed without taking his clothes off.

Promptly at 8:00 a.m. there was a knock on his door. "*Bonjour, Capitaine Delorme. Vous avez bien dormi?*"

"*Très bien, merci.*"

"We are having breakfast with General Beaulieu. He wants to go over some high-level details regarding your stay at the base."

The general's lengthy welcoming speech was accompanied by a breakfast of scrambled eggs, bacon, toast with maple syrup, and coffee.

"Look, Delorme, I don't know the details of your mission, but I trust my Israeli colleagues that they wouldn't risk compromising their country's relationship with Canada if it wasn't an important one.

Capitaine Brossard and I are putting our necks on the line to help our Jewish friends. The shorter the time you spend with us, the less likelihood of discovery.

"You and Brossard will spend the next two days in your quarters. You and he will go through a history of the regiment, its battle honours, its commanders, organizational structure, and UN service. On the third day, you and I'll go through a Q and A session to determine how much you retained.

"The morning after that I am sending you to the firing range to see how well you handle our weapons. Any questions? If not, good luck, and I'll see you the day after tomorrow. Oh, and by the way, while on the base, avoid at all costs any interaction with Sergeant-Major Favreau. He's a rabid anti-Semite of the old Quebec school."

Daniel hardly had a chance to gulp down what was left of his coffee, never mind ask any questions, before he was hurriedly ushered out of the general's quarters. It was quite evident from the "bum's rush" he got that his presence at Valcartier was less than welcome. He couldn't blame them; after all, it wasn't their fight.

Brossard murmured an apology. "The general's been stressed by a number of disciplinary issues on the base."

Over the next couple of days, Daniel didn't leave his room in the officers' quarters other than to use the washroom. Brossard would go to the officers' dining room and bring Daniel back his meals. He studied the papers provided by the general and committed their contents to memory.

On the morning of the third day, Daniel once again showed up at General Beaulieu's door, accompanied by Brossard, ready for his Q and A. The general greeted him with a broad smile, seemingly in a much better mood than when they had last met. "Come on in, Delorme. I've ordered us some fresh strawberries and pancakes with real Quebec maple syrup for breakfast. Coffee to start with?"

"Yes, please," Daniel responded.

"Now let's get down to business," the general continued.

With that, the session started.

Daniel could answer every one of the general's questions without hesitation.

"Excellent, Capitaine Delorme. Superb! And, finally, why is the regiment referred to as The Van Doos?"

"Twenty-two in English is *vingt-deux* in French."

"Okay, Delorme. No one will be able to tell that you have not been with the regiment for years. In the morning, I'll send Brossard or one of our NCOs to take you to the range for some target practice. Be sharp." The general shook Daniel's hand and patted him on the shoulder, sending him on his way with Brossard.

The two of them spent the evening drinking beer, playing billiards in the officers' recreation area, and discussing world affairs, in general, and women in particular.

CHAPTER 42

Life in the Weisz's hideaway at 14 Meineker Strasse became routine, after the first hectic days of getting themselves organized in the cramped quarters. They would mostly sleep during the day, and once the building quieted down in the evening, they would assemble in silence in the back two bedrooms of the apartment. They would wrap heavy felt rags around their feet so their footsteps would not be heard in the apartment below them. Ingrid and Esther would read fairy tales to the girls, while Arnold read books about America's Indians and the Wild West, written by German author Karl May, to Max. May, although he'd never visited North America, wrote vivid adolescent novels about the lives of Indians and cowboys living there. Occasionally, they would play out various roles from the stories.

Sometimes at night Arnold and Ingrid would quietly sneak up to the roof and sit on the chimneysweep's platform, observing Allied bombers emptying their deadly loads over Berlin. They would watch fascinated as the bright fingers of anti-aircraft searchlights would fix upon an unlucky aircraft as the flak from the batteries of 88s burst around it. They would listen as their neighbours scurried into the air raid shelters when the sirens sounded, which almost became a nightly ritual, as the war dragged into its fourth year. Even though they couldn't seek shelter with their neighbours, they felt insulated in their modest refuge from the orange bomb bursts that would light up the night sky of the German capital. They would play a game whereby the winner would be the one who could count the most explosions. Any diversion at all to pass the time and allay their fears of discovery and death.

It had been six months since they had gone into hiding when Max started to complain about boredom. He had now heard the same stories of the Wild West, and played the role of Winnetou, the fearless Indian Chief, countless times.

"Daddy, can we not do something different? I am really getting bored."

Arnold certainly understood the child's need for stimulation. *After all, hiding in an attic, while exciting at the beginning, was not something that would be healthy long term*, he thought. But what brilliant idea could he come up with to keep a seven-year-old boy interested?

"Well, Max, we have lots of lined paper and pencils, so why don't you start a diary? It may be something that we can have published after the war. Hiding from the bad guys from your perspective. I bet it would become a bestseller, Max!" He wanted it to sound adventurous and fun.

Arnold's infectious enthusiasm was quickly embraced by Max, who immediately started writing of their time in hiding.

My name is Maximillian Weisz, and my father had given me the idea to start writing a diary about our time in hiding from the Nazis. I will be eight years old, and because our family is Jewish, we have to hide in the attic of the apartment that we used to live in. My four year old twin sisters Elsa and Rachel, my grandmother, mother, and father are all hiding with us. Things are pretty bad because we cannot talk normally and my sisters are always bugging me to play girls games with them. I would really like to go with Father to sail our little balsa boats on the lakes. I am really unhappy and scared of what will happen to us. Father says that all bad things will end soon.

September 14, 1943

We have now been hiding for six months. I really miss going to the lakes with father to sail our boats. Life here is really boring. The girls never leave me alone. They want to play house with me all the time. I wish we had a cat or dog I could play with, but we can't even have goldfish. I am tired because the bombs kept us awake for most of the night.

My name is Maximillian Weisz, and my father had given me the idea to start writing a diary about our time in hiding from the Nazis. I will be eight years old, and because our family is Jewish, we have to hide in the attic of the apartment that we used to live in. My four year old twin sisters Elsa and Rachel, my grandmother, mother, and father are all hiding with us. Things are pretty bad because we cannot talk normally and my sisters are always bugging me to play girls games with them. I would really like to go with Father to sail our little balsa boats on the lakes. I am really unhappy and scared of what will happen to us. Father says that all bad things will end soon.

September 14, 1943

We have now been hiding for six months. I really miss going to the lakes with father to sail our boats. Life here is really boring. The girls never leave me alone. They want to play house with me all the time. I wish we had a cat or dog I could play with, but we can't even have goldfish. I am tired because the bombs kept us awake for most of the night.

November 18, 1943

We are getting very cold at night. Heldi bought us some extra blankets and makes us hot drinks at night. It's made from tree bark and tastes terrible. She says there is no more cocoa to be found anywhere. There was a raid in the building this morning. Father said that they took away some people because they were against the Führer. Bombs fell again last night, but they were far away. Heldi found a small Blaupunkt radio in one of the bombed out buildings and it still works. We now huddle under blankets and extra quietly listen to the BBC.

January 18, 1944

The bombing was very heavy and very close last night. Our building shook and Heldi said that the glass front door of our building was blown in. It's very cold and it is snowing. Father went out in the middle of the night to get us some meat from the zoo where some animals were killed by the bombing. I heard him say to Heldi that without it we might all starve. I haven't eaten any meat in a long time, but I don't think I could eat a zoo animal. While Father was gone and everybody else was asleep I snuck up to the roof to watch the snow fall. There were little fires everywhere.

March 12, 1944

It's my birthday today. Heldi has saved up some of the ostrich meat Father managed to get at the zoo after the bombing in January and that she had preserved, and she fried it up in some lard she managed to get with food stamps. It didn't taste as bad as I thought it would. She also made me a little birthday cake with whipped cream that she said she was able to get at a patisserie by bribing the clerk. It tasted delicious. Mother said that we couldn't have candles because it would alert the neighbours. No bombing today. Maybe they know it's my birthday.

March 18, 1944

A terrible thing happened last night. I again snuck up to the roof, but when I heard a noise I got scared and hurried to get inside and slipped and fell all the way down the ladder. Father says that both my ankles are broken. I am in very much pain and I cannot stand. Grandma and Mother wrapped some cold towels around my ankles, but they are still badly swollen. Heldi said that she would try to get some plaster and make me a cast.

June 7, 1944

We heard on the BBC that the Americans have landed in France. Father thinks that the war will be over very soon and that we may be able to move back into our apartment. Even though I am in a lot of pain I am very happy. Maybe life between these walls will soon be over and I can go outside again.

June 17, 1944

It's been exactly three months since I fell and broke my ankles. I still can't walk. I sit in a chair or lie on a mattress the whole day. It's horrible. Heldi says that they are getting better with the plaster on them. She thinks that I will be able to put weight on them in a couple of weeks.

July 21, 1944

My sisters and Mother have developed a very high fever. We don't know what's causing it but the reading is over 44 degrees Celsius. They are constantly throwing up and we are afraid that they will die if we can't find a doctor. Tonight we heard from the BBC that someone had tried to blow up the Führer. I hope they did.

July 22, 1944

Mother and the girls are getting sicker by the hour. It seems that whatever it is Grandma has caught it too. The only ones that are not sick now are Father, Heldi, and I. Father said they must find a doctor somehow or they will all die. I am very scared.

July 25, 1944

Everyone's been gone for two days and two nights now to try and find a doctor. Heldi went with them. They told me to be very quiet until they get back. I am very scared. I don't know what to do. I am all alone. I hope they come home soon.

Max's writing was interrupted by the scraping on the floor of the heavy cabinet blocking the entrance to their hideaway being moved aside.

CHAPTER 43

SPRING, SUMMER, AND FALL 1943,
MUNICH & BERLIN, THE EASTERN FRONT

In the year since their return from 1943's New Year's Eve festivities at the Air Ministry in Berlin, Bruno and Margit continued their illicit affair at every opportunity that presented itself. Bruno and Steffi grew further and further apart, spending less and less time together. Steffi, feeling herself slighted and ignored by her younger spouse, threw herself full tilt into charitable works. She would spend days and nights on end away from their home, visiting wounded soldiers in hospitals and shelters full of civilians bombed out of their homes. She led food and clothing drives for the families of soldiers at the front. The mental and physical stresses brought on by these unceasing activities took their toll on her appearance. As the war went on and the Allied air raids on Germany's heartland increased in intensity, so did her determination to help those most impacted by it.

Bruno and Margit took advantage of her absences to make love and future plans.

"Darling, when are you going to tell your wife about us? When are you going to make it clear to her that it's me you're in love with now?" Margit asked these questions on an-almost daily basis.

"Look, Margit, she is under a lot of stress right now. As you know, I hardly ever see her. It's something that will happen in good time. What's the sense right now anyway, in this world gone mad?"

"Because I want to have babies! Your babies! And I can't do that while you're married to another woman!"

It was mid-morning in late September 1943 when the phone rang as Bruno and Margit were having one of their interminable spats. Steffi had been gone the entire week working with a group of orphans in Hamburg.

"Good morning, Colonel Schmidt," came the voice over a crackling phone line. Without waiting for acknowledgement from Bruno, the voice continued, "This is Captain Rudolf from Reichsführer Himmler's office. The Reichsführer requests that you come to his office immediately on a top-priority matter."

"Certainly, Captain Rudolf. Please advise the Reichsführer that I will leave for Berlin forthwith."

"Heil Hitler," came the response before the phone was hung up.

Bruno rang Helmut Eckler and asked him to pick him up. He turned to Margit. "Darling, I have to go. Uncle Heinrich wants to talk to me. I should be back late tonight. We can continue our talk then."

"You son of a bitch, you'll never leave her, will you?"

With that, the pretty young Dutch farmgirl, her face red with anger, stormed out of the apartment.

Bruno and Helmut took back roads to get to Berlin. It was late afternoon by the time they got to Gestapo Headquarters at Prinz-Albrecht-Strasse. On the way, Bruno unloaded his romantic burden and marital entanglements to his old friend and driver Helmut.

"You know, these young women—no, girls—just have no idea of what life really is like. They think it's just parties and fucking, parties and more fucking. Steffi's looking pretty haggard these days, and I really don't want to sleep with her, but by God I would love some sleep and a whole day without any arguments about marriage and babies!"

"Well, good friend, as the saying goes 'You made your bed, now go lie in it,'" Helmut laughingly shot back. "Now you know why I've stayed a bachelor."

"I wonder what Himmler wants? That asshole Rudolf hung up on me before I had a chance to ask." Bruno changed the subject, seeing that he wasn't getting any sympathy regarding his women problems from Helmut.

✠

The two of them entered the imposing grey building covered by camouflage netting and surrounded by anti-aircraft guns. Bruno headed directly to Reichsführer Himmler's office on the second floor, while Helmut made for the cafeteria to get a stiff shot of schnapps. The drive had tired him out, as had Bruno's incessant complaining about his love life.

The bespectacled Himmler, with a permanent five o'clock shadow, greeted Bruno effusively. He looked dishevelled, his usually neatly combed jet-black hair standing on end. His uniform was badly creased, as if he had slept in it. The typically neat office was a mess, with papers all over the colourful Persian carpet and maps all askew covering the walls.

Looking around, Bruno thought, *We're obviously in crisis mode*.

"My dear fellow, thank you for coming here so quickly. I know that the roads can be treacherous in daytime. Any problems along the way?"

"No, Helmut's a great driver. Even on the back roads, he drives as if he was at Le Mans."

"Let me get straight to the matter. The Russkies are kicking our ass in the East. We lost over five hundred Panzers and close to a quarter-million men in the Kursk salient. Guderian and the other chicken-shit generals in the field are talking about a strategic withdrawal. That cannot happen!" Himmler's voice rose to a crescendo as he stabbed his manicured finger at a battle map pinned to the wall.

"It's only our boys, the Waffen SS, that have the backbone to fight and hold the line. That drug addict Göring can't even get enough planes into the air to provide air cover for a counter attack!"

"But Herr Reichsführer, what can I do? I am not a field officer."

"No, but you have balls, and the Führer trusts you."

"As you know, Herr Reichsführer, I am prepared to lay down my life for the Führer."

"The Führer has requested that you fly to the front, assemble the Waffen SS field officers and, along with them, confront the Wehrmacht Eastern Front commanders and personally deliver the Führer's message that there will be no withdrawal! Not one step back!" Himmler started to tremble and had to sit down.

"The Führer's order is crystal clear!" he continued. "Your SS comrades are there to back you up and to arrest any Wehrmacht officer that even breathes a word about withdrawal!"

"When would you like me to leave, Herr Reichsführer?"

"There is a Junkers Ju 52 warming up on the tarmac at Templehof. It's being flown by Hans Baur, the Führer's personal pilot. He attaches the utmost importance to this mission."

"Herr Reichsführer, please thank the Führer for allowing me this opportunity to serve the Reich. Heil Hitler."

"Best of luck, Schmidt. Our Führer is counting on you."

Himmler and Bruno shook hands, and Bruno turned and left the room.

As he ran down the stairs, he felt somewhat elated at the prospect of not having to go back to Munich that evening and continue his argument with Margit. Helmut was waiting for him at the bottom of the stairs, in discussion with Werner Best, one of Admiral Canaris' Abwehr officers.

"Hey, Schmidt, it's been a long time. What's new in your world?"

"Would love to chat, Werner, but Helmut and I have to fly," Bruno said.

As they got into the black Mercedes cabriolet with the SS logo on the door, Helmut asked, "Where to now?"

"Templehof. I'm flying to the Eastern Front tonight."

"Boy, must be important. Is the chicken farmer going with you?"

"No. He says the Führer needs him here."

Helmut raised his eyebrow and smiled sarcastically.

"Look, Helmut, I need you to drive back to Munich tonight after you drop me off. Steffi is not at home, but one never knows when she'll be back, and with Margit being in the state she was in, one never knows what could happen. Be a good friend and babysit her for me."

The tri-engine Junkers transport aircraft, with Bruno settled in the co-pilot's seat, lifted off the runway with its navigation lights extinguished, banked steeply to the right, and headed for the Eastern Front. Down below, the black Mercedes, with its headlights off, was racing along the Autobahn in the direction of Munich.

CHAPTER 44

JUNE 1973,

VALCARTIER, CANADA, & CAIRO, EGYPT

At 7:00 a.m. on the morning of the day he was supposed to go to the firing range, Daniel was woken by loud and insistent knocking on his door.

"Coming, Brossard, coming!" Daniel yelled, trying to rouse himself from a deep sleep.

As he flung the door open, rubbing the sleep from his eyes, Daniel was blinded by the early morning sun. Much to his surprise, instead of Brossard, in the doorway stood a tall, bald-headed, swarthy-complexioned sergeant major wearing freshly pressed green fatigues and carrying a swagger stick under his left arm. The man came to attention and raised his right arm to his brow in a stiff military salute.

"Good morning, sir! I am Sergeant Major Favreau, and I have been instructed by General Beaulieu to accompany you to the firing range for live fire practice. Are you ready to go, sir?"

Daniel was taken aback for a moment. He thought, *What the fuck is the general thinking? I thought this guy was the worst anti-Semite in the country and that he could tell a Jew from miles away. And this is the guy that's going to be with me all day with a loaded gun? Is he testing me or Favreau?*

His thoughts were interrupted by Favreau. "Are you ready to go to the range, sir? Now!"

"Yes, yes, Sergeant-major. Just let me grab my sunglasses. It's bright outside."

As the two of them drove in the Jeep, Favreau peppered Daniel with questions in a suspicious tone. "So, Capitaine Delorme, where were you born?"

"Trois-Rivières."

"Oh, I know it well. My sister lives there. What part of the city did you go to school in?"

Yoel's hammering a veritable encyclopedia of facts about French Canada into Daniel's brain during the week they spent together were paying off. They had established a credible background for him that would stand scrutiny.

"My parents and I moved to Montreal when I was fourteen, and I went to high school there. Villa Maria College on Decarie. It's a Catholic high school."

"Yes, I've heard of it. Very exclusive. You must have rich parents!" Favreau said in an envious tone.

"We did okay. My father was an executive with Canadian Pacific. After high school, I went to Collège Militaire Royal de Saint-Jean, in Saint-Jean-sur-Richelieu. Then on to a staff appointment at DND in Ottawa."

Seemingly satisfied with Daniel's answers, Favreau drove the rest of the way to the firing range, hidden behind some low hills topped with a row of poplars, in silence. There was no else on the range at that time of the morning, and the only sound was the chirping of tiny swallows playing hide and go seek amongst the tree branches and occasionally taking flight into the cloudless, brilliant blue sky.

After getting out of the Jeep, Favreau, handing Daniel a large paper target, suggested that he walk the fifty yards to the sand berm that acted as a backstop for fired ammunition and pin it to the splintered wooden post in front of it.

Daniel sauntered across the grass-covered range holding on tightly to the paper target, which a strong wind was threatening to tear out of his hand.

Favreau watched as the young officer walked nonchalantly away from him. He slowly and quietly undid the clasp on the holster of his 9 mm standard-issue Browning service pistol with thirteen rounds in the magazine, and carefully raised it by extending his right arm and clasping his wrist with his left hand. He took careful aim through the calibrated sight, and yelled out to Daniel, "You know, sir, Hitler was right. All the problems of this world are caused by the Jews! It's because of them that hard-working Catholic Quebecers like my kid brother can't get a decent job!"

He started to slowly squeeze the trigger.

Bang. Bang. Bang.

The three rounds whistled by, mere inches from Daniel's ears. They kicked up small plumes of sand as they hit the berm. A flock of birds, startled by the loud sound of the gun, flew skyward from the tree line.

It took all of Daniel's willpower to maintain his composure and to keep walking without looking back. He felt his sphincter contract but kept from soiling himself. In the few seconds that it took him to reach the target post, he contemplated his options. Should he run? Should he throw himself to the ground? Neither seemed very attractive, as the shooter, less than fifty yards behind him, would have no problem hitting him if that was his intent.

So, what's this all about? he thought as he calmly pinned the target to the wooden post. *If he wanted to hit me, he could have easily done that.* Knowing that wasn't Favreau's intent helped settle his nerves.

He turned around and slowly started walking back to the firing line. Favreau had a wide grin on his face as he lifted the Browning into targeting position once again. *Bang. Bang.* Two more shots rang out, both hitting the centre of the target that Daniel had just pinned up.

"Sergeant Major Favreau, will you please fucking quit shooting in my direction?" Daniel yelled as he quickened his pace, reducing the distance between Favreau and himself.

"Sorry, sir, the general's orders."

"How so, Sergeant-Major?"

Daniel had drawn even with Favreau. "I will explain on the drive back, sir. Right now let's get to some target practice." He handed the weapon to Daniel. "There are eight rounds left. Let's see what you can hit."

After expending two sixty-round boxes of high-velocity ammunition, the two headed back to the Jeep for the drive to base.

"Not bad, sir. For an art historian, that is. Wouldn't want to see you in a sticky situation, though."

"So, Sergeant-Major, what's the story about you taking pot shots at me?"

"It goes like this, sir. The general concocted this tale about me being a rabid anti-Semite to test your nerve when he assigned me to take you to the range. Had you panicked, your mission would be off."

"Well, I guess I'll be buying the drinks tonight, Sergeant-major."

"Please call me Dominic, sir."

The next morning, after a brief meeting with the general, Captain Brossard drove Daniel to the Royal Canadian Air Force base at Bagotville for the ten-hour flight to Cairo. The Boeing 707 would stop to refuel in Shannon, Ireland. Beside Daniel there were eight RCAF mechanics who were to take over the servicing of UN aircraft from their Polish counterparts. The aircraft landed at the El Arish Egyptian Air Force base north of Cairo at midday. Rows of shiny silver Soviet-built MiG-21 supersonic fighter jets were lined up wingtip to wingtip on either side of the runway.

The same way they were in June '67 when they were jumped by the Israeli Air Force, Daniel thought.

A colonel dressed in desert beige army fatigues greeted him in impeccable English on the tarmac as Daniel descended from the 707.

"Good afternoon, Captain Delorme, and welcome to Egypt." He beamed. "I trust you had a pleasant flight. I am Colonel Suweir, our country's liaison officer with the UN observer mission."

"Good day, sir," Daniel responded with a stiff military salute, sticking with proper military etiquette when addressing a senior officer. He was determined to stay in character.

"Too bad about Captain Ranpuil's sister. He was an excellent officer, very sympathetic to our viewpoint." Suweir paused, letting the comment sink in. "I hope that you are as well," the Egyptian colonel hinted.

At the terminal building they were greeted by Lt. Colonel Sadowski of the Polish Army. After the perfunctory greetings, they got into a white UN Jeep and headed for the noise and hubbub of Egypt's capital of eight million. During the ride through the teeming and dusty suburbs, Colonel Sadowski walked Daniel through the daily routine of the observer team and his duties but was constantly interrupted by a fawning Suweir.

"You know, Captain, we Egyptians are very fond of our Canadian comrades. We just wish that your government would take a world view more independent of the Americans. We love Canadians, especially your former prime minister, Lester Pearson. He understood the Arab world and our aspirations to rid our region of Zionist influence. You know, I was assistant military attaché at our embassy in Ottawa a number of years ago. A beautiful and very friendly city."

After an hour's drive through traffic of cars, trucks, donkey-and-horse-drawn wagons, cyclists and mopeds, not to mention pedestrians darting in and out, they arrived at the Cairo Officers' Club.

"Well, here we are, gentlemen. We will have cocktails and then dinner and go through the regular security briefing. Brigadier General Abdel Gamasy will join us for dinner. Now, Captain Delorme, I will take you over to the officers' tennis club next door to allow you to freshen up from your lengthy flight."

Daniel's heart skipped a beat upon hearing Abdel Gamasy's name. *Wow!* He thought. *I get to meet Schmidt or Müller tonight. I wonder which one it will be.*

CHAPTER 45

The Ju 52 descended through heavy clouds over the battle-scarred Russian landscape. As the wheels touched and the plane bounced along the grass landing strip outside the town of Svoboda, Bruno was shaken from a fitful slumber. He rubbed his eyes as he looked out the window and saw row upon row of stretchers with wounded soldiers lying on them beside the runway.

Baur turned to Bruno in the cockpit, shaking his head slightly. "Those are the lucky ones. We get to take them back home when we leave. We used to fly back the coffins as well, but now the numbers are too high, so they get buried where they fall. Not a pretty picture!"

The pilot taxied the plane to the wooden building that served as the control tower. Bruno opened his door and jumped to the ground, misjudging the distance and landing heavily. As he got up, he swore loudly and started to dust himself off. Then all hell broke loose.

The air raid warning sirens began to wail, and the anti-aircraft batteries situated around the airstrip opened up with a tremendous cacophony. Two Soviet Air Force P-39 Airacobras, obtained by the Russians under the American's Lend Lease program roared in barely above ground level, their 37 mm nose cannon and .50 calibre machine guns spewing bullets at the aircraft lined up along the strip, and the AA batteries protecting it.

Baur and Bruno ran, rounds kicking up dust and biting at their heels, and jumped into a trench by the side of the control tower. The raid was over as suddenly as it had begun, with one of the Russian fighters trailing smoke as they gained altitude and high-tailed it away from the shot-up airstrip. Two Messerschmitt Bf 109s were damaged beyond repair, as was a Storch utility aircraft. A quadruple 20 mm anti-aircraft guns was knocked out, with two of its four-man crew killed.

"One hell of a welcome, Horst!" Baur yelled to Base Commander Horst Wiederling as they climbed out of the trench and bolted into the building.

"It's been like this lately," Wiederling said. "They come out of nowhere, scare the shit out of everybody, then scoot out again. To what do I owe the pleasure of your visit?"

Bruno took an envelope out of his pocket and handed it to Wiederling. "This will explain it all," he said to the Luftwaffe officer.

"Oh, from the Reichsführer himself. Must be important!" Wiederling opened the envelope and started to read its contents. "Very well, then. Let's have a drink, and I will provide you with a car and escort to take you to Korennaya Hermitage."

The grey Luftwaffe staff car, with an escort of two armoured cars, wound its way through the heavily forested Russian countryside, sticking to dirt roads used more by farmers to drive their cattle to market than by motorized traffic. Bruno, sitting in the back of the car, was thankful that he had shared some schnapps with Wiederling as it fortified his nerves for the upcoming confrontation with the Wehrmacht field commanders.

They drew up in front of the elaborate wooden building topped by golden onion domes that had served as a monastery for a reclusive caste of Russian monks since the middle of the eighteenth century. The monks had been long gone, driven away by the misfortunes of war, and been replaced by a squad of fanatical Waffen SS troops wearing camouflage tunics.

Captain Egon Wolff, commander of the squad, came out to greet Bruno with a crisp "Heil Hitler" salute. "Good morning, Colonel Schmidt. I hope you had a pleasant journey," he continued, without waiting for a response from Bruno. "I have positioned my troops amongst the trees around the monks' compound. All entry and exit points are well guarded. I only await your orders."

"Well, Captain Wolff, let's hope that there won't be any need for drama today," Bruno said.

"I understand that the 'guests' should be arriving within the next half hour, sir."

"In that case, we should sit down and have a cup of coffee, no?"

"Yes, sir, but I only have the ersatz variety, and no milk."

"That's fine, Wolff, as long as you have some good schnapps to sweeten it."

"Colonel, what do you expect of my men?" Wolff asked, furrowing his brow in a worried expression.

"To take up position with their weapons in a threatening manner. If you know what I mean, Captain?" Bruno replied.

At around noon, as the sun began to filter through the tall pines, a variety of military vehicles started to arrive and disgorge their gold-braided passengers. Bruno greeted them one by one, dispensing with the usual "Heil Hitler," and instead shaking their hands.

The cream of the German Army's commanders who had participated in the terrible carnage around the Kursk battlefield were there – men who had aged years in months, grown old well before their time. The battles of Stalingrad, Kharkov, and Kursk had destroyed their nerves, their will to continue a fight that had turned against the Third Reich. They were ready to throw in the towel and retreat before the Soviet onslaught. Bruno was there to try to instil some courage and backbone and to halt their willingness to retreat. Or to have them shot to a man.

Once everyone was seated in the great hall, he began to speak. "I bring a message directly from our Führer. We all understand that the last few months have been hard, and that you and your troops have made terrible sacrifices to stop the 'Red Hordes.'

"Western civilization hangs in the balance, dependent on your courage and your troops' continued dedication to the Führer and the State. OKW has received a continuous stream of requests from most of you to withdraw two kilometres, to withdraw five kilometres, to withdraw to the next river or next town."

His voice rose. "Gentlemen, there will be no withdrawal! Not one centimetre! The Führer's orders are that all troops will stand their ground where they are or die! But *not one step back!*" He paused, letting his words sink in.

Field Marshall Walter Model stood up to speak. "You must tell the Führer that this is madness! Pure madness! To let the flower of Germany's youth bleed to death defending patches of Russian countryside of no use to anyone. Madness, I tell you!" He looked around the room to see a number of the other officers nod their heads in agreement.

Then General Hermann Hoth rose to add his voice to that of Model.

Bruno sensed he was starting to lose his audience. He gave Wolff a knowing glance. Without a word being spoken, six SS troopers entered the room, clutching Schmeisser machine pistols, and lined up at the back.

The field marshals and generals got the message.

While Bruno was strong-arming the Eastern Front commanders, Helmut had arrived at the Schmidt residence in Munich at midday. He was greeted at the door by Margit.

"Where is Bruno?"

"Himmler ordered him to fly out to the Eastern Front to deal with some important issues. He should be back in a couple of days."

"That bastard! That fucking bastard!" she screamed, tears flowing down her face. "He won't divorce that old bitch and thinks that I'll just sit around waiting while he kisses that chicken farmer's ass."

She felt like she was going to faint. The room had started to revolve. She grabbed onto Helmut's shoulders for support as everything went dark.

Margit woke up the next day sick to her stomach. It was obvious to her that she was carrying a child.

CHAPTER 46

JUNE 1973,

CAIRO, EGYPT—THE TENNIS GAME

After taking a shower and changing his clothes, Daniel joined Colonels Suweir and Sadowski and Lieutenant Commander Induran of the Indonesian Navy, the third member of the UN monitoring group, at the bar in the Officers' Club. They were soon accompanied by a number of Egyptian military officers from all three services. They were sitting in comfortable red-leather-covered armchairs, sipping their gin and tonics and discussing recent world events, when the manager of the club announced, "Gentlemen, Brigadier Abdel Gamasy."

They all stood up as the tall, well-tanned man with greying hair and gold-rimmed glasses strode into the room. Suweir saluted, and taking Gamasy by the arm, approached Daniel to introduce him as the new member of the monitoring group.

"General, this is Captain Delorme of the Canadian Army, who has come to replace Captain Ranpuil, who had to return to Canada on an urgent family matter."

Gamasy reached out to shake Daniel's hand, and in fluent French, said, *"Bienvenue au Caire, Capitaine Delorme. Je crois que vous avez eu un agréable voyage."*

"Oui, merci," Daniel responded with a smile, as he looked straight into Gamasy's pale blue eyes.

Was this really Schmidt? Daniel tried to recapture the image of the man whose picture he had seen at Mossad HQ the month before. He tried to superimpose the mental picture of the photograph on to the face of the man in front of him. *Definitely, the eyes, the forehead, the shape of the mouth all matched.*

However, he didn't have much time to ruminate as Gamasy continued in English, "Young man, you look very familiar. Have you been to Egypt before?"

"Non, monsieur, c'est ma première fois au Moyen-Orient," Daniel answered. He detected a slight trace of a German accent when Gamasy spoke English. He was now sure that Gamasy was his man.

Gamasy shook his head, and muttered under his breath, "I could have sworn … "

Their conversation was broken up by the club's manager. "Gentlemen, dinner is being served in the dining room"

Gamasy made sure to sit himself beside Daniel, with Colonel Suweir on Daniel's other side. "So, Captain Delorme, how long have you served in that illustrious regiment, the Royal Twenty-Second?"

Before Daniel could respond, Gamasy continued, "You know, Captain Ranpuil was a fine officer and a good tennis player. Do you play tennis?"

"I do, sir, however I am no Ilie Năstase."

"Well then, how about a game tomorrow morning? Let's say eight a.m.?"

"I would love to, sir, but I don't have any equipment."

"That's fine, Captain … may I call you Daniel? I will have the club's manager arrange a suitable racket for you. Do you have shoes and shorts?

"Yes, sir. I run every morning, so I bought those with me."

"Now, no running tomorrow! I don't want to be accused of beating a tired man." Gamasy laughed as he wagged a finger in Daniel's direction.

The rest of the evening was spent eating, drinking, and exchanging experiences in the military of the nationalities gathered around the table.

At around nine, Daniel said his goodbyes. "It was a long flight, and it's been a long day. I think I am going to turn in."

"Well, have a good night, and rest up for our game tomorrow." As Gamasy watched Daniel leave the room, he said to Suweir. "I can't help but feel I've met that young man before. My instincts are usually right. Make sure we keep an eye on him. Also, call General Haloub and ask him to join me for lunch after my game with the Canadian."

Daniel tossed and turned the entire night. The knock on his door at 7:30 a.m. startled him, as he had once again just fallen asleep. It was an Egyptian Army corporal carrying a tennis racket, who had been sent to fetch him.

"Good morning, Daniel. How was your night?" Gamasy, dressed in a crisp white shirt and shorts, greeted Daniel.

"Not great. I guess it's called jet lag."

"Well, don't worry, I will take it easy on you. Do you want to just hit balls or play a game?"

"Might just as well play a game; otherwise, what's the sense?" Daniel's competitive nature had kicked in. And he especially wanted to beat the German. The sun was already high in the sky, and the air was heavy as the two were set to finish their game.

"Forty-fifteen, game, set, match point," a sweating Gamasy yelled over to Daniel as he prepared to serve.

"Ahhh, yes," Daniel yelled back, his shirt and shorts drenched with perspiration. The ball, hit forcefully and with pinpoint accuracy by Gamasy, rocketed over the net landing at Daniel's feet. One bounce, and Daniel's return sailed over his opponent's head, landing outside the base line. The older German, in excellent shape, had beaten him handily.

Gamasy walked over and shook Daniel's hand. "Not bad for someone who travelled half way around the world only yesterday," he said, as he put one arm over the younger man's shoulder. "You know, I have a son about your age, but I haven't seen him in a long, long time. I wonder what it would be like to play tennis with him?"

An awkward silence followed as the two walked off the court.

"Let's go take a shower and then head for lunch back in the Officers' Club," Gamasy said to Daniel.

Colonel Suweir was waiting for them as they entered the locker room.

"Daniel, grab a towel I'll be along in a minute." Gamasy patted Daniel on the shoulder.

Daniel stripped off his clothes and stood under one of four showerheads and let the hot water cascade down on him as he lathered himself up. He thought about Gamasy's comment about having a son and wondered why Alexei had not told him about it.

Gamasy left the locker room for a quick conversation with Suweir. "Colonel, I have a bad feeling in my bones about this Captain Delorme. I am not sure what it is, but something's amiss. If he comes out of the showers ahead of me, put him under arrest."

"On what grounds, General? The UN will scream bloody murder and demand his immediate release."

"Don't worry, we'll make something up. I'll need some time to think about it, to figure it out. I just don't like it." With that, Gamasy re-entered the locker room, disrobed, and headed for the showers, just as Daniel was finishing up.

He looked at Daniel's naked body, and his gaze immediately focussed on Daniel's genitals. *Not circumcised!* He breathed a sigh of relief. *Maybe I am just getting too paranoid about the Jews,* he thought.

Daniel was by now towelling himself off and getting ready to put on his uniform. "I'll see you outside," he yelled over to Gamasy, who was now under the shower.

CHAPTER 47

Two days after the assassination attempt on Hitler at the Wolf's Lair in eastern Prussia, the roundup of conspirators across Germany was in full swing. Summary justice was the Führer's order of the day. No one, no matter how far removed they were from the plot, was to be spared.

One of those was Arthur Nebe, Steffi Hartmann's brother and Bruno's friend and mentor. By 1944, he and Bruno had drifted apart and were rarely in contact. The last time they saw each other was on July 22, at Plötzensee Prison in Berlin. Nebe had been caught up in the net cast by the Gestapo to detain everyone rumoured to have been involved in the July 20 plot against Hitler. On the afternoon of the 22, Heinrich Müller, head of the Gestapo, had called Bruno in Munich, where he was tending to a very pregnant Margit.

"Bruno, it's Heinrich," came the gruff voice over the telephone.

"Heinrich, what's going on? I've heard the news reports on the radio. How's the Führer? Who was the ring leader?"

"The Führer's fine, Bruno, shaken up, but all right. We're hunting down all the bastards, the traitors, the scum of German gentry that were behind this. It was led by Colonel von Stauffenberg. That's why I am calling you."

"How can I help?"

"Well, our agents hauled in your brother-in-law Nebe this morning. It appears that he had been in touch with some of the conspirators, including Stauffenberg, over the last few months. My boys were going to put him up against the wall when they bought him in, but I told them to hang on. I wanted to see if perhaps you can get some information out of him about the plot. He may talk to you to save his skin."

"Does Steffi know?"

"I let him call her, and apparently she's on her way down. She was at some orphanage near Hamburg."

"All right, I'll get Helmut to drive me down in the morning. Oh look, Margit is ready to give birth any day. I'll need to bring her to Berlin with me. Do you have a place we can stay at for a couple of days?"

"Lots of buildings have been bombed out here, Bruno. Space is very tight, but I'm sure we can find something comfortable for her. And until then she can stay with us. Bruno, this can't wait until morning. We've got to get to these vermin immediately, before they get a chance to go underground," Muller pleaded with Bruno.

"All right, I'll come right away."

In the middle of the night, Bruno and Helmut helped an expectant, slow-moving Margit into the back of the black Mercedes, where she lay down on the grey leather upholstery to try to be as comfortable as she could be for the drive to Berlin.

That same evening, Arnold Weisz was agonizing over the steadily deteriorating condition of his wife, mother-in-law, and four-year-old twin daughters. They had developed a very high fever and were vomiting and convulsing continuously. Their temperatures hovered above 44 degrees Celsius. Without medical intervention they would die. He knew they couldn't risk trying to find a doctor in daytime.

All the Jewish doctors in Berlin had already been shipped off to concentration camps, and he was only aware of one potentially friendly Christian doctor that he could attempt to contact: Dr. Egon Steinmeir at Königin Elisabeth Hospital. He was the young doctor who first saw Ingrid as she was about to give birth to Maximillian in 1936.

At around ten o'clock, Arnold made his decision. He entered the apartment from their hiding place to talk to Heldi. She was sitting at the kitchen table, reading a book by candlelight, as the Charlottenburg transformer station had been hit by bombs from an RAF raid earlier in the week and there was no electricity in the neighbourhood.

"Heldi, I am afraid that if we don't get Ingrid, my mother-in-law, and the girls to a hospital, they won't live much longer."

"That's why I am reading this book on medicine, Herr. Weisz. Trying to figure out what is wrong with them."

"I don't think we have time for that, Heldi. I am going to see if we can find Dr. Steinmeier at Königin Elisabeth tonight. He's our only hope."

Heldi gazed at Arnold in the flickering candlelight. He had aged decades in the six years since the death of his father-in-law. Most of his curly hair was gone, and what remained had turned white. His cheeks were sunken, and his skin had lost its colour, taking on a pasty grey colour. His dark eyes were devoid of the sparkle that they'd had when they had first met.

"I will come along with you, Herr Weisz."

It was a warm summer night. A light rain had cooled off the daytime heat as the five of them quietly descended the stairs of their building. The girls had been given Aspirin tablets to try to lower their temperatures and help them sleep. The streets were deserted as they slowly shuffled along in the direction of the hospital, their only hope. The Allied air forces seemed to have taken the night off as well, and with the blackout the only visible lights were the anti-aircraft searchlights scattered around the city scanning the sky.

Arnold had talked with Max prior to them leaving the apartment.

"Look, son. I have to take your mother and sisters to the hospital. It's their only hope of getting better. Heldi or I should be back by morning if we're lucky enough to get all of them admitted to a hospital. My hope rests with Doctor Steinmeir. You are to stay in our hiding place and not make any noise while we're gone. I love you, son."

Max hugged his mother and sisters as they shuffled through the door.

Arnold gave Max a hug and a kiss on the forehead as he left, carrying Rachel in his arms while Heldi carried Hannah on her back. Ingrid and her mother limped along behind them. It took them the better part of two hours of stumbling through dark and deserted streets to get to the doors of Königin Elisabeth Hospital. As they were walking up the steps, the double glass doors, taped to prevent them from shattering in case of a bomb blast, flew open and a bloodied corpse in a white medical lab coat was roughly thrown down the stairs.

"This is what happens to traitors!" a voice from inside yelled into the darkness.

Pandemonium reigned in the whitewashed entrance lobby of the hospital as Arnold and his family haltingly entered. SS and Gestapo officers in black uniforms were running up and down the marble stairs, some dragging bloodied bodies—a few still alive, others lifeless—behind them.

Screaming seemed to be the order of the day—high-pitched, commanding bellows from the Nazi officers, and unearthly howling from their victims. Every now and again a shot would ring out from somewhere upstairs followed by more banging and shouting. Doors were being slammed and furniture and medical equipment was being tossed about.

Arnold stood shell-shocked in the midst of this chaos, as if rooted to the ground. *Oh my God, what have I done?* But now it was too late to go back.

He didn't have much time to think, as a burly Gestapo officer came over and grabbed him by the arm. "What are you doing here?"

"I ... I ... I am ... sorry ... my wife and daughters are patients of Doctor Steinmeir, and they are deathly ill."

"Steinmeir the traitor is dead! Haven't you heard, man, they attempted to kill the Führer! Now, where are your papers?"

The only papers Arnold had was his passport, prominently stamped with a large J for Jew. He knew producing that would lead to instant death.

"Well, where are they?" the officer yelled, his voice rising as he stuck his face into Arnold's, the garlic on his breath overwhelming Arnold's olfactory senses.

"I ... I left them at home, sir," he stammered.

"What is your name?" He pushed his nose right against Arnold's. "What is your name, and where do you live?"

At this point, Arnold realized that the game was up. All he could hope for was a Nazi with some humanity left. "It's Weisz, Arnold Weisz, and we live at 14 Meineke Strasse in Charlottenburg. Apartment four, sir."

"A Jew? A Jew! I don't believe it!" The Gestapo officer started to laugh uncontrollably.

Arnold was confused. He could find nothing humorous about the situation as he backed up, frightened, and put his arm around a now loudly crying and trembling Ingrid. The girls were sitting on the cold stone floor, hanging on to Heldi's legs, both of them sobbing along with their mother. Esther just stood there as if in a trance, not totally comprehending where she was, or why.

Bruno had come to the hospital accompanying his brother-in-law, Arthur Nebe, who tried to commit suicide by taking poison when the Gestapo officers came to haul him out of his cell at Plötzensee Prison. Gestapo chief Heinrich Müller had asked Bruno to try to obtain information about the plot conspirators from his brother-in-law. Nebe was having his stomach pumped in one of the operating rooms while Bruno and Steffi waited in the lobby downstairs.

Bruno was distracted by the commotion and walked up to the group. "What is this all about, Major Lucke?" Bruno demanded as he approached the hysterically laughing Gestapo officer and the trembling and crying Weisz family.

"Colonel, this Jew and his sick family came to see that traitor, Doctor Steinmeier."

"Well, Steinmeier is dead." Bruno turned to Arnold. "I didn't think that any of your kind were still alive in Berlin. Where did you say you lived?"

"14 Meineke Strasse, sir."

"Who are the women with you?"

"My wife, my mother-in-law, my twin daughters and our maid. She's Catholic." He emphasized.

"Major Lucke. Get my driver Captain Eckler and take the Jews down to the *Sammellager* near Grunewald. They'll know what to do with them."

"Yes, Colonel. What about the maid?"

"I'll deal with her."

Lucke started to roughly shepherd the small group towards the door when Esther suddenly began to shriek and lunged at one of the SS soldiers in front of them. The man, surprised, turned around and in so doing, lost his balance and fell to the floor with Esther, still howling, ending up on top of him.

Another SS guard, alarmed and not knowing what was happening, but taking no chances in the chaos, bought the butt of his submachine gun violently down on the back of her head. Blood spurted like a fountain from her skull as her lifeless body rolled off the man.

"Lucke, get them out of here! Now!" Bruno screamed, as he motioned to some of the other guards to help the major hustle the Weiszes out of the hospital's lobby.

Ingrid fainted and Arnold had to half carry and half drag her while Lucke shoved them along. A brawny, bald-headed SS man took a red-headed twin under each arm, following their parents out the door, and unceremoniously flung them into the back of the waiting Mercedes staff car, with Helmut at the wheel.

Lucke jumped into the front passenger seat. "Captain Eckler, Colonel Schmidt ordered me to take these Jews to Grunewald. Would save us some time to just put them up against the wall around the corner."

The car roared off into the darkness with the two heatedly discussing what to do about their distraught charges in the back, Eckler wanting to follow Bruno's order and Lucke was all for disposing of the problem more expeditiously.

CHAPTER 48

JUNE 1973,

CAIRO, EGYPT

As Daniel exited the locker room, Colonel Suweir stepped in front of him, blocking his path.

Daniel didn't know what to make of the Egyptian's rude and forceful gesture. "Captain Delorme, I am putting you under arrest by authority of the Egyptian Military High Command for, for … " His voice trailed off to inaudible as General Gamasy hadn't given him any instructions as to what pretext he would need to arrest Daniel.

Daniel wasn't quite sure how to comprehend this turn of events. He didn't think there was any way the Egyptians could have figured out his true identity this quickly, unless someone either in Israel or Canada gave them a heads-up prior to his arrival. He decided upon taking a brazen tack and burst out laughing. "Very funny, Colonel Suweir, I guess letting a general whip your ass at tennis is an indictable offence in your country. Do I go directly to jail?"

Suweir was taken aback by Daniel's response and looked lost as to what to do next.

He was rescued from his quandary by Gamasy's exit from the locker room. The general looked at the two men and immediately realized that Suweir had acted on his instructions. "Colonel, I told you to arrest, jail and torture him only if he beat me at the game!"

He winked at Suweir, laughed, and put his arm on Daniel's shoulder. "Young man, let's go and have some lunch. All this running around has made me hungry."

Suweir followed them, shaking his head, uncertain as to what his superior officer had in mind with this apparent charade.

The others from the UN Mission and their Egyptian liaison counterparts were already seated at the long dining table. At the head of it sat General Haloub. On entering, Daniel immediately recognized the man as Heinrich Müller, the feared head of Hitler's Gestapo. His receding hair had turned grey, but the close-set, piercing black eyes Daniel had noticed in the picture at Mossad HQ had lost none of their lustre.

"Well, Egypt one, United Nations nil! Too bad it wasn't the Davis Cup!" Gamasy gleefully announced as he took a seat to Haloub's right and motioned Daniel into the empty seat to his left.

"General, this is Captain Delorme of the famed Canadian Van Doos. He has taken Captain Ranpuil's posting while he attends to family matters at home," Gamasy said.

Haloub gave an acknowledging nod in Daniel's direction and without saying anything else, returned to his conversation with the Egyptian officer seated on his other side.

As they ate their lunch of freshly grilled Nile perch, Gamasy queried Daniel on his family history, military experience, and schooling, probing for any inconsistencies. He found none but remained suspicious of the young Canadian officer. Gamasy's sixth sense was telling him there was something about the man that just didn't seem to fit the background he had just recited. It all seemed to fit too neatly, be too well rehearsed.

After lunch, all those in attendance returned to their duties, with Müller and Schmidt staying behind, nursing glasses of French chardonnay. Suweir hung around in the background until Gamasy dismissed him with orders to keep a close eye on Daniel.

With no one else in the room, the two of them conversed in German. "You know, Heinrich, we've been at this game for over twenty-five years now and I am getting tired. The constant looking over my shoulders is starting to wear on me. I imagine a Jew waiting to take revenge behind every tree, every doorway, around every corner. Why, I even suspected that young Canadian officer Delorme of being one until I saw that he wasn't even circumcised. Despite that, I still feel something odd about him. I can't put my finger on it, but I've got a strange premonition that everything is not as it seems."

"Bruno, could it be that it's because of that kid you and Margit had back in Berlin in '44 in that apartment that you confiscated from that Jew? When was the last time you saw him?"

"In May 1945 when I sent them with Helmut towards the American lines. I still have no idea what happened to them or to Helmut."

"This Canadian kid could be you twenty or thirty years ago, you know. Looks a lot like you did back then. Maybe that's what's freaking you out."

"I think I need some time away from here. These Bedouin don't know how to win a war. Sadat can talk all he wants, but at the end of the day they'll get whipped just like they did in '48, '56 and '67. Never thought the Jews could fight. When you think back to how they all went quietly into the gas chambers, you'd never think that these same subhumans would now have a country of their own and one of the best armies in the world.

"I would strongly suggest that you get the hell out of here as well. They are going to come and get us, and soon! Another war like Sadat's planning and the Jews will capture and occupy Cairo. The Mossad will look for us with a fine-tooth comb. This is all fucked up, I tell you!" With that, Bruno stood up, slammed his napkin on to the table and stormed out, knocking over the remainder of his glass of chardonnay.

That evening, sitting in the library of his comfortable, upscale home in Cairo's affluent suburb of Zamalek, he talked to Sama, his Egyptian wife of fifteen years. "Sama, I need to get away from Cairo for a while on my own. Not sure where, or for how long, but I need to get out of here."

"Are you still having those nightmares about Russia, about the camps?"

He just turned around, and without a word to her he walked out the door, slamming it behind him. He jumped into his two-seater MGB and, through light evening traffic, headed back to his office at Mukhabarat HQ. When he got there, he asked the night overseas telephone operator to put him through to Army headquarters in Asunción, Paraguay. After several rings a voice came on the line.

"*Buenos dias*. You have reached the Paraguayan Defense Ministry. How may I route your call?"

"Could you please connect me to General Martino Lopez?"

"Certainly, sir. May I tell him who's calling?"

"It is General Gamasy calling from Cairo. Please let him know it's urgent."

After a few moments' wait, the Paraguayan army's commanding general came on the line. "Schmidt, it's nice to hear from you, but what's the panic?"

"Well, Martino, I've been thinking over President Stroessner's offer of a high-ranking position with your military police and think that it's now time I acted on it."

"Splendid! I am sure that the president will be delighted. When can we expect you?"

"I will make travel arrangements tomorrow, but I expect to arrive within the next two weeks."

"Excellent, please let us know so we can prepare all the paperwork. Have a safe trip, Schmidt."

After hanging up the telephone, Bruno went to the safe hidden behind a picture of President Sadat on the wall by a filing cabinet. He took out a hundred thousand Swiss francs, and then he left his office for home.

CHAPTER 49

JULY 23, 1944,

GRUNEWALD TRAIN STATION, BERLIN—THE JOURNEY EAST

It was early on the morning of July 23, 1944, when the Mercedes SS staff car pulled up at Grunewald train station, the first stop on the road to Auschwitz's gas chambers and ovens for the great majority of Berlin's Jews. A light rain had continued falling, and the few miserable souls gathered on the platform under armed guard were shivering despite the summer heat. They were the last of the capital's Jews who had managed to evade the tentacles of the Reich's security apparatus. Some had been hidden by Christian friends or relatives, others had been employed in critical industries close to the capital and were now deemed as surplus.

Major Lucke jumped out of the passenger seat of the car and flung open the back door. He was angry at being inconvenienced by having to bring the Weiszes to the train station, and took it out on Ingrid, dragging the half-comatose woman to the sidewalk by her hair. Arnold struggled to get out of the back seat. Despite his weakened state, the courage and strength of his school days of confronting Jew baiters had returned, and he was ready to take on the Nazi bully abusing his wife. Helmut quickly sized up the situation and grabbed Arnold by the arm and pinned him against the side of the car, at the same time telling Lucke to take it easy on the poor woman. "Major, what's the sense of that?

Are you trying to protect these worthless *Jids,* Eckler?"

"Not in the least, but why work yourself into a frenzy over them?"

"Should have just shot the lot."

Their argument was interrupted by the high-pitched steam whistle of the train approaching the station. As it pulled in, its brakes squealing, Helmut took the still-sobbing twins by the hand and led them over to Arnold, who was holding onto a slumping Ingrid. The black, soot-covered steam engine, puffing dark clouds of smoke and cinders, was pulling six cattle cars behind it. The tiny windows in the corner of each wagon were covered with barbed wire.

The doors were being pulled open by the soldiers on the platform and the loudly protesting, crying and screaming Jews were roughly pushed, shoved or dragged onto the straw-covered wooden floors of each car.

Arnold hoisted himself up into one of the cars, and with Helmut's help pulled Ingrid up as well. Helmut then gently lifted each of the girls into Arnold's waiting arms. For a moment, their eyes met, then Helmut turned around and with quick steps strode off the platform. As the Mercedes sped away from the station, Helmut could hear the whistle and slow beat of the train's engine starting to pull out with its miserable human cargo. Destination Oswiecim in eastern Poland. He wondered what the world was coming to.

As Helmut was delivering the Weiszes to Grunewald, Bruno was at the hospital interrogating Heldi.

"How does a nice Catholic woman like you come to be employed by these filthy Jews?"

"If you permit me, sir, they are not filthy Jews. Jews they may be, but they are the nicest, kindest human beings. I've been employed by them for over twenty years and they treated me like family."

"Well, be that as it may, it's a crime punishable by death to hide or protect Jews."

"In that case, I am guilty, sir."

Bruno was taken aback by the honesty and bravery of this simple, middle-aged Austrian maid. The interrogation was interrupted by a doctor approaching Bruno.

"Colonel, I think that Sturmbannführer Nebe is now well enough to answer any questions. But please go easy, as he's still somewhat fragile."

Bruno turned to Heldi. "Don't go anywhere, I'll be back to you." He then ordered one of the soldiers to keep an eye on her.

He entered the brightly lit operating room, with his brother-in-law slumped in a chair in a corner, looking white as a sheet. Steffi was kneeling beside him and holding his hand. Without acknowledging his wife, Bruno bent down and quietly said, "Fine state of affairs, Arthur. What the fuck were you doing, getting mixed up with Stauffenberg and his motley cronies? What was in it for you? What did they promise you?"

"Bruno, for crying out loud, don't be rough on him. He nearly died," Steffi pleaded with her estranged husband.

"It's his own fucking fault. Turning against the Führer in his greatest hour of need. Now, Arthur, who were the others in on this plot? If you cooperate with us, I can guarantee that Himmler will take it easy on you."

"I honestly don't know why I was dragged into this. All I did was meet with von Witzleben and Goerdeler once. They didn't discuss any assassination with me, just some alternatives were the Führer no longer in control," Nebe responded in a quiet, hoarse voice.

"You asshole! That in itself is treason!" Bruno screamed at Nebe.

"Enough, Bruno!" Steffi pleaded. "I can accept that you cheated on me with that little Dutch whore, but I *won't* allow you to abuse my brother like this."

"All right, Arthur. I'll let the Gestapo's goons deal with you. See how you like that!" And with that, he stormed out of the room, returning to question Heldi.

"Now, Frau, Frau … "

"Fräulein Hinkelmayer," Heldi helped him out.

"Yes, Fräulein Hinkelmayer, where were we? Oh yes, being employed by Jews contrary to legal statutes of the Reich forbidding Christians from working for Jews. Where did you live? With them?"

"No, I lived in Pankow, and they lived in Charlottenburg."

"Oh yes, I remember the man telling me Meineke Strasse. Number 14, I think." Bruno lowered his voice and changed his approach to a kinder, less accusatory tone. "Well then, would you be kind enough to take me and show me the flat?"

Heldi had to think quickly. *Maximillian is still in the hiding place. If I don't take him over there, they will just go and pull the place apart. If I take him over there, maybe I can steer him away from it.*

She made up her mind to take him. "Yes, sir."

"Is Eckler back yet?" Bruno shouted out to no one in particular.

"I am right here, Colonel." Helmut responded as he walked through the front door of the hospital. Taking Heldi by the arm, Bruno escorted her outside to the car. The rain had stopped, and a crescent moon was peeking through the early morning clouds.

They drove from the hospital through bombed-out and seemingly deserted neighbourhoods. They arrived in front of an unscathed 14 Meineke Strasse after a fifteen-minute drive. Bruno allowed Heldi to take the lead, with him and Helmut closely following.

As there was still no electricity in the building, the elevator wasn't working, so they had to climb the four storeys. They got to the fourth floor and had to stop and take a breath. The exertion had exhausted all three of them. After recovering, they approached the front door of the apartment. Heldi made a big deal of finding her keys, creating a lot of noise in the process, hoping to warn Maximillian to stay quiet and in his hiding place.

"Hurry up, woman, I don't have all day for this!" Bruno admonished her.

Finally opening the door, Heldi mockingly and loudly announced, "Well, this is it, Colonel. The filthy Jews' luxurious apartment."

She hoped she'd been loud enough to alert Max to the presence of unfriendly parties with her.

Bruno and Helmutbegan walking through the apartment, looking into the kitchen, salon, and bedrooms. Helmut noticed the piano in the salon and sat down at it. It had been a long time since he played, but it returned to him quickly. He started playing Schubert's *Symphony No. 9*.

Bruno continued to look around and yelled back to Helmut, "You know, this would be perfect for Margit and the baby. No sense leaving it empty. The Jews won't be back, and Müller said that there was a shortage of apartments in Berlin. Let's go and pick her up and bring her back here."

Bruno was starting to feel better after his stressful encounter with his brother-in-law, Nebe, and his estranged wife, and euphoric at finding a well-appointed apartment for him and his mistress, approaching the birth of their baby. "All right, Fräulein Hinkelmayer, this will suit my pregnant wife and I just fine. May I have the keys?"

He put his hand out to Heldi. She didn't know what to do or say. She decided to feign feeling suddenly ill to buy herself time to think. "Sir, I am feeling ill. May I sit down?" she pleaded.

"Of course," Helmut responded, pulling out a chair for her to sit on.

Heldi slumped into the chair, trying to think of her next move. She was stumped, knowing her choices were all bad.

Bruno started pacing the floor. He came to the heavy oak cupboard concealing the entrance to the Weisz's hiding place.

"Hey, Helmut, look at this piece of solid German workmanship." He banged his fist a couple of times on the sturdy wooden furniture. Suddenly there was a nearly imperceptible sound from the other side of the wall behind the cupboard, as if in response to the banging.

"Helmut, did you hear that? Here, help me move this cupboard," he yelled as he drew his gun.

The two of them struggled to shift the heavy piece of furniture away from the wall, revealing the outline of a door.

Heldi rose out of the chair she had been sitting in and ran at Bruno, her nails ripping into the skin on the back of his neck, drawing blood.

Helmut grabbed her and threw her to the floor with one swift move.

The concealed door behind the cupboard opened slowly. Bruno saw a dark figure rising out of the darkness. He fired at it twice.

CHAPTER 50

JUNE 1973,

CAIRO, EGYPT—DEPARTURES

Daniel spent the next ten days after his arrival in Cairo inspecting Egyptian military installations, making sure they were adhering strictly to protocols established by the United Nations following the 1967 Six-Day War between Israel, Egypt, Jordan, and Syria. One of his trips took him to the east or Egyptian bank of the Suez Canal, where he looked through binoculars at Israel's Bar Lev Line fortifications. His mind was playing games, imagining Naomi and Alexei looking back at him. He shook his head and chased the thoughts from his mind.

After his encounter with Müller and Schmidt, Daniel didn't come into contact with them again, although he was aware of the fact that his Egyptian Army minders were reporting his every move back to them. He was quite anxious for his tour of duty to come to an end, as he was certain that the longer he stayed, the more probable the discovery of his true identity and mission. On the eleventh day, word finally came that Captain Ranpuil would be returning to his post in Cairo after his compassionate leave in Canada.

Colonel Suweir drove him to Cairo International Airport along with Colonel Sadowski, whose tour was over as well, and who was returning to Warsaw via Paris along with Daniel. After shaking hands and saluting the Egyptian Colonel, the two of them mounted the stairs to the Air France Sud Aviation Caravelle jetliner that was scheduled to fly them to Paris and then connect them to their flights on to their homes in the USA and Poland.

Across the tarmac, Bruno sat in the first-class cabin of a British European Airways Hawker Siddeley Trident, sipping his Glenlivet with one ice cube, observing Daniel's Air France flight taxiing for takeoff. His memory raced back to late July 1944 in Berlin, and the birth of his son, named Heinrich, after Müller. He wondered whatever became of him and his mother as he watched the Air France plane gain altitude. His flight to London and then on to Buenos Aires, with a final destination of Asunción, Paraguay, was next in line for takeoff.

CHAPTER 51

Arnold, Ingrid, Rachel, and Elsa were sitting jammed together with forty-two other miserable, suffering souls on the wet, stinking straw covering the floor of the cattle car slowly being pulled eastward by the coal-fired steam engine of the Deutsche Reichsbahn. With the monotonous, rhythmic clacking of the wheels on the rails, the only indication of passing time was the amount of light entering the wagon through the small opening in the upper corner. It was dark when Ingrid began convulsing and vomiting blood, soaking Arnold's shirt and pants. The girls had mysteriously started to improve since the start of their journey, but Ingrid's condition had quickly deteriorated. She thrashed around and attempted to get up but collapsed in a heap. Arnold yelled out in desperation, "Is there a doctor here?"

"Yes, yes!" came a hoarse voice in response.

An elderly man with a white beard pushed and shoved his way through the sweating and stinking humanity crammed together in the wagon. "I am Doctor Eisenberg from Dortmund. How can I help?"

"My wife just fainted. She's had a high fever now for weeks."

"Do you have a light?"

Arnold reached into his pocket and retrieved a small box of matches, lighting one of them.

Someone shouted, "You're crazy! You're going to light the straw on fire! Put it out now!"

"Good God, give me a second to see the condition of this poor woman!" Eisenberg yelled back, as he searched for a pulse, first on Ingrid's wrist and then on her neck. He found none. The light from the match had gone out and Arnold couldn't see the look of sadness and disappointment on the doctor's face. Eisenberg shook his head in the dark and placed his hand on Arnold's shoulder.

"I am sorry, my friend, but your wife is gone. She may be better off than the rest of us."

Arnold sobbed uncontrollably, clutching the twins to his chest. Others placed her body in one of the corners of the freight car, and Arnold covered her up with his jacket. As morning came, and light started to filter in through the tiny opening, a group of men gathered to say Kaddish, the Jewish prayer for the dead, over the bodies of Ingrid and three other unfortunate souls who had passed away during the night.

A few hours later the train pulled up at the gates of hell.

As the doors were slid open, bright summer sunshine flooded into the car, blinding all those who had been in darkness for four days.

"*Schnell, schnell, raus!*" the SS guards on the platform yelled at the hapless passengers who were still able to get down from the wagons on their own. German shepherd and Alsatian dogs, held onto by SS men, straining on their chains and barking fiercely, were nipping at those who were too slow to move.

Arnold hesitated, holding on tightly to both girls, as he looked back at Ingrid lying on her back, his jacket pulled away, exposing her face. Her sparkling green eyes were now lifeless, surrounded by red circles, and her beautiful black hair had turned an ashen grey, as had her complexion. His thoughts raced back to the time he first set eyes on her at the law firm in Berlin in 1930, and tears began to run down his face.

"You filthy Jew. Get out of here with your pathetic runts!" the tall, heavy-set Ukrainian camp guard, reeking of alcohol, screamed at Arnold, hitting him square in the back with his wooden stick. Weakened by the four-day journey without food, devastated by the death of his beloved Ingrid, he collapsed, losing consciousness. The guard grabbed the loudly crying twins and roughly threw them down into the arms of a blond-haired, blue-eyed SS officer.

"Gently, gently, Sergei. The good doctor doesn't want any damaged goods. They are twins, be careful with them."

The officer looked down at the two of them and smiling, softly whispered, "It's all right, girls, you'll be just fine. Dr. Mengele will have some candies for you."

Then, taking them by the hand, he started to walk through the chaotic crowd of recent arrivals being herded by camp guards and *kapos* in the direction of tall, red-brick chimneys belching black smoke and soot.

One of the *kapos* threw a bucket of cold water on Arnold. "Come on, man, get your filthy ass out of the wagon or the SS will shoot you!"

"Where are we, and where are my daughters?" Arnold asked with panic in his voice and a sad and frightened look on his face

"Auschwitz, and your girls will be fine. The SS took them to see the camp doctor."

Arnold slowly lowered himself to the platform. He could hardly stand, his back giving him a great deal of pain. He didn't have long to think as another guard shoved him in with a group of men, most dressed in shabby clothes, shuffling along in line, as *kapos* on either side rained insults and blows from their sticks or bare fists on them. They stopped at a windowless, low concrete building. A tall, balding SS officer was standing on an upturned wooden crate in front of the only entrance.

"Welcome to the labour camp at Auschwitz. Here you will be put to work for the benefit of the Führer and the German Reich. Before you are assigned to your work detail, you will need to be deloused in the showers. Before going into the showers, you will take off your clothes, glasses, and empty your pockets and pile them neatly on the benches outside the showers. You will be issued new work uniforms after your shower. Now, please proceed through the entrance in a quiet and orderly manner."

As he removed his pants, shirt, and undergarments in the jam-packed room, buzzing with a cacophony of different languages and accents, surrounded by naked, dirty, and sweaty bodies seeing the doors closing behind them, Arnold felt somewhat comforted by the thought that a doctor would be taking care of Rachel and Elsa, and that at least Maximillian was safe in the hiding place at 14 Meineke Strasse. Above, on the roof of the building, two men wearing gas masks were breaking open metal containers of deadly Zyklon B, or hydrogen cyanide pellets, which they then poured into the roof vents.

CHAPTER 52

JULY 1944,

BERLIN—THE THEFT OF AN APARTMENT

As the deadly gas started to enter the "shower" room, the more than seven hundred people, coming to the realization of what was happening, began to scream, cough, and vomit, shoving and pushing each other towards the exit. The ones closest to the barred and locked door were jammed up against it and trampled by the ones behind them. Arnold's last moments of consciousness took him back ten years to the salon in the Charlottenburg apartment and his debate with his deceased father-in-law about what was to come under Nazi rule. A faint smile crossed his face and then everything went dark.

A couple of days earlier in the fourth-floor apartment at 14 Meineke Strasse, Berlin, the sound of two gunshots reverberated around the whole building, followed by a woman's screams.

Helmut grabbed a loudly screaming Heldi by the arm as she jumped from her chair, running at Bruno.

"What have you done? What have you done?" she shrieked.

Bruno looked at her blankly, lowering his arm with the smoking gun in his hand, as Helmut restrained her, pinning her arm behind her back. He then gazed down at the blood that had begun pooling at his feet.

"He was only a child. Not even nine years old," she sobbed.

Bruno knelt down to take a closer look at the apparition that he had fired at as it had slowly risen out of the darkness in the back of the heavy wooden wardrobe. Indeed, it was a young boy. He felt for a pulse but couldn't find any. He turned to Heldi. "Who was this boy?"

"Maxwell Weisz. Can I see him?" She pleaded with tears in her eyes.

It didn't take long for Bruno to put two and two together. Obviously, it was the son of the Jewish family with the two red-headed twin girls he'd had Helmut drive from the hospital to Grunewald Station. He stepped aside, leaving a bloody boot print on the floor, allowing Heldi to kneel beside Maximillian's body.

She lifted his head and planted a kiss on each cheek, while stroking the boy's dark hair. She quietly whispered, "Maxie, you are better off where you are headed than in this cruel, cruel world."

Without another word, she entered the space that had been the Weisz family's hiding place for the last few months and, taking a blanket from one of the mattresses on the floor, gently covered up the boy's body.

"Helmut, take the body downstairs and see where you can get rid of it." Then Bruno turned back to Heldi and in a solicitous tone asked, "Madam, could we sit down and talk?"

"You have the gun," she coldly responded, continuing to wipe the tears from her eyes.

As Helmut rolled the boy's slight body in the blanket and hefted it over his shoulder, a blood-stained notebook fell to the floor.

Bruno kicked it back into the hiding space and escorted Heldi into the kitchen, where the two of them sat down. "Look Frau—what was your name again?

"Hinklemeyer."

"Whose apartment is this?"

"Mine."

"Do you have some proof of this?"

"I sure do," she said defiantly, as she reached into her purse and pulled out the deed prepared by Ziggy Guthausen. Bruno examined it closely, drawing his finger along each line.

"I see, so the usual Yiddish horseshit where we'll transfer the property from a Jew to an Aryan in name only and then hopefully back again when the war is over. Well, Frau Hinklemeyer, it won't work in this case. You know that the penalty for hiding Jews is loss of all possessions and deportation to a labour camp?"

Heldi didn't even acknowledge hearing Bruno's words. She just stared out the kitchen window as grey clouds started to gather and a soft rain continued to fall outside.

"So be it, madam. When my friend returns, the three of us are going in front of a judge and you will legally transfer this apartment to me. My wife is going to have a baby anytime now, and we need appropriate accommodations. This lovely apartment will do just fine."

A half hour later Helmut returned.

"Helmut, help me push this wardrobe back against the wall. I don't want anyone entering the hiding space of those cursed Jews. I especially don't want Margit to find out what has gone on here. Now let's go and find a judge."

The three of them drove through the bombed-out streets of Berlin, with sullen civilians rummaging through smoking ruins for anything useful. The RAF had paid a visit to the German capital a few nights before.

"Let's see if Judge Oberhofer is still in his office. He's been busy handing out death sentences to the conspirators, so he could be around."

Bruno had the names and addresses of a coterie of judges that he had dealt with in his lawyering days through the early and mid-1930s. He knew that none of them would have any compunction or be bothered by a guilty conscience in affecting the transfer, even though they would be fully aware that it was "transfer by theft." Judge Oberhofer's office was the closest, and they found him in his office, busily signing execution orders. Bruno, Helmut, and Heldi were welcomed by the elderly judge.

"Come on in, my boy. Great to see a loyal face in these conspiratorial times. I am sending a great many of these traitorous 'upper crust' bastards to hell. I am happy to understand that you're still one of the

Führer's few favourites. But enough of an old man's blabbering. How can I help you, and how is Steffi?"

His assistant broke in, "May I get you some tea or coffee? Unfortunately, we only have ersatz, but it's hot."

"We are fine, thank you. We only wanted to interrupt the judge for a few minutes."

"Well, Judge, Steffi and I are divorced," he lied, "and I have a new fiancée who's about to give birth to our child. We found a wonderful apartment in Charlottenburg, whose owner is willing to sell it to us." At this point, Bruno gave a dark and threatening look at Heldi. "And I need you to prepare the transfer and ownership deed."

"Gladly, my boy. Now what's the address, whose name is it being transferred from, and whose name is it being transferred into?"

After getting all the paperwork drawn up and signed, the three of them headed out into the darkening street. The air raid sirens began to wail just after they started driving towards the Müller residence outside of Berlin's Treptow district. It was night by the time they had dropped Bruno off, and Helmut stepped on the gas and drove back towards SS headquarters with Heldi. They had just reached the outskirts of the city when the bombs from the RAF Lancasters began to fall. Helmut pulled the Mercedes up behind some previously bombed-out buildings. He turned to Heldi in the back. "Fräulein Hinklemeyer, run, hide, and don't show your face until this horrible war is over. And good luck."

"Thank you, sir. God bless you." She took off at a gallop, hoping to make her way during the night to a friend's apartment in Berlin's Pankow District. The next day, American Liberator bombers were back to hit Berlin again. One of their targets was the industrial district of Pankow. It was a week before Heldi's body was found by workers clearing the rubble from the American raid.

The next day, Bruno, Helmut, Margit, and Heinrich Müller were back at 14 Meineke Strasse, surveying what used to be the Grossman-Weisz apartment.

"Well, darling, what do you think of our new home?" Bruno smiled at Margit.

"This is wonderful. Such a nice place for our new baby to be born in," she enthused.

"Have you chosen a name yet?" Müller asked.

"Yes, Heinrich, after you."

"And if it's a girl?"

"Annabel, after my mother."

"Are you sure you want to have the baby born here, at home?"

"Absolutely. My sisters and I were all delivered on the farm in Holland. And look how healthy we grew up to be."

"Well, in that case, I'll have Helmut drive me back to the office now. I will arrange for two SS nurses to come and stay with you and help with the delivery."

"Thank you so much, Heinrich, and please thank Traudl for her hospitality, as well." She gave both Helmut and Müller a hug before retiring to one of the bedrooms.

Two days later, during a heavy RAF night air raid, Margit, after nine hours of heavy labour, helped by the two SS nurses, delivered a healthy, screaming baby boy. Helmut was also there to lend a hand in Bruno's absence.

Bruno was high in the Austrian Alps at Berchtesgaden, Adolf Hitler's summer home, along with Martin Borrman and Heinrich Himmler, working on plans for an alpine redoubt should Germany suffer more reverses on both fronts and be forced to retreat within Germany's borders and undertake a guerilla war against the invading Allies. Bruno was given command of an elite unit of the SS, dubbed *der Werwolf*, to conduct operations against any occupying forces.

Himmler and Bruno walked out to the expansive terrace to converse.

"Too bad about your brother-in-law, Nebe," Himmler said. "He seems to have been a good sort. Did a splendid job with the *Einsatzgruppen* in Russia. Frank tells me that they eliminated more than half a million Jews."

Bruno just nodded in response, his thoughts on what was happening with Margit and her impending delivery of the baby back at 14 Meineke Strasse.

Himmler continued, "Strictly between the two of us, I have been in contact with the Jewish Agency in Budapest through Eichmann. I am negotiating for ten thousand American trucks in return for stopping the shipment of the remaining Hungarian Jews to Auschwitz. These Jews will agree to anything to save the skin of their few wretched co-religionists.

"Eichmann is fighting me wanting to kill Jews, not trade them. He and Auschwitz Commandant Hoss say that the gas chambers and crematoria have to be supplied with raw materials." chuckling at his own turn of phrase, and without any reaction from Bruno, he continued talking. "Have you ever been to Auschwitz, Bruno?"

"No, but I recently sent a few Jews from Berlin for holidays there, including a couple of red-headed twins." He laughed.

"Well, I am sure that Dr. Mengele will honour you with a thank-you note. He's been doing an excellent job of medical research on twins, but I understand that he's running low on candidates."

They stood in silence, each with their own thoughts, taking in the majesty of alpine scenery surrounding the Eagle's Nest, as the sun slowly sank behind the high, snow-peaked mountains, painting them pink. With Hitler having retired, they saw no further reason to remain, and they had Himmler's chauffeur drive them back to Berlin. They stopped in Munich, where Bruno went to see Steffi.

"Steffi, I am sorry about Arthur, but after his stupidity, there was nothing I could do to help. I am sure that Himmler will try to do everything to ensure that they go easy on him in Dachau," Bruno lied, trying to ease his wife's pain.

She looked terrible, years beyond her age, with dark circles around her tear-reddened eyes. She had also taken to drinking copious amounts of alcohol, which did not help her appearance. "You know, Bruno, you're a lying bastard with not a stitch of humanity left in you.

I wish that you and that little Dutch tart rot in hell," she yelled, and started crying.

Bruno just stood there staring at her. *How beautiful, sexy and alluring she had been.* He thought back to the passion, the fire of the early years. It was all gone now. He looked at her as if looking at an empty shell.

"She will be giving birth to our baby any day now, something you could never do," he said. With that final twist of the knife, he turned, slammed the door behind him, and walked out to the car, joining Himmler in the back seat. It would be the last time the two of them would see each other alive.

"I guess that didn't go so well," Himmler chuckled under his breath.

CHAPTER 53

Elsa and Rachel stood trembling in fear in front of the SS officer with the wide space between his front upper teeth. They were holding on to each other, their little bodies wracked by sobs, tears running down their cheeks.

A nurse, dressed in white, in total contrast to the black uniform of the officer, was trying to console them. "Girls, there is no need to be afraid of Dr. Mengele. He just wants to check you out to make sure that you're both healthy. Here, have some candy."

She reached into her pocket and gave each of the girls a lollipop.

Dr. Mengele bent down and stroked the girls' red, curly locks, and, turning to the nurse said, "Erika, please give these girls a bath, some fresh clothes, take them for a haircut, then bring them into my office. Oh, yes, and get them something to eat."

That evening, the girls, helped by sleeping pills, would have their first full night of uninterrupted sleep in many months.

The next morning they underwent a thorough physical examination, conducted by Dr. Mengele, to ensure that they were fit and suitable for experimentation.

Hauptsturmführer, or Captain Josef Mengele, recipient of the Iron Cross 1st Class, entered Auschwitz in May 1943 as an educated, experienced medical researcher. With funding for his experiments, he worked alongside some of the top medical researchers of the time.

Anxious to make a name for himself, Mengele searched for the secrets of heredity. The Nazi ideal of the future would benefit from the help of genetics, according to Nazi doctrine. If so-called Aryan women could assuredly give birth to twins who were sure to be blond and blue-eyed, the Thousand Year Reich could be saved.

Mengele, who worked for Professor Otmar Freiherr von Verschuer, a biologist who pioneered twin methodology in the study of genetics, believed that twins held these secrets. Auschwitz seemed the best location for such research because of the large number of available twins to use as specimens.

"Good morning, girls. Did you have a good sleep?" Mengele asked as he entered his office and offered some candies to the Weisz twins. The girls had been taken there by Erika, and had been sitting curiously eyeing the many formaldehyde-filled jars containing various human organs. They didn't answer, averting their eyes and looking at the shiny linoleum floor.

"Well, then, what are your names?"

As there was still no answer forthcoming from the girls, Mengele decided to play a game.

"All right, how about we play a little game? I will try to guess your names. If I get the first letter right of one of your names, then that person has to tell me what the second letter is. How about an H?"

The two girls looked at each other and exchanged a slight conspiratorial smile, as if to say to each other, "Hm, he doesn't know much, we have him fooled." It was the first time they had smiled since they had left their apartment in Berlin.

Mengele continued with the game until he learned the names of the girls and gained a small level of trust. "Girls, Nurse Erika is going to take some blood samples from you, so we will know how to treat you if you get sick again. Don't worry. It won't hurt at all."

Dr. Mengele's trials began with the simple blood test. It was the beginning of a slippery slope that over the next four months exposed the twins to horrific medical experiments designed to try to perfect the "creation" of twins.

In early January 1945, just weeks before the liberation of Auschwitz by the Soviets, Elsa was injected with a virulent strain of typhus, and Rachel with what Mengele had concocted as an antidote, to see whether Elsa would recover from her twin sister having received the "cure." She didn't, and as a final indignity, the four-year-old's body was shipped off to Germany for an autopsy to examine the effects of that particular strain of typhus on adolescent, pre-pubescent females. Rachel did not die from the antidote; however, it had rendered her infertile.

She was liberated by soldiers of the 322nd Rifle Division of the Soviet Army on January 27, 1945. A young Hungarian Jewish woman by the name Klara Gerber, who had lost both her husband and daughter at Auschwitz, took Rachel under her wing, and the two of them made it to the Greek port of Salonika by the end of the year. They had travelled through Poland, Romania, and Bulgaria with a group of other camp survivors of various nationalities. Sometimes they would walk along roads, other times they would hop on freight trains or transport trucks.

At one point, Rachel refused to continue with Klara because the train carriage they were trying to climb on to resembled the one that had bought her and her family to Auschwitz and death.

"Klara, please don't make me go on this train. It's like the one that carried Father, Mama, Elsa , and I to that horrible camp. Please don't make me," she pleaded with tears in her eyes.

"Rachel, please, darling, this train is not the same," said the young Hungarian. "It's going to take us to Palestine, to the 'Promised Land,' where nobody can hurt us. Where you can eat as much as you want and play all day. Please believe me, little one."

Rachel finally relented and the two of them arrived in Salonika at the end of December 1945. In February 1946 they boarded the Jewish refugee ship *Henrietta Szold*. The ship—with over 500 Jewish refugees on board, all survivors of Nazi concentration camps—was interned by British authorities when it docked in Haifa, Palestine.

The passengers, including Klara and Rachel, were transferred by the British military to an internment camp on the island of Cyprus. They didn't arrive in Palestine until the declaration of nationhood by Israel in May 1948. Klara and Rachel were invited to join Kibbutz Degania Alef, an agricultural community established in 1907 southwest of the Sea of Galilee that had a large number of orphans whose parents had been murdered in the Holocaust. There they both adopted Hebrew names, with Rachel Weisz becoming Rivka Ban'Or. It was here that she met and became inseparable friends with Naomi, a survivor of Bergen-Belsen.

CHAPTER 54

JULY 1944 — MAY 1945,
14 MEINEKE STRASSE, BERLIN

Heinrich Karl Schmidt, named after Heinrich Müller, head of the Gestapo, and his paternal grandfather, Karl Schmidt, first saw the light of day on July 28, 1944. He was born a healthy, blond-haired, blue-eyed boy, the perfect image of an Aryan as imagined by the Nazi hierarchy. Present at his birth beside his mother, Margit, were Helmut Eckler, his godfather, and two SS nurses, one of whom acted as a midwife. His father, Bruno Schmidt, didn't meet his son until a few days after his birth, when he returned from the Eagle's Nest, high in the Bavarian Alps.

As he came through the door, Margit, in a house coat she had found in a closet, with the baby in her arms, greeted him. "Sweetheart, let me introduce you to four-day-old Heinrich Karl Schmidt."

Helmut emerged from the kitchen holding three glasses of Berentzen Winter Apfel Schnapp that he had discovered in what used to be the Weiszes' liquor cabinet

"The great warrior returns," he announced somewhat sarcastically. "How is that genius of a strategist, our Führer, doing in his alpine redoubt? Moving armies that don't exist, around maps that are no longer relevant?" He let out a laugh.

Margit gave him a disapproving look.

"Well, let's not dwell on the musings of a megalomaniac," Helmut said. "Let's drink to the next generation! One without the swastika branded on their behinds!"

Helmut had obviously been sampling the schnapps well before Bruno's arrival.

"Helmut, I would caution you with that kind of talk. I've seen people shot for a lot less than that. *Prosit!*" Bruno clinked glasses with Margit and Helmut and downed the golden, viscous liquid with one swallow.

Life at 14 Meineke Strasse continued on uneventfully for the rest of 1944. Miraculously, the almost-nightly air raids seemed to leave their immediate vicinity untouched. Helmut had moved into the apartment, occupying what used to be Maximillian's room. Neither he nor Bruno ever again broached the subject of what had transpired there in late July. Cobwebs had started to populate the entrance to the Weiszes' hiding place behind the large oak cupboard.

Bruno spent weeks at a time away from Margit and rapidly growing little Heinrich. On Christmas Day, 1944, he was in the Ardennes region of Belgium, urging on the advancing SS divisions that had begun a counterattack against Patton's Third Army, with the aim of capturing the Belgian port of Antwerp. The war was not going well for the Germans.

In late April 1945, Bruno came to the apartment. Berlin was under direct attack by the Soviet armies, who were fighting in the capital's suburbs. He arrived in the sidecar of an SS dispatch rider named Kurt. Margit rushed to greet him, with little Heinrich in her arms. He asked Helmut to join them.

"The war is over. The Russkies are everywhere. You must get out of Berlin and head west towards the American lines while you still can." He paused for a moment to let it all sink in. Then he continued.

"Helmut, you take the staff car and Margit and the baby and drive out of the city towards the American lines. Kurt, my dispatch driver, will join you. The two of you can split the driving. There are numerous roads still open and passable."

He then turned to Kurt. "Here, take my ID papers and ID disc. It should get you through our lines." The sound of artillery drowned out some of his words, and he had to repeat himself a number of times.

"What about you, darling?" Margit asked with tears in her eyes.

"I still have work to do. I'm heading over to the Führerbunker. The Führer needs me. I will figure out a way to get out of the city and join you as soon as I can. Once the fighting is over, let's plan to meet up in Magdeburg on the Elbe. From my information I believe that it's the furthest forward line of the Americans' advance to the east."

He turned to his friend and confidant, saying, "Helmut, take good care of Margit and Heinrich."

He then embraced Margit and kissed the baby, shook hands with Helmut and Kurt, and headed out the door as the building shook from a barrage of rocket fire from nearby. Margit looked out the window and saw him ride off on the motorcycle.

"Well, let's wait for nightfall before we begin our journey," Helmut suggested, taking another swig from the schnapps bottle.

As darkness fell, they gathered together blankets and food for their escape from the hell that was Berlin. It would take them many days to get to the American lines, through German checkpoints on the lookout for deserters, and avoiding Russian troops closing the circle around Berlin. They would travel only by night, laying up in various hiding places during the day.

CHAPTER 55

As the Air France jet winged its way across the Mediterranean, Daniel leaned back in his seat. He soon fell asleep, waking only when the plane's wheels touched down on the tarmac at Paris Orly Airport. Enveloped by the crowd in the arrivals lounge, he slowly made his way through French Customs and Immigration, to be greeted on the other side by a beaming Alexei.

"Welcome to Paris, my boy." Alexei gave Daniel a bear hug before asking, "What's the conclusion, Daniel?"

"It's definitely them," he answered. "Without a doubt, both Müller and Schmidt."

"Good, we'll have our boys take care of them. Now your flight to New York is starting to board. Your parents, I am sure, will be happy to see you!"

He had his arm around Daniel's shoulder as he walked with him to the departure gate. He once again embraced Daniel and whispered in his ear, "Israel owes you its gratitude, and it shall not be forgotten."

And indeed Daniel's work had resulted in the Israelis being ready to repel the Arab nations' attack on their country in October of 1973 in what was to become known as the Yom Kippur War. The fourth Arab-Israeli war of the twentieth century.

"By the way, did you know that Schmidt had a son?" Daniel asked.

"No, I did not, but what difference does that make?"

"None, I just wondered."

Daniel boarded his flight for New York's La Guardia and a welcome reunion with his parents.

The British European Airways plane with Bruno aboard followed Daniel's Air France flight down the runway and rose into the air bound for London, with a connecting flight to Asunción, Paraguay, aboard Pan Am.

A few nights later, cloaked by the darkness, agents of Israel's Mossad silently approached Bruno Schmidt's and Heinrich Müller's suburban Cairo homes. Their mission, based on Daniel's positive identification, was to eliminate the two Nazis who were helping the Egyptian Army develop rockets capable of raining destruction on Israel's cities. Bruno Schmidt had flown the coop; however, Heinrich Müller was shot while sleeping in his bed.

Upon arrival in Asunción, Bruno was hustled into a waiting Paraguayan army vehicle and driven to meet Alfredo Stroessner, Paraguay's dictator since engineering an army coup in 1954. The two men greeted each other effusively.

"Schmidt, so grateful that you accepted my offer from many years ago to come and work for our State security police. We have underground Communist cells working to overthrow our government. Your background equips you with certain talents to deal with this kind of threat."

Stroessner smiled at Bruno and grasped and shook his hand warmly in a gesture of welcome to the former SS colonel.

"General Stroessner, thank you for your confidence in offering me the job. I won't let you down."

"Well, there are a few of your old comrades working in our police and military, so you'll find yourself quite at home."

With that, Bruno assumed his post and set about fighting the Paraguayan underground.

Daniel, back in New York, applied for and took up the position of Assistant Curator of European Old Masters at New York's famed Metropolitan Museum of Art. He never discussed his secret mission in Egypt with anyone.

CHAPTER 56

JULY 1974,

PARQUE NACIONAL TINFUNQUÉ, PARAGUAY

After his arrival in Paraguay, Bruno Schmidt set about destroying the Paraguayan underground that was fighting to unseat Alfredo Stroessner's dictatorship. In interrogations of suspected underground members, he used the methods developed by the SS during the Second World War. He proved to be an able enforcer for his new employer. He heard about Müller's assassination by the Mossad through the grapevine, having severed all relationships with his Egyptian associates, for fear of being tracked to his new home.

In July 1974, he was invited, along with his former SS colleagues working for the Paraguayan military, to a gathering of ex-Nazi officers from Paraguay and Argentina, to be held at a Paraguayan National Park at Tinfunqué, on the River Pilcomayo. It was a safe meeting place in the middle of the rainforest, away from prying eyes and publicity.

As the arriving Germans were greeting each other, Bruno spotted a long-forgotten face amongst the Argentinians. He approached the man. "Helmut, my friend, it's great to see you again!"

He went and hugged his old driver, whom he had not seen since leaving the apartment at 14 Meineke Strasse in April 1945.

"Bruno, you old dog, you survived the war. So happy to see you!"

The two friends had not had any idea as to each other's fate. They walked through the trees and found a fallen log to sit on.

"Tell me what happened after we saw each other the last time. And what of Margit and Heinrich? How are they?" Bruno asked excitedly from his wartime driver and subordinate, not in the least attempting to hide his anxiety about the whereabouts of his mistress and infant son, about whose fates he was in the dark.

"No, you first," said Helmut. "How did you manage to get out of Berlin?"

"After I went to the Führerbunker, I saw that there was no hope of convincing the Führer to try and escape, so a group of secretaries and officers decided to try and break out. I joined this group and made it out into the suburbs, where I was arrested by the Soviets. After interrogation, I was sent to a prison camp in the Ural Mountains, where I spent four years. There I was given the opportunity to join a group of former SS officers to assist the Russians with their secret service, the NKVD, and teach them our methods.

"In 1956, after the Sinai War, the Russians wanted to help Abdel Nasser build up his army and his secret service. So, Müller and I were sent to Egypt to help them set up their Mukhabarat, or secret service, and to keep a watchful eye on German scientists who were helping the Egyptians start a guided missile program based on our development of the V2 rockets. I was made a general in the Egyptian Army and was there until 1973, when I came to Paraguay at the invitation of Stroessner. But tell me what happened with you, Margit, and little Heinrich?"

"Well, when the four of us left the apartment that night, I drove through the battle-scarred streets, trying to avoid the Russians, who seemed everywhere. We managed to get as far as Potsdam, where we hid for the day. As darkness fell, we continued on our journey, circling Russian checkpoints. Every now and again we would encounter a stray SS patrol, looking for deserters to string up. Lucky that Kurt had your ID; otherwise, we would have been put up against the wall.

"When we got close to the Elbe, I decided to try and make a run for the American lines during the daytime. I managed to get across a half-destroyed bridge near Magdeburg and was roaring towards the

Yanks when we were jumped by a Russian fighter patrolling the wrong side of the Elbe. I am sorry to say, my friend, that Margit and Kurt were killed instantly, but little Heinrich was shielded by Margit's body, and didn't have a scratch on him."

Helmut paused at this point, letting Bruno absorb the information about Margit and little Heinrich's fate.

A vacant look came into Bruno's eyes as he lowered his head into his hands and sat silent for a short time. Helmut continued, recalling what took place on that early May day back in 1945.

"I was wounded. A bullet had shattered my shoulder and another one just missed the main artery in my thigh. An American army doctor and his driver happened upon the scene and took us to a field hospital. There they stitched up my leg but had to amputate the arm."

At that point he showed Bruno, who was still clutching his head in his hands, the empty sleeve of his shirt.

"So, Margit's dead!" Bruno sobbed. "What about Heinrich?"

Helmut continued with his story.

CHAPTER 57

MAY 1945,

AMERICAN FIELD HOSPITAL NEAR

MAGDEBURG, GERMANY—THE BABY

"Corporal Murphy, you accompany this wounded German to the operating theatre. Let me take a look at his injuries," Colonel Sam Singer, with the usual authority in his voice, commanded the enlisted man.

"What about the bodies and the baby, sir?"

"After you escort the man, get a detail together to bury the bodies. I'll take the baby." Clutching the hysterically screaming baby boy to his chest, he entered one of the large tents used as sleeping quarters.

He approached a senior nurse and handed her the baby. "Here, Lieutenant Hunter, please take care of this baby until I come back. I think he needs to be fed. See what we can scare up for the poor little bugger." With that, he turned around and went into the operating theatre to tend to Helmut's wounds.

"I think that we'll be able to save the leg, but we'll have to amputate the arm," he said matter-of-factly, at the same time organizing his surgical team to perform the operation. Helmut's arm was amputated just below the shoulder, leaving only a stump. The wound on his leg was stitched up.

Dr. Singer washed up after the operation and went to find Lieutenant Hunter, who was tending to the baby boy. "Well, Lieutenant, how does babysitting suit you?"

The nurse was cradling the baby in her lap and feeding him milk from one of the GI ration packs. The baby had stopped crying and was ravenously sucking on the jerry-rigged nipple made by the nurse. "It's fine, sir, now that he's done screaming. Poor little guy. What an experience!"

Dr. Singer went over to the baby and gently stroked his head. *How long have Agatha and I tried to have a baby? This little guy has no parents, it seems. We could raise him as our own. I'll telephone Aggie and discuss it with her!*

It was getting to be nighttime, so he decided to put the call off until the morning.

Early the next morning he headed over to the divisional headquarters to see if he could be connected to his wife back in Larchmont. The field operator succeeded in getting a connection.

"Aggie, it's been so long since I heard your voice." Samuel spoke into the receiver in an excited tone.

"Yes, sweetheart. Are you okay? Is everything all right?" Agnes responded, reflecting Samuel's excitement.

"Yes, yes, I'm fine. But there's something I want to discuss with you."

"Sure, go ahead."

"Well, you know how long we've been trying to have a baby." Samuel's tone took on a pleading intonation, which caught Agnes somewhat off guard.

"Yes, and it's all my fault that we haven't been successful."

Sam could tell that Agatha was about to break into tears, as she always would when the question of having children arose. "Well, Aggie, what would you think if we adopted one?"

Sam continued without waiting for a response from his obviously distraught wife. "A baby boy was brought into the field hospital today. His mother has been killed, and I'm not sure if there is a father around. He's a real cute little blond guy! I could put in a request with SHAEF to authorize the adoption. What do you think?"

"I ... I am speechless. It's not something we ever discussed. How would we know about his background?"

"He's just a child. Can't be more than about nine months old. We would be saving a life."

"Well, Sam, you seem pretty committed to doing this, so what can I say? Let's go ahead with the adoption process."

"Oh, thank you, darling. You'll see that we made the right move!"

Sam went back to check on Helmut after the operation. He was drifting in and out of consciousness. He had gotten Helmut's last name from his SS ID card. "Look, Mr. Eckler, you've been grievously wounded, and I don't expect you to clearly answer any of my questions. Do you understand English?"

Helmut, having studied English at university, nodded.

"We have taken steps to bury the two people that were with you in a cemetery in Magdeburg. I am assuming that the woman was the baby's mother?"

Helmut once again nodded.

"As the baby seems to be without parents, I would like to make arrangements to have the baby adopted by a responsible US family. Do you understand?"

Although Helmut was only half conscious, he understood enough of what Sam was saying. Not knowing what the future would hold for him, not aware of Bruno's whereabouts, and realizing that Margit was dead, he felt that what Sam was proposing would be in little Heinrich's best interest.

"Good. I will arrange for the papers to be drafted to allow for the baby's adoption by a US family."

Sam knew he had to get the US Army's okay to affect the adoption. It would be a long and arduous process. So, he thought he would call on his old friend, Mickey Marcus, to help smooth the way. He was aware that Mickey was in Germany, dealing with the upcoming war crimes trial of major Nazi war criminals. He contacted SHAEF to see where Mickey was stationed and found him with the 157th Regiment in Dachau, the infamous German death camp near Munich, which they had liberated the previous month.

"Mickey, glad to have found you. I need your help. I know you have some pull with Ike at SHAEF, and I'd like to talk to you about something that I am trying to accomplish. You'll think I'm crazy, but can you come up to Magdeburg so we can talk about it?"

"Yes, I can to come up. I'm now with the judge advocate general, working on what these Nazi bastards did to our people and bringing them to trial, but for you I'll take the time. After all, you did save my leg in Normandy. I'll see you in a couple of days."

After a long day's drive through Russian and US checkpoints, a weary Mickey Marcus pulled up in front of the field hospital.

Sam had laid down for a nap after completing several surgeries on wounded GIs and some German civilians. He was roused from his sleep by a corporal.

"Sir, there's someone here to see you, a Colonel Marcus."

"Mickey, it's great that you could come up!" Sam hugged an exhausted Mickey. "Here, why don't we get you settled away and we can talk in the morning."

"Okay, can you accommodate my driver as well?"

"Sure, we'll have both of you taken care of. I'll see you tomorrow."

Next morning after breakfast, Sam and Mickey drove down to the banks of the Elbe. It was another bright day, the sun's rays dancing on the swiftly flowing river's surface.

"So what's so important that you have me hightail it here from Munich?" Mickey asked.

"Well, as you know, Aggie and I have been trying to have a baby forever, without success. The other day, I happened on an SS staff car that was shot up by a Russian fighter. The driver survived, I just operated on him, but his two passengers died. There was also a baby in the car. He was untouched. One of the dead was the baby's mother."

"I know where you're going with this, Sam, and it's a harebrained idea. Taking on a German baby. Who knows who his parents could have been? Nazi war criminals, perhaps? They were in an SS staff car, after all. And you know how upper brass feels about contact with German civilians."

"That's exactly why I asked you to come up. You have the ear of the generals at SHAEF. You could convince them to allow Aggie and I to adopt the little tyke. He's so cute, around nine months old. The nurses at the field hospital have fallen in love with him."

"This is crazy, Sam. Have you and Aggie thought it over well?"

"Aggie is somewhat reluctant, but she hasn't seen how sweet he is."

"Okay, if you're set on it, I'll have a talk with Bedell Smith, Eisenhower's right-hand man, to see if we can wangle this somehow. Get some form of authorization or waiver to the rules forbidding fraternization with enemy civilians."

"I knew I could count on you, Mickey. I don't know how I can ever repay you."

"Don't worry about that, just bring the kid up as a true American."

With a letter of authorization signed by General Eisenhower, Sam was able to have the baby flown on a US Air Force transport to New York, where the baby was picked up by Agatha and Bernard, Sam's father-in-law. Sam flew back to the United States a couple of months later, having received his discharge papers. They settled in Larchmont, New York, and set about bringing up the little baby boy. Sam took up residency at Zion Hospital as assistant chief surgeon, while Agatha doted on their adopted little boy, whom they named Daniel, after Mickey Marcus.

CHAPTER 58

JULY 1974,
PARQUE NACIONAL TINFUNQUÉ, PARAGUAY

Helmut finished his recounting of what had transpired at the American field hospital near Magdeburg in May 1945.

"So, Heinrich is alive?" Bruno enquired, lifting his head from his hands.

"I presume so. From the way he was talking, I think that it was the American doctor who operated on me and his wife who adopted him. I managed to swipe a card with his name and US address on it. I may still have it somewhere."

The two of them sat in silence for a while, each deep in their own thoughts about the past and what the future might hold.

Bruno spoke up first. "I would love to see Heinrich but cannot take the chance of travelling to the US, as I'm sure that I am still on the FBI's list of Nazi fugitives. Do you think you could go and locate him?"

"That would be quite the journey, if I can even find the doctor again."

"Well, I would pay for your flight. The Paraguayans are good payers."

"I could try to find him, I guess. Would you want me to tell him about his real parents, or just let it be?"

"I think that telling him about his roots and how he came into this world would clear some mysteries up for him."

"I'm not sure. Let me play it as things develop with the good doctor, if I can find him. How do I get a hold of you?"

Bruno took a pen out of his pocket and scribbled down his telephone number. Then the two of them rejoined the rest of the boisterous group of ex-SS men, regaling each other with stories from the war while drinking copious amounts of Löwenbräu, the famous German beer.

The telephone rang in Bruno's office one morning the week after the meeting of the former SS comrades.

"Hello, Schmidt here."

"Bruno, it's Helmut. I found Doctor Singer's address. He's in New York, or at least was at the end of the war."

"Oh, good. Do you have the time to fly to New York?"

"Life is kind of quiet here in Buenos Aires. Not much happening in the import-export side of things. I could take a few days off. I've checked on flights, and there are two direct flights a week, at around three thousand round trip."

"I'll wire you the money. Good luck!"

CHAPTER 59

AUGUST 1974,
NEW YORK CITY & BUENOS AIRES, ARGENTINA

Helmut's plane landed at New York's La Guardia Airport on a sunny and sweltering early August morning. The overnight flight from the Argentinian capital had worn Helmut out. He hadn't slept for a moment.

Helmut took a taxi into downtown Manhattan, looking for a hotel to rest up in before he began his search for Dr. Singer. He found a room at Manhattan's historic Algonquin Hotel. It was a bit pricey, but he thought, *why not sleep in comfort at Bruno's expense?*

Following four hours of fitful sleep, he decided to take a walk around Times Square and take some pictures with the small Leica camera he'd bought along. After eating a hot dog from a street vendor, he returned to his hotel room, where he took out the city's Yellow Pages directory to look up the address of Zion Hospital in Brooklyn. He contemplated phoning to connect with Dr. Singer, but then thought the better of it, and decided he would just show up the next morning.

That morning, he went for breakfast in the hotel's dining room, after which he hailed a taxi on the street, to take him to Zion Hospital. Helmut showed up at reception, asking to see Dr. Singer. He paced the snow-white reception area with pictures of the hospital's benefactors beaming down at him from the walls, along with warnings about infectious diseases and washing your hands. Thinking about how he would approach Samuel occupied him, and he played various scenarios over and over in his mind. After all, they hadn't seen each other since 1945, and he wondered whether the surgeon would even remember him.

The receptionist interrupted his thoughts. "May I tell Dr. Singer who is asking for him?"

"Please just tell him that it's an old friend from the war."

After a short discussion, the receptionist instructed Helmut to go to the fourth floor and office number 406.

When Samuel received the call, he wondered who the old friend could possibly be. Chewing on the stem of his unlit pipe, he thought, *could it be his driver, Corporal Murphy? Or perhaps Lieutenant Hunter, the senior nurse at the field hospital, who looked after Daniel? Or possibly Douglas from London, whom he hadn't seen since he passed through the British capital on his way to Palestine in 1948?* He didn't have long to wait as the knock came on his door.

"Come in."

Helmut opened the door slowly and carefully and stepped inside. Samuel came around from behind his desk and looked at Helmut without recognition. He couldn't immediately recall who the man standing in front of him was, although a faint familiarity passed through his mental memory bank.

"Hello, Dr. Singer, it's been a long time. I don't blame you for not recognizing me. Helmut Eckler." He held out his hand to shake Dr. Singer's.

Several thoughts ran through Samuel's brain as he absent-mindedly shook Helmut's outstretched hand.

Why is he here? How did he find me? Did it have anything to do with Daniel? "Oh yes, now I remember. We had to amputate your arm. Bad wounds. One on your leg as well, if I recall correctly?"

"Yes, yes, I am the one," Helmut responded, as his eyes wandered around Samuel's small office, with papers piled high on the metal desk, and bookshelves with medical texts lining the walls. He also noticed the picture of a smiling woman with a young man on the credenza behind the desk. The boy in the photograph looked to be about twenty years old, with blond hair and blue eyes, and wearing graduation robes.

"So, how can I help you, Mr. Eckler? Is it something about your wounds?"

"No, not at all, although I do get ... what do you call it, where my arm used to be?"

"Phantom pain. It's quite usual. But, then, why have you come to see me?"

"It's about the baby boy that you were arranging to have adopted by someone in the US. Have you been in contact with the adoptive parents?"

"Actually, yes. My wife and I adopted him."

"And how is he doing?"

"Well, he's thirty now and works at an art gallery."

"I presume that the photograph behind you is of your wife and the boy?"

"Yes, it is."

Just then the intercom on Samuel's desk came to life. "Dr. Singer, you're wanted in the second-floor ICU."

"Please sit down. I shouldn't be too long."

With Samuel gone from the office, Helmut quickly took his camera out of his pocket and snapped a couple of pictures of the photograph of Agatha and Daniel, putting it away before Samuel's return.

As Samuel re-entered his office, he apologized to Helmut. "Sorry, Mr. Eckler, but duty called."

"That's fine, doctor. Now, can I ask you if I may meet the boy? By the way, his birth name is Heinrich."

"We named him Daniel. I honestly don't think it's a good idea for the two of you to meet. He believes that he was born in the USA and we don't want to change that perception."

"Don't you think that it would be beneficial for him to find out about his true birth parents and his heritage?"

"No. I don't!" Samuel's voice rose in anger, and his complexion reddened, as he was quite emphatic in denying Helmut's request. "Now, is there anything else I can do for you, Mr. Eckler? I have a busy day ahead of me."

"No, and thank you for your time, doctor." Helmut once again proffered his good hand to Samuel.

"Goodbye, Mr. Eckler, and be assured that the young man is in good hands, loved and nurtured by us. I don't think it would be a wise idea to turn his world suddenly upside down."

Helmut took a cab back to the Algonquin Hotel, and left New York for Buenos Aires the next day. Once he had returned to the Argentinian capital, he phoned Bruno.

"That was a short visit, Helmut. Didn't you manage to locate the doctor?"

"Yes, I did. And I was right, it was he who adopted Heinrich. But he refused to allow me to meet him."

"How is he doing?"

"From what the doctor said, he'd doing all right. I think that the doctor is Jewish."

"That's poetic justice for you. The son of a Nazi war criminal being raised as a Jew." Bruno chuckled at this strange twist of fate.

"I managed to take a picture of a photograph of the boy that the doctor had on his desk."

"Could you send it to me?"

"Sure, after I have it developed."

"Instead of sending it to me, perhaps we can meet again, and you can give it to me then?"

"You're welcome in Buenos Aires any time, my friend."

"I'll plan to be there the middle of next week."

A week later the two of them met in a bar at Buenos Aires' Ezeiza Airport.

"Nice to see you again, my friend." Helmut hugged his Second World War superior.

"Great seeing you as well. I'm anxious to see the photograph you took of Heinrich."

Helmut reached into his pocket, pulled out an envelope, and handed it to Bruno, who took the picture out of the envelope. His face went white.

"Shit, he certainly has balls," Bruno spoke up loudly.

"What do you mean, Bruno?"

"You are sure this is a picture of Heinrich?"

"Well, the doctor said he and his wife adopted him. Why, what's the matter?"

"This guy came to Cairo as a Canadian United Nations officer. I knew there was something odd about him when I first met him. I just couldn't put my finger on it. I think that he was working for the Israelis. He sure has balls."

"Look at his face. It's you at the same age when we were in university," Helmut chimed in.

"I need you to get his address for me."

"What do you plan to do?"

"I want to bequeath him an inheritance. For him to find out who his real parents were. I am going to leave him the apartment at 14 Meineke Strasse. I still have the deed that was signed by Judge Oberhofer in 1944."

"It should be an easy matter to find out his address. I'll just call the New York City information line or get hold of a telephone book."

"You do that, Helmut. Also, please contact one of my old colleagues at any of the law firms I used to work with back in the days. See which is still in business and have them draw up a will. I want you to be my executor. I'll pay for your flight to Germany and I'll mail you the deed."

Helmut noticed a vacant look come into Bruno's eyes, as if his thoughts were many miles away. And they were. Back to the war, his days in captivity in Russia, his life with Steffi. They were all coming back to him as he wondered about how he would react if he did get to meet Daniel face to face again.

"Is everything all right, Bruno?" Helmut asked.

"Yes, yes. Just marvelling at the strange twists of fate that life throws at us."

CHAPTER 60

SEPTEMBER 1974,

BERLIN—DRAWING UP A WILL

It didn't take much time for Helmut to locate Daniel through a New York telephone book he found at the US embassy in Buenos Aires. After receiving the apartment's deed from Bruno by mail, he made arrangements to fly to Berlin.

He arrived at Berlin's Templehof airport on a muggy afternoon at the beginning of September. He hadn't been back to Germany since the war ended and he had immigrated to Argentina as so many other Germans did to escape their past.

After checking into a hotel, he looked through the business directory of Berlin's telephone book in order to locate a law firm that he would have been familiar with. He had no trouble finding the firm of Keller, Czinner and Hugo. They hadn't even changed their name after the war. Helmut remembered that old man Keller had done a lot of work for Bruno and his SS cronies before the outbreak of war, and Helmut felt certain that he would now help an old colleague.

He picked up the telephone and made an appointment. He had met Gustav Keller with Bruno once before the war but was sure that Keller wouldn't remember him.

"*Guten Tag*, Herr Eckler. How may I be of service to you?"

"Herr Keller, I would presume that you don't recall who I am, but I was Colonel Bruno Schmidt's driver before and during the war."

"Oh, yes, Bruno Schmidt. I did a lot of work for him during those troubled times. I haven't heard of him since the war. I think he was in trouble with the Americans."

"Well, he's alive and felt that contacting an old colleague to get some legal forms drafted wouldn't be out of the question. Yes?" Helmut cocked his head to the side, looking at Keller and waiting for a response.

"That depends on what kind of work he wishes for me to perform and why he hasn't come himself."

"It's a simple will that he needs to have drawn up. And for obvious reasons, he couldn't come himself." Helmut gave a nod and a wink, which Keller immediately understood. "So, let's get to it."

After a half-hour drafting session, the document deeding the apartment at 14 Meineke Strasse to Daniel Singer of New York, upon the death of Bruno Schmidt, was completed.

"Thank you, Herr Keller. Bruno will be most grateful. Oh, and here are five-hundred marks for your trouble."

"You give my best regards to Herr Schmidt, please," said Keller as he pocketed the cash.

Helmut had gone to the Meineker Strasse address and taken some photographs of the building, which he attached to the copy of the deed he left with Keller, along with instructions on what to do the next time he heard from Helmut.

CHAPTER 61

MAY 1988,

ASUNCIÓN, PARAGUAY

Life had slowed down considerably for Bruno in the intervening fourteen years since he joined Paraguay's anti-Communist police force. Alfredo Stroessner remained in power and continued to protect Bruno from those looking at his past.

He retired from active police work in 1976 and married a German immigrant woman significantly younger than him. He and Helmut went on to correspond regularly and meet occasionally at the SS get-togethers. Bruno flew to Buenos Aires one time to introduce his wife, Elspeth, to Helmut. She reminded Helmut of Margit, with her blonde hair and blue eyes. The three of them sat at an outdoor café, with Bruno and Helmut recounting their wartime exploits and adventures.

One day in late May, Helmut's telephone rang. It was a tearful and distraught Elspeth that was on the line.

"Herr Eckler, something terrible has happened. Bruno's dead. He had a heart attack last night, and they couldn't revive him."

"I am so sorry, Elspeth. Is there anything I can do?"

"If you could be so kind as to contact his old friends? The funeral will be next week."

Bruno was buried with full State honours befitting a general in Paraguay's police force. Paraguay's dictator was in attendance, as was

Helmut, and many of Bruno's old SS comrades living in exile in various South American countries.

Upon returning to Buenos Aires, Helmut sent a telegram to Gustav Keller's law firm, advising him, as Bruno's estate's executor, to act on his instructions regarding Bruno's will.

CHAPTER 62

LATE JULY 1988,
NEW YORK CITY—THE WILL

Daniel, Madelaine, and Eric Bender listened attentively as they sat in the small coffee shop at the bottom of Deutsche Bank's New York office, with Eric translating the German document Daniel had received in the mail. Upon hearing the name Bruno Schmidt, Daniel's thoughts went back to his mission in Cairo fifteen years ago. *What does this document mean? What does Bruno Schmidt have to do with the document or me?*

"The document says that SS Colonel Bruno Schmidt and his wife, Margit Angelika Hootveg, had a baby boy born in July 1944 in Berlin. The boy was named Heinrich Karl Schmidt. So this is a birth certificate for the boy. The documents that this is attached to are the last will and testament of Bruno Schmidt and the deed to an apartment in Berlin.

"It says, 'Bruno Schmidt, who died in Asunción, Paraguay, in May of this year, and Margit Hootveg, the boy's mother, having died in 1945, buried in Magdeburg, Germany, and his only relative being the surviving son, Heinrich Schmidt, now residing in New York, USA, under the name Daniel Singer, hereby inherits the apartment in which he was born, at 14 Meineke Strasse, Berlin, West Germany.' It is signed by the will's executor, Helmut Eckler."

Daniel's jaw dropped at the revelation that he wasn't born at Zion Hospital in New York, the son of an American soldier killed in Italy, but the son of a convicted Nazi war criminal, whom he had himself marked for assassination in 1973. Daniel was having trouble dealing with the facts and started to get queasy. Standing up, he excused himself, going outside into the brilliant sunshine. He thought about Gamasy's comments about having a son that he hadn't seen in many years, and now realized the little secret his mother had been about to tell him before he left for Rome. Returning to the coffee shop he sat down again.

"What do I do?" he asked aloud, not so much from his two companions, but a higher entity.

"Why, you go to Berlin, take possession of the apartment and sell it or use it as a European pied-à-terre. You know, it's in a very swanky part of the city," Eric chimed in.

"Yes, that's what you should do," Madelaine added.

Daniel was still wrestling, coming to terms with his past and his roots. He wondered about his father's motivation, the enigma that was exclaimed by Alexei in Tel Aviv. Was he a cold-blooded killer or just an opportunist taking advantage of turbulent times? He couldn't quite figure it out. He decided he would fly to Berlin, look at the apartment, and then decide what to do. Eric offered to help him by contacting the Deutsche Bank office in Berlin, asking them to assist Daniel in any way possible. Daniel booked a flight the next day, advising his superior at the MET that he was taking two weeks' holidays to look after some family matters.

That evening, he and Madelaine had a long discussion about the document and his plans to fly to Germany.

"You know, Maddy, I can't believe what I found out today. How could my parents have kept it from me?"

"They wanted you to grow up a healthy boy, without the guilt that having been born in Germany during the war would burden you with. They might not even have known who your father was."

"It's such a small world. To think that I was together with my father without either one of us knowing the identity of the other! For God's sake, I played tennis with him."

"You need to go to Berlin and look at the apartment. You never know what it may lead to."

Daniel couldn't get to sleep that night, pacing the floor, a glass of wine in his hand, playing over in his mind the events of the day. He packed his bags in the morning, boarding a flight to Germany the next evening.

CHAPTER 63

AUGUST 1988,
BERLIN—VISITING A BIRTHPLACE

Upon arrival in Berlin, Daniel contacted Kurt Hammerstein, Eric Bender's associate at Deutsche Bank's Berlin office.

"Hello, Mr. Hammerstein, it's Daniel Singer from New York."

"Oh yes, Eric had mentioned that you might call. How can I help?"

"First of all, could you recommend a reasonably priced hotel near Meineke Strasse?"

"Certainly, let me look at the directory." There was a pause on the other end of the line, then Hammerstein said, "Well, there is a B and B on Meineke Strasse. Let me call them to see if they have a room available. Hang on." He came back on the line a few moments later. "You're in luck. They have a room open. Would you like me to pick you up?"

"Not necessary. I'll just take a taxi. However, why not join me for dinner?"

"That would be excellent. Let's meet at your hotel, at say seven thirty?"

"Perfect."

When the two of them met, they hit it off immediately. Over beers in a neighbourhood restaurant, Kurt asked Daniel the nature of his trip. "Eric didn't tell me much, other than to offer you any assistance you may need. So, I am at your service."

"I've inherited an apartment in Meineke Strasse from my father, who recently died in Paraguay. I've come to look at it and determine what I should do with it. Would you like to come with me tomorrow to take a look at it? Perhaps help me out if I run into any problems? And since I don't speak German, perhaps translate for me?"

"I would be delighted to."

"Why don't we meet at the apartment then, at ten. The address is Fourteen Meineke Strasse."

The next morning, not having keys to the apartment, they went to the flat of the building's superintendent, who looked at them with great suspicion.

"What can I do for you gentlemen?" he asked, only emerging halfway from the entrance to his flat, keeping the door behind him half open.

Since he asked in German, Daniel looked quizzically at Kurt, who translated. "He wants to know why we are here."

Daniel reached into his pocket and pulled out the deed and the will, and handed it to the portly, balding man with a heavy hint of garlic on his breath, who perused them line by line, stopping every now and again saying, "Ahem, ahem."

"Please tell him that I am here to take a look at the apartment, but I have no way of getting in."

Kurt translated for the superintendent, who asked them to wait while he went back inside. They could hear drawers being pulled out and the rattle of metal. After a few moments, the man emerged holding a key ring with a couple of keys attached.

"Very strange, nobody has lived in that apartment since the end of the war. My father, who was building superintendent before me, said that a high-ranking Nazi and his wife and baby were the last ones living in there. Apparently, he took it from a Jewish family who were sent away, if you know what I mean." He raised an eyebrow. "I see from the papers that you've inherited it. Do you plan to move in? It's a big space for one person."

A woman's voice from behind him interrupted his questions. "Who is it, Hans?"

"Oh, some people want to have a look at that empty apartment on the fourth floor."

"Well, we'd best get going, and thank you for your help," Kurt said, as they proceeded towards the elevator.

"There are two sets of keys there. Be sure to bring back a set," the man called after them.

They opened the front door and entered the apartment, which was in total darkness. They drew back the curtains to let the daylight in. Everything had remained the same since Bruno's departure in April 1945. A thick covering of dust was evident, highlighted by the faint rays of sunshine filtering in through the windows.

The furniture was in its place as it had been on that day. There were cobwebs everywhere and a musty odour permeated the apartment. They threw open the windows to let the fresh August air in. They walked around the place, peering into the bedrooms and the salon, and they inspected the kitchen.

"Beautiful apartment, you should be able to do real well selling it," commented Kurt. "You will, of course, need to get it cleaned up. I can highly recommend my cleaning lady."

"That would be very kind."

They continued to walk around the apartment, examining the various nooks and crannies, when they noticed the scrapes along the floor, by now mostly obscured by the dust, by the large oak cabinet.

"Looks like this had been moved," said Kurt.

"Must be something behind it."

The two of them strained to move the cabinet aside to reveal the secret entrance to the space behind it, where the Weiszes had been hidden for a good part of the war.

"Whoa! It smells in here," exclaimed Daniel as he entered the Weisz's hiding place. Everything was covered in dust and with cobwebs. He couldn't help but notice the dark red stain on the wood floor inside the door. He also picked up a small notebook, whose cover was also stained dark red. "I wonder what went on here? Perhaps this notebook will tell us something."

"It's handwritten in German, can you read it for me?" he said, handing the book to Kurt.

Kurt started reading and translating for Daniel.

> *"My name is Maximillian Weisz, and my father had given me the idea to start writing a diary about our time in hiding from the Nazis. I will be eight years old, and because our family is Jewish, we have to hide in the attic of the apartment that we used to live in."*

"It seems that the people who used to own this apartment hid here from the Nazis until late July 1944. This is a diary written by an eight-year-old telling of the terrifying times they had, until it abruptly ends."

> *"Maybe life between these walls will soon be over and I can go outside again."*

"What would life have been like between these walls, hiding from the horrors of the persecution they endured? And what happened to them? Tell me, Kurt, are there city archives where we can trace the history of this place?"

"Certainly. We'll have to go down to the *Rathaus*, or city hall, and see if we can examine the documents."

"Could we arrange to do that tomorrow?"

"Sure. I'll beg off work for another day. But why are you so interested in its history?"

"Because I was born in this apartment."

The revelation shocked Kurt. He didn't know what to say, so he just kept his mouth shut, thinking, *we'll see what tomorrow brings.*

Later that afternoon, Daniel walked around the city of his birth. He went to the Brandenburg Gate, the Reichstag, and to Checkpoint

Charlie, the dividing line between the American Zone and Soviet-occupied East Berlin. While he walked, he thought over what he had seen that morning, and it troubled him.

A number of questions arose in his mind. *Who did the original apartment belong to? What happened to them? How did my father end up with ownership? What will I do with the apartment if I find out it was obtained unlawfully?*

He figured that the visit to the city archives the next day would provide some answers.

Over breakfast the next morning, he and Kurt talked family histories. Daniel explained how he was brought up in New York thinking he was born in the USA, only to find out that he was the son of a Nazi war criminal.

Kurt, having been born in West Berlin well after the end of the war, had a less than favourable opinion of Adolf Hitler's regime. He went to university and learned about the excesses committed by the Nazis during the war. He understood Daniel's shock at learning of his background and was willing to be helpful in researching his family's past.

They arrived at the city archives mid-morning. After the payment of fifteen marks they were ushered into the archives to begin their search. They requested to see the documents relating to 14 Meineke Strasse, which was brought out to them by a young and pretty clerk. Kurt quickly found the pages relating to apartment #401 and started to read it, while translating aloud into English.

"Apartment #401 at 14 Meineke Strasse was purchased by Alexander Grossman, haberdasher in July 1924 for 20,000 Marks from Hugo Eberling, furniture maker. According to the 1927 census figures, the apartment was occupied by Alexander Grossman, his wife Esther, and daughter Ingrid. It was then sold in December 1942 to a Heldi Hinkelmayer for one thousand Reichsmark, or five percent of the original purchase price."

Daniel cut in, "That's crazy, why sell it so cheap?"

"Back during the war, deals were made whereby Jews would sell their properties and valuables to trusted Christian friends with the idea that they could buy them back when the war was over. It's obvious that's what happened here."

"What then?" Daniel asked.

"Well, in July 1944, title to the apartment was transferred for zero consideration from Frau Hinkelmayer to Bruno Schmidt, a colonel in the SS. The transfer was signed by a judge. So, it appears that the apartment was appropriated by Schmidt, and the transaction blessed by a friendly judge. Ownership is still in the name of Bruno Schmidt. We will have to go see a lawyer while you're in town to get ownership transferred to you."

"Is there somewhere we can go and see what happened to the Grossmans?" Daniel asked Kurt.

"Let me do some research. My secretary can look into it. The Nazis kept pretty good records, so we should be able to discover what happened to them. I have to get back to work now, but I will be in touch as soon as I find out something. What are you going to do for the rest of the day?"

"I think I'll go back to the apartment and figure out what to do with it."

Daniel returned to the place of his birth. Feeling as if it were haunted by ghosts, he went into the attic, the Weiszes hiding place. He saw the mattresses on the floor, the children's toys strewn about, and wondered how life would have been under such circumstances.

Walking into the salon, he sat down by the dust-covered piano and looked at the notebook with its childish penmanship and thought about what could have become of the eight-year-old writer, wondering, *If I had known Bruno was my father, could I have shot him while we were together in Cairo?*

That night, back in his room at the B&B, he fell into a fitful sleep. Nightmares from his mission to Cairo came back to haunt him. How he wished Samuel were alive so he could seek some guidance.

He received a telephone call from Kurt the next morning.

"I have good news for you Daniel. My secretary found the International Tracing Service office in Bad Arolsen, northern Germany. They keep information on persons living in Germany at the beginning of the war sent to concentration camps across Europe, based on Nazi documents. The Nazis kept excellent records. We can either drive up there or request documentation concerning the Grossman and Weisz families to be faxed to my office."

"Thank you, Kurt. I don't want you to take another day off work, so why don't you have them fax the documents to your office, and I'll come down to look at them."

"Fine, I'll ask for them to be sent down."

It took two days for the documents to arrive. During that time, Daniel spent his days continuing to explore the city. He didn't return to the apartment, as he found it too depressing. He arrived at Kurt's office in the afternoon. Kurt laid the document on his desk and invited Daniel to sit on the other side. He began to read and translate the handwritten papers authored and signed by SS Captain Helmut Eckler:

1. *Esther Grossman, Jewess, living at 14 Meineker Strasse, Charlottenburg, deceased from natural causes at Königin Elisabeth Hospital on July 23, 1944.*

2. *Ingrid Weisz, Jewess, daughter of Esther Grossman, also of 14 Meineker Strasse, delivered to Grunewald Station for transport to Auschwitz Concentration Camp on July 24, 1944.*

3. *Arnold Weisz, Jew, husband of Ingrid Weisz, same disposition as his wife on same date.*

4. *Elsa Weisz and Rachel Weisz, twin daughters of Arnold and Ingrid Weisz, same disposition as parents on same date.*

"So, they were sent to Auschwitz on the orders of this guy, Eckler, who is my father's will's executor," Daniel said under his breath. "Is there any way of finding out what happened to them after they were sent to Auschwitz?" Daniel enquired of Kurt's secretary.

"Let me call the Tracing Service and find out," she replied. After a short conversation on the telephone she turned to Daniel.

"There is the Holocaust Survivors and Victims Database at the United States Holocaust Memorial Museum. I can try to get information on them from there. Would you like me to call?"

"Yes, please."

She got on the telephone, and after a lengthy conversation, in which she provided details on the Grossmans and Weiszes while taking notes, she hung up and turned to Daniel.

"There are no notations on the fates of Arnold and Ingrid Weisz in the database; however, there are on Elsa and Rachel. It's a good thing that the SS kept such detailed records on those sent to the camps. Being twins, they were registered into the Auschwitz medical facilities in August 1944. There they underwent various tests, with Elsa passing away from typhus in January 1945. It seems that Rachel survived until the end of the war and was amongst those liberated by the Russians. And that's where it ends."

"I wonder if there is some way that I could locate Rachel Weisz?"

"Well, the woman I was talking to at the Tracing Service did mention that if someone were registered with them, they could attempt to locate that person. Should I give it a try?"

"That would be much appreciated."

"Should I give our office as the place for them to contact you should they be successful in locating her?"

"Yes, that would be ideal. Thank you. Not much more I can do in Berlin, so I'll fly back to New York tomorrow. Kurt, could you please keep an eye on the apartment for me?"

"Yes, and I will contact you at your work if we hear anything back from the Tracing Service."

CHAPTER 64

OCTOBER 1988,
NEW YORK CITY

Back in New York, Daniel picked up where he had left off, working at the MET. However, he couldn't get the image of the apartment out of his mind and kept replaying what life for the Weiszes must have been like while in hiding. He was determined to try to make up for their suffering and locate Rachel Weisz, if at all possible. He had long, nightly conversations with Madelaine, unloading on her the burden he carried of being the son of a Nazi. It became an obsession with him.

It was a Monday afternoon in the middle of October when the telephone rang on Daniel's desk.

"Hello, Daniel. It's Monika from Kurt Hammerstein's office in Berlin. How have you been?"

"Well, thank you, and you?"

"Just working hard. You know what a slave-driver Kurt is. But I have good news for you. I just heard from the Tracing Service, and they have located Rachel Weisz."

"Wonderful!"

"Would you like her contact information?"

"Yes, please."

Daniel couldn't contain his excitement, so called Madelaine. "Maddie, guess what? They located Rachel Weisz. She's living in Israel!"

"Great news, Daniel. Will you try to contact her?"

"I will, first thing in the morning. It's midnight in Israel. I'm so excited."

That evening, over dinner with Madelaine, Daniel revealed his plan on how he would deal with the apartment.

"I'm going to transfer the deed to Rachel Weisz. The apartment rightly belonged to her family until my father seized it. I can set things right in small measure by gifting it back to her, to do with as she wishes."

"That's awfully generous of you, but do you know whether she'll want it, or even what her current circumstances are?"

"Well, I'll find out tomorrow, but in any case, I'll sleep better tonight."

Early the next morning Daniel dialled the number in Tel Aviv given to him by the Tracing Service. The telephone was answered by an answering machine in Hebrew. Daniel left a message in English, hoping that Rachel would understand.

Later that afternoon, Daniel answered the ringing of the telephone at his work.

"Hello, Mr. Daniel Singer?" came a voice with a heavy Hebrew accent from the other end of the line.

"Yes, this is he."

"I believe from the message that you left that you were looking for me, Rachel Weisz. By the way, you wouldn't be the Daniel Singer that visited Israel in 1973 and did some work for the Institute?"

"Why, yes, that's me."

"Daniel, it's Rivka, Naomi's partner. So nice to hear from you after all these years. But what can I do for you?"

Daniel fell silent. After all those years, the memories of his time in Israel came flooding back to him. Yes, of course, Rivka, the red-headed Israeli soldier cum guide who was having an affair with Naomi. He recalled what Naomi had told him about Rivka and her background.

"Hello, Daniel, are you still there?"

"Yes, of course. How's Naomi?"

"She's well, rising in the ranks. We've adopted a beautiful little baby girl. Named her Elsa, after my sister."

"Rivka, it's a very small world. You were born at 14 Meineke Strasse in Berlin as Rachel Weisz. Correct?"

"Why, yes, but what does that have to do with you?"

"I have found out some very interesting and important information about your and my family that I would like to discuss with you, but not over the telephone. Would you be willing to meet me in Berlin?"

"If you feel it's that important, I'll consider it. However, I don't retain good memories of life in Germany, so it won't be a happy journey for me."

"Believe me, Rivka, it will be worth your time to come. When will you let me know?"

"Let me discuss it with Naomi, and I will get back to you in a few days. It was really nice talking with you, Daniel."

It was the end of October before Daniel heard back from her.

"Hello, Daniel," Rivka said. "I've talked it over with Naomi, and we will come and meet you in Berlin. We won't be able to get there, however, until somewhere around Christmastime. Would that be okay?"

"Yes, absolutely. Just let me know your travel plans, and I'll make arrangements to pick you up at the airport. Please give my best to Naomi."

CHAPTER 65

DECEMBER 1988,
BERLIN—THE REUNION

Daniel arrived in Berlin on a snowy mid-December afternoon. He called Kurt upon his arrival and made plans to meet him for lunch the next day.

"Good to see you again, Daniel. I assume that you've made up your mind as to what you want to do with the Meineke Strasse apartment?"

"Yes, and that's where I'd like your help. I need an introduction to a real estate lawyer to transfer the deed into my name and then to transfer it once again to the individual I want to gift it to."

"And who is that?"

"Rachel Weisz. Thanks to you and Monika, I was able to contact her in Israel, and she's coming to Berlin to meet me."

"That's wonderful, Daniel. I'll make arrangements with a lawyer friend of mine to look after the paperwork."

A couple of days later, Daniel took a taxi to the airport to pick up Rivka and Naomi. The three of them hugged warmly at the arrival gate.

"Hello, Naomi. Beautiful as ever."

"Daniel, I am mystified by all of this. What is the reason you had us fly here from Tel Aviv?" Rivka asked.

"Well, you'll find out soon enough. After we drop your bags off at the hotel, I am going to take you to a place that should bring back some memories."

They caught up on each other's lives in the cab on the way from the airport.

"How are Alexei and Yoel doing?"

"Alexei is retired from the Institute, and Yoel in now the director of the French Section."

"And how is your father? Such a sweet man."

"He died several years ago."

"Oh, I am sorry."

"And you two, still working at the Institute?"

"Naomi is now a major. I look after our daughter, Elsa."

After dropping their bags off, they proceeded to 14 Meineker Strasse. The taxi stopped in front of the building and the three of them got out. Rivka looked enquiringly at Daniel.

"Do you recognize the building, Rivka?"

Rivka gazed at the building's façade and something stirred in her memory. It had been forty-four years since she last set eyes on the building, but things slowly started to come back to her.

"Why, this is the building that my family lived in. Where we hid during the war, and where we were taken from by the Nazis."

Daniel pushed open the glass door, and they headed to the elevator.

"I used to love riding in this elevator," Rivka reminisced.

They got off on the fourth floor and Daniel led them to the door of apartment 401. He carefully pushed the door open.

Memories began flooding back, overwhelming Rivka as she looked at the piano in the salon. Tears came into Rivka's eyes when Daniel led her to the hiding place. From the dining room table, Daniel lifted the notebook Maximillian had kept a diary in and handed it to Rivka.

She began to read, then started to feel faint and had to steady herself on the window ledge. "I wonder what happened to him?" she sobbed.

"There's no information on him in the SS records. You, your twin sister Elsa, and your parents were shipped to Auschwitz, but there is nothing mentioning him."

"So, Daniel, how do you come to this apartment?"

"Like you, Rivka, I was also born in this place. But a couple of years after you. After you were transported to Auschwitz, my birth father, a colonel in the SS, took over. Naomi, he was Bruno Schmidt. If you remember, he was the one I was sent to Cairo to identify in Operation Berlin on the Nile."

"You're the son of an SS officer? How could you be? You're Jewish, for God's sake!"

"My mother was killed in the war, and I ended up at an American field hospital. I was adopted by my father, Samuel Singer, a surgeon working at the hospital. I had no idea who my birth parents were until I received a package in the mail containing my birth certificate. My parents never told me that I was born in Germany. My mother was Dutch—that much I know. I intend to visit her grave before I leave Germany."

It was too much for Rivka to comprehend. She sank into one of the upholstered chairs in the salon, which used to be occupied by her grandfather, Papa Grossman, buried her face in her hands and started to cry.

Naomi went and sat on the arm of the chair, wrapping her arm around Rivka's shoulder, trying to console her.

"Rivka, this apartment belonged to your family," Daniel said. "My father seized it illegally, and I have made arrangements to transfer title back to you, to do with as you wish."

The only sound in the apartment was Rivka's continued sobbing. "That won't bring my family back!" she shouted at Daniel in frustration.

"Nothing I can do to bring your family back, but handing over this apartment, where both you and I were born, might give your daughter a start in life as she gets older. It is rightfully yours." Daniel paced the room, stealing a glance in Rivka's direction every now and again. He could understand her feelings, being faced with the memory of her family and her time in hiding and in Auschwitz.

Finally, she stood up and said, "Let's go. I need to get out of here."

"We must go to see a lawyer that my contact in Berlin introduced me to. We need to draw up the papers for the transfer."

"If that is your wish, Daniel." Rivka responded, her face sad, trying to hold back her tears.

The next day, they all went with Kurt to the lawyer's office to affect the transfer of the apartment into Rivka's name. Afterwards, they took a cab to the airport so Rivka and Naomi could begin their journey back to Tel Aviv.

Daniel hugged the two women. "It is a small world, Rivka, and the past cannot be undone. Fate and history bind us together. I am sorry for your loss and what you went through, and hope that this insignificant token of apology for what my father had done will be accepted in the spirit it's being offered."

"You're a wonderful man, Daniel," Rivka whispered as she and Naomi began walking to their gate.

The next afternoon, Daniel boarded the train for Magdeburg. It was raining heavily. He located the small church with the cemetery behind it where Corporal Murphy's burial detail had buried his mother. He stood by the grave and thought back over the years it took to get him here, wishing he had something of his mother's, but he didn't even have a picture. He bent down, planted a kiss on the simple cross, and whispered, "Thank you, Mother, for giving me life."

He then turned and walked away to catch a train to Frankfurt, from where he would fly to New York.

CHAPTER 66

Although both Heinrich Müller and Bruno Schmidt had passed away, the German scientists they had watched and nurtured in Egypt continued to work on developing and miniaturizing missile guidance systems and explosives for Muammar Gaddafi's regime in Libya. Libya and Egypt had been Allies against Israel under the banner of the United Arab Republic until 1977.

Dr. Hans Niedermeyer, who during the Second World War worked under Werner von Braun on the development of Germany's V1 and V2 rocket programs, was in charge of Gaddafi's weapons program. In November 1988, he met with agents of the Libyan secret service at the research facilities in Tripoli.

One of the agents turned to the German, "Dr. Niedermeyer, I come on the orders of Colonel Gaddafi. As you know, American bombers tried to assassinate our great leader in 1986 under the pretext that he had ordered the explosion at a nightclub in Berlin that year. He wants to teach the Yankees a lesson and get revenge. Colonel Gaddafi has ordered the building of a miniature bomb that will be hard to detect and have enough explosive power to bring down a commercial airliner. Can you come up with one in a relatively short time frame?"

"I think that's entirely possible."

Three weeks later, Dr. Niedermeyer delivered the explosive device to Libyan secret service headquarters. From there, Libyan agents would smuggle the device into the luggage hold of a Malta Airways jet headed to Frankfurt.

CHAPTER 67

Daniel boarded Pan Am flight 103, flying from Frankfurt to Detroit via London and New York. He settled into his seat, 32A, in the 747 that was to fly him home to a very pregnant Madelaine, who was expecting in March. All the baggage was loaded, and the plane taxied for takeoff. It reached a cruising altitude of 30,000 feet over northern Germany, then turned west towards the United Kingdom. The flight landed in London at 8:30 p.m., where it took on additional passengers and then began its transatlantic journey, flying over Scotland before heading out over the North Sea.

Daniel adjusted his seat into the reclining position, put on his headphones to listen to one of the year's hits, "The Flame" by Cheap Trick, and started to doze off. Daniel felt satisfied that he had transferred ownership of the apartment where they were both born to Rivka. He wished he could have done something more significant to atone for his father's sins but was nonetheless happy that he was able to make the gesture and was wondering what his adoptive parents would have thought.

Thirty thousand feet below, Ian McLeod had just left his favourite watering hole, the Black Bull Inn, close to midnight, where he had played darts and consumed a couple of pints of Guinness with friends.

A thunderous roar and flash lit up the night sky. McLeod took shelter by a stone garden wall as pieces of aircraft began to drop all around him.

A journey that had begun forty-four years ago beside the German Autobahn ended in a Scottish farmer's field.

In New York, Madelaine had just sat down for dinner. She was eagerly awaiting Daniel's return the next morning, and she rubbed her belly, feeling the baby move inside her. She wouldn't find out until the next day that Pan Am flight 103 had been blown up over Scotland during the night by agents of Libya's secret service.

Bruno Schmidt had been dead for months, and he undoubtedly would have found it ironic that his activities in Egypt would lead to the death of his only son. A small world, indeed.